Callback

Silhouette Studios

KATANA COLLINS

CHAPTER ONE
Marly

"WHEN MY CAREER goes to shit, under no circumstances are you to allow me to go on a reality show. Got that? No Celebrity Survivor or sad MTV seasons about how far I've fallen."

The other end of the phone line was heavy with silence. I could practically hear the grinding gears in my agent's brain.

I waited, gripping the steering wheel with blanching knuckles. I was good at this game. Good at silence. Good at waiting. I smirked, holding the wheel steady and passed a slow driver in the middle lane. Eventually, Kyle said, "Marly, I think you're over-reacting. Stop planning for doomsday when you haven't even stepped into your audition yet."

True. But planning was what I did. It was who I was. I flicked a glance to the spiral bound turquoise planner in the front seat beside me. My travel buddy. Without that planner, I was lost. I swallowed, the sight of it bringing bittersweet memories of my dad. "I hope for the best, but plan for the worst, Kyle," I recited Dad's words, ignoring that vicious, painful ache behind my ribcage and the gaping hole in my heart since his passing.

"Don't I know it," Kyle muttered. "You ever heard of self-fulfilling prophesies?"

"Having a *plan* isn't going to cause a disaster." I tossed a quick look over my shoulder before swerving into the next lane and slipping off the exit ramp. "Who am I meeting with again? It's not just some 'producer' with a camera in a rent-an-office, is it?"

An audition at Silhouette Studios *should* mean I'd be safe from that sort of audition. As one of the largest production houses in Los Angeles, it should mean that I was stepping into a professional audition, where nothing out of line was expected of me. This wasn't some B-Movie audition with a greasy guy named Chet filming me on his cell phone. It was a top three studio. It *should* mean I could trust them.

But I know better. It only takes one burn from a candle to be wary of all fire. And sometimes, the more powerful the person, the more they don't believe the rules apply to them.

"No, no. Today is the real deal. You'll be meeting with the casting director—Nicole Stevens of Stevens Casting. Probably a couple of producers, the director. There's nothing to be wary of with this one. Trust me, you'll see."

"You can't trust everything you see—even salt looks like sugar." Another Dadism.

Kyle sighed again. He was the king of sighs. "But Marly, you should know—"

"Let me guess ... the producer expects a blow job under his desk in exchange for the part? Don't worry, I have a plan for that, too. And it involves my foot being lodged so far up someone's ass, I could file my toenails on their tonsils."

Kyle grunted. "Jesus, Marly. Graphic much?"

I sneered. It *should* be a ludicrous statement. It should

be such a ridiculous notion for a proposition like that to happen at a huge Hollywood production studio ... except that it had happened to me already. Twice.

Shame and guilt burned hot in my stomach and my grip on the wheel tightened. What the fuck did I have to feel guilty about? I had done the right thing. I refused him, shoving his hand away from beneath my skirt and walking out of that audition. Without the part. Without the callback. But with my dignity. Even with being a well-recognized face in this town, it still wasn't enough to halt the advances. To sway the rumors. Maybe it wasn't happening *despite* my well-recognized face, but because of it.

From the other end of the phone, Kyle sighed again. "Do you really think I would knowingly send you into an audition where they expect sexual favors?"

I opened my mouth to answer—*of course not*—and yet, nothing came out. My throat felt tight, my skin hot and prickly and my ears flushed in the way they always did when I lied. Kyle was a good agent. I liked him. He had always had my back in the years we'd been working together. I did trust him ... to an extent. So why couldn't I just say that?

My silence earned me another sigh. "Thing is," Kyle said, "you don't have to trust them. But you do have to trust *me*. And those propositions should stop now that you and Omar went public with your engagement."

I smiled while cutting across three more lanes of traffic to take the next left. Omar Blake. My best friend and "fiancé," according to US Magazine's latest report. Our plan had worked perfectly. Omar needed a beard and I needed directors to stop thinking I would use my vagina as some sort of magical ticket into Hollywood. "That's true," I replied. "Nothing's happened since we announced our engagement." The diamond on my ring finger caught a gleam of the Los Angeles sunlight, nearly blinding me. My mother's ring. Once more, my heart squeezed with memories so faded, that I almost couldn't call them memories anymore. "Then again," I sighed, "I also haven't gotten any parts since the announcement, *either*." Omar, on the other hand, was in the final stages of callbacks for a huge franchise movie deal. At least six movies contracted and potentially more within the franchise. He needed that deal. Especially after he'd spent most of his savings to stop his jackass ex-boyfriend from outing him to the press.

"Well, this audition could change that. It's a great role—buzz around town is that it has Oscar potential."

The yellow light in front of me changed to red and I slammed my foot onto the brakes, screeching to a stop. Damn—that came out of nowhere. Butterflies fluttered around my belly at the thought of being in a film well-regarded by the Academy. I loved my romantic comedies, but I wanted—no *needed* to show people the kind of chops I had. Back in my college days, I had played Antigone and Lady Macbeth. I had brought audiences to tears with my parts in the Laramie Project. I swallowed, turning into the Silhouette Studios lot, easing off the gas as I approached the guard. "Hold that thought, Kyle," I said into the ear piece, then leaned out the window. "Marlena Taylor," I said to the guard. "Here for my meeting with Stevens Casting."

"Yes, Ms. Taylor." He scanned a list on a clipboard in his hands before he pointed beyond the first few buildings in front of us. "Studio Eight. You're gonna go straight and take a right at the water tower, follow that road down to the end."

"Thank you."

"Marly," Kyle pulled me back into the conversation. "As I was saying, you know the film's about Dominant/submissive lifestyles, of course—in the same vein as *Secretary*. But it requires nudity. Lots of it."

I rolled my eyes. "That's fine, Kyle. I don't have a problem with tasteful nudity."

"Full frontal?" He gulped on the other end of the line. "Look. I know it's not my place. And as your agent, the last thing I should be doing is trying to talk you out of an audition. But as your *friend*, I have to say ... maybe it's something you should think about considering the rumors Jack started—"

"Jack doesn't get that kind of power over me," I snapped. Jack Seaver. The ass I gave my heart to while filming Bridesmaid Retreat. When I ended things with him, he smeared my name all through Hollywood with awful rumors that I'd offered sexual favors in exchange for my leading role in his movie. And Los Angeles, being the town it is, believed him. "This isn't porn, Kyle. It's a film—an *Oscar*-worthy film. Nobody berates Julianne Moore or Jennifer Connelly for nude scenes."

Kyle's voice wavered on the line. "I know you pretty well, Marly, and I don't think you'll be able to handle the backstabbing and whispers happening at Hollywood parties behind your back. I'm just worried for you, that's all."

My inhalation was shaky at best and the single butterfly in my stomach was now in full flight. "I'll be fine, Kyle." Catching my reflection in the rearview mirror, I realized I almost believed it myself. Leaning forward, I wiped beneath my eyes where the smoky eyeliner had smeared a touch too much, then pinched my shimmery cheeks. When I was done, I hardly recognized the woman behind the thick coating of makeup. Long, thick lashes blinked back at me in the rearview mirror.

And what if you aren't fine? I squeezed my eyes shut, closing the proverbial curtain to my reflection. That little voice of doubt had been whispering for a week since I got the script for this audition.

What if I'm only auditioning for this role to step out in front of the rumors? Because maybe if I show my tits and ass on screen, directors and producers will stop asking to see them in person? I rolled my eyes in spite of myself, pulling into a parking space.

Yeah, because that's how sex works. People see you in movies and *stop* fantasizing about fucking you. "This film is an amazing opportunity to show studios that I can do more than be a cute airhead on screen."

"You're right," Kyle said, his voice shifting into something harder. Business-like. "It's an amazing opportunity and you're a talented actress. Show them your vulnerable side. Just keep your nose clean in there. No sarcastic jokes, no flirting. Nothing. Keep it kosher."

I nodded, looking up at the tallest building in the lot. My butterfly-filled stomach flipped and a chill ran down my spine, despite LA's latest heat wave. *Oh, God, keep it together.*

My nerves bounced as the reality of the upcoming audition hit me. I inhaled, taking the dry, warm air into my lungs and exhaled it slowly.

"Marly?" Kyle prodded.

"I'm nodding," I said. Then, with another deep breath, I turned the car off. "All right, Kyle. I have to go or I'll be late."

The car locked with a beep and my heart fluttered as I entered through heavy glass doors with my planner tucked safely under my arm. "Stevens Casting?" I asked a young, beautiful woman sitting at the front desk and took note of her perfectly applied makeup and smooth golden hair. Aspiring actress perhaps? Hoping to get auditions through entry level work, most likely. I ran a hand through my own glossy locks, pulling all my red hair over to one shoulder.

The girl pointed to the end of the hall. "Third door on the left," she said, smacking her gum and flipping the page of a magazine.

As I walked down the hall, anxiety jumped low within my belly ... worse than the damn butterfly. So much worse. Slowly, the walls seemed to be encroaching, closing in around me. I fell against the wall, my back pressed against the cool paneling and took a deep breath, glancing at my phone. My stomach lurched and the time on the screen spun. I only had one minute to pull it together or be late going in.

My stomach was in my throat as the wave of nausea rushed over me. I doubled over, putting my head between my knees. You'd think after hundreds of auditions, I'd be used to the nerves. And yet, here I was, bent over, nauseated with anxiety. The same ritual as always. After a few deep breaths, I opened my eyes. My knees trembled within my dark wash jeans and I swallowed the little bit of bile that rose in my throat with a hiccup.

On a final deep breath, I pushed off the wall, making the move to enter the audition. Only that same cleansing breath caught in my throat when I lifted my gaze to find the famous Jude Fisher, American heartthrob and two-time

Oscar winner, standing in front of me. Wow, he was magnificent. Everything from the top of his sandy brown hair, down his muscled physique, to his European loafer-covered toes.

I inhaled once more, only this time I was met with his cool, spicy scent. A scent with hints of sandalwood and pine. Whatever that cologne was, it was fresh and clean and so made for this man, that the manufacturers should call it *Eau du Jude Fisher*. That smell sent tingles spiraling down my arms, along with his intensely heated gaze, directed right at me.

He raised an eyebrow. His gaze flared within my already heated body and inside my peep toe heels, my toes curled in a motion that was so completely out of my control, I hadn't even realized I was doing it.

My spine stiffened and I pulled myself to a standing position, a little too quickly. Stars flooded my vision. I cleared my throat, forcing my body not to sway with the dizziness as I distracted myself with smoothing my blazer. A ping came from my cell phone—the alarm signaling that I should be standing inside that audition room right this second. Shit, I was officially late.

"You okay?" Jude asked, resting a hand to my elbow. The gentleness of his touch startled me more than the action itself. There was a power in its tenderness; a strength behind the gentle curve of his fingers. Despite the soft touch of his hand, his gaze was hard.

I smiled, though it felt shaky, like my knees. "I'm fine—I just … um …" I pointed to the door. "I'm due in there for an audition." Was that me speaking? My usual raspy, low voice had been replaced with a squeaking mouse.

He flicked a glance over his shoulder toward the fridge

in the common area. "I was getting some water—let me get you one," it was a command, rather than a question. "They can wait a moment." Thick lashes framed green eyes. Not dark like emeralds, but fair, like a light jade color that was so unique, I found myself entranced by his gaze.

My throat was suddenly lined with cotton and I nodded, managing to rasp, "That would be great, thank you."

Those eyes assessed me for only a moment longer. I glanced away, busying myself with the false act of flipping through my planner. His gaze cut to the book in my hands, then back to my face. I could feel his stare, as sure as if it was his fingers brushing over my flesh. Finally, he stalked to the refrigerator and grabbed two bottles from the bottom shelf. Twisting the cap, he handed the first to me. "Drink," he said quietly. "Have a seat if you need to."

I took a sip and as the cool water glided down my throat, I kept my eyes fastened on Jude. Dang, he was gorgeous. The top button of his crisp shirt was undone and the slightest bit of chest hair curled at the base of his throat. Once I swallowed, I gave him another smile, this time a little more confident. "Sorry about that," I said. "I-I get nervous right before walking into an audition."

He nodded, taking a swig of his water as well, wiping his chin with the back of his hand.

When he said nothing more, the uncomfortable silence itched across my skin like an outbreak of chicken pox. "It never matters how prepared I am, either. I've spent the last week on FetLife prepping for this role; researching and joining chatrooms. Hell, I even watched BDSM porn. Preparation doesn't stop the nerves. I've tried everything to calm myself before an audition—meditation, Alexander theory, a glass of wine. I even tried peeing right before.

Nothing helps." Oh, God, did I really just tell Jude freaking Fisher that I watch porn and pee before an audition to calm my nerves? Why was I still talking? *Shut up, shut up, shut up …*

His amused smirk tugged higher. "Feel better now?"

Before I could answer, a small group of tourists walked by, phones up, snapping photos and video as the guide gestured to the closed doors. "This is where we hold many of our auditions …"

Jude sucked a breath so sharp, his chest inflated with it. He spun, facing away from the crowd, dipping his head back into the refrigerator. But it was too late. An older woman pointed beside me to where Jude stood with his back to everyone. "Is that Ju—?"

"That's right!" I said, stepping in front of him. "Marlena Taylor here." I don't know why I did that. Why I jumped in to spare him the studio tour. Behind me, I heard the slow, relieved release of his breath. And something in that small sound ignited a fire low in my belly. Warmth spread from my core, stretching out around my torso and limbs and coiling around my spine. He had helped me moments ago and it was my turn to repay the favor. A small part of me delighted in it; delighted in helping him; in pleasing him. And that hit of pleasure was like an adrenaline shot to my veins.

"Come on," I said, waving the small group of five over to me. "Let's get a selfie!"

I hugged the crowd of smiling, laughing people into me. "One, two, three!" The snaps of their phones were comically loud.

With another wave, the tour guide shuffled the group back down the hall.

Jude turned, his face so close to mine, that I could see every crease framing his eyes. Every dark dot of stubble. "How did you ..." He cleared his throat, his voice fading away and as he shook his head, his scent breezed across me, surrounding my body like I was submerged in him. It left me breathless. "Thank you for that," he said, his breath still heavy and deep. "I've never been good in crowds, especially not since...." He touched his watch with thick fingertips. "I've never been good in crowds." And whatever he'd been about to reveal was swallowed along with his panic.

For a few moments, I stared at his face. The dread was melting; dissolving like a single grain of sugar into a steaming beverage. Likewise, whatever anxiety I'd been feeling evaporated with helping Jude. "It was nothing."

Those jade green eyes flared, then softened, like a flame that had been stoked with a sharp gust of air. "It wasn't nothing." He touched his watch again, looking at the time. "And you're now officially late for your audition."

"Oh, shit." How had I forgotten? The whole damn reason I was here. The whole reason for Jude getting me the bottle of water. My audition. Placing my cool palm to my forehead, I sighed. "I'm gonna have to go in there and explain—"

"No, you won't," he cut me off in a gravelly voice. Though his jaw was stern, his eyes were kind. Holding the door open, he gestured for me to enter, leaning in to whisper, "And ... you should embrace that nervousness. Especially for a role like this one."

Jude placed a hand at the small of my back and guided me into the room. The heat of his touch permeated my clothing and I took another sip of water to calm the flush of heat spreading across my cheeks. Never in my life had I been starstruck—and yet, around this man, I became a stammering idiot.

Wait a minute. He was coming into the audition with me? Why would he be doing that unless he was involved in casting—

"Sorry, everyone," Jude announced while entering the room, "I was trying to get a bottle of water when one of those backlot tours came through. Thank God for this girl—she saved me from an onslaught of selfies. Threw herself under the bus for me." He offered me an encouraging smile before taking his chair at the long table of people ready and willing to tear my soul apart.

Though the table of people acknowledged me, said hello, and welcomed me, there was an energetic wall. A wall that separated them from us—it was an unspoken audition rule that yes, they speak to you, but no, you are not on equal ground. And yet, Jude got me water. He helped me through my panic attack and I repaid the favor in the face of the crowd. And now, he sat at the table of power. He was both my peer and my superior. Both peasant and king. He knew how it was on both sides of the aisle and his kindness, his humbleness touched some flame deep inside me that I'd been almost positive Hollywood had long ago tamped out.

A woman stood at the end of the table and held out a hand. "I'm Nicole Stevens," she said, then quickly directed me to another man who stood from behind the table.

He took my hand and offered a lopsided grin, curly red hair flopping over onto his plastic rectangle glasses. "I'm Seth, an executive producer. This is Ash Livingston—he'll be directing the film." He continued down the line of people, introducing them one by one until he finally reached Jude. "And of course, I'm sure you know Jude Fisher already. He'll be playing the role of Leo."

Jude hadn't torn his eyes from me since we had entered. I felt his stare, heady and electric through every handshake and pleasantry. And now we were face to face, shaking hands. While every other member at the table sat behind their glass wall, he sat on top, teetering over the edge. I swallowed and it felt like a ball of yarn going down a sand paper tunnel. "Yes, of course. Thanks again for the water."

"Here you go," Seth handed me the audition sides. "Jude will be reading opposite you today."

I gulped and my knees locked. Jude terrified me in a way I couldn't describe. Our chemistry was as palpable as an active volcano and I was the lava, ready to erupt at any moment.

Seth continued, walking around the table and taking his seat. "Today's audition is just all about the chemistry. We want to see you—well, Holly, submissive to Leo. We want to see sparks."

Sparks? The way I was feeling inside, I could give them a freaking Fourth of July fireworks display.

Seth grinned. "And … off you go."

CHAPTER TWO
Marly

"THANK YOU SO much for coming in, Marlena. We will be in touch in the next couple of days."

Crap.

Crap, shit, motherfu—

"Thank you for the chance to read for Holly," I said, ignoring the sailor inside my brain throwing curse words around. I nodded graciously, but inside, I was a screaming, raving mess. Could I have screwed up that audition more? I'm usually so strong and solid in my character choices. But in that room, I was stuttering and blushing like a friggin' virgin on prom night. I'd even tripped—*actually* stumbled backwards as Jude approached me during the scene. We were supposed to have chemistry for God's sake, and I could barely look the man in the eyes.

I grinned at the table of producers, directors, and casting directors; but even my smile felt too tight. Frigid. "Thank *you* for meeting with me," I went down the line, shaking each of their hands, hesitating when I got to Jude. "Thanks again."

"It was a good read," he said. "You really seem to level with Holly." He licked his lips, his hand lingering on mine.

Kyle's words flashed in my mind. *Keep your nose clean. No flirting.* I wrenched my hand from Jude's—perhaps a bit too hard. "Well, I think she and I have a lot in common."

Why the hell did I say that? Holly and I have nothing in common.

His mouth twitched as he dipped his hand into his pocket.

"Thanks again for the opportunity," I addressed the group, backing out the door, and exhaling in sweet relief when I was finally alone. I shuffled down the quiet hall and found a ladies room to slip inside. Turning on the faucet, I wet a paper towel and placed the cool cloth on the back of my neck.

What would I say to Kyle? That I let my nerves get the best of me? (Again.) And screwed up another audition? (Again.) I read those scenes completely wrong. If this bad audition streak kept up, it didn't matter how much Kyle cared for me; he was going to drop me as a client. And then I'd be back bartending at the Comedy Cellar. Or worse yet—back to filming commercials. Was there anything more embarrassing than a once well-known celebrity peddling Atkins meal bars or some shit like that?

Yeah, I'd had a one hit romantic comedy, but I wanted something real. Something raw. And this was that project … I could feel it. If only I could make the producers realize it, too. Did I love Holly's character? Not really. A submissive woman who lets a man dictate everything from what she wore, to what she eats, to when she worked out?

It's not exactly a character I connected with. *Which is exactly why I need to do it.* If I could tap into a character that made my skin crawl and still make it authentic, then maybe I could also eradicate those whispers of doubt that echo *you're not good enough* in my mind at every freaking audition.

I needed another chance; another audition. I flicked

through the faces I'd just met—who had been the most approachable? Seth seemed reasonable; maybe if I spoke to him before leaving?

Tossing the wet paper towel in the trash, I shoved a shoulder into the bathroom door and steeled myself to march back into that room and show them just how perfect I'd be as Holly. The corner of the door bounced into something on the other side and swung back, knocking me onto my ass.

"Ow," I croaked, rubbing the heels of my hands.

The door creaked open slowly and there, on the other side, pinching the bridge of his nose, was Jude. I muttered a curse under my breath as he crouched in front of me, concern marring his face. "Are you okay?"

I shook my head. "I ... I'm fine. I was just—"

"In a hurry, apparently," he cut me off, extending a hand.

I pushed off the bathroom floor and winced at the jolt of pain that bolted up my wrist. I hesitated for just a second before dropping my good hand into Jude's. A surge of power pulled me to a standing position and his hand cradled mine, large and warm. What the hell was it about this guy that had me so unnerved? I gulped a panicked breath before rushing to the sink, washing my hands. "I'm so sorry—is your ... did I hurt you?" If I broke that beautiful face of his, I would never forgive myself.

He put a hand to his nose once more before dropping it to his sides. "I think I'll live. You sure you're all right?"

Oh, hell. With how much I fall down? This was nothing. I rolled my eyes in spite of myself. "Oh, I'm fine. That's nothing compared to some of the falls I've taken." I shrugged, shaking the water from my hands.

In the mirror, I watched as Jude's lush mouth curved into a grin, revealing a delicious dimple on the side. "Why are you in such a hurry?"

I swallowed, frozen, as though captured by those sparkling green eyes of his. Damn, he had an effect on me. And I hated him for that. "Um, actually, I was going back into the room—to see you all again."

"Oh?" His eyebrows twitched higher. "Forget something?"

"No. It's just ... my audition ... was a bit lacking. And I want them—um, you—to see what all I'm capable of."

"Ms. Taylor, I think we know perfectly well what you're capable of." His voice was soft, but no less intense and my blood heated, running thicker through my veins as I forced my breathing to remain steady. I resisted the urge to take a step back—was that ... was he *hitting* on me? No. This could not happen at yet another audition.

I crossed my arms, elongating my neck. Even with my three-inch heels—he still had a good six inches on me. "And what's that supposed to mean?" I challenged quietly, eyes narrowing.

Jude's smirk twitched higher on one side before it dropped completely. "You thought your audition was lacking?" he repeated. I opened my mouth to answer, only Jude continued talking, before I could even get a word in. "You thought the scene we read in there together wasn't good?" He took a step closer and what little air was left between us buzzed to life.

Again, I tried to answer, but Jude cut me off, leaning against the wall beside the sinks. "You're joking, right?"

I huffed a breath and his eyebrows arched, awaiting my answer.

I touched a hand to my sternum, lifting my brows. "Oh, me? You actually want me to answer this time? Yes, I think I could have done better. A hell of a lot better." I dropped my arms, willing them to relax. I was on high alert, but that was no excuse to alienate the freaking *star* of the movie. I'd have to be an absolute idiot to do that. This man did things to me; things I didn't want to feel in an audition, but he hadn't come right out and done anything wrong yet.

His eyebrows crumpled together, and he shook his head. "Marlena—"

"Marly," I corrected him.

"—you got the callback."

Wait—what? It took me a moment to hear him. *Really* hear him. And it took me longer to believe him. I narrowed my eyes. "No ... there's no way. My audition was terrible."

"Your audition was not terrible."

I shook my head. "It *was*. I was nervous and stammering and—and they wanted to see sparks and I could barely look at you without blushing and dropping my eyes to my feet—"

"Marlena," Jude said. "Look at me." He placed two gentle hands on my arms, punctuating the demand. I lifted my gaze, powerless to ignore his command. "You. Got. The. Callback." He lowered his voice to a whisper. "There's only one other actress in the running for the part right now. If you go storming back through those doors, you're going to ruin it for yourself. Whatever it is you *think* you did wrong, it just isn't true."

"But ... I was so bad."

Jude sighed, dropping his hands from my arms. "Do you know what BDSM stands for?"

"BDSM: Burritos, Doritos, Snickers, and M&Ms," I joked without thinking. Oh, God … I'm such a shit. It was an inside joke between me and Omar because of my obsession with junk food. But as soon as the words left my mouth, I flushed bright red, horrified. "I'm so sorry—I was kidding, but it was a stupid joke—"

Before I could finish my apology, Jude threw his head back and barked a laugh. "Okay, for some that might be what it means. But for this movie, it's Bondage/Discipline. Dominance/*Submission*. And Sado-Masochism. *Submission*. Holly and Leo wouldn't have the sort of forward chemistry most people consider. Your understanding of her was spot on."

His words were finally sinking in. "So … I got the callback?"

He nodded. "You got the callback. Your shy version of Holly was exactly what we were looking for."

What the hell was his angle here? No one in this city helped anyone for nothing. He was either lying or he wanted something. "How do I know you're not just saying that?"

Jude's face twisted in confusion. "Just saying what? What do I gain from lying to you about your callback?"

I shrugged. "I don't know. Maybe you're trying to sabotage my audition. Or you know one of the other actresses up for the role …"

He ran a hand down his face, scratching at his jaw before shaking his head, defeated. After another moment, he tugged a gold watch from his wrist and dropped it in my hand. "I'm giving you my Rolex. Bring it with you to the callback. Now," he shifted his weight, pointing to the watch in my hand. "Would I give this to you if I wasn't going to see you again?"

My jaw dropped as I stood there speechless.

"That's what I thought. I'll see you *soon*." He turned slowly, sliding both hands into his pants pockets, sauntering out of the bathroom.

I looked down at the heavy watch resting in my hands and gulped. The weight of it, both figuratively and literally, was heavy and warm from his body heat. Jude's body. A shiver ran down my spine, rattling each vertebra, despite the warmth of the gold in my palm. If what he said was true—*holy shit*, then I was getting a callback for this role! I swallowed a scream, peeking out the door to make sure he was gone. With the hallways clear, I ducked back into the bathroom with a silent, joyful shout, jumping up and down in front of the sinks.

CHAPTER THREE

Jude

I CLOSED THE door to Ash's corner office behind me, falling into the leather chair across from his desk with a sigh. He wasn't back yet from the audition and I could use the moment alone, anyway. Most actresses in Los Angeles weren't exactly demure, submissive types. That personality just didn't breed the "spotlight" mentality. But Marlena Taylor? I groaned, leaning back. She was the perfect combination of timid and passionate. Almost every actress who came in played the role as a dominant woman trying to be submissive for the man she loved—and almost every actress had it wrong. But Marlena got it. She got Holly—a woman who was naturally submissive, overcompensating for her lack of control by a false sense of dominance. Holly finds her true self in the BDSM lifestyle. The problem was … Marly didn't *know* she got it. *She doesn't know who she is.* Though it was clear Marly didn't quite grasp the lifestyle to its fullest extent, that was easy enough to coach. A true and natural chemistry and understanding of the character? Not so easy.

I lifted her headshot from Ash's desk where she grinned at me through the image. Goddamn, she was beautiful. Even her physicality was exactly what I had pictured Holly to be in this movie. Glossy red hair, blue eyes. Thin, but not hard-bodied. I dropped the headshot back down on the desk where it had been and released a sigh, trying to shake her image from my mind. Shit, I needed to snap out of it. Yes, she was perfect for the role—that didn't mean I needed to spend the whole fucking afternoon daydreaming about her.

Beside Marlena's headshot was an image of Layla Hutson, nearly naked on the beach. If that wasn't the damn biggest difference in personalities, I didn't know what was. After all we had been through, I still couldn't believe Rich had brought Layla in for this audition. Yeah, her agent was the biggest bulldog in the industry and when the script crossed his desk, he was relentless until Silhouette Studios gave her an audition. As a producer, I get it why Silhouette Studios auditioned her; the studio owed her one after they canceled her latest movie. And even I couldn't ignore the fact that she would draw an audience. Dumb frat boys would come in droves at the chance to see Layla Hutson full frontal. But as her ex-husband and the other lead character of this movie, I had to say ... she was all wrong for Holly. And not because she was a bad actress—Layla was actually a good actress. But there was an honest vulnerability Marly brought to the role that Layla simply didn't have. And hand to God, I'm not just saying that because she had used me to climb Hollywood's social ladder.

There was a knock at Ash's door and I hopped to my feet as Richard Blair, the CEO of Silhouette Studios walked in. "Jude," he bellowed. "The auditions went well." Other than a few smile lines around Richard's mouth and some salt added to his pepper hair, he looked almost exactly as he had twenty years earlier in his prime. And he damn well knew it, too.

"With one or two, yes." I pushed the headshots toward Richard who gave a wolf's whistle, holding up Layla's image.

"Fuck me," he grunted. "Layla will cost the studio a pretty penny, huh?"

I shrugged, doing my best to act indifferent. "I think you mean a pretty million."

"After canceling production on her latest movie?" Richard sighed and dove a hand through his hair. "We owe her."

I snorted. "Yeah. And she knows it."

"She was good in the audition, Jude. You have to admit she was the best actress we saw."

I swallowed the thick knot lodged in my throat. "She was good. But Marlena Taylor was better." I tapped Marly's headshot with an index finger. "And if we're serious about this being an award movie, then we're better off going with the actress who can show Holly's vulnerability in a subtle way."

Ash entered at that moment, closing the door behind him. My best friend since college ... God I hoped he'd be on my side with this one. "Richard," Ash said with a nod. Then, he flashed a quick smile at me.

Richard ran his tongue across his teeth, examining Marly's headshot more closely. "Does this girl have a body shot like Layla's available?"

"She does," Ash said, crossing to his desk and pulling an image out of his top drawer. Where Layla's body shots oozed confidence and sex, Marlena's were playful; sweet even. Innocent, if half naked photos could be such. There was a twitch behind my zipper and I shoved the feelings that stirred low in my gut aside. I'd been down that road before and I knew from experience that it ended abruptly at the edge of a cliff. No more dating actresses. Never again. I tore my eyes away from the images.

"She's that girl from the Chase Evans movie, right? The Wedding Dance or some bullshit?"

Ash nodded. "Yeah, that's her. Bridesmaid Retreat."

I inwardly groaned, swallowing the sound. Romantic comedies are great. But it's also the sort of movie that could really hurt Marlena in future auditions. It's hard to move beyond that cutesie typecasting. "She's ready to break out, though. I think this part is perfect for her."

Ash's smirk climbed higher and he flashed me a knowing look. "I have to admit, you guys had some intense chemistry in the audition." His eyebrows jumped suggestively with the statement.

Richard set the images down on Ash's desk, pointing a finger at each of us. "Careful. After the class action harassment suit being brought against Harris Lewendon, we are issuing a studio-wide no-fraternization policy." Richard grumbled something inaudible to himself and tugged at the sleeves of his dress shirt before going over to Ash's liquor cabinet and dropping some ice into a glass.

Ash snorted and Richard shot him a stern look. "I mean it … Absolutely no fucking anyone you're working with."

"Well," Ash said, sarcastic regret tightening his face. "That could be a problem … Because I fucked the receptionist last night."

Richard hissed a curse from under his breath and poured a scotch.

"What?" Ash asked in false innocence. "It was consensual. Go ask her … She already texted me about meeting up again tonight."

"You better not," Rich said, pointing at Ash. "Not without getting her to sign a non-disclosure first."

"Yeah," Ash huffed a laugh. "Because that's some hot foreplay. Hey, baby, sign *this* …"

I groaned, dipping my hands into my pockets. "You don't have to worry about that with me, Rich. I'm done with actresses." After Layla? Never again. Especially not one I had to see every day on set.

"It goes beyond actresses. Anyone on the crew. Anyone who might see you in a position of power over them," Richard said, tugging the cap off the scotch bottle. Then he held it up, sloshing the liquid around in an offering. "Anyone else want one?" He didn't wait for an answer as he poured three drinks.

We clinked glasses and Richard sipped with a satisfied sigh as the amber liquid went down, looking to me after he swallowed. "So … You don't have faith in Layla?"

My spine stiffened at the mention of her name, and I hated that she still had this power over me. Hated that the mere thought of her face or sound of five little letters could make my skin crawl. "No," I managed to say calmly. "I don't have faith in Layla." Not because she was a bad actress. But because I didn't have faith that she and I could successfully be in a movie together—that we could successfully act like two people falling in love. Fucking been there, done that, and it ended in a train wreck.

"And this has nothing to do with your failed marriage? It's based solely on talent?"

I saw the fear in Richard's eyes. The fear of a lawsuit. Part of me wanted to lie … but I couldn't. Not to my boss; not to the man who had taken a chance on giving two broke kids a job on a whim years ago. "I can't tell you that my history with her isn't influencing me. Of course, I don't want to act with Layla. Of course, I don't want to do a movie with the woman who used me and stomped on my fucking heart and then sold the footage of it to TMZ. But all that aside … This girl," I grabbed Marly's headshot and help it up. "This girl is an even better actress than Layla is. She brings an innocence and vulnerability to the role that Layla's read didn't have."

Richard was silent as he took another sip. "I don't know. We're already taking a risk on this script as it is. Do we really want to also risk the casting on someone so green?"

My face turned brittle and my teeth gnashed over top of each other, but Richard hardly seemed to notice. He just kept right on talking. "Layla would secure future projects for the studio, too. Ginger, here, is a risk on a lot of levels."

I pressed my lips together in a tight line. "Well, that's why we do callbacks. We'll see how they both do in the second audition, right?"

Silence sat heavily between us. Ash took a long pull from his whiskey before setting it onto a carved wooden coaster on his desk. "With your permission, Rich," Ash said, "I'd like to bring in a third party to the callbacks to help us decide between Marlena and Layla."

Richard jerked his gaze from the tumbler in his hand, wreaking of disapproval and whiskey. "A third party?"

"Yep. I think having a professional submissive in the room will offer us insight that a bunch of men wouldn't necessarily think of." Ash sat at his desk, rifling through papers and looked up at Rich over the top of one rustling sheet. "Don't you think?"

Richard's brow creased on an exhale, and he shook his head. "All right then. I guess you have it all worked out." He tipped his head back, finishing the rest of his drink in one swift swallow, setting the glass down on Marlena's headshot. The sweat from the glass dripped down, creating a circular stain on her face. "You'll have a hell of a time filming with either one of 'em, I bet." He winked, slapping me on the back as he made his way out the door.

Ash wiped a hand across his eyes, taking a drink from his whiskey. I fell back into the chair across from my longtime friend, crossing my feet at the ankles. "Well? Let's hear it," Ash finally said.

"Layla and I acting together will be a disaster. You know it and I certainly know it."

Ash sighed and his drink splashed over the lip of the glass as he set it down. "But she'll sell a hell of a lot of tickets."

My face fell. I was exhausted. These fights, these debates about casting were too much. Layla was too much. "I can't do it, Ash," I finally said quietly. "You've known me how long now? You knew me when Layla and I were a couple and before we met and since we broke up. I can't act with her again. I'll end up killing her." Then, I added quieter, "Or it will break me." The latter was more accurate, as much as I didn't want to admit that.

Ash leaned forward onto his knees. "Buddy, I can't hire another girl just because you've had your heart broken. I have to do what's best for the movie."

"That's what I'm telling you!" I pushed off the chair, pacing the room like a caged tiger. "Layla's a good actress. I'm a good actor. But together? We'll be awful—all that Oscar buzz you assholes have been pushing, will be out the window." I stalked over to the desk. Lifting Richard's sweating glass off her headshot, I pushed his finger into Marlena's image. "*This* girl and I have chemistry. Natural chemistry, not forced. And she's a good actress. She would nail this part."

Ash smirked. "She *was* good. Did you see the way she stuttered around you?" He chuckled. "L-L-Leo, I can't do this," Ash impersonated Marly's high-pitched voice.

"Exactly." I lifted a brow. "Holly needs to be enamored by Leo. *Intimidated*. You think Layla's really going to be able to act intimidated by me? Christ, that woman wouldn't be intimidated by the devil himself."

Ash shrugged. "Look, I admit it, Marlena's audition was better, but she doesn't have the audience. She doesn't even have the sex appeal."

"Fuck the fucking audience," I growled.

Ash raised his hands defensively. "Whoa, man. Calm down. I'm on your team, remember? I want the best movie possible."

I swiped a hand down my face once more before leaning my elbows onto the desk. Was it just sex appeal that Marlena needed? That was easy enough to work with. Have her ditch the blazer she wore to today's audition, swap her skinny jeans with a short skirt and a low-cut shirt and she'd be just as worthy a sex symbol as Layla. And one that American women can relate to. "All right, Ash. Marlena needs to be sexier by day, but demure in her acting. What else?"

He took a deep breath, holding her image to the light. "She really didn't seem to understand what BDSM is all about. I could tell she had done some research, but when it comes down to it, a Google search isn't going to cut it with this part. We all know Layla knows the lifestyle—"

"Okay, fine. But can I just add that Holly doesn't know the lifestyle in the beginning of the movie, either. It could work to our benefit that she's all flush faced and innocent." I clapped my hands together, dropping back into the seat. For the first time since I'd found out Layla was auditioning, I felt a glimmer of hope. "I can work with those things. What else?"

"She'd have to be willing to do some serious PR prior to the movie coming out. Some Maxim covers, maybe even a Playboy interview. Really pump up her image and get her in the spotlight like Layla is. Basically, she was really good in the audition. But not so good to make us forget about Layla."

Excitement pulsed in my veins. The thought of Marlena under my command; listening to my demands, working to please me, paddling her curvy ass when she disobeyed my orders. I inhaled to calm my racing heart, clenching my eyes shut as my pulse hammered in my ears. *No, stop that.* This was acting. No fraternization. And in no way could Marly feel like I was using my position of power as a producer to be with her sexually. This was purely business. Two method actors—one helping the other prepare for a role. I could get Marlena ready for this part and then I could finally break those ties that Layla had over me. Standing, I gripped Ash's palm in a firm handshake.

"I need to resign from the casting committee."

Ash lowered his gaze, studying me. "What are you up to, Fisher?"

"It's better you don't know. But I guarantee that after Marlena's callback, you'll leave there saying, 'Layla who?'"

CHAPTER FOUR
Marly

"HONEY, I'M HOME!" I called out, skipping into the stunning condo Omar and I shared. There were days I couldn't believe this was my life. When I moved to LA five years earlier, I never would have imagined that I'd be living in three-thousand square feet of luxury with my gay "fiancé" and starring in movies.

The smell of roasted vegetables wafted in the foyer, along with Sister Sledge blaring through the speakers. I inhaled, following my nose to the kitchen.

"Hey, boo," Omar leaned in, pecking me on the forehead, spatula in hand and a red apron tied around his waist. It was a stark contrast to his 6'5 massive frame. Bulging, veined muscles dipped and curved over his arms and even through the frilly apron, I could see the definition of a six-pack.

I smothered my laugh in my palm. "You better hope we don't have any paparazzi planted outside the window," I said, gesturing to his outfit.

He placed his hands on my waist and circled his hips against mine, thrusting. Then, he spanked me playfully with the spatula. I ducked away as he was about to give me a second swat, narrowly escaping the swinging cooking utensil. Laughing, he danced back over to the oven. "That ought to keep the tabloids happy for a while," he winked, pouring me a glass of wine. "How'd the audition go?"

I inhaled the spicy wine before taking a sip. Unsuccessfully, I tried to hide my grin behind the lip of the glass. "I got a callback."

"What?" Omar threw down the spatula. "Already?"

If possible, my smile stretched even wider, as I nodded.

"Oh, hell yeah!" Omar rushed over, lifting me in a hug with a quick smack to the lips. "Did they just tell you right there on the spot?" He lowered me to my feet, his massive hands still cradling my hips.

I flushed, buying myself a moment with another sip of wine. "Actually—I thought I sucked. I was preparing to go back in and beg for a mulligan ... but on my way, the actor I read with stopped me, telling me I would ruin it by going back." I shrugged, avoiding Omar's questioning gaze.

"So, they haven't actually called you back yet?"

"No—but he gave me this." I held the watch up for Omar to see. "And told me I could bring it back when I come in for the callback."

Omar's face crumpled into skeptical lines, taking the Rolex and turning it over in his hands. "Who is this guy? Why were you alone with him?"

I chuckled, loving how protective he was of me. Growing up, it was always just my father and me. And as loving and organized as my dad was, he was also a single parent and not exactly the over-protective, shotgun-bearing father you see in movies. And these days, Omar was the closest thing to family I had. "Careful, Omar. You actually *sound* like an overprotective fiancé, now." I brushed my hands over his furled brow, rubbing gently at the worry lines. "And if you don't watch it, you're going to end up needing Botox before I do."

His face softened, but he caught my hand in his. "Sorry," he said, shaking his head. "I guess someone in that audition liked you enough to look out for you, huh?"

His statement needled me. Liked me how? For my talent as an actress? For my ass? Or for the rumors he'd heard? I swallowed, hating that whisper of doubt that always crept into my mind after an audition. If I wasn't careful, I'd start believing the rumors myself soon. Pushing the thoughts away, I climbed onto the barstool across from where Omar cooked. "I guess."

"Even still, sweetie, don't count your chickens and all that." He moved back over to the oven, picking up his spatula once more. "For all we know, that's not even a real Rolex."

I cleared my throat, playing with the corner of an envelope on the kitchen island. "Actually, the guy who helped me—it was Jude Fisher."

"Are you kidding me? Mr. *I've won two Oscars and I've only just turned thirty* gave you his watch?" The words were playful, but Omar's grip on the spatula tensed.

I shrugged, trying to play it down. But inside? I was freaking out, too. "He's already cast as the lead in the film and so he was there in the audition room." I took another sip of wine, swallowing down the giddy feeling that rose in my belly. "Have you met him before?"

"Once at a party." Omar muttered, stirring the vegetables. "Be careful with that one. Rumor has it he and that ex-wife of his were more than a little wild." He threw a glance at me from over his shoulder, eyebrow raised.

My stomach lurched. "He didn't seem wild. Intense, yeah."

"You know what else is intense? Tigers. Intense, wild,

and powerful...." Omar studied me and a flush crawled up my neck. I inwardly cursed, knowing my freckles would flare at any moment. I hated how telling my fair skin was. "You like him?" Omar whispered.

Shit. Stupid revealing freckles. I didn't want to like Jude. It was stupid. Immature. And dangerous to get involved with someone who was a potential costar. Omar dropped the spatula into the pan and walked over to me, his finger curling under my chin. My heart raced, pounding in my ears as I lifted my gaze to his. "You like him." This time, it wasn't a question.

I shrugged the comment off, grabbing some mail on the counter and flipping through it to busy myself. "I don't even know him," I chuckled in an effort to ease the tension.

"Okay," Omar said, backing off. He knew me well enough to know when to leave things be. "Keep in mind, though, this little arrangement we've got is only supposed to be until you find someone more appropriate."

I sighed, reaching for the wine bottle. "And what if I *don't* find anyone?"

Omar rolled his eyes, holding out his glass for a refill as well. "Oh, c'mon. If you don't find anyone, it's because you're not even making an effort. And sweetie—that clock is rounding midnight. You're gonna turn into a pumpkin soon if you don't get some."

I held my glass up, clinking his. "Then I guess I'll just have to find a man who loves pumpkin pie, now won't I?"

Omar's laugh bellowed through the kitchen. "Too bad I'm an apple crumb kind of man myself." He winked, rubbing a hand over his smooth head.

"And what about your drama with Simon?" I asked. One look at Omar's expressive eyes, and I knew I shouldn't have brought it up.

"He wants another two hundred thousand to keep quiet," Omar muttered, eyes cast down into saucepan.

My stomach twisted, hatred dripping out like acid. I didn't hate many people in the world … It was a strong word and I didn't like it … But I *hated* Omar's ex-boyfriend, Simon. "Another two hundred thousand? When you already gave him three hundred grand? Have you ever seen this alleged video he has of you two?" Though I couldn't see Omar's eyes, his shoulders slumped, defeated. A lump lodged, thick and heavily in my throat.

I slid off the stool, walking over to where Omar stood and wrapped my arms around his torso. My cheek fell against the hard muscles of his back and his ribs collapsed with a long exhale. "I have some royalties from Bridesmaid Retreat you can use, if you need it," I offered.

I felt, rather than saw, Omar shaking his head. "I have a little left over from my other movie. And I should know about whether or not I got the part in this new franchise. Six guaranteed movies." He let out a low whistle. "That'll help me recover from this payout."

Anxiety coiled at the base of my chest. I didn't like it. Paying off Omar's ex—hell, not even an ex. A man he had a few weeks with down in Cabo. As soon as Simon got wind of this new movie deal, he'd just ask for more money. "Are you sure paying him is the right move? Maybe—"

"Yes," Omar interrupted. "I have to pay him. After I get this part—sign the contracts, maybe I can consider coming out. My agent and manager both think it's the way to go."

I curled my fingers around his elbow, turning Omar to face me. His large, brown eyes were wet with a sheen of unshed tears that he only ever revealed to me. "What about what *you* think? What *you* want?"

His fingers brushed over my face, gently. "I want the least drama possible."

I cringed. Why was this industry so hard? Why couldn't you just be an actor on screen and do your own thing in private, without tabloids and fans and people constantly trying to fit every actor into one of four archetypes. "And the least drama is really paying half a million to an asshole? Denying who you really are? Lying to your fans … Who I bet that same half million you spent on Simon, would support you? Pretending to be engaged to a woman you aren't in love with?"

For a quick moment, I thought he might agree with me. But just as quickly as I saw the action-hero mask slip, revealing the beautifully vulnerable side to Omar he hardly ever exposed, it vanished. Leaning down, he pressed a chaste kiss to my cheek. "How could any man not love you?" Before I could answer, he swept me into his arms and spinning us across the kitchen, two-stepping beside me. "We need to celebrate your successful audition tonight! After dinner—some dancing, maybe?" Tugging me against his warm body, he waltzed us through the kitchen like he was some sort of contemporary Gene Kelly. Then, slanting my body into a dip, he paused in that position, kissing the tip of my nose. My heart warmed as his lips brushed my nose. How did I get so lucky? In a town full of leeches, I found a butterfly. My phone buzzed, vibrating across the counter. Omar spun me out of his arms and I swayed on my feet, using the counter to steady myself. Dang, I needed to get myself into some dance classes to keep up.

When I reached my phone, my heart jumped to my

throat. The text was from Kyle—*Callback next Thursday, 1pm. Congrats!* I held the phone up to Omar, "See? Told you I wasn't counting my chickens early."

CHAPTER FIVE
Marly

"ARE YOU SURE about this outfit, Omar? I really don't want to end up on Celebrity What Not to Wear tomorrow!" I tugged the too-tight dress down and in doing so, I swore I almost had a nip-slip.

"Stop fidgeting with it. You look *hot*. And you are up for a sex-pot role, so get used to these sorts of bare-all outfits."

I groaned. "Right," I hissed. "Because the only way to be sexy, is to show a shit-ton of skin."

"Baby, I hear you. And I acknowledge you. But you and I both know this bullshit is part of the industry." Grabbing my hips, he tugged me in front of a storefront window display, pointing to my reflection. "Look at that woman and tell me she isn't the star of the next Jude Fisher movie?"

Heat flushed from my face down to my core as I took in my outfit. It wasn't that I didn't know I was sexy. I just freaking hated this game we played in Hollywood. The glad-handing to get award nominations. The chauvinism. The power dynamic between the studio executives ... almost all of whom were men. But at least with my "engagement" to Omar, the propositions had stopped.

"If you are uncomfortable, we can go home and change," Omar whispered in my ear. His deep voice rumbled through me and though the change was slight, the Omar portrayed in public vs. the Omar he was at home, was notable. He wasn't ever a passive man, but while out and about, he became even more commanding and intense.

I found myself shaking my head, unsure of why. Maybe it was because this outfit was tame compared to the full-frontal nudity I'd have to display if I got this part. Or maybe it was as simple as the fact that I felt sexy, and for someone who usually gets cast as 'cute'… 'sexy' felt pretty damn good.

Omar slipped his hand in mine and with a gentle tug, he pulled me beyond the velvet ropes to the front of the line. "You wanna be a star?" he whispered. "You have to act like a star. And stars don't wait in lines. Come on." Without stopping, he nodded at the bouncer and pulled me with him into the club.

The music vibrated through my body, my pulse thrumming with the bass. "What's your poison tonight?" Omar lifted my hand, pressing a sweet kiss to my knuckles before tugging me close into his body. I had to crane my neck to see him.

"Bourbon on the rocks."

He rolled his eyes, smiling to soften the gesture. "Do you even like that stuff? Or do you only drink it because your dad did?"

"I *started* drinking it because of my dad. I *continue* drinking it because I like it." I raised a challenging brow. "Do you drink IPAs because you like them, or because you think the Hops will put hair on your chest?"

His laugh barreled out of him and he spun me out, releasing me onto the crowded dance floor. "Touché, pussycat," he said before heading to the bar. *Oh God*, these heels! I stayed a moment amidst the writhing bodies because I definitely didn't trust myself to walk anywhere without Omar's shoulder to balance on.

Once I caught my balance, I moved to the line of VIP tables and hesitated before Omar's words resonated in my mind. *Stars don't wait in lines.* I pushed beyond the massive group of people to the front of the line and gave an apologetic smile to those waiting. A bouncer with a clipboard nodded at me before he unclasped the rope and let me through. "You have the back table, Ms. Taylor."

"Thank you," I said as I walked up the stairs— carefully, God, so carefully in these dang shoes. A giant assortment of peonies caught my eye at the back table and warmth seethed through me. I put a hand to my heart while brushing the other over the soft petals. Beside the crystal vase, was a small box of salted caramels ... my favorite. Carefully, I plucked the note taped to the top of the box and unfolded it.

> *Congrats, love. Some salted caramels to go with that inevitable bourbon you will order tonight.*
>
> *~ Omar*

"Someone out there takes good care of you."

That warmth turned cold as a shiver shimmied down my spine. The good kind of shiver. That voice—but it couldn't be ...

I turned to find Jude just over my shoulder. His eyes were sharp, alert, and his stance, rigid. His gaze slid the length of my body and his eyes widened before they snapped back to my face. "Different look you got there tonight," he said, nodding to my outfit. "The producers at

Silhouette would certainly approve."

"And you?" I asked in a moment of bravery.

His jaw locked and a breath filled his chest. "I approve of anything that will get you the role of Holly."

But, why? Why did he care? Only the bravery from a moment ago melted away, and instead, I said nothing as I looked around for cameras. Jesus, with cell phones these days, just about anyone could sell a picture to TMZ. "To answer your earlier question, yes, someone out there takes great care of me." It wasn't even a lie, I thought with an inward smirk. "Would you like to join u—" I moved to step into the table, only my stupid heel caught on the red carpet, hurling me into Jude's chest. He caught me around the waist and as I tilted my chin up to look at him, his eyes darkened.

"You weren't kidding when you said you fall a lot." Humor flashed across his eyes and a momentary amused smile tipped the corners of his lips.

Instinctually, my hands slid up his broad shoulders as I caught my balance. His hands gripped my waist, doing all sorts of things to my pulse and our eyes locked, the intensity robbing me of breath. Right there in the middle of a crowded club, I was pressed against a stranger. My pulse kicked up a notch as Jude's brows crept up his forehead.

A crimson stain burned across my cheeks as I pulled back from him. "Be near me at your own risk." From over Jude's shoulder, I watched as Omar sidled up to the bar, putting our drink orders in.

"I think I'll be all right," Jude said. "I do all my own stunts."

I lowered myself onto the plush bench. "Do you want to sit? I think it's a little too dangerous for me to be standing in these heels." I lifted my leg, showing off three inches of pure danger.

Once more, that grin of his lifted. It was breathtaking. Literally. His smile was stunning. He whistled, curving his fingers around my ankle, taking a look at the heels. "No wonder you fell. Look at those things. They should be registered as deadly weapons."

His touch against my ankle was soft and tender as his fingers brushed the straps. I jerked my foot back and scanned the VIP section. "Are you here with someone?"

Jude sank beside me, crossing an ankle over his knee. "I'm actually here to see you," he said quietly.

My heart jumped with his admission. "Me? How'd you even know—"

"I have friends here at the club. They saw Omar's reservation and I figured you'd be here with him."

I swallowed the lump in my throat as guilt tweaked in my belly. For the first time since Omar and I went public with our engagement, I regretted the massive deceit. "So ... you're here to see Omar?"

His head moved slowly from right to left. "I wanted to congratulate you on the callback. You *did* get the call from your agent, right?"

I nodded, warning signs popping through my body like little teeny firecrackers going off in sequence. "Yes, a couple of hours ago." I glanced around the club, adding, "I don't have your watch on me, though."

He flipped a hand in the air with a dismissive wave and then leaned back on an elbow. "Oh, I'm not worried about that."

Goosebumps rose on my arms, but I refused to acknowledge them. With each ambiguous answer he threw at me, my blood heated more and more. "Well, then. Why don't we cut through the bullshit and you tell me why you're *really* here?"

His face dropped, eyes widening before he chuckled. "All right." Uncrossing his legs, he leaned forward on his elbows, his body—his intense presence invading my personal space. But I couldn't be the one to lean away. Not with a man like this. The second I gave him that power, he'd eat me alive. Like the tiger Omar referenced earlier, Jude was simply waiting for the right moment to pounce.

His eyes flicked over my body, almost as if he knew exactly what I was doing by standing my ground. "You're right," he continued. "Let's cut through the bullshit. There's one other actress up for the part. Layla Hutson."

Layla freaking Hutson? I inhaled a sharp breath. Crap. Jude's ex-wife was my competition? Though, *competition* didn't seem like quite the right word for it. I didn't stand a chance when paired beside the walking Playboy Centerfold. I didn't know much about their breakup, outside of the ridiculous footage that was blasted all over TMZ. But I knew better than anyone not to believe everything you saw or read. "So?" I tilted my chin in a false act of confidence.

"So … you and I both know that beating Layla out for this role is a long shot."

Was he kidding with this? I snorted, shaking my head. "Well, *great*. Thank you so very much for coming out here tonight—where Omar and I were *celebrating* the callback—to tell me I don't have a shot in hell at the part. Thank you, Jude Fisher. Now if you don't mind, I think I'll take my bourbon, and my caramels, and my peonies—"

"Let me *finish*," he snapped through thinning lips. "Beating Layla at this role is a long shot, *but* I can help you.

And with my assistance, at least you'll be walking into the lion's den armed rather than empty handed."

"A couple hours ago, you told me I nailed that audition. Now I'm an unarmed Daniel in the Lion's den?"

"I meant what I said—your audition was great. The problem is, even though *I* know you're perfect for the part, all the studio sees is a girl who doesn't yet have a fan following."

I gulped. He was right. If I went into this callback next week the same as I did today, there was no way I'd get the part. And I *needed* that part. "So, what do you suggest?" I asked quietly.

Jude's mouth lifted into a barely there smile and he leaned in even closer. His breath was hot and he smelled of gin and peppermint. Green eyes pierced into me with an intensity beyond anything I'd ever seen in my life. "We have a week until your callback. I can teach you the BDSM lifestyle, prep you for the character, help you with your image and make it so they'll be begging you to sign the contracts."

Sweat gathered at the nape of my neck and a wave of prickly heat seared my cheeks. "I'm not sleeping with you," I said bluntly.

Jude's gaze softened, thoughtfully and he shook his head. "I'm not asking you to. How I teach you will be strictly professional. Omar can even be there, if you want."

That was a bold move … inviting my fiancé to join us. I narrowed my eyes at him. Was it a bluff? "How are you going to teach me this lifestyle if we're not having sex?"

As he took a long, lingering sip of his martini, our gazes locked over the edge of the glass. "The director, Ash, said something very poignant in our meeting today. He said, you can't really learn this lifestyle through a Google search. And he's right, Marly," Jude said, his voice lowering as he leaned forward. "Sex is the least of BDSM. Yes, it's a component, but anyone can have sex. It's everything leading up to that which is important."

Thoughts swarmed my mind. BDSM wasn't about sex? That didn't make sense. My expression must have shown my confusion, because Jude released a breath, and clarified some more. "BDSM is about control. It's about the power dynamic between two people. It's sexual in nature ... but it's not always about sex." I wasn't sure when it happened, but somehow, we had moved closer together. The light cotton of his dress pants brushed my bare knee, deliciously soft against my flesh. "Control," he said again. "And it has nothing to do with a male/female power dynamic. There are female Dominants. Male submissives. Sexual orientations that vary. Above all else, BDSM is about trust. Trust and control."

"And ... pain?" I asked. Everything I knew about BDSM involved pain and punishment. Whips, paddles, ropes, that sort of thing.

If Jude was surprised by my question, he hid it well, slowly shaking his head. "Sometimes, but not always. That's probably the biggest misconception about BDSM." His eyes wandered over to the box of caramels and he turned his wrist over, freezing, his eyes locked on his bare flesh. Was he looking for his watch? It was at home on my nightstand. Then instead, he looked at his phone for the time. "Here's a small taste," he said, reaching for the caramels. "Have one." He held the box out to me.

It felt like a trap, but I took one carefully as he gave me an encouraging nod. "Indulge me," he said.

I unwrapped the candy and even though it was small enough to pop the whole thing in my mouth, I bit into half of it. The dark chocolate coating cracked and gooey caramel melted over my tongue in a splash of creamy sweetness. I closed my eyes, sighing as a burst of salt sprinkled on the top contrasted with the decadent caramel. I swallowed, eating the second bite and sucking the little bit of melted chocolate from my fingers. When I opened my eyes, I found Jude's gaze affixed to my mouth. Darting out my tongue, I licked the corners of my lips, wiping away any excess chocolate that may have gotten on me. "Okay ..." I said carefully, shifting against the plush bench. "Not sure how this fits into BDSM." I reached out to take another caramel from the box, but he swiftly slid it out of reach.

His smile was gone. Replaced with an intense expression that had his eyebrows low over his eyes and his mouth dipping in a way that wasn't quite a frown, but also definitely wasn't a smile. "I had to see what you look like when enjoying these. And if I was your Dominant, I might tell you to have only one more caramel tonight. At exactly 10:45." He leaned over, taking one wrapped caramel and dropping it into his breast pocket. "And at exactly 10:45, I'll have my caramel. We may still be here at the club, looking at each other from across the room. Or I may be gone already, but no matter where, we will be sharing this caramel together."

I narrowed my eyes at the box of chocolates. "What would we get out of that?"

"Well, it's a small example of the power dynamic. For me, I love knowing that my submissive is enjoying her treat and I get to think about her pleasure at the exact moment it's happening. I get to imagine her expression, imagine her smile as she bites half, allowing the chocolate to melt over her fingers so that she can lick it off after."

"Yeah ... but the box is right there," I said, pointing at it. "We could also just each enjoy a caramel now. Instead of imagining my face enjoying it, you could actually see my face enjoying it."

"And as a Dom, there might be times I choose to do that." His voice dropped, husky like he'd just taken a mouthful of cigar smoke. "But we are in a time where pleasure is a constantly running spigot. Any time you want, you can stick your mouth over that overflowing water and gorge yourself in pleasure. In a world of instant gratification, you could absolutely eat those caramels now. Or you could wait. Eat only the two I tell you and indulge in the flavor, knowing that's all you get tonight. Knowing that I am pleased by you following the order. And knowing that in those moments, I am picturing the way that tiny string of caramel fell over your bottom lip as you took a bite. By withholding, that pleasure will intensify with the second caramel."

My mouth went dry, but other more important areas were completely wet. "You can't know that," I managed to rasp.

He nodded. "Oh, yes, I can." The tip of a pink tongue darted out, running along the seam of his full lips. Did he know the effect he was having on me? Did he know that the mere sight of that tongue nearly drove me to my knees?

I shook myself out of the Jude Fisher fog. This was absolutely out of the question. "And what about Omar?"

"Tell him," Jude said, sitting back against the bench once more. "Tell him *everything*. You have to both be on board. Your needs and comfort are the most important.

Which is why, if you want Omar there by your side, I can arrange that." Relief flooded me. Jude's care and caution and respect for both Omar and me only made me like him more. "If you agree, I'll bring you into my world. I'll be trusting you with a side of myself not many people see."

"But that's going to change," I said. "As soon as this movie premieres, people will know ... Or at least, suspect." His face tightened.

"Not necessarily. In theory, *most* people will only think I am a talented actor." He leaned forward, humor flashing in his eyes. "Only you, Omar, and I will know what a real hack I am," he whispered with a wink. "If you decide to learn my lifestyle, I'll show you what it is to relinquish control of a situation. We'll do trust exercises. Role play different Dominant/submissive behaviors, rehearse the callback sides. But absolutely no sex."

I arched an eyebrow. "No sex, huh?"

"No. Even if you were single and interested, as soon as actors fuck in real life, all chemistry on screen is lost."

I never believed that urban legend. It was ludicrous. Just because you were together in real life, didn't mean you couldn't act like new lovers as well. Hell, it was what acting was. But the fact that Jude Fisher seemed to buy into that mindset was curious. "You and Layla were together for years. And you acted in films together and—"

Words weren't needed to silence me. One look from Jude's green eyes and I snapped my mouth closed. Those eyes, which moments before had been heated, froze into an icy glare. I cleared my throat, desperately wishing I had a bourbon in hand to keep myself busy. Instead, I twisted my hands in my lap, bouncing my knee. "Oh," I whispered. "So, you're offering to help me because—"

"Because if I have to act alongside Layla, one of us may not live to wrap the movie. And I honestly think you're the better actress," he interrupted, voice sharper than a knife's blade.

"Thank you," I whispered. I was dying to know the whole story about Jude and Layla, but I also knew better than to pry.

"The only question is … are you up for this? Method acting isn't easy. And it's not for everyone."

There was a little voice in the back of my brain screaming to run in the opposite direction. To get the hell away from Jude and this audition. But my gut was saying something entirely different. I trailed my gaze around the club; no one seemed to be watching. No one seemed to care that I was sitting here all alone with an actor I had just auditioned with, while my 'fiancé' was off somewhere in the bar on his own. Kyle was going to kill me when he found out about this. *If* he found out about it.

"If I do this, no one can know. *No one.*"

Jude nodded, tilting his head to the side. "If anyone finds out about this, I'm in just as much shit as you are."

He pushed to his feet, smoothing a palm over his pants. I stood too, my gaze drifting with his movement, powerless to stop where my eyes roamed.

"Tomorrow night, meet me at Daisy's Diner on Kings Ave at 10:30 pm. If you accept my help, come with a week's bag packed. I'll be there waiting." He reached into his jacket pocket and pulled out a business card. "If you eat that caramel tonight … text me. Let me know how it felt, what your thoughts were. And if I don't see you tomorrow night at Daisy's, I'll understand. And I'll be rooting for you at the callbacks."

From over Jude's shoulder, Omar approached. He stood a handful of inches taller than Jude, with massive shoulders that were beyond what any normal man would need. And yet, with the two men side by side, Jude's figure set my body on fire, while Omar's did nothing for me.

"Jude Fisher," Omar's voice boomed, handing me the bourbon and sliding his hand around my waist. "This is a surprise."

Jude grinned, taking Omar's hand. He didn't flinch, didn't cower; didn't back down the slightest bit in Omar's presence. Impressive. Most men, no matter what their status, quaked at least a little around Omar. He was that kind of guy.

I caught the glint in Omar's eyes and smirked. He had noticed it too, that lack of flinch in Jude.

"I saw you both come in and I wanted to congratulate Marly on her audition."

Omar nodded, sipping his pint and squeezing my hip. "I heard you already congratulated her … with a Rolex."

Jude smiled in a rehearsed way I was beginning to recognize. It was his camera smile; not the real one. Not the one that crinkled his eyes and caused divots in his cheek. "Yes," Jude said, pointing playfully at me. "And I want that back after your callback."

Omar pressed his lips in a slow, lingering kiss behind my ear and I wiggled, nearly giggling at how much it tickled. Jude's eyes stayed fixed on me, narrowing at the moment between us. Shit. I needed to learn how to do this fiancé thing better, because right now? I sucked at it. With a silent sigh, I leaned into the kiss. When Omar pulled back, he offered me a content smile and brushed his thumb over my bottom lip. His gaze shifted to the opened box of caramels and he grinned. "Already dug in, huh?" Then, looking to Jude, he added, "She can't resist those."

"I noticed." Jude's mouth twitched into a smile and he waved at the VIP server. "I got you some champagne. To celebrate. Of course, that was before I knew you were a bourbon drinker."

"Thanks, man. That was nice." Omar said, his grin widening.

"Thanks, Jude," I echoed. "Would you like to stay for the first glass?"

"No, no. I've got to get going." He leaned over, taking Omar's hand once more in a firm handshake, then leaned in, slowly, brushing his lips gently across my cheek. Even though it was chaste, the sensation fluttered in my stomach.

He turned and headed out of the VIP section as Omar raised an eyebrow at me.

"Don't start," I puffed, finishing the rest of my bourbon in a gulp.

"Wasn't gonna," Omar grinned. "Now, let's get this celebration started." He sat down and pulled me into his lap, curling his body around mine in a hug.

I FOUND MYSELF checking the time every five minutes. I was powerless to stop, even from the dance floor. Of course, Omar noticed and at around 10:40, I tugged my phone out of my small glittered purse, the bass from the music still pulsing around us. His gaze narrowed, eyeing me with a scrutiny that only Omar could get away with.

"You got another date later tonight?" he joked.

My cheeks warmed. With a final sip of bourbon, I shook my empty glass. "I'm going to use the bathroom and get another bourbon. Want one more?" I asked, lifting my chin toward Omar's nearly empty pint glass.

He tipped the glass back, finishing the rest and handed me his empty cup. "Sure. Thanks, boo."

I wasn't lying exactly, telling Omar I was getting another drink ... and yet, it definitely didn't feel like the truth. But I had to know; had to find out for myself what this pleasure was that Jude talked about. What would it feel like to eat that caramel in the same moment he would be eating his and thinking about me? I swallowed, my mouth suddenly dry as I weaved through the VIP lounge. I checked my phone again as I reached our table. 10:43. The peonies still decorated the table like pink, fluffy balls of cotton candy. I put my phone down, face up, watching the minutes tick by. 10:44. My stomach fluttered and I took one of the salted caramels in my hand. Normally, this box would be half gone by now and I'd be feeling guilty, with plans to punish myself with an extra 30 minutes on the treadmill. This was different. I was excited for the bite. For a nibble of a treat I'd had dozens of times. The flutter in my stomach waved up my body, cresting at my breasts, and beneath the flimsy dress, my nipples tightened.

Was Jude doing the same thing? Was he at home, caramel in hand, watching the clock, anticipating my bite? Was he in bed? On his couch? Wearing his suit or pajamas? Or better yet, nothing.

Shit. No. *No.* This was research for a part. That's all. The time on my phone switched. 10:45 exactly. Those were his words. With the change in time, that wave of excitement I'd been feeling turned into a monsoon. Chill bumps skated down my arms. Why was I nervous? Why was I so excited? I lifted the caramel to my lips, closing my eyes and slowly took a bite. My heart slammed against my ribs, beating wildly and I felt that same pulse between my legs. I bit the caramel, chocolate cracking against my teeth, immediately melting against the warmth of my lips and breath. It was dark ... still sweet, but also bitter. The caramel spilled over my tongue, sweet and rich and gooey, and as I chewed, I saw Jude's face. His slightly curved smile. His jade green eyes, so cool and collected. What would he look like wild? Unhinged? Would he be pleased knowing I was eating this salted caramel just as he had instructed? Was he eating his, too? Did he swallow it in one big bite? Nibble it like I did? Lick his lips clean of melted chocolate as he finished?

I swallowed, my stomach tight and crossed my legs to relieve the ache at the apex of my thighs. Then, I placed the other half of the caramel in my mouth, sucking the melted chocolate from my thumb, rolling my tongue over the tip of my finger, imagining it was the tip of Jude's cock. As the caramel dripped down my throat, thick and creamy, my mind exploded with imagery of Jude and caramel drizzled on various parts of his body.

A moan escaped from somewhere low in my throat. The guttural sound unlike any noise I'd heard myself make in the past and my eyes shot open. *Did anyone hear that?* My face burned and I scanned the room, looking for anyone who might be watching me; laughing at me. No one looked my direction. Most bodies were still writhing on the dance floor. Or at the bar ordering. Omar was just to the side of the dance floor, facing the opposite wall talking on his phone.

What is wrong with me? This was a chocolate covered caramel for God's sake. Not a vibrator. Not porn. Not a sexy romance novel…. One single piece of candy and I was so damned hot, I was considering rushing home to have a little quality time with my battery-operated boyfriend.

My gaze settled back onto the nearly full box of caramels beside the peonies. I wanted another. Wanted more of what I'd just had. But Jude had specifically said only one more for tonight. Heat curled around my spine and I clutched my hands together. If I was a submissive, following this rule would be part of what made it sexy. And if I was being completely honest with myself, it *was* sexy.

Knowing he was at home, turned on, thinking about me. And knowing I made him happy. The disease to please, my dad called it. But no, it was more than just that. Maybe it was the delayed gratification Jude had mentioned. The fact that this was the only chocolate I was having tonight and so I anticipated it. Waited for it, longing for it. Nervous for it. And it made the caramel so, so much better. Jude's pleasure was only part of that.

Dipping my hand into my bag, I pulled out Jude's business card, running my finger along the cornered edge of the paper. Then, grabbing my phone, I punched in his number, texting him.

I'll see you tomorrow at Daisy's. My mind was made up. Whatever that was I had just experienced? I wanted more of it. Needed more of it. For research, yes. But also for myself. That intense moment of pleasure was unlike anything I'd had before. My phone buzzed in my palm.

So, it was good then?

Good didn't even cover it. I swallowed, my thumbs tapping the keys. *It was the best salted caramel of my life. How was yours?*

If I closed my eyes, I could almost hear his low rumbled

chuckle. Could almost smell his earthy, spicy scent.

I loved every second of it. And I love it even more knowing you enjoyed the experiment, too.

The experiment. Was that all I was? Some sort of twisted BDSM Pygmalion?

It didn't matter. The point was, I wanted this part. And it was clear I had a lot to learn about this lifestyle—about Jude's lifestyle—despite the hours I'd spent Googling and on FetLife. Three little dots appeared above Jude's name. He was typing more.

You did a great job tonight. Have fun, be sure to drink some water and take a Tylenol before bed.

"I was wondering what was taking so long." Omar's voice boomed above me and I jumped, startled, clutching the phone tighter. He laughed. "I should have guessed you dug back into those caramels. I'll go get us the next round."

He turned toward the bar.

"And a water," I blurted out, my eyes falling to Jude's text. "Please."

"Water and a bourbon coming up," Omar said, walking away.

I sighed, leaning back and slid the phone into my purse. If I was going to try this submissive thing for a week, I was going all in. *Except for sex.* Which, based on how turned on I got from one damned chocolate, might be harder than I thought.

CHAPTER SIX

Jude

IT WAS 10:46 p.m. when my phone rang with an unknown number. My mouth was still coated with the chocolate and caramel and my cock was hard. A little detail that wasn't going unnoticed, but was completely fucking unwelcome. There was no place for my damn arousal when it came to me and Marly. Now if I could just convince my dick of that.

My breath hitched as the phone buzzed against my coffee table. Was it Marly calling? Shoving my hand into my hair, I grabbed the phone, pressing the answer button.

"Hello?" *Shit, why is my voice so graveled?*

"Jude Fisher." I recognized the deeply masculine voice immediately.

"Omar," I responded, surprised. "What can I do for you?"

"We need to talk," Omar said. He didn't sound mad … he also didn't sound all that happy.

"Where's Marly?" I asked and immediately regretted it. Asking the whereabouts of Omar's fiancé was probably not the best way to start this conversation—whatever this was. Then again, if Marly and I were going to do this education for a week and perhaps be in this film together, we had to find a way to become Leo and Holly without Omar being threatened.

"She told me she was going to the bar to order us a drink, but then she went back to have another caramel." Omar chuckled. "God, I love that girl." There was something in his voice ... I noticed it when I watched Omar and Marly together at the club, too. There was affection there, absolutely. But chemistry? Sexual tension? It was non-existent.

I stretched out my legs, putting my feet up on the coffee table, sinking deeper into my leather couch. "She's just eating the one?" I couldn't resist asking.

There was a pause before Omar answered. "As far as I can tell, she just had one."

A satisfied smile curved my mouth. *Good girl.* "What can I do for you, Omar? And how'd you get this number?"

"You're not the only one with friends you can call in favors from. After Marly told me about the Rolex from today's audition, I got your number from a mutual friend."

Up until that point, Omar's voice had been calm and collected. But instantaneously, it shifted, his voice suddenly tight, aggressive even. I swallowed, ignoring my instinct to snarl back. This man was Marly's fiancé. The real man in her life. Whereas I was just the stand-in for a role in a movie. I had to respect the man she chose to be her life partner, while at the same time respecting Marly's right to privacy. She was trusting me. And I needed to honor that trust.

So instead of saying anything, I slung my arm over the back of the couch, settling in for the angry fiancé lecture that was sure to come.

"Look," Omar said. "Marly is an incredible actress. And the fact that you believe in her means a lot. To her. And me. I just want ... no, *need* you to know ... I am all for her getting this part. But if you're using her in any way, I will ruin you. I don't care if it means I never get a job at Silhouette Studios. I will take you fucking down in flames with me."

Well, shit. I could respect that. I cleared my throat. "I'm not trying to take advantage of Marlena. I believe in her. Without a doubt, I know she is best for the part. That being said, she has a lot of work to do, studying the BDSM lifestyle. And I have to tell you … if she gets the part, she and I will be doing exercises together. Exercises and scenes that are very sexual. And sensual. When we film, we'll be naked—and I don't just mean our bodies. Emotionally, we'll be raw. Vulnerable. Is that going to be a problem?"

I wasn't trying to be an asshole. But Omar had to know; he had to understand what it was going to mean for Marly to do this movie. Three months of us working closely together. Full frontal nude scenes, but even more intense would be the bonding; the chemistry we needed to discover together. Not a lot of partners could handle that kind of intimacy … even if it was only onscreen.

"What Marly and I have is special. And I trust her to do what is needed in her career. I'm not threatened by whatever onscreen or off-screen relationship you two have," Omar said. "Marly can handle herself. But as her best friend, I'm calling to tell you I have her back. And if you do anything to threaten or hurt her within the process, you will regret that. Am I clear?"

"Understood." *Best friend*. Omar called himself her best friend, not her fiancé. I couldn't resist asking. "When you have her back, do you have it as her best friend or her fiancé?"

There was a pause on the other end of the line. "Both,"

Omar said. "We are best friends first and always. No matter what happens. And fiancés second."

Emotion knotted in my chest. What was that feeling clawing up my throat? Envy. I was envious of their love. Their bond. It was the very thing Layla and I had been missing in ours. We weren't friends ... we never were. Not even in the height of our passion. Our bond was purely sexual. My lust for her was the fog that clouded around us, convincing me it was love. But I didn't fucking know what love was. Who was I to judge what I saw between Marly and Omar? Maybe that chemistry I *thought* they were lacking was just my own fucked up idea of what a relationship should be.

"Omar, I promise you, I'll take care of Marly. Onscreen and off-screen. I have no intention of taking advantage of her. I only want to help her get this role and I know I can. I'm a member of the Los Angeles BDSM community and I think I can help her grasp the character even more than she already does."

Another long pause. "Wow," Omar said finally. "I can't believe you told me that. It's so ... personal."

"You deserve to know. But I'd appreciate your discretion."

"Your secret's safe with me."

My phone pinged in my ear and I looked at the screen, seeing a text from Marly. "I need to go, Omar."

"You have a good night." With that, we disconnected the call.

Well, that was ... interesting.

IT WAS ABOUT nine-thirty p.m. when I slipped into the club

the following night—I had roughly an hour before Marly arrived at the diner. Well, hopefully. If her nerves didn't get the better of her. And if she didn't show? My stomach twisted at the thought and I sighed, with a quick glance around the crowded dance floor. Bass pounded through expensive speakers. Sweaty bodies writhed against each other, despite the early hour.

My stomach flipped as I made my way through the maze of people to the back rooms of LnS—an abbreviation for Leather n' Silk. It had been over a year since I'd stepped foot inside these walls. But nothing had changed. It felt like just yesterday that I was here every weekend.

On the surface, LnS looked like any other thriving nightclub. It had a light BDSM/Burlesque theme to it, but it was just that. Light. The people who frequented the downstairs were first timers. People who saw the lifestyle as a fun gimmick. They'd put on leather and carry whips, and at the end of the night, they went home, spanked a few asses and called themselves edgy.

But those with a key to LnS knew that it was so much more. I turned down the small hallway, passing the bathrooms and came up behind Claude Guille—star of the most recent teen heartthrob movie and the main love interest to most girls ages thirteen and under. I snorted to myself. *Claude Guille.* At an audition, just a couple of years ago, "Claude Guille" was Clyde Grimes—a pimply blonde kid from Texas reading for featured background roles. A bony brunette with far too much eyeliner clung to his arm, eyes foggy and dilated. The bouncer stood about triple the size of Claude with arms folded. A massive wall, blockading the way up the stairs into the *real* LnS.

"C'mon, man!" Claude whined, holding up a one-hundred dollar bill. "I can double this."

Pete's eyes darkened and his crossed arms flexed with the bribe. These guys get paid more than that and then some. The last thing he needed was a hundred bucks. "Upstairs is off-limits. I'm sorry, but you'll have to leave."

"Baby," the girl's nasal voice clipped my ears and I winced at how closely she sounded like Layla. Fuck. "I'm tired."

Claude snaked his arm tighter around her waist, tugging the girl into him. "Thanks a lot, asshole," he muttered, turning and practically dragging the girl beside him.

Claude's eyebrows jumped when he saw me. "Good luck, man."

I nodded, waiting until Claude was completely out of sight, then pulled a gold keycard out of my wallet.

"Jude," Pete looked at me, his eyes widening for only the briefest second. "It's good to see you here again. Welcome back."

"Thanks," I did my best to give him a smile. So much for trying to slip in without making a big deal of my return. "Rough night?"

Pete exhaled through tight lips, shaking his head. "It's a Tuesday, man. Thought it'd be a slow night." He took my keycard, swiping it through a reader and holding the screen out to me.

"My voice is my password," I said into the microphone.

Pete handed the card back to me.

"I have a guest coming tonight, but we need to be really discreet. More discreet than usual."

"Back entrance?"

I nodded. "We'll be meeting down at the diner on Kings Ave in about an hour."

"What's her name?"

"Marlena Taylor."

Pete typed something into the tablet, his face revealing nothing. One of the attributes LnS prided itself on— absolute apathy toward everything and every*one* you do inside its doors. The second I walked up those stairs, Pete would be on the internet, researching the hell out of Marly and putting together her file ... essentially a blackmail file if she were to ever leak information about the *real* LnS. It was the best and most secure way to keep those within its walls hushed. The types of people who came to this club had money—more than they knew what to do with. A monetary fine would do jack shit in keeping people quiet. But dirt on you that will be spilled if you spill? Yeah. That was enough to keep mine and most everyone's mouth shut for sure.

"You know the drill," Pete continued. "You can explain the privacy code to her yourself. I'll have a temporary contract in your room in a few minutes. It will cover her for the basics for a night."

"I might need something a little more involved. I want her to learn about the lifestyle and see more than the average girl I bring."

Though his face didn't show it, interest vibrated off of Pete's body. I haven't been to the club, let alone had a sub with me in a long time.

"Not a problem. I'll get you the beginner's contract. If she decides to join, the process will be more involved, as you know, but this should give her a taste of the community with safety to you and the others."

"Thanks, Pete. Have the contract be good through Thursday." I took off up the stairs, two at a time. The question was, what would they find on Marly as leverage? Damn, I hoped I never found out.

Marly

I SAT IN Daisy's Diner sipping my second cup of tea. I was early, but hoped that the extra time and the warm beverage would calm my frazzled nerves. Steam billowed from the top of my porcelain cup and the warmth of it surged from my palms up my arms, heating me both inside and out. I set the glass down, my hand trembling as it clattered against the saucer, then picked up my pen, twirling it in my fingers. My turquoise planner sat next to my cup like a reliable friend and I tapped my pen rapidly against the binding. With a quick glance at the clock, I chewed my lip and tugged on the raven black wig. It itched like hell and sweat gathered at the base of my neck. I still had time to back out. It wasn't yet ten thirty; I could still leave.

My heart jumped with each jingle of the door, only to relax again when it wasn't Jude. If I continued this way, I'd have a heart attack before the guy ever showed up. My leg bounced and I chewed the side of my fingernail. It was an awful habit, and yet I could never break it. I managed to nix poor eating habits, cracking my knuckles and popping my gum—but chewing my nails? Nope, that one was ingrained into my DNA.

My phone buzzed from inside my purse and I dipped my head inside, catching the vibrating cell in one hand. I smiled as a text from Omar illuminated the screen.

Thinking of you. Stay safe, boo, and knock 'em dead.

With one glance at those words, I tugged my fingers

from my mouth, calmness washing over me. What would I do without that man? I uncrossed my legs, my jittery bouncing knee subsiding. As I typed my response, awareness buzzed over me, shooting pins-and-needles sensation down my arms. When I glanced up, Jude was frozen in the open doorway, his eyes fixed on me. I slapped the phone down onto the table, nudging my toe against my rolling luggage. The weight of it, oddly comforting. Familiarity in unknown territory.

His gait was strong, confident as he made his way across the room. "You came," he said simply, his eyes traveling over my wig and heavy makeup. I even contoured my face, hoping to look like an entirely different person. A smile tipped his lips.

"I told you I would be here."

"Yes. You did." The subtext *but I didn't believe you* sat just below those words. Like kelp floating beneath the surface of the ocean. "Let's get to it, then." He slid the chair out from under the table, dropping into it. "You'll be in my possession from tonight—"

The hot tea burst through my nose and I coughed, pressing a palm to my chest. "Excuse me, *possession?*"

He blinked, pulling loose papers from a leather folio. "Yes. *Possession.* Much in the same way that Holly is in Leo's possession throughout the film."

Oh, good lord. Panic rose in my chest like a bathtub filling with water. Red flags waved everywhere and yet, I nodded for him to continue. He set the papers down, the lines at his eyes and forehead softening as he draped his hand over mine. His touch sent a jolt of electricity from the soft flesh of his fingers up my arm. My skin prickled, heating beneath his touch and I shivered despite the surge of warmth. "Marly," he said quietly, "this is the language I use as a Dominant. It's only words, okay?"

His green eyes were bright and I blinked slowly, moisture clinging to my lashes. Throat dry. Eyes wet. I cleared my throat. "But … it isn't *just words*," I repeated. "It's a lifestyle. Your lifestyle. Leo's … Holly's lifestyle. Don't feed me some line about how they're meaningless phrases."

As Jude leaned back in his chair, his hand slipped away. It felt deliberate. Intentional. Like he was purposefully withholding his affection because I spoke up which only made me want to fight harder, louder.

"You're right," Jude said quietly. "They're just words, but at the end of the day, they represent action. In this world—" he coughed, covering his mouth with his fist briefly. "*My* world, possession isn't a negative thing. It means safety. Security. Because as your Dom, as Holly's Dom, it's my job to care for you. And you for me. This relationship is all about anticipating each other's needs and fulfilling them by—"

"By beating the shit out of each other?" I interrupted, regretting it immediately when the soft lines of Jude's face tightened and his mouth turned down at the corners.

He gave a humorless chuckle and shook his head. "Sadomasochism is only a small part of BDSM. For someone who claimed to do her research, I'm surprised you would say something so … incorrect."

Incorrect and hurtful. I squeezed my eyes shut. "I'm sorry," I whispered. "I didn't mean that."

"Yes, you did." Jude observed me, licking his lips and watching me so closely, my skin tingled under his gaze. If his touch was all heat and fire … then his gaze was the opposite. Cool, collected. "If I do my job right this week, you'll understand by Monday why those thoughts are inaccurate." He cleared his throat and leaned forward, taking a stack of papers in his hand. Tenderly, he traced the edges, not saying another word. The slow movement of his finger as it curved around the corner, brushing over the pointy edge had me squeezing my legs tighter together. That touch. So light. Gentle, but firm. I could almost feel it from yesterday when his hands caught my elbows as I nearly fell at the club. "Do you want me to continue?" He didn't look up from the stack of papers. Couldn't see me nodding yes. Or maybe he wanted me to speak.

"Yes, please continue."

From over the paper's edge, his eyes aligned with mine. We were like the sun and the moon, both orbiting around a common goal. We had hardly anything in common. Two different worlds trying to collide—and so far, failing miserably. "Are you sure? Because in these contracts, I reveal things about myself that I only share with a select few. And I need your word that—"

"You have my word, Jude." He looked so vulnerable. Sad, even. The contrast was jarring—from the man I saw and met in the audition room, to this man sitting in front of me, nervous and exposed.

"Unfortunately, I need your word *and* your signature on these contracts." He slid over a short, two-page document. A non-disclosure agreement. "My lawyers insisted you sign this first. It just states—"

"That I am not allowed to discuss anything I see or hear regarding your lifestyle," I read aloud. Grabbing my pen, I scribbled some notes, adding Omar's name into the contract, then initialed and slid it back to Jude. "I tell Omar everything. He has to be the exception to this."

Jude initialed and signed the change. "Then I'll need Omar's signature, too."

I nodded. "Fax it over to him. I'm sure he's fine with that."

Jude released a heavy sigh, his eyes drifting closed. "Okay, then," he whispered. "Until Omar signs his contract, you can't talk to him about this though. Fair?"

"More than fair," I agreed.

"Here goes nothing," Jude murmured to himself, pulling out the next stack of papers. "This is a copy of my Dominant-submissive contract," he said. "If you and I were entering a true relationship, this is the stage where you would list your hard limits—i.e., things you will never do and I should never attempt—and your soft limits—things that you might be open to eventually."

I took a long sip of tea. "So, like ... anal would be a soft limit." Oh, my God. Did I just say that to a practical stranger? I'd never tried anal, but all my friends seemed to think it was incredible and I was ... well, intrigued.

I stared into my teacup, awaiting Jude's response. Silence came from the other end of the table and when I glanced up over the lip of my small ceramic cup, Jude was staring. Like, *really* staring. Jaw tight. Eyes shrewd. Lips wet and plump. When I met his eyes, something between us shifted. The air felt tighter, like there was less oxygen between us and we were breathing the same small pocket of air. "For some, yes," Jude finally said.

"And ... um, what would be a hard limit?"

"Well, what is something you would never in a million years do? In fact, if I did do it to you, it would be a betrayal?"

I brought my fingernail to my lips, nibbling the edge.

"Public nudity, sharing, voyeurism. Whatever I do in the bedroom stays private, just between me and my partner."

Jude nodded, a smile curving the corners of his lips. "We have that in common."

He slid his submissive contract across the table. Was that …? Was his hand trembling? He scraped his other palm down his face over his mouth.

He was nervous. So nervous, he was shaking. Without thinking, I covered his shaking hand with mine, curving my fingers around his knuckles. He gasped from the other end of the table. "Jude, I promise you, you're safe with me. All these secrets … I would never do to you what Jack did to me—" my voice caught and I swallowed, trying again. "I just … I would never do that to you. You can trust me."

Each deep breath he took was like Xanax for my nerves. Our breathing evened, until we were inhaling and exhaling together like some sort of fucked up, naughty yoga class. "Thank you, Marly." He breathed my name like it was a mantra. A whisper on his lips. I'd never liked my name … but coming from Jude? It almost sounded sexy.

"Thank you for this. You're helping me … and … and I'm still not entirely sure why."

"I already told you why," he said. Could it really be this is all just because he doesn't want to act alongside his ex-wife anymore? It seemed extreme. He cleared his throat and tugged his hand from beneath mine, tapping the contract. "So, this is an example of what I expect from my submissives. Before we begin, I have her look it over, make any amendments she wants to it. We agree to everything expected and of course, we revisit the contract from time to time, discuss any new scenes before they happen."

I lifted the contract, reading over it.

"You don't need to sign that now. Or ever. I think it would be a good exercise for you ... for us ... but it can take a while, hashing out the Dom/sub contract."

"Shh," I chastised him playfully with a wink. "I'm reading here." I gestured at the contract and Jude's smile lifted once more.

"Reading about Burritos, Doritos, Snickers and ... what was the last one?"

"M&Ms."

"Right. M&Ms." His grin widened and I tore my gaze back to the contract.

Jude Fisher's daily rules:

1) Every day, sweet girl must wear an item that reminds her of Jude. It must be an item given to her by Jude and it must stay on her from the moment she gets dressed, to the moment she goes to sleep.

2) Every morning before leaving the house, sweet girl must text Jude a photo of her outfit. Not to be approved, but so Jude can praise her and tell sweet girl how beautiful she is.

3) Every morning by 7 a.m., sweet girl will receive a good morning text from Jude and every evening by 11 p.m., she will receive a goodnight text. She must respond within 15 minutes of receiving these texts or prepare for punishment during their next playtime.

Holy shit. This was intense. "Sweet girl?" I asked, looking up.

His smile shifted, turning unsure. And he shrugged one

shoulder to his ear. "It's always been the term of endearment I've used for my subs."

Unease twisted in my belly. I never liked being one of many. "Even Layla?"

His smile dropped. "Yes," he answered hoarsely. "Even Layla."

Grabbing my pen, I scratched out all of the sweet girls on that paper. "I don't know what I should be called yet, but I'm unique. And I don't want my nickname to be one you've ever used for any other sub, especially your ex-wife."

"Noted."

I kept reading.

4) Every day at lunch, ~~sweet girl~~ must perform 100 kegel exercises and text Jude while she is doing them.

5) Every day at 6 p.m., ~~sweet girl~~ must insert Ben Wa balls and wear them until after dinner.

I paused from reading to take a sip of tea.

"You should start thinking of safe words, too," Jude said. "Just to get in the habit of using them."

Safe *words*? Plural. Before I could ask Jude about that, he started talking again. "And you should know, I'm officially no longer involved in casting the movie. I have no say in whether you get this part. Anything you do or don't do this week has no bearing on your getting hired. Understand?"

"Yes," I whispered, taking another sip of tea. It had cooled considerably. Jude's eyes dropped from my mouth to the tea cup, then lifting a hand, he gestured for the waitress to bring more hot water. Without me saying a word. If that were Jack sitting here? The hot tea could have been delivered over ice cubes and he wouldn't have noticed. *Or maybe he noticed and just never cared.* I clutched the contract tighter, sadness sitting heavily in my chest. Instead of dwelling on it, carving the sadness out like a cavity, I ignored it and kept reading. Because everyone knows if you ignore a cavity, it just goes away, right? Right.

6) If ~~sweet girl~~ chooses to masturbate, she must call Jude, wearing her collar of bells so that he may listen to her as she orgasms.

My blood roared in my ears and the tips of my breasts tingled. Holy hell, that sounded hot. And twisted. A collar with bells on it? Like some sort of fucked up elf from Santa's workshop? I cleared my throat, uncrossing and crossing my legs again and squeezing them to ease the throbbing ache of my clit. "So ... this um, bell collar thing ... does your sub say anything when she calls you?"

His lopsided smile was wicked and sexy and I wanted to run my tongue along the crooked curve of his lips. "No," he answered. "That's part of the fun. The collar of bells is kept in her nightstand. She calls, puts the phone down, says nothing ... and that's how I know what's happening, when I hear the bells. Sometimes I talk to her while she's masturbating. Other times, I just listen."

Holy. Shit. I licked my lips and set the paper down, clenching my hands beneath the table. "I can tell you now, I won't be doing that. Hard limit."

"I understand. Keep in mind, you can try these things with Omar. This week is about you learning the lifestyle, experiencing parts of it ... but it doesn't have to be with me."

A laugh snuck up on me and came out like a honk. "With Omar? God, no." The words were out before I could stop them and I pressed my lips together so hard, that my teeth bit into my soft flesh. "I just mean ... uh, I can't see us doing something like that—"

Jude shrugged, but the intensity of his eyes betrayed the casualness of the gesture. "You don't have to explain anything to me, Marly."

I set the contract aside. "Why don't I finish reading that later? Like you said, it can take a while, right?"

He nodded. "Okay, then. As I was saying before, you will be in my 'possession,'" he threw finger quotes around the word, punctuating it with his damn dimples, "tonight through Wednesday afternoon, at which point you'll go home and spend the rest of the evening relaxing before your Thursday audition." He clicked a pen with his thumb, setting it precisely parallel to the paper. "This is the last contract and it's from the BDSM club we'll be at for the week. It's the most important. The club protects both of us; it makes it so you can truly see the lifestyle without participating. You can watch what BDSM sex looks like, without us ever having to touch. Are you okay with that? Is there anything you don't want to see inside those walls? Let me know and I'll keep you from those areas."

I might be watching people have sex alongside of Jude? I closed my eyes, imagining what sorts of scenes we might see inside of the club. Would I be able to keep my wits about me? Yes, for the love of God, why would I risk everything for something as fleeting as a night with Jude? If I were to give in to these feelings, then all the rumors ... everything Jack had ever said about me would be right. I felt things with Jude I've never felt in my whole damn life with anyone else ... but maybe that's what method acting was all about. Maybe I was only feeling these things because I was already tapping into Holly in a way I never needed for other roles. And now ... we'll be watching others have sex. Together.

The bottom line was ... I wanted to see what this sort of intimacy looked like. How could I expect to play the part of Holly if I'd never seen the effect it had on women? Porn wasn't the same. Those women were essentially actresses, too. I needed to see a real orgasm. The real pleasure. The real pain. Not the over-dramatic screams of a young woman getting paid to act like she was having fun. "I want to see everything. But if I'm uncomfortable, all I have to do is say my safe word and you'll get me out of there?"

"Exactly. Your safe words will be your safety net," Jude said. "If you are uncomfortable with anything at any time, you simply need to state one of the safe words created tonight and the act will immediately stop."

"Safe words," I said, repeating him. "You keep mentioning them in the plural ... I thought you only had one?"

"Most submissives have at least three—one that means slow down, one that means stop, and one, um, non-verbal signal. For example, yellow to slow down—meaning you need a breather or a quick break, but you don't necessarily want to stop. Red would be to stop. You need everything to cease immediately. And the non-verbal ... usually, it's snapping. Something easy to do if your hands are tied and you're gagged."

Holy. Shit. What was I getting into? How far was Jude going to push me? Was he intending to make me use these words?

I gulped hard, a shiver tumbling down my spine.

"So," Jude said, "while I grab our check and use the restroom, you read the LnS contract." He stood, walking across the diner to the cashier.

I scanned the page and wet my lips at the legalese. The language in this one was completely different than the other two. Much more formal ... threatening almost. The standard non-disclosure agreement was different. I'd seen a million of those in my career. Every time a new script passed my desk, I had to sign one. But this? It was different. And Jude should know it was different. He could have sent this paperwork ahead of time. Could have messengered it to my house or faxed it. What was he hiding?

I sipped my tea once more, the cup clattering as I set it back down. My hands trembled and I lifted the pen, resting my other hand against my planner. Steadying me. I took a deep breath, skimming over the first two pages, only understanding every other word. I sighed, frustration rising from my stomach, lodging in my throat.

I could feel myself retreating. Backing away from the opportunity of a lifetime; the opportunity to learn the lifestyle, learn insight about Holly I couldn't get from a freaking Google search. *Backing away from being taken seriously.*

"Oh my God, are you Marlena Taylor?" A middle-aged woman at the table next to me leaned over, squinting as she tugged her glasses from atop her head down to the bridge of her nose.

"Uh—no," I tried to say, my voice cracking as I tugged at the wig.

"It is you!" she cried, clapping her hands together. "Oh, my daughter and I loved you in Bridesmaid Retreat."

"Um, thanks."

The woman crinkled her nose, smiling in a way that I've been smiled at my whole life. Like I was meant to look cute and smile pretty. Vapid. A pretty face, nothing more. "Is this new look for a role?" she asked, whispering.

"Something like that." I strung my fingers through the plastic strands of the wig. Even with the wig, I was still recognizable. As a rom-com girl. Nothing more. I was interchangeable. Clutching the pen tighter, I scribbled my name at the bottom of the last page. "I, uh, have to go. Have a good night." I collected my things off the table and tucked them into my purse before grabbing my rolling bag and rushing for the door. Jude could find me outside … I needed to get the hell out of there before anyone saw us together. Recognized me out with another man.

It didn't take him long to find me. He came barreling through the doors, heaving a sigh when he found me outside, leaning against a parking sign. "I thought maybe you left," he said, his breath heavy. His words quiet, but urgent.

"No," I said. "A woman recognized me and I didn't want her seeing us together."

He nodded, but offered nothing more. I grabbed the contract from within my purse and handed it to him. "Here you go."

"That was fast. You read it all?"

My lungs tightened with a deep breath, working hard to regulate each inhalation. "Yep. Read it all."

A muscle in his jaw ticked and a bit of his hair fell across his forehead. My fingers twitched, aching to thread them through his hair and push the fallen strands out of his face. "And … you're okay with everything?" Jude pointed that glower of his directly at me.

Crap. He's going to see right through my lie. "Yes," I said, as Jude reached across and took the rolling bag from me. "It was a bit unorthodox, but I … understand." I tilted my head, angling my chin at him. What did Jude say about this contract? Dammit, I should have just read the stupid thing. Think, Marly, think! What was one thing it said inside? "I mean, like you said, the club has to protect themselves somehow, right?"

I held his steely gaze, those intense, jade eyes glittering back at me. "That's right."

Heat flashed across his gaze and as quickly as I saw it, it was gone. "Come on," he said, lifting my bag effortlessly. Heading for his car, his palm hovered at my lower back, not quite touching but seeming to give an electric pulse as though he had some sort of supernatural power. How could I *feel* him without really feeling him? It made no sense. Jude hit the button on his keychain and from across the parking lot, a black car beeped, the headlights flashing as it unlocked. "Will Omar be coming?"

Omar? Oh, right. He had invited Omar multiple times so that I would feel more comfortable. I shook my head. "No. I have to do this alone."

"Well," Jude whispered, bumping my elbow with his. "Not *alone*."

I smiled up at him. "You know what I mean." Shoving my fingers inside the wig cap, I scratched at the base of my scalp. Damn thing was *so* itchy. And hot.

"By the way, the wig was a smart idea," Jude said.

I snorted, the dark hair catching against my glossy lips. "Lot of good it did, since I was *still* recognized."

"That doesn't mean it wasn't a good idea."

"Well, we can't have any cameras catching me out and about with Hollywood's most notorious bachelor, can we?"

Jude bellowed a laugh as he opened the door to a sleek, black Bugatti, gesturing for me to get in. The noise caught me off guard—it was such a different laugh than the throaty chuckle I was accustomed to hearing from him. "You make a strong point, Ms. Taylor."

My gaze flicked from the Bugatti to my own car parked across the lot. "Leave it," he answered, reading my thoughts. "My assistant will come pick it up tonight and bring it back to my place. We'll park it in the garage where no one will see it."

I slid into the plush leather seats. There was a groan and I wasn't sure if it was me or the sound of leather buckling around my weight. Jude tossed my bag in the trunk, then circled around and dropped himself into the driver's seat.

"Well," I said, "according to you, if it's something the media reports on, it's likely not even close to the truth, right?"

He winked and the car purred to life. "You're learning."

"What can I say?" I flipped open the passenger side mirror, fiddling with the dark curls. "I'm a quick study." I swung my head wildly back and forth like an exaggerated supermodel on acid. "So, what do you think of the dark hair?" I asked, dropping my voice deeper. "Should I make it a permanent change?"

Omar would have laughed. Jack would have pulled me into his lap and kissed me. But Jude simply stared. His eyes were intense; fixed onto my mouth and they slowly slid up to meet my gaze. He stared until I shifted in the seat. Heat surged in my cheeks, flushing my face. It was like some sort of convoluted game of chicken. One I was definitely going to lose. "I-I was kidding."

"I know." There was a crinkle at the corners of his eyes that suggested a smile and yet those lips—dang, those lips, were nowhere close to lifting. He leaned over, reaching forward with one hand and adjusted the wig. It shifted on my head and the curls symmetrically fell to each side of my shoulders.

Then, he stretched beyond my body, reaching across my shoulders and taking hold of the seatbelt. With a tug, he pulled it across my chest and clicked it into place at the base of my hip. "Safety first," he whispered, but didn't make any move to stop staring. A blush crawled from my itchy hairline down to my painted toes. Flirting with him was major league and I was still in the minors, learning the rules of the game. His eyes darted back and forth, skimming my features. The grin slid lazily across his face this time. "Not used to being looked at so closely, Ms. Taylor?"

I swallowed. "I'm an actress. Scrutiny comes with the job." Then, after a pause, I added. "I'm just trying to figure out what it is you're looking for."

"Me, too," he muttered as the car glided out of its spot.

CHAPTER SEVEN
Marly

JUDE PULLED AROUND the back of a nightclub, swinging into a spot near a small set of iron stairs and an unmarked brown door.

A woman wearing a black skirt, patterned tights and a black corset stood outside with her foot propped into the cracked open door. A sliver of ambient light leaked out into the night, creating a yellow illuminated wedge onto the paved parking lot.

Jude held the car door open, offering me his hand out of the deep bucket seats. "Where are we?" I asked, wrapping my fingers around his warm palm. It sent electricity zinging up my arm and I tilted my chin to look up at him as I stood.

His grip on my hand tightened and he froze, his stance turning frigid. "LnS ... from your contract. The one you said you read."

Shit. "Right. LnS. Guess I spaced for a second."

Instead of looking up at him, I busied myself, digging in my purse for a stick of gum. Anything to stay occupied rather than engage in another staring contest.

He grunted a single, gruff sound. His voice, hoarse and heavy, skimmed the air between us so thick, I could have run my fingers through that punctuated grunt. Then, he lifted his finger, curled it under my chin and tugged my gaze to his. The movement was gentle, but one glance at those green eyes was like whiplash cracking at the base of my neck. *He knows*, a whisper echoed in my mind and I swallowed hard against my sandpaper throat. But more terrifying than the fact that he might know I was lying, was the swell of lust that rose from my core; building and growing like my body was a pressure cooker and Jude was the valve refusing my release. My toes curled within my heels as his finger stroked my jaw. "Just to sum up that contract ... You are not allowed to discuss anything or any*one* you see inside. Not even to Omar. That contract can't be scratched out and initialed. LnS is very particular. You understand?"

I nodded. Not understanding ... because stupidly, I didn't read the fucking contract. "I understand," I lied, closing my eyes momentarily against the stroke of his fingers. For all of a second, I wished they would coast down my neck, between my breasts, across my navel, until he reached between my legs. My eyes shot open with a deep breath. What was wrong with me? The whole point of this method research was to move away from people thinking I slept my way to the top.

I took a step back, away from his touch. The absence of it left me chilly and ... and alone. Which was ridiculous. He was literally right there in front of me. "Um, just curious ... what if I do tell someone? Omar, or my agent—"

Jude's expression widened, horror filling his eyes and he shook his head. "You can't. There is no 'or.' There is no 'what if'. You simply can't do it." He turned, walking away.

"Yeah, but ..."

"But nothing," he hissed, spinning to face me. Each breath lifted his chest, then collapsed with his exhale and the rims of his eyes narrowed.

My spine stiffened. Oh, *hell* no. I stepped into his personal space, shoulders back and eyes glaring. Who did he think he was? I barely had a second to acclimate to my new surroundings and he was already yelling at me? *Well, fuck that.* My scowl deepened as I brushed against his chest. "Do not yell at me as if I'm below you. We are colleagues. We are equals. And *this* submissive thing is just acting. Don't fucking forget that just because I'm a damn good actress." Okay, yes, part of this was my fault. I should have read the fucking contract. I should know inside and out what I was getting myself into. But this attitude he was giving me? That shit had to stop. "I have every right to ask questions. I'm walking into an unmarked door with a man I barely know."

His set jaw twitched as he glared at me. I held my ground, crossing my arms until the tension melted and he ran a hand over his face. "Sorry," he mumbled on a sigh. "You're right. It's a touchy subject for those of us who are members. Upstairs, it's very exclusive and we all have images and personal lives to protect. You can understand that, right?"

Oh, yes. Good lord, could I understand that. I nodded—it was all I could do, since I didn't trust my voice to answer just yet.

"Good," Jude rubbed my arms, his hands gliding down my bicep to elbow, then back up again. "I'm sorry."

"You said that already."

"Well, sometimes the important things need to be said twice." His fingers curled around the backs of my arms with a gentle squeeze and despite the cool evening, heat flared in my core. How in the hell was I going to keep my cool around this man for a whole week?

As his hand slid from my arm down to my lower back, it hovered just above the waistband of my jeans. He walked us over to the corset-bound woman waiting at the door and nodded a hello. "Chloe," he said, dropping a peck to her cheek.

"Mr. Fisher, it's nice to see you back. Do you have the contract?"

I smiled at Chloe. She was all hardened beauty and pure business. And I loved that about her. If only I could be more like this Chloe chick, maybe this industry would stop walking all over me.

"Here you go," Jude said pulling one of the contracts I had signed from his folio. "Here is your copy and I'll give Marly hers back once we're inside."

With a quick scan of the paper, Chloe nodded, opening the door for us. "You know the way. I'll lock up behind you."

As Jude led the way down a dark hallway, he reached behind, holding out a hand for me to take. I ignored it. We weren't in character yet. And the last thing I needed was his hands on me more. Touching me. Heating me. With a glance back, Jude seemed to get the picture and fisted his hand, shoving it deep in his pocket instead. "Your first task," Jude said, holding open another unmarked door leading to yet another dim-lit hallway, "is to take that wig off and wash that makeup off your face."

"I—what? But no one can know—"

A thick breath lodged in my chest as he jerked to a stop, turning slowly. "No one will say anything. But people here will know who you are." Jude's face tightened into a scowl that was deep and beautiful in a way that only *he* could make look sexy. He scanned my face, his eyes roaming slowly over me like some sort of human lie detector. "Tell me, Marly ... what did the contract say about the common room?"

Shit. He was quizzing me. *Because he knows. Come on, Marly. You skimmed that contract ... recall something useful.* "That ... it was the area where all patrons of the club can meet." Okay, so that was a pretty lame guess. Anyone could have deduced that.

"And what is not allowed in the common room?"

Double shit. What would the hard limit be on a common area in a BDSM club? "Uh—" It wouldn't be nudity. It wouldn't be sexual acts. Maybe punishment?

His eyes dipped to my mouth where I was chewing my fingernail. Triple shit. Biting my nails was a dead giveaway. I dropped my hand, threading my fingers together and clenching them in front of me.

"You didn't read the contract at all, did you?" A chilly grimace twisted his mouth and disapproval seeped from him like sweat out of a runner's pores.

"We needed to get out of that diner fast," I said, justifying my actions. My stupid actions. Bitterness spiked inside of me.

He shook his head, his eyes dropping to where I twisted the engagement band on my left ring finger. "You lied to me," he said, shaking his head. Shame spiraled through me, burning like acid down to my belly. "That document is intense. The most important thing you had to sign. I *told* you that. And you ... you didn't even read it. And what's worse? You *lied* to me about reading it." His whisper was so low, that it was barely audible. He stepped back, the movement small in its action, but huge in meaning. "It was my fault. I should have made sure you had read it before letting you in here."

"*Letting* me in here?" I said. "You aren't *letting* me do anything, Jude. This week, these exercises, these lessons ... they are my choice. It is *my* choice what I sign and how I understand it."

Jude's inhale hissed through his clenched teeth. Spinning, he walked in a circle, scrubbing his hands down his face. "Goddammit, Marly. Part of this week is about us taking care of each other. Trusting each other. If I was your Dom, it would be *my job* to ensure you read the contract and understood it. It's my job to keep you safe. And it's your job to communicate with me and be honest." He swallowed so hard, that I could see the tension lining his throat. "We both failed. Less than one hour in and we failed."

"You told me to trust you. Trust you as my 'Dom' for the week, right? Well, would my Dom have given me paperwork I *shouldn't* have signed?" It was circular logic. It was stupid. I knew that. My stubborn, hot-headedness had taken over.

"As your Dom, I wouldn't let you get away with that behavior. It's not acting in your own best interest. You disobeyed me ... if you were my sub, you'd be in for a punishment." The words were threatening if you boiled them down without inflection or meaning. But the glint in his eyes was naughty. Playful. "You need to read this contract." He gripped the paper in his tight fist, holding it in front of my face. "You need to understand it front and back—"

"Okay, I *will*. I promise. Can you just ... I don't know, show me around first? I promise I will not tell a soul what I see inside these walls. I won't tell Omar."

"You need to know what you've signed away—it's not just a monetary fine if you tell someone. LnS will ruin you—"

"Please," I plead. "Just … let me read the contract later. I fucked up. I know. You don't need to rub it in."

Jude sighed. "I'm not trying to rub anything in. Or make you feel guilty—"

"Bullshit," I snapped. Jude's eyes widened and he jerked back as though I'd struck him. "You *were* trying to make me feel guilty. For lying to you." I sighed, softening my tone with a quick glance over my shoulder. Thank God the hallway was empty. This argument was embarrassing enough just between Jude and me. "You don't need to make me feel guilty. I already am for lying to you. I'm … sorry. But also, don't stand there and lie and tell me your motives have nothing to do with a little bit of a guilt trip."

His mouth twitched. "You're right. Honesty goes both ways and I was trying to make you feel a little guilty. I'm sorry, too." Reaching out, he took my hand and gave it a warm squeeze.

A tremble vibrated through my body as his touch slipped away. Jude hoisted my overnight bag onto his shoulder, leading the way down to room number 218. The keycard slid into the lock and the door beeped open, like a hotel room. "After you," he kicked the door and it swung open, revealing a lavishly decorated bedroom, equipped with bathroom, kitchenette and a wall lined with built in cabinets.

I cautiously entered, looking around the corners for all my friends to pop out and shout *'Surprise! Just kidding!'* But the room stayed eerily silent, except for the deafening thrum of my heartbeat.

On the same wall as the bed, was a door. Not the bathroom … I could see it on the other side. Maybe a second closet?

"That goes to my room," Jude said, gesturing to it. "All members get two rooms." Jude followed me inside, closing the door behind him.

"Why wouldn't you want to sleep in the same room as your sub?"

He carefully set my bag on the bed, then straightened his cuff links with a quick, taut tug on his sleeve. "Usually I do. But sometimes, part of her punishment is time apart. Or sometimes …" he paused and his mouth ticked into a small grin. "Sometimes it's sexier. Delayed gratification, right?"

I licked my lips, the memory of the salted caramel from last night still lingering in my mind. "Right," I said, my voice hoarse.

"So," Jude stepped to the center of the room, his hands outstretched in a dramatic display. "This is the true LnS club—a BDSM club where memberships are highly exclusive, not to mention expensive. It's a place for those of us in the community to keep our kink without being found out by wandering ears and eyes. And for a few days, you will be privy to those secrets. Which is why your discretion is of the utmost importance."

I swallowed. "I get it, okay? I will never tell anyone what's in here."

"Good." He punctuated the word with a short, sharp nod. Then, with a heavy sigh, he stabbed his hands into his hair. "Marly, have a seat," he said, gesturing to the bed, his hair now disheveled in a way that made him even sexier.

Which wasn't freaking fair at all. When my hair was windblown? I landed on Page 6 with a big DON'T stamped across my ass. But Jude? The tousled look suited him.

I sat at the edge of the bed, watching as Jude paced in the room. "Look, I want to take you outside of this room tonight. But you need to know what you're getting yourself into by staying here. LnS knows its patrons have money. Monetary fines wouldn't keep some of the people here quiet. But a dirty secret that they could spill on you?" Jude paused, kneeling in front of me.

"A dirty secret? Like ... if I tell on them, they'll tell on me?"

"Exactly." He nodded. "That's why you can't tell anyone who or what happens behind these doors. LnS has dirt on all of us. Don't get me wrong, I trust this club with my life. I know they'll never leverage anything if they don't have to. They don't want to use this information. But they will if they have to."

I gulped. "So, they're looking into something about me?"

Jude sighed, his face sagging with the deep, thoughtful breath. He put a hand to my arm and moved it up and down in soft, reassuring strokes. "They're not looking. If you're in the club, that means they have something."

A breath stuck in my throat and anger burned inside me. I wanted to hit something. But then, that anger turned to panic and pressure clamped onto my chest as I thought of Omar. It wasn't just my secret I was keeping. I yanked my arm from his hold. "Oh, my God."

"That's what was in your contract."

"The one I didn't read," I whispered, lifting my eyes to

the soft, golden light in the center of the room. "Shit."

"It's not too late for you to leave. If we leave now, chances are we won't run into anyone in the hallway. As long as you don't see anyone, I'll tell Chloe that you changed your mind. You still can't tell anyone about me or this room, but it'll be a much easier secret to maintain."

I hissed a curse, pushing the hair out of my eyes as I shot to my feet. "Yes."

He seemed startled and pushed off his knees to stand as well. "Yes?"

"Yes. Get me out of here. I won't tell a soul, but I can't be a part of something that might reveal my secret to the world."

Jude reached out to touch me once more, but I flinched, pulling back. His face tightened and a sharp breath traveled into his flaring nostrils. "Okay." He bent, lifting my bag and cracked open the door, peeking into the hallway. "Come on," he said, without looking back and stretched out his hand behind him. Practically beckoning me to grab hold of his.

This time, I did. Despite every cell in my body screaming that it was a bad idea. Our palms connected, all warmth and tingles and a wave of electricity surged from the point of contact up my arm. The tips of my breasts tightened and a stab of breath pushed through my lips as he tugged me gently into the hallway to follow him.

We barely made it two feet before Ash Livingston, the director I had just auditioned for, turned the corner.

"Shit," Jude hissed.

Shit didn't even begin to cover it.

CHAPTER EIGHT
Marly

"**H**E MIGHT NOT recognize you," Jude whispered over his shoulder.

Right. The wig. And the makeup. I lowered my chin, pulling the acrylic hair over my face, draping it in front of me like a curtain.

"Jude? You're actually here?" Ash's voice was a deep baritone, rich and velvety and I could practically hear the inquiring smirk in his voice. "You haven't been here with anyone since …"

Jude cleared his throat. "Yeah, well, we were just leaving."

"What?" Ash asked. I peeked up through my lashes, trying to get a glimpse of the scene in front of me. "Come on. Stay for one community drink? Eve and I were just headed there."

Oh my God. I hadn't even seen the girl standing behind him. She was thin with lush curves and short white-blonde hair in a pixie cut. And she was glaring at me with her liquid lined eyes, a smirk tilting one side of her mouth.

"Marlena?" Ash asked.

Shit. I clenched my eyes shut. Why'd I have to look up? Why'd I have to stare at Ash's submissive so hard? If I had just kept my damn head down, maybe we could have gotten out of here.

I darted a glance to Jude, who sighed, giving my hand a light squeeze. He lifted his brows, and the unasked question of *What do we do now?* hung limp in the air between us.

"What are you two up to?" Ash asked. Moments ago, he'd seemed so relaxed. Happy even that Jude had been here with another sub. But now? Anger tightened his lips and his shoulders seemed to lift higher around his ears, bunching with rage.

Instead of shrinking against Ash's display of anger, Jude stood taller, stepping closer to his friend. "Marlena, go back into the room. And take care of that first assignment." He held the keycard out for me to take. I took it, our fingers brushing.

"First assignment?" Did he mean reading the contracts? That seemed unnecessary now …

He glanced over his shoulder, pointing to the wig. *Oh, right.* Take off the makeup and wig. I nodded, backing up toward the room. Placing my palm at the crest of the wig, I slipped it off. Guess it didn't really matter if anyone recognized me now. I was in this. *Really* in this. If Ash knew I was here, it was all going to shit anyway. I might as well stay and learn something. "Yes, *Sir*," I said, rolling my eyes and sliding the keycard into the lock. With a beep, the door opened.

"Good girl," Jude said. It was a compliment. Good girl. And yet, my spine bristled at it. "Only next time, say it without the attitude."

I LOOKED LIKE myself once more, though my hair was a little flatter than I would have liked. Luckily, underneath the wig, I had twisted sections of my hair into curls, so it fell in soft waves down my shoulders. Even though Jude said to wash my face, I still dabbed on some concealer, mascara and lip gloss, out of habit.

Jude had been in the hallway with Ash for about five minutes before he lightly knocked on the door. I opened it and he slipped inside, scanning me up and down. "Well, that's more like it."

I cast him a sidelong glance. "What happened? Is Ash going to tell Silhouette what we're doing here?"

Jude shook his head. "Nope. That whole dirt thing LnS has on people? It works to *protect* you as well as threaten you. If Ash told anyone, he'd be in just as much deep shit as you and I."

"Why was he so mad?"

"Who says he was mad?"

I dropped my cheek to my shoulder, giving Jude my best *cut the shit* look. His face broke into a smile and his chuckle rumbled through the room. "Okay, he was pissed. But that didn't have anything to do with you. Not really, anyway. I think he just got excited to see me here with someone ... and then, the fact that it was you, and not a *real* submissive, took away from his misguided happiness."

"You don't come here much anymore?"

"No."

For such a verbose guy, it was an unusually short answer. But I knew not to push. I doubted it would get me very far, anyway.

"So," Jude said. "What now?"

I shrugged. "Well, Ash seeing us is probably the worst that'll happen here. No one else from Silhouette is a member, right?"

Jude's grin was back, thank God. I preferred it much

more to his scowl. "I can't answer that. But I can tell you … that seeing Ash is probably the worst that'll happen."

I smiled back at him. "Which is basically like answering my question."

"And yet, I didn't break any rules." He winked. "Does that mean you're going to stay the week?"

I nodded. "Yeah. I think it does." It was a different story when I could have snuck out without seeing anyone or anyone seeing me. Now? Well, now it was different.

He jerked his head toward the door. "Come on. I want to show you the common area tonight. It'll be a mellow night—I just want you to observe and follow the other submissive behavior you see in there. Get a sense of the community we've got here at LnS."

Bending, I grabbed my planner, holding it like a varsity cheerleader holding a textbook.

"What's that?" he asked, taking it from my arms.

"It's just … my notebook. You know, to take notes and stuff."

I resisted the urge to wrench it away from him as he flipped open the pages. "That's personal, you know."

"It's a planner," he said, stating the obvious.

I snorted, yanking it back and closing it. "It's so much more than just a planner."

His smile curved higher. "It has stickers in it."

"Shut up," I said, hugging the planner to my body. "Anyone who likes to plan has stickers."

"You had little acting stickers that said *Lights, Camera, Action!*" He huffed a laugh, pressing his lips together to suppress it and covering his mouth with his tightened fist.

Though I couldn't say why exactly, I laughed too, and

lunged at Jude, smacking his arm with the planner. "Don't make fun of me. This thing is my life. *If you fail to plan, then you plan—*"

"—to fail," Jude said, finishing the quote. "Benjamin Franklin, right?"

My stomach clenched, hardening into a wall of muscle. *Well, that was unexpected.* And both comforting and jarring. "You know that quote?" We were standing closer than I realized. I wasn't quite sure why my breath was so heavy, but there was a glorious feeling of camaraderie between us in that moment. Finally. And for the first time since we sat down to tea, it felt like maybe, just maybe, we had something in common.

If I had more self-control, I wouldn't stare at his defined neck that curved into broad, muscled shoulders. Every dip, every contour of taut muscle flexed with each breath he took and I wanted to reach out and run my hands over the strong column of his bicep.

His eyes shifted from my planner, still clutched in my hands, up my body. Slowly, tortuously slowly, his gaze scraped upward over my tingling breasts, tensed neck, parted lips, until finally landing on my eyes.

His attention was like a sedative, calming me in ways that yoga and meditation have never been successful. "While I appreciate your ... hobby," Jude said quietly, taking the planner again, "you won't need this in the common room." Leaning down, his lips moved merely a breath away from mine and he walked me backwards until I bumped against the wall. His breathing increased. Deeper. Faster. And he put both hands on the wall above my head, caging me in.

There was a playful glimmer in his eyes, and while in

this position some women might feel afraid, I felt breathless. Exhilarated. He swallowed, not pulling away, but his gaze fell to my neck. "Did you choose your safe words yet?" he asked.

My smile twitched. "Let's use 'planner' for stop. And 'sticker' for slow down."

"Oh, my God," Jude said slowly. "Those are the least sexy safe words I've ever heard." He grinned, pushing off the wall and held out his hand for me. "Those will work well, then. There is no reason in hell you should be talking about planners or stickers." He winked. "On the walk down the hall, I want you to say your words over and over in your head. Memorize them. Planner, stop. Sticker, slow down. Planner, stop. Sticker, slow down ..."

"Planner, stop. Sticker, slow down."

"Good girl. Repeat that over and over in your head."

Planner, stop. Sticker, slow down. He opened the door for me and tucked the keycard into his pocket. "And" he said, "we need to find a new term of endearment for you other than sweet girl."

Planner, stop. Sticker, slow down. "Damn straight we do."

We stopped in front of another door, this one was carved on the edges with intricate designs and swirls, while the other doors along the hallway looked like generic hotel room doors. His fingers curled into my hair, twisting and tangling around a lock. With a gentle tug, he lifted it to his nose and sniffed.

"Creepy, much?" But if I was being honest, it wasn't creepy. It was sexy as hell. The red of my hair was bright against his tanned skin.

He ignored me, whispering, "Poppy."

I scrunched my nose. "What? Did you just call me a nickname for a *grandfather*?"

"Popp*ies*," he clarified. "Like ... the flower. They're red, like your hair. You even smell floral."

I dug my fingernails into my palm, repeating, "Poppy." He came up with that fast. Really fast. "You've never had another submissive with that nickname, right?"

He shook his head no, finger still twirled into my hair. "I've never had a redheaded submissive. Or anyone I've nicknamed Poppy."

It wasn't that I wanted a relationship with him—physical or otherwise. But the thought of being one of many made my skin crawl. I was unique. I deserved a nickname as unique as I was. "Poppy. I think I like it."

"It's important to you," Jude said, dropping his hand from my hair. "Feeling special. Different than the others."

I nodded, finding my voice despite my tight throat and dry mouth. "Yes."

Cupping my jaw with both hands, he lifted my gaze to his. If someone saw us right now, standing like this, facing each other in a dark hallway, his hands holding my jaw ... it would look like we were about to kiss. *Were* we about to kiss? Would I let him kiss me? Involuntarily, I licked my lips, a shuddered breath tearing through my wet mouth.

"Marly, you are special."

"I am?" I meant it to be a statement, but it came out a question.

"Even if what we're doing here this week isn't 'real', ... it's a huge step for me. I haven't had a woman here with me since—"

"Since Layla?" I finished for him.

The rims of his eyes tightened, causing the small lines

around them to deepen. "Actually, no—"

The door to the common area swung open and Chloe came barreling through. If she cared about us in the hallway, she didn't show it. Not even for a second. She walked fast, barely giving us a second glance as she passed. And even though Jude stood firmly, I jumped like a freaking mouse was underfoot, wrenching away from Jude's touch and putting a couple feet of space between us.

He gave a throaty chuckle. "You'll be fine, Marly. This common room is a safe place. It's casual ... like playtime for most of the Doms and subs. We're going to go in there and I'm going to treat you like you're my submissive. What the others in the group do with their submissives may not be as playful ... but what I do with you—it'll be a light introduction. You might get a light spank. A bit of ordering you around, but nothing dramatic." A light spank. In public. My face burned and I took a cool, calming breath. If I get the part of Holly, Jude will be spanking me fully nude. On camera. For everyone to see. If I can't handle a small group watching, then maybe it's not the role for me. "And," Jude continued, "if anything I do is too much ... what do you say?"

I closed my eyes and dragged a deep breath through my nose, letting it out through parted lips. "Planner for stop." Probably the stupidest safe word in all of existence.

"Right. Or ..."

"Sticker to slow down."

"Good girl, Poppy."

Good girl. Why were those two words so damn satisfying?

"And you have to trust me. Trust that when I demand something of you, it's for your best interest."

"Okay," I nodded, "let's go."

Jude's eyes flashed as he opened the door. Taking my hand, he pulled me into a lounge area. I blinked into the lights; it was much brighter than the dimly lit hallway. Around the edges of the room were a few kiosks. One, a fully stocked bar, complete with a bartender. Another was a Starbucks stand and barista. There was a fireplace and several circles of leather club chairs nested together for intimate conversations. But at this moment, the group was in one large circle in the center of the room.

I scanned the group. Holy crap. Was that—Yep, that was the creator of MediaShark, the number one fastest growing media share site to date. Across from him was Kari Baron, a bluesy singer who took home a Grammy this past year. Next to her, a dude who looked larger than life—like a Marine or something else. His right pant leg hung strangely. A prosthetic. He had a prosthetic leg. And seated at each of their feet was a partner. Well, a submissive.

Emotion seethed through me ... the subs didn't even get a *seat*? They had to sit on the floor at their Master's feet, like some sort of ... of ... *pet*.

Sitting on the floor were two other film actors. Evan Reiks particularly took me by surprise. That guy was a sub? He was a Vin Diesel look-a-like, playing equally tough, gun-toting characters. Oh, God. I'm staring. I quickly averted my eyes. And that's when my gaze collided with Ash sitting in the club chair right beside us. Heat burned in my cheeks as Ash glared at me. Like ... *seriously* glared. What the hell was his problem? Sitting at his feet was the same stunning woman from the hall. She brushed long, blonde bangs that swept long across her forehead away from her coal-lined eyes.

But then quickly, her ice-cold stare flicked to Jude and narrowed, frosty pink lips curling in a smile so fleeting, it left me wondering if I even saw it. Ash tugged hard on a leash that was clipped to a collar. And just like that, the moment passed. Gone, as the girl's eyes dropped back to the floor.

I glanced at Jude and his eyes were also on the girl, his expression completely unreadable. Stone-faced. "Who's that?" I whispered.

"No one," Jude said. His neck muscles roped and his teeth gnashed together so hard, I could see his jaw muscle working. Maybe now wasn't the best time to ask about her.

I gulped and it went down heavily, as though I were swallowing a fistful of marbles. "So, what do we do now?"

"Have a seat," he gestured to the floor beside one lone empty club chair. "Every night, whoever is in the club can choose to meet here at 11:30 p.m. nightly for a quick hello and drinks. It's like an optional check in."

I had just barely dropped to my knees beside him, when he brushed his fingers through my hair. "Actually—could you get me a drink, Poppy? Martini, very dry. And get yourself a water, too."

I bit my cheek to stop a snarky retort—a water? What was I, sixteen? And was there a reason why he couldn't have asked for the drink *before* I sat down? I pushed myself to my feet, and with a polite nod, answered, "Of course."

A satisfied smile stretched across his face and I couldn't stand to look at the smug grin any longer, instead turning toward the bar. Before I got one step, he grabbed my hand, stopping me. "Of course ... what?"

I swallowed, remembering his contract. *Sweet girl must always address Jude as Sir during playtime, whether in public or private.* "Of course, *Sir*," I whispered.

"Good girl, Poppy." Pleasure rushed through me and I walked quickly to the bar. I put in the order for him and asked for a water, drumming my fingers across the marble counter.

It wasn't often I needed a drink. But here? Tonight? I was so far out of my comfort zone, I could really use a little liquid courage. "Actually," I said, glancing quickly at the bartender—a young girl with golden blond hair. Her nametag read Andrea, and I reached out a hand, stopping Andrea as she grabbed for a water glass. "I'll have a Woodford on the rocks. A double." Because damn, did I need it.

It only took Andrea a few minutes to prepare both drinks and as she finished, she slid them across the counter with two small, royal blue square napkins. "Oh—oh my God, I don't have my wallet," I said, sliding my hands in my jeans pockets to see if I had any cash tucked away that I had forgotten about.

"It's okay," Andrea said. "All drinks are billed to your Master."

"My Master," I whispered, taking a heavy sip of bourbon. "Right. And that includes your tip, too, right?"

Andrea nodded. "Masters and Mistresses are usually very generous," she whispered. Her smile was sweet, her bright blue eyes, kind. "I'm kind of new here, too," she added. "But everyone is really nice. Chloe takes good care of anyone who steps foot inside here. You need anything, you find her, okay?"

"I will. Thank you," I said, lifting the martini and the bourbon. The glasses were cold and felt good against my clammy palms. The circle stared at me as I approached, every single person's eyes wide, and one of the subs even gasped as I sat down beside Jude.

"What?" I handed the martini up to him and took another sip of bourbon.

Jude placed his martini on the table beside him and leaned forward, resting his elbows onto his knees. His sigh hissed through his nose. "I told you to get a water."

I shrugged, looking down at the bourbon in my hand. The glass was beginning to sweat, beads of cold condensation running over my fingers. "Yeah, but I wanted a bourbon. I kind of felt like I needed it."

"In these walls," Jude whispered, "you don't get to choose what you need. I choose what you need. And you're supposed to trust me to make the right choice. I would have ordered you a bourbon next—but I wanted you to hydrate first."

I narrowed my eyes, glaring up at him from the stupid seat on the floor. "You're fucking joking, right? I'm an adult. I've been drinking for years. I think I can handle *one* bourbon."

"First of all, that's not the point," he whispered. "I didn't tell you to get yourself a drink. And in this world—in my world—that's the sort of action that requires permission. Second of all, that's a double pour. So technically, you ordered yourself *two* bourbons."

I opened my mouth to argue, but thought better of it. "Well …can I have it now? It'd be a waste if I didn't—oh!"

Jude pulled me off the floor, some of the amber liquid sloshing out of the tumbler and splattering beside my toes. He pulled me over his lap, taking the bourbon from my hand and placing it on the floor at his feet. Leaning down, his breath was hot against my ear as he whispered, "What's your safe word?"

I swallowed. "Planner for stop. Sticker for slow down."

His palm came down onto my ass in three fast strikes. His spanking wasn't hard in the least, but it did things to me. Things that I didn't want to admit, even to myself. My belly pressed into the firm musculature of his thighs and with each strike of his hand, an erection pressed a little harder into my stomach.

Heat blasted from my blushing cheeks down to … well, my other cheeks. Thank God I was wearing jeans, otherwise my bare ass would have been on display for the entire membership of this bizarre club. But even without that added gem, the situation was humiliating enough. And yet—despite the embarrassment … despite the humiliation, longing stirred between my legs. A tight pressure built and I could feel my muscles flexing with each spank.

As his hand came down with the final slap, it lingered on the curve of my backside. He stroked where he had so violently spanked only seconds before and the vast difference between gentle and aggressive caused a shiver to tumble down my spine.

Only a few seconds passed, but it felt like eons. Jude helped me back to a seated position on the floor. Then, handing me the remaining bourbon, said, "Now, go get a water. After you drink the entire glass of water, you may have your bourbon."

Only, I didn't need the alcohol anymore. That display had been intoxicating enough.

Jude

I PINCHED THE stem of my martini glass with such force, I was afraid the fragile glass might snap in half. The liquid slid down my throat, chilled to perfection and smoother than water. Damn, they made a good martini here.

I needed to get a grip. I enjoyed spanking Marly's ass way too much—and based on the way my cock pushed against my slacks, most everyone in the circle would know it too. Ash sent me a knowing glance, hiding his smirk with his scotch.

It has nothing to do with Marly, I reasoned. I haven't spanked anyone in over a year. Haven't fulfilled this dark, aching need inside of me to control and release. Nope. Doesn't have a damn thing to do with Marly.

But that moment ... out in the hallway. I closed my eyes, the feel of her hair lingering on my fingers like silk. The way we leaned into each other, so close to kissing ... so intimate. My gaze fell to where Marly was sitting in front of me, eyeing the flushed pink color of the back of her neck, clashing with her red hair. Her bourbon gathered beads of moisture around the sides which dripped onto her jeans, leaving dark spots of saturated denim. The empty glass of water sat beside her thigh.

I worked my throat, swallowing beyond the dryness and leaned down, pressing my lips to her ear. "Drink slowly," I cautioned. What had she eaten for dinner? Or was she drinking on an empty stomach? The thought made my chest tighten. If she spent half the day tomorrow sick, it would be partially my fault.

She held my gaze, her glare lowering as she wet her lips. Then, slowly, she brought the glass to her mouth, and in several gulps, finished the bourbon. The muscles in her neck tightened as she swallowed and worked her jaw in a way that I feared she might crack a molar. There was a twitch against my zipper and I groaned inwardly. Upon finishing, she smacked her lips and set the glass down on the floor beside the empty water glass.

What the fuck was that? Did she *like* the punishment? Want more of it? Because if that was the case, I had to adjust my tactics. A punishment that felt too much like pleasure wouldn't work for either of us. Or was she feeling feisty? Defiant? Fuck if I knew.

My fingers bit into the leather armrests of the chair as I shoved against it to my feet, stepping around Marly and walking over to the bar. "Andrea," I said quietly, with a quick glance at her nametag. I had never seen her before, but that wasn't saying much since I hadn't been here in over a year. "Could I have another martini and a glass of water, please."

She dipped her chin. "Of course, Mr. Fisher," she said, lowering her gaze. Bartenders at the club weren't expected to adhere to submissive rules. Yes, they had to address everyone as Ms. or Mr., but they could look Masters and Mistresses in the eye. This girl was a submissive by nature. Did she know yet? Was that why she was working here?

"Do you have any crackers or cookies or something behind the bar?"

"Um …" she paused, looking around beneath the bar. "I don't over here, but I can grab you something from the coffee counter. Anything in particular?"

Salted caramels. Her favorites. Not that she deserved a treat. And frankly, those wouldn't do much to soak up the alcohol in her stomach. "Maybe a biscuit or some scones?"

Andrea nodded. "I'll check."

This was a stupid idea … inviting Marly here. Maybe the common room was too much, too soon for her? Everything seemed fine right up until I asked her to trust me to take control. The second I asked her to order water, she rebelled.

The tips of my fingers brushed across the cold marble bar top, the swirling gray lines like veins along an alabaster skin. Marly is a talented actress ... but not everyone is cut out for this kind of role. *Not everyone is cut out for this kind of life,* my brain corrected me. Here, she thought this was the shallow end of a pool she was dipping her toes in, when in reality, it was a whirlpool ready to suck her under its murky depths.

"We have a blueberry muffin, a cranberry scone, or a caramel apple scone. I can also order delivery for you, if you need something more substantial—"

"The caramel apple scone will be perfect. Thank you, Andrea."

"I'll bring your drinks over for you."

I thanked her and took the scone. Marly's glare seared into me from the other end of the room, the heat between us growing with each step closing in. I sat back down, placing the scone on my thigh and spread my legs wide. "Eat," I demanded.

Her mouth twisted, horrified as she looked from the scone to my face. "Do you know how much fat is in a scone—"

"Eat the goddamn scone, Marlena."

She swallowed, her jaw tight, molars grinding across each other like unoiled gears. "Fine," she snapped, and reached for the scone.

I smacked at her hand and she gasped, recoiling. "What the fuck?" she whispered.

"Eat the scone. Off of my leg."

She held my gaze, her stunning features cold like the

marble countertops. But mine was colder. I could be a scary son-of-a-bitch when I wanted to be. There was something else in the depths of her blue eyes. She didn't seem frightened by my games. Angry, yes. Which was annoying as hell because she knew why she was here. She knew this was all part of the process to learn. But beyond that anger, curiosity piqued.

"Eat it off your knee like *a dog*?" she hissed.

Andrea walked over, handing me the martini and setting the glass of water on the floor.

I took a slow sip, then set the glass on the table beside me. "If this is too much, you know what to say, right?" I lifted my brows, my eyes boring into hers. "What are your safe words?"

Her nostrils flared, her expression a swirling tornado of fury and intrigue. And like a tornado, I was sure she could destroy everything in her path. She was wild and beautiful and dangerous. "Planner for stop. Sticker for slow down."

"Do you want to use them right now?"

I curled my fingers tightly around the leather armchair, my insides twisting. *You can do this, Marly,* I thought. I didn't think I was moving too fast for her, but if I was, she needed to learn to speak up. To trust me that I will stop as needed. But only if she uses her words. Leaning down, I whispered, "I need to trust that you will be able to use those words when you need to. If a Dom is constantly stopping, wondering if his or her sub is okay because there's a concern she isn't using the words, that's a problem." Her marbled expression softened—though barely. Once marble, now soap stone, her eyes tilted, glossy and blue like the sheen of a still lake. "Now … do you have anything you want to say to me right now?"

A shiver oscillated through her body, so strong it was visible in the way her shoulders pulsed. She shook her head no.

"Good. Then eat."

She returned her attention to the scone, shifting to her knees and scooting between my legs. *Fuck me.* Maybe this was a bad idea. Then, clutching her hands behind her back, she bent at the waist, biting off a bit of the scone. "If it falls," I said, "Then you eat off the floor."

I watched, aware of every shift of her weight from one knee to the other. Each time she wiggled her hips or shoulders or swiped her tongue out to clean the crumbs sticking to her glossed lips, my cock got harder. I closed my eyes, swallowing a groan as her head bobbed up and down over the scone, inches away from my tenting pants.

Reaching out, I brushed her fallen hair away from her face, my fingers skimming her neck as I flipped the curtain of siren red hair to her other shoulder. Her cheeks flushed at my touch and her neck tightened as she nibbled. She lifted her eyes, meeting mine, her face serious and heating to a delicious shade of pink that would have matched the shade of her ass after I spanked her.

She likes it. I swallowed hard, moving my fingers to her jaw and following the line of tension as she swallowed the bite of scone. *Maybe she's more like Holly than I thought. Yeah, she's fighting this tooth and nail, but it's only an hour in. We have a whole week.* My doubt dissolved faster than an ice cube on the LA sidewalks.

Her lips were swollen and wet and she ran her tongue along them once more. It wasn't even meant to be sexy—if anything, it was clumsy and she was trying to reach a crumb far off the corner of her mouth. I dragged my thumb across her jaw, collecting the crumb and held it out in front of her mouth, lifting my brow.

Her gaze shifted quickly between my legs where my cock was standing tall, tenting my dress pants with a vengeance. Practically saluting her for the good work she'd done. She darted her gaze away, the flush on her cheeks turning a deeper shade of mauve. Then, parting her lips, she took my thumb in her mouth, wrapping it around the soft pad and sucking the crumb off my flesh. Fuck me. Her tongue flicked over the top, scraping over the edge of my fingernail.

This time, there was no swallowing my satisfied groan. It rumbled out of my chest like a caged animal, crying for an escape. I wanted to kiss her; grab her by the back of the neck, pull her lips to mine and ravage her mouth until she couldn't stand without my assistance. I wanted my tongue sliding between those ripe, wet lips of hers. My body slamming her back against the wall, while I plunged inside of her.

Shit. Only one hour together and I was already derailing into uncharted territories. This can't happen. It is my responsibility to keep this tame. To not cross any lines. And to make matters worse, Marly was engaged. I had made a promise; not only to her, but to myself. No sex. I could not take advantage of a method actor researching a potential role. Just because she made me feel things I hadn't experienced since Layla, didn't mean it was excusable to act on those feelings.

She was halfway finished with the scone and I cleared my throat to get her attention. "Are you full?" I asked, my voice deeper than usual.

She nodded and I moved what was left of the scone to

the side table. Tan crumbs sat like a Pollock painting against my gray dress pants and her eyes were fixed on my thigh.

I couldn't resist. It was too good. She was too fucking sweet. And how much farther would she go? "You made a mess," I said.

She didn't remove her eyes from the crumbs.

"Do you have something to say to me?" I prodded.

She lifted her chin, meeting my eyes, reluctance twisting in her expression. "I'm ... sorry?"

"You're sorry, *what?*"

"Sir. I'm sorry, Sir?" She spat the words, doubt and frustration curling her mouth in a wry grin.

Yes. Fuck me, yes. "Is that a question?"

She heaved a sigh, her breasts straining with the tight breath against her button-down blouse. "*No.* I'm sorry, Sir."

It was hard for her to say that, which only made the victory that much sweeter. Sexier. She shifted uncomfortably and I noticed the way she moved her weight back and forth on her knees.

"Do your knees hurt?"

She nodded. "Yes."

"Yes, *what?*"

"Fucking hell," she muttered.

Bending, I scooped my hand into her hair, squeezing, wrapping the strands around my fingers and gave a small tug. It shouldn't have hurt. Or if it did, it was nothing compared to the spank earlier. "You don't get to curse at me, Poppy. Now ... yes, what?"

"Yes, Sir," she whispered. "My knees hurt. High school soccer injury."

I released her hair, grabbing the pillow from behind my back and placed it on the ground. "Here," I said gently. "Kneel on this."

"Aren't we ... aren't we done?"

I leaned down, ready to scoop my hand back into her hair as she quickly added, "Sir?"

"*I* decide when we're done. Now," I glanced down at the crumbs on my pants. "Clean up your mess. With your tongue."

I expected some resistance. A moment of hesitation. Anything. But she didn't. She leaned down, running her tongue along the ironed crease of my pants, lapping up the crumbs with several strokes of her tongue.

My hard cock pulsed with that obedience. It was so good. So fucking good. "Good girl, Poppy." I stroked her hair and with her body pressed into my thigh, I felt, rather than heard, her satisfied purr. Her tongue stroked my cotton dress pants, only one layer between that tongue of hers and my flesh. She tilted her head, licking the inside of my thigh, dangerously close to my aching, tight balls. My breath hitched in my chest, my grip on the armchair tightening. "That's enough. You can relax now."

Marly lifted upright once more and looked over her shoulder to Ash whose eyes were steeled onto us. Red heat stained her cheeks, spreading in a flush across her nose. I was pretty damn sure Ash had been watching the whole time. Shit, the whole room had been watching. That was the problem with taking a hiatus from a club like this. When you came back? You were the talk of the town.

I took Marly's chin gently in my pinched fingers, pulling her gaze away from Ash to me. "You don't need to look at them. I've got you, Poppy. Trust me?"

She swallowed, moisture brimming her eyes. A shattered breath dragged in through her parted lips. "Sticker," she whispered, so low, I almost didn't hear it.

Sticker, slow down. I jerked back, shock nearly overtaking me. Fuck. I'd been so certain she had been enjoying that—the scone, the crumbs ... even the spanking from earlier. "What's wrong, Marly?" I asked, not releasing her chin.

"I don't know how to answer when you ask me to trust you. We're in playtime... I know I'm supposed to say yes, Sir. But ... that would be lying. And I'm not supposed to lie to you."

"You don't trust me," I said, summing up what she was trying to say. It was like a punch to the gut, knocking the wind right out of me.

She pressed her lips together. "Trust takes time," she said, shrugging. The shrug, meant to be casual, but it looked forced. An attempt to turn a heavy statement lighter. "And we barely know each other."

Nothing else about the exercise caused her to pause. Not eating the scone off my lap. Not the spanking. Not the fact that my cock was fucking nearly brushing her cheek as she was between my legs, bobbing up and down, mimicking the movement of a blowjob.

Releasing her chin, I brushed my fingers into a stray piece of hair falling across her forehead. "Thank you for being honest with me. That's how this trust is built. If I ask you something during playtime ... you can be honest. You will never be punished for being honest, Marly."

"So ... when you asked 'Trust me' ... what should I have said?"

"You could have said, 'I'm trying, Sir.' That would be

honest, right?"

She nodded, the movements tight. Still unsure. "What else is bothering you?"

"It just … it feels weird that our first lesson is in front of … of a bunch of strangers."

Aha. There it was. "Here's the thing. My job this week is to respect your hard limits, while also pushing your boundaries … never crossing them. It's a challenging position. But that's my job. And that's also why I love it. Your job is to trust me … or learn to trust me… and open yourself up to the idea that this process, these games, are all for your and my benefit. Starting here, in front of the group is a little like throwing you into the deep end of a pool. But all these people in this room, are going to be roaming around the club this week. It's better for you to see them now. Meet them now in a controlled, safe environment. So that later in the week, when you see one of them getting whipped in the chambers, you already know them in a more human element."

She looked up at one of the candles burning on a post. The warm glow caught in her eyes, flickering orange against the bright blue. "That … actually makes a lot of sense."

"Good." I nodded toward the circle. "Now sit down, relax. Watch the group. Watch their interactions," I whispered. "See how they speak to their Masters and Mistresses. And likewise, how the Doms address their subs." Those azure eyes of hers took an extra long moment to sweep my body and the walls of my stomach muscles tightened as her gaze landed briefly between my legs. Through parted lips, she let out a small gasp and reluctantly, it seemed, jerked her head away, spinning to sit back down on the floor. This time between my spread legs.

From the profile of her body, the tips of her breasts were tight, as if the room was sub-zero temperature. Only, I knew the thermostat was set at a balmy 72. Which meant one thing. Marlena Taylor was just as turned on as I was.

Across from us, Kari wore a burlesque-ish corset and an above the knee pencil skirt over fishnets that crisscrossed down her slender legs. "Henry," she said, swatting her sub with a leather riding crop. "I'm feeling a little dry."

Her sub hopped to his feet, grabbing baby oil from the basket next to her chair. The stream squeezed from the bottle into his palms and he warmed the oil in his hands. Then, starting at her bare shoulders, he massaged the oil in, his hands traveling over her creamy skin in slow, tender movements. Kari sighed, closing her eyes and sipping her drink.

The other Doms chatted quietly about how life had been since they had all last seen or spoken. While doing so, Tim, a Dominant who was also some sort of internet mogul, tugged the hair of his sub, pulling her face to his crotch. She immediately unzipped his pants and went to work sucking him off.

I never really understood the appeal of that sort of instant gratification … blow jobs were earned. By both the Dom and the sub. But Tim was used to power and having things when, where, and how he wanted them. As his sub moved to her knees, bending over his erection, it was clear that beneath that short skirt of hers, there were no panties.

Another thing I never understood. I did not share. Whether she was my sub, my girlfriend, or my wife—she was for my eyes and my eyes alone. Something Layla never quite understood. Of course, in acting, it was different. In theory, it was not you on screen with another person … it was you in the mindset of a character. But I had to face it; in this business, lines blurred all the time. And with Layla? Well, hell. She didn't think the lines applied to her. She somersaulted over them.

Marly ran her fingers over the edge of her water glass, her painted nails grazing the lip. She was either fascinated by her glass of water or uncomfortable with what was happening across the circle. When I looked up again, I was met with Ash's raised eyebrow. Could practically hear his thoughts. *She can't even handle a girl's bare ass. How was she going to manage full frontal nudity and gratuitous BDSM scenes?*

She leaned back, her cheek brushing against my knee, sending a jolt of electricity through my veins. "How long are we supposed to stay out here?" she asked.

"Why, Poppy? Are you feeling a little shy?"

I cast a sidelong glance to Ash. Even though his attention was on his own sub sitting at his feet, I knew he was listening to every word we said.

"*No*," Marly answered quickly, then ran her tongue over her lips. "No," she tried again, quieter this time. "I just thought I should go back to the room ... read over my LnS contract." Her slurred words tripped clumsily over her tongue.

I sipped my martini, almost finished with it. "Once I finish my drink, we can go. Have a little more water."

A breath puffed out of her pink stained lips, but she lifted the water glass regardless, taking a sip.

With a final glance around the circle, I swallowed the rest of my martini, chewing on one of the olives. "All right, I'd say you've seen enough for the first night." I pushed off the armrests and onto my feet, holding out a hand for

Marly. She looked up at me, all big blue eyes and pouty lips and I was tunneled back to our second meeting in the bathroom when I had accidentally knocked her on her ass. Or maybe she knocked herself on her ass ... *she* was the one who swung the door open hitting me.

She inched her feet beneath her, swinging her legs around. Shoulders stiff, back straight, she reached out her hand and dropped it into mine as a sliver of pink tongue swiped across her bee-stung lips. I sucked in a sharp breath. Holy hell if that plump mouth of hers didn't fall right in line with my zipper. A small part of me, a little spec no bigger than the scone crumbs that she licked off my lap, loved that she was as affected by this as I was. It was comforting, not feeling alone.

Leveraging her palm against mine, she stood, bringing her water glass with her. She turned to deposit it at the bar, but I held tightly onto her hand, tugging her back into me. I glanced with a side eye at my own empty glass. After a second, recognition swept over Marlena's face as she nodded, rolling her eyes. She grabbed my empty glass and brought them both over to the bartender before slipping out the door, not even bothering to wait for me.

CHAPTER NINE
Marly

I REALLY SHOULDN'T *have slammed that bourbon so quickly.* I was in a haze and even though I wasn't wasted necessarily, I was definitely teetering on the edge between tipsy and drunk.

"Where are you going?" Jude's voice boomed from somewhere behind me. I just kept walking, not bothering to stop; not bothering to turn around. Even though I had zero clue where the hell I was or where I was going. I also had zero fucks to give for Jude. Yeah, that might be the bourbon talking.

His footsteps behind me were heavy and fast, and in a moment, I heard his breath at my side; could feel its warmth on my neck.

"Answer me." He wasn't shouting, but there was a danger to his voice that set my nerves on edge.

His hand wrapped around my elbow and even though I had expected it to be rough, Jude was gentle and his fingers danced in little circles over my tender skin, sending pleasure rippling across my flesh. "You can't just walk out ahead of me like that. Not to your Dom." He added quieter.

"But you're not my Dom—you're Holly's."

"Damn right. And for this weekend *you're* Holly."

I moved to pull out of his grasp, only my limbs seemed heavier than normal. Like my body was trapped in molasses and as I shrugged his hands away, my head spun.

"Are you—are you drunk?" he whispered.

My face flamed and heat surged to my cheeks. God, could this be more embarrassing? I had one stupid drink and the effects were already fogging my mind. Maybe everyone was right; maybe I just wasn't cut out for this kind of role. Hell, I doubted Layla Hutson would have blinked an eye at the public blow job in that room; she may have even jumped right in.

"Come on," Jude said gently when I didn't respond. Wrapping an arm around my waist, he guided me back to the private room and slid his keycard into the lock. "Sit," he commanded, pointing to the bed in the center of the room.

"No," I clenched my jaw, my fists mimicking the movement.

Bent over the fridge, Jude lifted slowly to a standing position, spinning to face me. An eyebrow lifted in my direction. "*No?*"

"That's right," My voice was thick with frustration and coated with bourbon. "No. Or have you forgotten the meaning of the word?" Holy hell ... this *had* to be the alcohol talking. Marlena Taylor just didn't *do* things like this. Ever. Then again ... Holly did. And as Jude so calmly pointed out ... I was Holly this weekend.

Excitement pulsed inside of me, the heavy thrum of a buzzing electricity. Would he spank me again? *Please, please spank me.* It wasn't enough through the jeans. I wanted the skin of his palm cracking against my raw, stinging flesh.

His walk toward me was slow and he moved like fluid. "You knew the rules when you signed on for this. You agreed to them. While in my possession, you do as I say.

That's what you signed. That's what your safe words are for. If you truly mean 'no' … you know what words to use, right? Even drunk?"

His eyes flashed and I nodded, my eyes flicking to the turquoise planner, still on the bed where I left it. "Planner, sticker. Yeah, I got it." I swallowed and steadied my wobbly knees by clenching my thighs. Below me, the floor spun. I moved forward, even closer to Jude than he had dared to come to me and the tips of my breasts brushed against his crisp shirt. "Holly would have said no … especially on the first night … the first command with Leo. Right? Is that not why we're here?"

Light danced in Jude's green eyes, making them appear even lighter than they actually were. There it is … he got it. Somewhere between my anger in the hallway to now, I'd started acting. Started playing. His lips curved into a wry smile. "Then, *Holly* … that 'no' deserves a punishment."

The muscles between my legs spasmed with the sexy threat and a chill skated across my skin, leaving a trail of goose bumps in its wake. Surprise flickered in Jude's expression as comprehension replaced his frustration. "You *do* like the punishments," he whispered, as though he suspected all along. He trailed his fingers along my jawline, then cupped my face. "I thought you might." His touch was firm, commanding, while still tender as his fingers stroked gently over my skin. I couldn't help but wonder, if that simple touch to my jaw could send electricity jolting through my body … what else could those talented fingers do? He dragged his lips to my ear and his breath was hot. "You liked being spanked, Poppy? You want more, don't you?"

I couldn't answer and a whimper pushed past my trembling lips. Excitement skittered down my throat and landed low in my belly. I knew in all rational areas of my mind that I should step back; move away from this man. He had bad news written all over him. And yet, I wanted nothing more than to dive in head first to this world with Jude. I didn't want to step away; I didn't want this pleasurable sensation to end. My entire life, I planned everything to the minute. I knew how every moment of every day would go and I traveled through life with my nose in my planner. Jude was forcing me to look up. Look up and relinquish control. And *damn,* did it feel good. I was fighting it ... it was in my nature to fight it. As unnatural as a mouse befriending a cat. But at the edge of my anxiety ... my nervousness about giving up control, I felt a little glimmer of relief. And arousal. How long had it been since I felt desired? Since a man had looked at me the way Jude does?

I should step back. Step away. But instead, I moved a final step closer, pressing our bodies flush against each other. If I was doubting Jude's interest in me, it was quickly secured as a steely erection pressed between my thighs. His words may have been an act, but his body? This reaction? That was no acting. A short breath caught in my throat and as he pulled back from my ear, my hair got caught against the stubble coming in from his morning shave, tethering us together.

His sharp nose brushed along the swell of my cheek as the smooth stroke of his thumb along my jaw sent little jolts of anticipation through me. Tipping my gaze up to his, I was rewarded with his smile and glistening eyes. His other hand glided down my neck as the back of his knuckles stopped just before the swell of my breast began. I arched my back, pressing into his touch. "Don't stop," I pleaded, closing my eyes and tipping my neck back, giving it to Jude like an offering. He ran the backs of his knuckles over the side of my breast. The ache deepened, my nipples growing tighter and breasts deliciously heavy. A gasp involuntarily broke through my parted mouth and I ground into his body, hips bucking toward him. A raw, insanely sexy sound rumbled from deep in his chest. With a shallow inhale, Jude's lips parted and my eyes fluttered closed.

I knew better—God, did I ever know better than this. But I had never known it was possible to ache so deliciously from a simple touch. And when Jude tipped my chin, I didn't resist. He hovered there, his lips centimeters from mine. *That fucking delayed gratification.* I'd had enough of that. I pushed onto my toes, moving my lips to his. He managed to pull back a second too late and my mouth brushed across his, just barely fluttering against his moist mouth.

I moaned a frustrated sound.

"You're drunk," he whispered, curving his pelvis back and away from me. My grip on his waist tightened, clawing at him, pulling with all my strength to get his cock flush against my arousal once more. Blood thundered through my veins like rapids, rushing along with my quickening pulse.

"Jude," I cried, his name a strangled gasp parting my lips. I was drunk and it was the reason I had the courage to do this. To risk everything—my reputation, a potential Oscar-worthy role and my whole career for one night of pleasure.

Those hands scraped up my back, gripping my shoulders and then the heat, the throbbing, the ache tore away from me as a cool breeze disrupted our hypnotic warmth. I blinked, finding Jude on the other side of the room, a hand scraping down his weary eyes.

"You need rest," his voice was freshly wounded, like an old gash that had been ripped open.

"Jude," I took a step forward, and shivered, running a hand over my goose-fleshed arms.

He held out a palm, stopping me mid-step. "Don't—" He cleared his throat, pressing his fist to his mouth. "Please. You're drunk."

My eyes dipped to the hard outline of his cock, pushing against the front of his pants. "But you're not."

"Exactly," he said. "Have a seat on the floor, facing the bed. Wait for me there, eyes forward."

"The floor—"

"*Marlena.*" His no-nonsense tone snapped through my body like a cracking whip. Before I knew what I was doing, I lunged for the floor, sitting cross-legged, facing the bed. "Good girl, Poppy."

The tension in my back released, warmth spiraling around my spine. A few minutes passed with me sitting there like that. What was he doing? What was taking so long?

I looked over my shoulder, catching Jude's eyes in the mirror over the sink. He had his hands buried in my toiletry bag. "Eyes forward, Marlena," he scolded. His voice was no-nonsense, but in his eyes, a glint of humor. With a huff, I turned back around, staring at the boring damask comforter and lush embroidered pillows. A few minutes later, his legs appeared in front of me and he sat on the bed, setting a few things beside him. He curled his fingers under my chin, tipping my head up toward the light. "Eyes closed," he commanded.

I did as I was told, feeling my lashes sweep against the tops of my cheeks. The room spun in the dark and then a warm cloth swiped across my face. Over my forehead, eyes, cheeks. In long, gentle strokes, Jude was washing off what little makeup remained on my face.

My eyes jolted open. I had a process for removing my makeup. An intricate process that involved eye cream and moisturizer and essential oils. "Relax," Jude whispered, dapping the cloth at the tip of my nose.

"These products are—"

"*Marly.* I'm an actor. You think I don't know how to apply moisturizer?"

Well, that was true. I was about to object, but stopped myself. This was part of the research. Part of the process. *Trust the process.* "Okay," I said. "I trust you." *And I can always fix whatever you do wrong after you leave.*

"Good girl, Poppy." The cool cloth was more abrasive on my face than I was used to, but wasn't entirely unwelcome. And paired with Jude's gentle circular movements, my skin felt refreshed. More exfoliated than usual. I had no doubt my cheeks, forehead and chin were bright red. Stupid fair, sensitive skin. I pressed my lips together, stopping myself from telling him to not use a washcloth.

With my eyes still closed, I relaxed my neck as Jude tilted my chin right … then left. Then, peeking out of one eye, I caught the way Jude's eyes flashed, examining my skin. "I'll use cotton balls tomorrow," he said, practically reading my thoughts. "Something softer to wash your face."

"I could have told you that," I whispered, an arrogant smirk lifting the corners of my mouth.

The rough sound of his chuckle percolated in the air between us, churning, brewing inside my body. "But isn't there something more fulfilling about me discovering it on my own? About relinquishing the control and realizing that …" he paused and taking a dropper full of oil, added a few drops to his palms, warming it in his hands. Then, leaning forward, he whispered, "I've got you."

Was it more fulfilling? Surprising, yes. Unusual, for *sure*. He pressed the oil onto the tender skin beneath my eyes and around my forehead and chin, sweeping his fingers up my neck. "Turn around for me."

After I turned, he scooped his hands into my hair and then slowly worked the hairbrush through, carefully working out the knots.

"Think," Jude said. "Close your eyes and tell me about how me taking care of you makes you feel."

When I closed my eyes, Jude was everywhere. Behind me, in front of me … even inside me. In my lungs, in my thoughts. His musky scent was thick and consuming. *How do I feel? … Weird. I feel fucking weird.* But I couldn't say that. Even though I was new at this, I was pretty sure that would earn me a punishment. "I feel a little … childlike," I answered.

The hairbrush paused for a second at the crown of my head before it started moving down my hair once more. "What does that mean?"

My mom popped into my thoughts. I didn't often think of Cynthia Taylor. I didn't *let* myself think about her. "It makes me feel nostalgic. My mom used to brush my hair before bed every night."

"Why do you think she did that?"

The sweet memory was painful and tore a bitter laugh from my throat. Sweet. And like too much sugar, thinking about my mom would cause a cavity if I wasn't careful.

"Because I was three. I barely knew how to wipe my own ass, let alone brush my hair." There was a sharp tug on my hair… a warning.

"Don't use humor to protect yourself."

Damn him. Damn him for seeing right through me. And damn him for calling me on it. "Sorry," I said. "You've shown me a side of yourself today you don't reveal to many people. And I'm just … I'm shitting all over it."

A single burst of short laughter snorted through his nose. Even his laugh was intense. "I wouldn't say you're shitting all over it. And I'm going to let it slide that you haven't been addressing me as 'Sir' this whole time." He rapped the hairbrush against my lower back. "Turn back around."

I spun back to face him, giving a shrug. "Sorry," I said. "*Sir*."

"You know how you can make it up to me?" Jude asked. A million filthy thoughts whirred through my mind. "Tell me how this makes you feel. Without using humor to protect yourself."

He'd made himself vulnerable all night. It was the least I could do. I watched closely as Jude took my moisturizer, screwed open the lid and dipped his fingers inside. A dollop of cream gathered on his forefinger. It was strangely erotic—the way he plunged his finger inside, with intent. Curving it around the rim of the jar, swirling it. "I think my mom used to brush my hair because it was like … a bonding ritual. Every night, she would brush it and then braid it. Then, she'd tuck me into bed. I was never a good sleeper—I had all kinds of anxiety and fears as a kid. It's why my dad got me my first planner. Taught me to control the fear by having a plan. But my mom had a different approach … she would meditate before bed and when she tucked me in, she put quarters on my closed eyes. Then she told me that if I managed to wake up with the quarters still on my eyes, I could keep them." I chuckled, a sad, wilted sound. "I never did … I think it'd be impossible for anyone entering REM to sleep the whole night with quarters on their eyes. But … it made me feel safe. Our nightly ritual."

"Does this make you feel safe?" Jude massaged the moisturizer into my temples and forehead, dabbing his fingers lightly over my skin.

"Yes." One word. And yet, it was really hard to admit. So hard to say. "My mom died right before my fourth birthday."

His fingers froze along my cheekbones. A frown tilted his full, pink mouth and I couldn't help another sad laugh. "Come on," I said, "You're too beautiful to frown like that."

His mouth curved into a tiny smile, but his eyes … those green eyes still frowned back at me. "You're one to talk." He brushed his thumb below my eye and gathered a single bead of moisture. One lone tear I hadn't even realized had slipped out. Then, he lifted his thumb to his mouth and sucked my tear off the tip. He was literally drinking my sadness. "I'm so sorry for your loss, Marly."

"Thanks," I whispered, barely recognizing my own voice. "My dad … he tried to take over the nightly ritual, but it just wasn't the same. He knew it. I knew it. And after the first couple clumsy attempts, I just started braiding my own hair after I brushed my teeth. He never said so, but he was relieved. I remember the first time I came out of the bathroom with the braid a knotted mess at my nape, he smiled and told me how proud he was of my independence.

And as he tucked me in, and kissed my cheek, he whispered to me, *"Let the fire inside you burn brighter than the fire around you."*

Jude stood, walking around behind me and kneeling. "Did you and your dad develop your own bedtime ritual?" I felt the gentle pull of my hair and recognized the pattern as his hands worked three sections into a braid.

"Not really. He would usually come upstairs and tuck me into bed. But that was it."

Jude worked silently. Did I feel safe here with Jude? Cared for? I hadn't talked about my mom in years. Dad loved me; had cared for me, in his own way. He was never super affectionate, but after mom died, I was always provided for. He showed his love with gifts, and lessons and active time together—golfing and tennis and teaching me practical life lessons. But this sort of attention? Brushed hair and handsy affection ... even Omar didn't often show his love like this. "Is this aftercare?" I asked, remembering my research for the audition.

"Yes," he said, leaving it with that simple one-word answer. As he got to the end of my braid, he held out his hand. "Hand me your elastic, please."

I tugged the hairband off my wrist and passed it back to him. After he secured the braid, he stood, tugging back the comforter. "Lay down, Poppy."

I stood and as soon as I did, the floor and the ceiling switched places, a staggering reminder that I wasn't yet sober. *Whoa.* Jude caught me around the waist, guiding me to the bed.

"Still a little tipsy, huh?"

I nodded, falling back onto the soft mattress. "Guess so."

"Do you get sick when you drink?"

I shook my head no. "The last time I threw up from drinking too much was when I was seventeen at my graduation party."

"Good," Jude said, grabbing a wastebasket. "I'm going to put this here anyway. Just in case."

I lowered onto my back until I was looking at the smooth ceiling. The bed dipped as Jude sat next to me.

When my eyelids grew heavy, I fought them to stay open. He was too beautiful to look away from. His deep voice broke the silence. "Close your eyes, Poppy."

For what felt like the millionth time that day, I did what I was told to do, letting my eyes close and darkness engulf me. The room spun, but less than before. Beside me, I heard a rustling sound and then two cool, metal circles rested on my closed eyes.

Tears filled beneath my flattened eyelids. If I thought hard enough, I could almost still smell the lavender oil on my mom's hands. His lips pressed against my forehead, firm, but gentle. "Good girl, Poppy. Sleep sweet."

The bed dipped as he stood and I heard every footstep he took toward the side door. There was a creak as it opened into what I assumed was Jude's adjoining room and then a quiet click as I drifted off into the deepest sleep I'd had in a long, long time.

CHAPTER TEN
Marly

THE NEXT MORNING, I woke with a long stretch, reaching my hands overhead. The sheets were tangled around my legs, the comforter in a heap beside me. I was always a wild sleeper. Gliding my hands back down my sides, my pinky brushed the cool metal quarter that had slipped off during the night.

Tears flooded against the backs of my eyes and one spilled down my cheek. The salty drop pooled over my lip and I darted out my tongue to catch it. Last night was special. For the first time in years, maybe even decades, I had let myself be taken care of. It wasn't exactly comfortable. Actually, at times, it was downright awkward. But undeniably, I had slept better last night than I had in years.

I threw the thick cotton sheets aside, and pressed my bare feet into the lush threads of the area rug. Still groggy, I moved to the sink and grabbed my toothbrush. A few minutes later, there was a light knock on the door. I had barely finished brushing my teeth as I hopped over, buttoning my pants. I swung open the door finding Jude there with a giant silver tray.

My eyes widened at the matching silver pot on top. "Please tell me there is coffee in there," I grinned, my stomach fluttering. There was nothing better than a strong cup of coffee in the morning.

Jude matched my smile and the creases around his mouth deepened. "You know it," he said, setting the tray down onto a side table. He tipped a small coffee cup over and poured the rich, steaming coffee into a mug. "How do you take it?"

"Just cream. Well, half and half preferably—milk turns my coffee a grayish color." *Ick.*

"Hmm," Jude pressed his lips together staring at the creamer.

"Or whatever. Whatever you have is fine." I waved it off like it wasn't a big deal. I mean, it was just milk. I didn't love it, but it was fine. I'd survive.

Jude looked up, his green eyes sparkling. "It's not a problem at all ... just one second."

"Seriously, Jude ... it's not a big deal."

But he didn't let me finish. He backed out of the room, leaving me there with a mystery tray of breakfast. I lifted the cover to find a plate of fruit, steaming oatmeal, bacon, eggs and sausage. I dropped the silver lid back onto the plate, falling back onto the bed. *Ew, meat.*

Jude was back in a minute with a little cup of half and half and he slowly poured it into my mug. "Just say when."

I laughed, shaking my head. "When. But I could have poured it myself, you know."

He smirked, handing me the piping hot coffee. "I know ... but you're going to spend the week subservient to me. I might as well give you a full-service breakfast prior to that." He winked and I couldn't help but laugh. He made a damn good point.

"Well in *that* case, I could really use a massage—"

His gaze narrowed playfully, with just a hint of a smile curving his lips. "Don't press your luck." But his eyes skimmed down to my shoulders, sweeping quickly over my body before he glanced away. He joked no, but his eyes said yes. Pulling the side table in front of me, he lifted the lid on the breakfast. "I wasn't sure what you like, so I got you a little of everything. You're going to need your energy, so eat up. I've got a lot planned."

My stomach turned at the meat. "I'll have the fruit and oatmeal. I'm a vegetarian."

Regret flickered across Jude's face and he quickly scraped the eggs, bacon and sausage onto a separate plate. "I'm sorry—I had no idea." He muttered a curse, hands clenched onto his hips. "Damn."

I shrugged, spearing a piece of pineapple with my fork. "Why would you?" I laughed. "We only just met the other day." Chewing the fruit, delicious tangy sweetness exploded on my tongue.

"That's my job as your Dom to know ... to take care of you." he said, sitting beside me and eating the eggs himself.

"So, would that have been in our Dom/sub contract? No meat play?" I grinned and nudged him with my elbow.

He shot me a humoring smile. "I know you're joking ... but yeah. It's the sort of thing you would have told me, or put in your contract. Plus, it would have been easy enough for me to research on my own and find out you're a vegetarian." He waved his fork, falling back onto his elbows while eating. "Guess your first lesson of the day is being learned the hard way—it's a Master's job to take care of his sub. He or she is supposed to provide all things necessary to a comfortable life."

I lifted a brow at that, taking another sip of coffee. "Oh, really? *Comfortable?*"

He laughed, shaking his head. "I mean ... not everything we do to our subs is comfortable for them. But just because something's uncomfortable, doesn't mean it's not also pleasurable."

"Like what?"

Jude thought for a moment and then answered, "Nipple clamps."

Coffee nearly spurted out my nose at that. I wasn't sure what I expected the answer to be ... but 'nipple clamps' were the last thing I ever thought I'd be discussing with Jude Fisher over breakfast. "How are they pleasurable?"

Jude shrugged. "Some of us have higher pain tolerance than others, so we need more ... extreme means of pain for punishment."

I swallowed, awestruck. "You? You enjoy pain."

He nodded, taking a final bite of egg before setting the plate back onto the tray. "Occasionally. I started as a submissive. Most Dominants do."

I set my oatmeal down next to his empty plate. I guess I didn't delve far enough into FetLife. "What's your skeleton?" I asked quietly.

Jude's eyes darted up to meet mine. "My what?"

"Your skeleton. What is it the club has on you that keeps you hushed about this place?"

His lopsided smirk tipped higher. "Show me yours and I'll show you mine?"

For a moment, I considered telling him everything. About me and Omar and Simon blackmailing him and how Jack spread all those rumors after I dumped him. If I got this part, we would inevitably be spending a lot of time together. And if trust for this week was important? Maybe I should lay it all out on the table.

Jude's eyes widened and his mouth dropped open.

"Oh, my God," he said quietly. "You're actually debating telling me."

Heat flooded my cheeks and the flare of warmth dipped all the way into my belly. Or maybe I'm just an idiot.

"No, Marly—that's great," he leaned forward, placing a hand on top of mine. "Really. The fact that you trust me enough to tell me a secret like one they find here for the contracts—" the catch in his voice threw me off. Was he actually moved by this? By me? He did a sort of half grunt, half chuckle thing and shook his head. "Well, let's just say it's been a long time since a woman's been so up front with me."

I opened my mouth to speak, but Jude cut me off. "My secret they have on me isn't that exciting. It's the mere fact that I'm in this lifestyle as hardcore as I am. My mother is a senator in Montana and a huge feminist. Even though everything I do is consensual, my lifestyle becoming public would hurt my family. Not to mention my career. All anyone would see is Jude the Dom who whips women. Not Jude, the Academy Award winning actor and loving son. She's worked her whole life to get to where she is, I can't let my kinks take away from all the good she's done for women's rights."

"But ... aren't they going to find out after this movie comes out?"

His brows creased in the center of his face. "Why would they? Yeah, I'm acting in the film. And one of the producers. But to the world, it's just that ... *acting*. No one thinks Jamie Dornan is a real Dom, do they?"

"Well ..." I lowered my cheek to my shoulder, shooting him a grin.

Jude laughed, the sound deep and rich like the coffee I had earlier. He narrowed his eyes, studying me. "So ... *your* demon. It must be a doozy, huh?" he asked as a quiet afterthought.

I looked away, shrugging. "Something like that."

"It's okay," his thumb moved in circles over my knuckle. "You don't have to tell me. Just the fact that you were considering it is ... well, special."

I sighed, relieved. Even though I *wanted* to be upfront with Jude, I just couldn't. Not yet. Because I wouldn't just be outing myself ... I'd be outing Omar.

CHAPTER ELEVEN
Jude

I WAS IN full-on teacher mode. My mom was always trying to get me to go for higher education—get a job teaching at a collegiate level. Being a Hollywood actor? It was just about the most appalling profession I could have picked in her mind ... outside of a gigolo. No, scratch that. She would have seen a male escort as being progressive. Just like she'd probably be fine with my BDSM lifestyle, had I stayed a submissive. Not that she'd want it out in the public ... but privately? She would have applauded that shit.

Marly and I sat on the floor across from each other. We'd already gone over the Dom/sub contract in detail and filled it out as if we were entering a real relationship. Ass play, a soft limit. That one shocked me. And if she was mine? Truly mine? That soft limit would be explored. Literally. With lots of lube.

Shit. I took a deep breath, trying to clear my mind. Get it off of anything sexy with Marlena. I imagined a cold shower. Diving into the Atlantic Ocean in the middle of January. Baseball. Anything to calm down my raging libido.

Hard limit. Public nudity. Sharing. Exhibitionism. We had that in common. Although surprisingly, she wasn't opposed to watching others. I'd asked her specifically to clarify that, especially since she seemed so uncomfortable with the public blowjob happening in the circle across from us yesterday.

She laughed, her cheeks turning pink and her freckles darkening with the flush. "I just wasn't ready for it. If you prepare me... give me a head's up what we're walking into ... I think I'll be okay watching."

"Watching ... a Dom have sex with his submissive?" I asked and she nodded. "Watching him tie her up?" Another nod. "Watching him take a paddle to her ass until there are welts covering her naked body?" She swallowed ... hesitating. Then, nodded. "Okay, then," I said, surprised, making a note on the contract. "I will let you know before we walk into a scenario like that. LnS has designated rooms for it, so I doubt you'll accidentally walk in on it any-where."

Marly's red hair was down, framing her heart-shaped jaw like a glossy, rippled curtain. *That fucking hair is incredible,* I thought, remembering the satin strands as I brushed it last night. Would it feel just as silky cloaking my thighs as she worked my cock in and out of her mouth?

I squeezed my eyes shut quickly, taking a sobering breath. *Get your head in the game, Jude.* When I looked up from the contract, she had moved from picking at her cuticles, to biting her nails. Something was on her mind. Reaching out, I tugged her finger free from her lips and her face fell. Seemingly embarrassed, she wrung her hands together, dropping them to her lap. "What is it?" I asked.

She sighed before answering. "I always thought BDSM was like a giant orgy. Or ... maybe not an orgy. Maybe more like a sequence of one night stands. I thought it was casual. But this ... God, this is like, a lot of effort just to have sex."

"Not everyone does it like this … but they should. Without mentioning names, some people do the one-night stand thing. They go over rules quickly with submissives that they know are trained in the lifestyle. But they don't have anything like this." I lifted the contract like a visual aid to drill my point home.

"But not you?"

"No. Not me." The silence stretched between us like chewed bubble gum around a finger. Did she need more of an answer than that? "They don't always last a long time," I clarified. "Sometimes, I only have a submissive for a weekend. Other times, we stay together a few weeks. But for me? I need this piece of paper. I need control. I need to know that we are entering a relationship with all the facts laid out in front of us."

Marly swallowed. "When was the last time you had a submissive?"

"Seventeen months ago. Layla left me almost two years ago. And after her, I had a couple submissives who only lasted a weekend or two, as I mentioned." My stomach tightened, an acid-like burn rising up my throat. "And one who lasted a few months." I tried to swallow that lump down, but it got lodged at my Adam's apple. "But it's not a time I really like to talk about." In other words: Please don't ask me anymore.

Her lips pressed into a tight line. "Okay," she said. "Just answer one more question and I promise to stop prying."

Fucking hell. I wanted to say it was fine. It was her job to pry this week. That my life was an open book. But those seven months after Layla? It was anything but an open book. It was a fucking diary. Locked in a safe. Sealed in the basement. "Okay," I managed to say.

"Did all your submissives have to go through this?" She pointed at the contract. "Or were any of them casual? Like ... one night stands?"

By her blade-sharp tone, I expected a much heavier question. One that would slice me down the center and spill my past all over the floor by her feet. Did I ever cross a hard limit line? Or did any of my subs ever go running and never look back? *Yes, and yes.* This question? This, I could handle. "Poppy," I said, a smile relaxing my face. "I've never liked *anything* casual. Not sex. Not submissives. Hell, not even jeans."

"Okay," she said, matching my smile. "So, what's next? We've got almost a week together. What the hell are we going to do for a week?"

"Well, to start with ..." I stood up, moving to check my watch, only to be met with my bare wrist. Damn. I kept forgetting I gave my Rolex to Marly. Instead, I tugged my phone free from my back pocket. "As you saw in our contract, before I enter a weekend with a submissive, I pamper her the day before."

Marly turned her head to the side, looking at me from the corner of her eyes. "Okay ..."

"You, my sweet Poppy, have a massage coming in fifteen minutes. After that, Lynne will give you a facial."

Her grin widened and she leaned forward, fake whispering, "I thought we said 'no sex.'"

God, she was sweet. "Not that kind of facial, dirty girl." She rose to her feet and rested her hands on her hips, still smiling in a way that robbed me of my breath. "After the facial, you'll get a manicure and a pedicure and we'll meet up for dinner after that."

"Wow," she said. "A whole day of pampering. And you're not even getting laid afterward."

I barked a laugh that caught me by surprise. "At some point before the week is over, I'm going to get through to you that getting laid is the least of this lifestyle."

Backing out of the room, I gave her a final wink. "Enjoy, Poppy."

CHAPTER TWELVE
Marly

HOLY SHIT. OKAY, so yes, celebrities tended to get pampered a lot. Yes, I get facials once a month and as often as I can, I get myself to a nail salon … mostly because it helped me not bite my damn nails when I pay a hundred bucks for nail art. Pampering in this industry is not uncommon.

But *this* kind of pampering. I had never experienced it before. And I go to the best salons in Los Angeles. I moaned, too relaxed to care about the embarrassing sound as the manicurist massaged my hands and forearms.

Hours later, they finished and packed up the traveling massage table and supplies, then left. I had just wrapped myself in a lush robe that was left hanging on the bathroom door when my phone buzzed at the bedside table. Omar's name flashed across the screen. "Hey, babe," I said, answering.

"Hey, boo. How's it going?"

"It's really great," I said, combing my fingers through my hair. "So far, I got drunk, then spanked, and tucked into bed like a four-year-old. Then today, I was rubbed down in an oiled massage."

Omar's silence was fraught with unasked questions.

"Don't worry," I added, "the rubdown was by a professional masseuse. Jude wasn't even in the room."

"Then why are you whispering?"

Was I? Shit, I *was* whispering. "Would you believe for dramatic effect?"

He gave a deep, rumbling laugh that could have rattled the phone in my hands. "Not for a second. But I trust you know what's best for you."

"Any word about Simon?" I asked, hoping for a change in subject.

He sighed. "Nothing new. Haven't heard back yet about my callback either."

Instinctively, I put my hand to my heart, aching for him. "You'll get it. I know you will."

"You don't know I will. You *hope* I will ..."

"How about this? I know you're talented and hard-working and you *deserve* that part. Whether or not you get it."

"Right back at you, boo."

I smiled, a breath escaping audibly through my nose— half-laugh, half-sigh. "Whatever happens, we'll get through it."

There was another pause, before Omar said, "Hey, you got that little calendar on you?"

"It's a *planner*, not a calendar. And yes. When don't I have it?" I grinned, picking up my turquoise planner.

"Well, do me a favor. Open it up to next Thursday, after your callback ... and pencil me in for a dinner date." There was a light knock on the door. I tightened the knot of my robe at my waist and pranced over to open it. "You've only been gone 24 hours, but I miss you already," Omar said.

Jude peeked in, grinning, and I held up a finger, asking him to hold on a moment. "I miss you, too, babe. I've gotta run though. Talk to you tomorrow?"

"Talk to you tomorrow."

I hung up and tugged the lapels of my robe tighter across my cleavage as I bent over. Using my blue pen, my specific 'Omar' pen, I wrote in curly cursive our dinner date.

"How's Omar doing?" Jude asked, shutting the adjoining room door behind him.

"He's good. I think he's a little lonely."

His neck tightened and his eyes flashed, erupting into an emerald flame. It all lasted only a second. One fleeting moment of pure, undiluted intensity before he relaxed and settled into a smile. "Is it the first time you two have been apart since getting engaged?"

"Actually, yeah. I didn't realize that. We've spent a night here or there apart, but never a whole week." Even though I didn't do anything wrong by admitting that, I still lowered my gaze, embarrassed. Or maybe uncomfortable was the better word. Which was ridiculous. Omar was my fiancé … my fake fiancé, but for all intents and purposes with Jude, I had every right to talk about him. In fact, Jude was the one who asked the question. But if I've done nothing wrong, then why did I feel so damn guilty?

"I got you something," Jude said.

My concern was muted—replaced with a fireball of excitement. I always loved presents. My dad wasn't always the greatest at showing affection, but he showed love with gifts; showered me with them until I became accustomed to getting them nearly every time we saw each other. Sometimes they were small gifts—a set of stickers for my planner or a new roll of washi tape. Sometimes they were big. Like when he became ill and gave me both his wedding ring and my mother's wedding band and engagement ring.

I shifted my weight, feeling restless and suddenly aware of how naked I was beneath the robe. Damn, I wish I'd thought to put on something more than just a thong after my massage.

"Sit down," Jude instructed, gesturing to the bed. I sat and crossed my legs, careful to tug the robe tightly shut, covering any bit of flesh at the tops of my thighs. "Remember rule number one in our Dom/sub contract?"

"Ummm," I thought back to that morning. Between the massage, the facial, the nails, the pedicure, and Omar's phone call … it felt like a lifetime ago.

"Every day, Poppy must wear an item …"

"… that reminds her of Jude," I finished for him.

"Well …" From behind his back, he produced a long, slim jewelry box. "This is what I got for you to wear."

I cautiously took the box. The royal blue velvet was lush and thick and screamed money. But whatever this was, it didn't come from a box store. There was no *Cartier* logo or Tiffany's signature bright blue box. If anything, it seemed old and there was a faded navy inset of damask within the royal blue, decorating the box. Already, without opening it, the box itself was gorgeous. "It looks like an antique," I said, dragging my fingertips across the textured velvet. Like petting a cat in the wrong direction, it sent a chill down my spine.

"It *is* an antique," he said. "Open it."

The hinge of the box creaked in protest as I flipped it open. Inside, a silver choker lay flat against the royal blue satin padding. At the center of the necklace was a cream-colored cameo; the profile of a Victorian woman, with her hair in curls piled on top of her head. "Wow," I exhaled the word on a sigh. "It's ... it's gorgeous."

Jude reached over, taking the necklace from the box and held it up for me to get a better look. "It's from 1879. I went shopping to find an item to remind you of me ... as said in our contract. I was at all these shops on Rodeo Drive, and nothing stood out to me. Nothing seemed like you ... not Chanel, not Hermes. And then, I was driving home and came across this little antique shop. And there it was."

"I haven't worn a choker in ..." I laughed. "Hell, I don't think I've *ever* worn a choker."

"May I?" he asked, holding the necklace up, gesturing to my neck.

I nodded, gathering my hair on top of my head, feeling a little like the woman in the cameo, with all my hair clenched in my fist at my crown. Jude reached around and the cold silver brushed my clavicle as he dragged it up my throat, hinging the clasp at the back of my neck.

"There," he said. "It reminded me a little of the dog collars a lot of subs wear."

My head snapped around to look at him. A dog collar? That's what he thought of?

His grin widened. "Easy, there, Poppy. I knew you weren't the dog collar sort of sub. But this necklace, it will give you a small taste of what it's like for the subs who do get collared. It's similar, yet different. More ... you. Or at least, the you I've gotten to know in twenty-four hours."

I stood, walking over to the mirror and brushed my hand over the necklace. It was gorgeous. Unlike anything I'd ever worn before. The diamond from my mother's engagement ring caught the light and I couldn't help but compare the two pieces of jewelry. "My mom loved antique jewelry," I said.

"You do too, right?" Jude said, walking toward me. I tilted my head at him. What made him say that?

"Your engagement ring," Jude said. "It's got to be pre-World War Two."

I wrapped my hand around my left knuckle. "You noticed that?"

Jude nodded, reaching out and taking my hand. "These etchings here ... the filigree, it's usually found in pieces from the 20s. Very deco. Very Gatsby of you." He winked and released my hand.

"It was my mother's ring," I said. "She had a love for ornate, old jewelry." I laughed, "Actually, she had a love for ornate old *anything*. My dad told me that she bought this fainting couch before they got married. They had a big fight about it because he thought it was so impractical and that she'd never use it. So, she dragged it over in front of her desk and used it instead of her office chair every day."

Jude laughed, his smile wide and beautiful, creasing his eyes in a way that warmth and happiness seemed to radiate from him. "I wish I could have met her."

"Me, too." I said. And meant it. How weird was it that Jude had me talking about my mom twice in two days?

"But maybe I can meet your father."

My throat went tight. "He died, too. Right after New Year's." Once more, my eyes drifted to where my planner rested beside the bedside. That planner was the last gift I got from him on Christmas right before he died. "This will be my first Christmas without him."

"Marly," Jude whispered. "I'm so sorry."

My right hand curled around my left knuckles, clutching my fingers; my mother's ring. Hiding it. A sharp breath punched out of my lungs and I forced myself to focus on the sharp edge of the diamond setting. How it pressed into my tender palm, indenting my soft skin. I took a breath and gave Jude my best smile. But it felt too forced. Rickety, like one of my mom's stupid antiques that needed fixing. "It's fine," I said. "But thank you." How many times had I said different iterations of that phrase to people? *I'll be okay, thank you. Everything's fine, thanks. Thank you, but I'm fine. Fine. Fine. Fine.* I'd said that word so much in my life, that it had lost all meaning.

And I was pretty sure Jude saw right through it. Saw through *me*. Because the man noticed *everything*. Every time he watched me, his gaze was sharp and cutting; like a machete, able to hack through brush and weeds. He was able to slice through my bullshit and see the truth behind my words.

Even as I said those words again ... *it's fine* ... for the millionth time in my life, the misery of loss twisted in my chest, wringing out like wet laundry.

Then, on cue, practically like he could read my thoughts, Jude brushed his hand over mine, meeting my stare head-on. "Don't be afraid to wear your pain, Marly," he said. "Wear it proudly, like your mother's diamond ring. Wear it proudly like you'll eventually wear Omar's wedding band. Don't shy away from that pain. But also, don't let the jewels or the pain you wear outshine the sparkle in your eyes. Or," he touched his hand to my chest, directly over my heart, "the sparkle in here."

My breath caught and I was entranced by his gaze. The gentle touch of his fingers sparked inside of me and I wasn't sure if I was affected more by his touch or by his words. But something in those words struggled inside me. *Wear my pain?* It went against everything my stoic father had taught me. "I'm not hiding anything." Jesus. I sounded defensive, even to myself. "Sometimes you just have to put on a strong face and keep going ..."

Jude nodded and stepped back. The absence of his touch was devastating. "Earlier today, you asked me why anyone would want pain. Why they would willingly accept it."

"Yeah ..."

"Well, a lot of people believe that being strong is not feeling pain. Pretending something doesn't hurt, right? The whole, 'put on a happy face' bullshit. In my opinion, the strongest people are the ones who feel the pain. They feel it down to their bones ... no, beyond their bones. They feel it in their soul, so deeply that it transcends any sort of physical pain. They feel it, first. They understand it, second. And they accept it, third."

Those words resonated, hitting a chord inside me, and for a fast second, I heard the harmony in my heart. But just as quickly, doubt edged its way back in. "You're telling me that in order to fully accept the pain and loss of my mother and father's deaths, I need a Dom to whip the hell out of my ass?"

"I'm not telling you anything of what you need, Marly. I'm just saying that there's a place for darkness, pain, and acceptance. And how a submissive might see a situation differently than you."

"But ... sometimes, you just need to put on the happy face. Sometimes you need to smile and be the sunshine you want to see in your life and ignore the pain. Ignore the shadows," I fought back. What Jude said went against everything I believed. Everything my dad had taught me.

"Sometimes that can work. But too much sunshine is

just as bad as not enough. It can cause dehydration … drought. Sometimes you need that shady tree to sit beneath. Sometimes you need a little darkness to gain perspective."

"But—"

"Just think on it tonight after we go to bed. When I leave you alone with your thoughts, let it roll around in your mind. And now? Let's have some dinner."

My stomach growled and I looked at my phone. Eight o'clock already? Holy shit, the day flew by. "What's for dinner?"

Jude pulled out his phone, opening up a delivery service. "Anything you want. Literally. The rest of the night is all about you and your pampering. You choose the food. You get to pick what we do after dinner. You can even wash your own face tonight," he said, laughing. "Then, tomorrow? It really begins. Tomorrow, we transition you more into sub-life. Sound good?"

Good? I wasn't sure 'good' was the word I'd use to describe my feelings. "So, I'm in charge for the rest of the night?"

Jude shrugged. "Yep. It's always part of the fun with prep. Some of my subs don't know what to do with it, so I skip this stage with certain women. The ones who are so in the lifestyle, they wouldn't get pleasure from a prep day of control." He slid his hands in his pocket. "But something told me, you above all else, would appreciate it."

A wry grin pulled at my lips. "The first thing I want to do is change into clothes. Then, I want to order sushi. Cucumber and avocado rolls for me. Then … after dinner …" I pointed to the adjoining door. "I want to see your room."

CHAPTER THIRTEEN
Jude

S HE WANTED TO see my room. My fucking *room*. No sub, other than Layla, had ever stepped foot in there. Even with this tradition of giving my submissives one day of power and pampering, none of them had asked to see it. Almost like despite the day of power, I still had drawn an invisible line across the door. An unspoken hard limit.

I swallowed the last of my spicy tuna roll and watched as Marly nibbled on a piece of ginger, her eyes forward on the computer screen I had grabbed from my bedroom. Granted, Netflix on a 17-inch laptop screen wasn't the most luxurious, but we were comfortable together, sitting on the floor with the laptop between us as some cheesy show about a hospital and bunch of doctors fucking each other played.

The credits rolled and Marly covered a jaw-popping yawn with the back of her hand. "Ready for bed?" I asked, secretly hoping she totally forgot about wanting a tour of my room.

She shook her head, slowly moving it back and forth. "Nuh-uh. I want to see what's behind door number one," She pointed her finger to the adjoining door. "You're not getting out of this that easily." She moved that same finger she'd used to point to the door to my face and it took every ounce of my self-control not to nip the tip of her finger.

"You seem tired, Marly." God, I was such an ass. What was the big damn deal, right? It was just my room … it wasn't even my room inside my *home*. It was just like a studio apartment I rented from the club. *And in some ways, that makes it worse.* My real home? It was perfectly designed with only a few BDSM toys in the closet. I had always been diligent to keep my two lives separate. *Until Layla. Layla fucked everything up.* But my room here? It housed all my secrets. Every deviant act, every wicked toy … if walls could talk, they would tell Marly what a fraud I was.

"I'm not tired," Marly said. "And it's my night, right? If I want to spend it playing Boggle until five a.m., I *can*."

"Well," I said, sliding the plastic sushi containers to the side and shutting my laptop. "If we're going to get technical about things, your day of control and pampering ends at midnight." I checked my phone for the time. "You have 36 minutes." Maybe she'd run out the clock. Or maybe she'd see my room and be bored. It looks like any other bachelor pad. Hell, it *was* just like any other bachelor pad—if said bachelor was an affluent Dominant. It wasn't like she would really find anything too telling in there. It was the principle behind it. That room was mine. Supposed to be off-limits until I decided the relationship was ready.

"What?" Marly checked her phone as well. Like she didn't believe me that it was nearing midnight. "How is it almost midnight already?"

"Pampering takes time," I joked. "Ninety-minute massage, ninety-minute facial, sixty-minute manicure, sixty-minute pedicure … it adds up."

She jumped to her feet, brushing invisible dust off her yoga pants. "Okay, 36 minutes." She walked to the door. "Show me your room."

I stretched my neck to each side. "Fine." I stood, turning the knob to the adjoining door and holding it open for her. She stepped cautiously over the threshold, looking around. Her look of bewilderment was so intense, you would have thought it was the fucking door to Narnia.

My room was bigger than the sub's room. All Master's bedrooms were. That's just the way LnS designed the space. Mine was shaped like a studio apartment rather than a hotel room, like Marly's. Against the front wall was a small kitchen. Next to it, a full bathroom with white marble tiles. Next to the window, in the corner of the room was a California King size bed. And what Marly couldn't see? The restraints connected to that bed beneath the mattress. The anal beads in the nightstand drawer. The journal I kept of my submissives, detailing every single one of our dirty acts.

She circled the room, running her hand along the small prep area in the kitchen. Pacing to the front door and peeking into the bathroom. Then, wandering to the window. Each step she took deeper into my space felt like a threat. Like I was a cat being cornered and she was encroaching on my safe space. The first time Layla had seen this studio, she had opened every drawer. Took out every piece of clothing I owned and examined it. Went through my journal and read every word about every sub I'd ever had and then threatened to burn the book. It turned into a battle of who was the real Dom between us ... and I was always fighting to prove my position. My jaw clenched painfully. Would Marly do that? Walk around and judge every aspect of my life?

She threaded her fingers into the edge of the tasseled curtains and peeked out the window. "We're only on the second floor. Have paparazzi ever tried to photograph in here?"

"It's reflective glass. We can see out. They can't see in."

She nodded, seemingly pleased by that answer and turned to the bed. Her eyebrow crept higher, arching over her blue eyes. "That is one big bed."

"You and Omar don't have a King?"

"Uh …" She jerked her eyes from mine, stumbling over her words. "No. I mean, not yet. I have a queen—*we* have a queen. For now."

Something was off about their engagement. I'd felt it when I first saw them at the club together and whenever Marly mentioned Omar. Even now—her reaction was extreme. Asking what size bed she and her fiancé shared shouldn't make someone so flustered. I examined her. The way her newly manicured fingers flew to her mouth and as she began chewing, she stopped herself, lengthening her strong, lean arms out in front of her. With an outstretched hand, she sighed, admired her manicure, then clenched her hands around her hips.

She stared at my comforter—it was simple with slate grey pleats and black and grey matching ornate pillows. Then, she quickly moved past the bed, toward my walk-in closet.

"Marly," I warned as she reached out a hand to the doorknob of the closet. I rushed in front of her, blocking the entrance with my body.

She didn't say anything, but her shrewd eyes flashed and she lifted that same challenging eyebrow as before. "I'm in charge for how much longer?"

I sighed, glancing at my phone. "24 minutes."

"Okay, then." She waited, standing her ground.

I couldn't let her go in there. Anywhere but that closet.

She'd barely had any time to adjust to LnS. Other than a brief excursion last night to the common room, she hadn't left her room all day.

"Jude," Marly snapped. "*Move.*" The hollow in my chest plummeted to my stomach. With tense shoulders, I stepped aside and waited. Waited for the other shoe to drop, even if I wasn't sure what that was going to look like.

Turning the knob, she opened the door and peeked into the walk-in closet. Some of my suits hung at the front, but mostly … it housed my toys. My paddles. My ball gags. My ropes. All the stuff I refused to bring home with me rested on shelves, perfectly organized.

"I tried to warn you," I said.

She was silent for a long moment, the tension palpable. God, I would give anything to know what was running through her mind. "Marly …" I said. "You're killing me here. Please say something."

"That's … that's a lot of stuff."

"Yeah," I whispered.

Her chin tilted as she looked up and down the shelves. "Most of it I recognize. I mean … not from experience. But like movies and stuff." She stepped deeper inside the closet; deeper inside the dragon's lair.

"Marly, maybe you shouldn't look too closely in here." I followed her into the walk-in closet, that sick feeling spreading like a virus to other areas of my body. "I haven't even been in here in over a year—" Marly stopped at the back wall so abruptly, I nearly slammed into her. She paused at a hook, where a diamond studded collar dangled off of it.

My blood turned cold. No, cold didn't even begin to describe it. It turned to dry ice. Brittle and so desperately freezing, that it would physically harm you to touch it. That's what I transitioned into. I'd forgotten that collar was there.

Marly gently lifted the collar off of the hook and ran her newly manicured nail over the largest center diamond. "Wow. Was it Layla's?"

She doesn't know. She doesn't know how fucked I am. How fucked up Layla made me. And the monster I turned into after she left.

Chest heaving, I launched toward her, wrenching the collar out of her hands and put it back on the hook. But Marly didn't seem phased. She stood there, maintaining her wide stance, her hands now falling to her slim waist and her spine went rigid.

Her tank top showed the taut, smooth skin of her shoulders and sternum. Tanned and silky-looking and the low neckline offered an exquisite view of her neck. A view that I shouldn't be taking.

"What happened to *me* having the control until midnight?"

"What happened to respecting a person's limits—hard or soft?"

Her gaze dipped briefly between my legs and I felt the ice in my veins thaw. Not only thaw, but spike to molten lava with one second of her attention directed at my cock. Jesus Christ, what was I … twelve-years-old? A girl glances at my penis and all of a sudden I'm rock fucking hard and ready to plunge inside of her?

"How can I respect your limits when you didn't *tell* me what they were?" Her voice grew louder with each word and her chest heaved. Each angry breath sent her breasts pulsing with the inhale-exhale.

"Part of being the one in control is reading your partner's signals." Couldn't she see? Couldn't she tell I didn't want her in there? I tried to stop her from coming into my room. She wanted to regardless. I tried to block her from entering the closet. She barreled through anyway. I tried to convince her not to go deeper inside ... and that's when she found the collar.

Her face softened, albeit only slightly. "Yeah," she whispered. "Well, I'm pretty fucking new at this. Maybe you could cut me a break."

I *should* cut her a break. Every cell in my body screamed in agreement. "I'm always cutting everyone else a break. When does someone finally give *me* that courtesy?"

We stayed locked in each other's narrowed gazes a moment longer before Marly spun away and stomped out of the closet, heading back to her room. Everything about this woman put me on the defensive. She made me feel brittle, when I'd worked so goddamn hard to become impenetrable. She made me feel vulnerable, when I'd spent the last two years building walls so I'd never feel so exposed again. She enraged me. Ignited me. I hated it.

I hated it so much ... that I might actually love it.

I ambled after her, catching the door as she stomped into her bedroom. "I'll come in to tuck you in after a few minutes." A few minutes. That's what I needed. A few minutes to calm down. Pull myself together.

"Don't bother," she sneered, barely looking over her shoulder.

"Marly—" I didn't mean it to sound so threatening. But her name rolled off my tongue in a growl.

She spun around and even as she leaned against the sink's counter so casually, so carefree and composed, her eyes gave her away. They were shrewd and assessing. Anything but aloof. "What time is it, Jude?"

I sighed, checking my phone. "Twelve minutes until midnight. But—"

"Then *I* am still in control. And I want to go to sleep *without* you tucking me in."

"Going to bed angry is never a good idea."

"Neither is blaming someone else for your own baggage." Her blue eyes flashed like a flame that had just been doused in accelerant. "You said it yourself." She pushed off the counter, stalking toward me in slow, predatory steps, backing me out the door. "Respect the limits. Read your partner's signals." Her eyes went wide, but her mouth stayed pressed into a firm line.

"Fine. But if you're the one in control, then as part of your *lesson*, you should know it's your job to make sure your submissive is okay. And pushing the person you're in charge of out because you're angry, isn't the answer."

The tense curve of her mouth relaxed. "So, what do you do when you're at an impasse like this? You need some sort of validation—to tuck me in or something affectionate to try to smooth this over. And I need to be left alone to process." She shrugged. "What do we do?"

I closed my eyes. I knew what I needed to do. "It starts with me apologizing."

She was quiet for a long moment. "That's a good start."

"I'm sorry for snapping at you, Marly. The last woman to step foot in that room was my ex-wife. I thought I could handle you in there, but … obviously, I wasn't ready."

I glanced up from my lowered gaze. "Okay," she whispered. "I'm sorry if I didn't read your signals. I was so focused on being 'in charge', I steamrolled right over them."

I exhaled in relief, the tension melting from my shoulders, but my stomach was still twisted in knots. "Can I please tuck you in now?" I needed it. With that intense fight … I needed to feel her touch, brush her hair, put her to bed so I knew she'd be there in the morning. My stomach was dense; heavy and felt like it was lined with led as I awaited her answer.

"What time is it?"

Fuck. "Seven minutes 'til midnight."

"Then, no. I need one night this week where I put myself to bed."

My heart fell. What if she was gone in the morning? What if I'd ruined the only other potential candidate to play Holly in this movie? What if I'd ruined whatever friendship was blooming between us? *Friendship.* It didn't seem like quite the right word. She had a fiancé. But still … whatever it was, it was more intense and calling her a friend didn't do it justice.

"But," she said, "as a compromise, I'll let you brush and braid my hair. In *your* room."

"In my room?" Back where we'd had our fight. Back where Layla haunted me at every corner. Did she know? Could she sense how badly I needed a connection right now? Warring feelings of tension and relief coiled around my spine—I didn't want to go back in that room with her. But also, thank God she was allowing aftercare in some form. That she was learning to read me. It was a double-edged sword.

"Yes. Because as a wise Dom once told me, it's part of the job to push those boundaries without crossing them." A smirk tugged on her lips and I couldn't but chuckle. It was a sweet release—her smile, my laugh.

"He sounds like a smart man."

She shrugged, grabbing her hairbrush and whooshing past me into my room. "He can be. But I'm also learning he can be a stubborn jackass sometimes, too."

Oh, Poppy. You don't even know the half of it.

CHAPTER FOURTEEN

Jude

EVEN THOUGH I apologized last night, I still tossed and turned all night. It would have been worse if Marly hadn't allowed me some aftercare time. Most of the night, I lay in bed with my palm pressed to the cool wall between us. Marly's bed was right on the other side. If I listened carefully, holding my breath, I could almost hear the creak of the bed as she rolled around in her sleep.

Around 5:30am, I gave up entirely. After showering, I ran out to get breakfast—chia seed pudding for Marly. Whatever the hell that was, the woman at the café assured me it was vegetarian. And an egg sandwich for me with two of the largest coffees they sold. With half and half. *Because milk turns her coffee grayish.* I grinned as I slid my keycard into the lock. Never in my life had I heard anyone say that about coffee with milk. It was fucking adorable.

I had a lot to make up for today. Yesterday was supposed to be easy. The easiest day of the whole fucking week and I had managed to screw it up. *Easy for who, though?* That's the thing ... most submissives already in the lifestyle don't want to push a Dominant's boundaries too much. They want to please me, even while they're in control. Except for Marly. *And Layla.* But there was an innate difference between the two—yes, Layla was a switch. And based on Marly's behavior, she likely was, too. But Layla was an experienced submissive. She made choices very intentionally—to punish. To control. And to hurt. And not in my best interest. But Marly didn't know any better. Even though our apologies last night were brief, it was what we both needed. The softness of her eyes ... the way she knelt on the floor in front of me and let me take care of her, touch her, even though she was still mad, it demonstrated a base knowledge—no, not knowledge. An instinct that in this relationship, caring for each other comes first.

Now, it was my turn to show her I was willing to step out of my own comfort zone for her, as well.

At 7a.m. on the dot, I pulled out my phone and texted Marly.

Good morning.

As per our faux Dom/sub contract, she responded within a few minutes with her own good morning and texted a photograph of her outfit for the day.

Jeans. And a tank top. Casual. Stunning. My cock saluted her, twitching to life. I groaned and cursed my stupid libido. Maybe if I hadn't let it go dormant for over a year, I wouldn't be so overactive. "Not fucking now," I said to no one. But the photo was missing something. Something important. Her bare neck taunted me, teased me that she wasn't really in this.

You look beautiful, I texted. **But you forgot something**.

Oh, shit, she texted back. A few seconds later, my phone dinged again with another picture message. This time, she wore the antique choker.

Much better. Ready for breakfast?
Omg, I'm starving.

I opened the side door leading into her room. She was

157

standing a few feet away, leaning against the sink, running a lipgloss wand across her bottom lip.

Holy shit. The photo didn't do her justice. That salute from my cock? It went to full-on attention.

It was just jeans and a goddamned tank top. I needed to pull it together. She had a fiancé who was already way more fucking understanding than I would ever have been. Letting my future wife come to a BDSM club with another man? What in the hell was Omar thinking?

She paused, looking up at me. "Where's breakfast?"

I jerked my head through the open door. "I thought we'd spend today in my room."

"You don't have to do that." Her mouth tipped into a small smile.

"Yes. I do." She may not know it yet, but I did. "Come on."

I turned, heading into my room, trusting she was behind me. I heard the soft click of the door shutting behind me as I walked to the small eating nook that was near the window.

When I turned to face her, Marly was grinning. "You did all of this for me?"

"I overreacted last night and I'm sorry."

"You already said you were sorry ... last night."

"I know. But what good is that apology, if I don't back it up with action?"

Her smile widened. "I guess it would be pretty worthless." She slid into the chair I held out for her, taking the cloth napkin and draping it over her lap. "You know, I'm sorry, too. For pushing you last night."

I took my seat across from her. "Giving me some time with you before bed was apology enough."

"Only ... it wasn't." Regret tightened her features and that smile of hers dropped. I immediately missed it and started scheming all the different ways I could bring it back. "What good is action without the words to back it up?" she said, trying to reverse my phrasing.

I took a bite of my egg sandwich and gave her a skeptical look. "It doesn't quite work in reverse, does it?"

A laugh bubbled out from her and she shook her head, taking a sip of coffee. "Guess not. But I *am* sorry. I shouldn't have pried ... I shouldn't have pushed you that much. I was thinking back to what if someone pressured me to revisit some of Jack's old things at the back of my closet? The thought of watching someone holding his stuff, treating it like something precious ... well, anyway. I know it's different, but I understand why you got upset."

"I appreciate that. But you also helped me realize something last night. I need to move on from this paralysis she has over me. Over this room."

"That comes in baby steps. Not with an actress you hardly know, barely trust, and isn't even a real submissive barreling through all your shit like a tornado."

I grinned. A tornado. It was the exact comparison I had used a couple of days ago.

Her eyes widened. "What?"

"Nothing. You're just something else, you know that?"

"Something else being a disastrous weather system?"

I laughed, the feeling shaking my diaphragm. It was like a muscle that had been in hibernation for years; like stretching after a long, deep sleep. She took a bite of her chia seed pudding and moaned. "Oh my God, this is good. Is that honey in it?"

"Maple syrup," I said. "I wasn't sure if you ate honey

on a vegetarian diet. You know ... bees and stuff."

"I do eat honey. But the maple is delicious, too."

We ate the rest of our breakfast more or less quickly, with the occasional chit chat. I wasn't the kind of Dom who wanted my sub to be silent and constantly serving. If anything ... I preferred to serve her; as long as I was the one in control of that. We finished eating and she cleared some of the plates.

"So, what's on the to do list for today?"

I took a long, low breath. "You're going back into my closet. You're going to look around at the various toys and ask all the questions you need to. You're here to learn."

She lifted a brow and dropping her hands from her hips, sauntered over to the closet. "Do *you* need a safe word for this?"

Maybe. "No, but we're going to play it like a game. I'm going to go in first and sit at the back of the closet. And we'll play like red light-green light, until you reach me and have your fill of looking around."

"Okay," she drew the syllables of the word out. "So, if you say red light, does it mean you're uncomfortable and you need me to stop looking at something?"

"Yes. Yellow light will mean that I want you to slow down and look harder. It may mean that something you're looking at deserves extra attention."

"And what happens when I get to you?"

"That's the catch ... you're not allowed to speak. The only words you're allowed to say in that closet are your safe words. And when you reach me, that's when you can ask your questions. But while you're looking around ... I just want you to see. Experience. Touch as many of the toys as you want."

Her nose scrunched, a disgusted look on her face. "Are they ... I don't know, *clean*?"

I chuckled at that. "Every toy, every anal plug, every paddle gets thoroughly cleaned after each use. You don't have to worry about that."

"You want me to touch someone else's anal plug?"

I paused. To an outsider, yeah, it would seem weird. "I want you to trust that I would never put you in harm's way. I want you to touch and experience what you're comfortable with. And I want you to trust me that everything in that closet has been soaked and sanitized. Even after you touch everything, after this week, I'll personally clean everything in there."

"You don't have a cleaning service for that?"

"LnS does, but I prefer to do it myself. Then I *know* for a fact that everything has been cleaned to my standards."

"For a guy who tells others to trust him, you don't seem to trust many people yourself."

Boom. There it was. And it had only taken her a day and a half to see right through me. It was like a shiv to the kidney and it knocked me down for the count. "I don't. Not since Layla."

With the strappy little tank top she wore, her red hair fell in wisps down her shoulders, brushing her neck. She was classically beautiful in an effortless way. It made it so easy to get lost while staring at her. "I don't either." She tucked a hand into her back pocket and brought one of those bare, pale shoulders to her ear. "Trust many people, I mean. I'd like to blame Jack, because I prefer to blame him for everything," she snorted despite herself and rolled her eyes. "But the truth is, I've always been this way."

I shook my head. No way. "No one is born distrusting.

There is a catalyst in your past ... you're just either unaware of it, or ignoring it."

Her arm, still angled behind her, tightened visibly. The muscles at her triceps bunched into a tight little ball and her nostrils flared. "You just know everything, don't you?"

"Until we know our greatest weakness, we'll never know our greatest strength."

"Who said that?"

I shrugged. "Someone dead probably." I turned, opened the door to the closet, then with a quick flick of my finger, I turned on the light inside. She watched me; watched my every step as I backed into the closet, dragging a chair behind me to the farthest wall. Her eyes were peculiarly feral with a savage, predatory gleam I hadn't seen in her before. Slowly, they dipped down my body as I lowered into the chair, spreading my legs and getting comfortable. Her unguarded gaze landed at my hips before lingering on my cock for an extra moment. Then she blinked, and it passed. The lustful, hungry gaze was gone. Replaced with a stony indifference that I knew was a complete and utter act.

"Green light," I said, starting the game. Oxygen stalled in my lungs as she brushed her right index across the cameo at the center of her throat and took her first step inside the closet.

Marly ran her hands along the sleeves of my cashmere suits at the front of the closet.

"Green light," I said again. The suits the least interesting thing in the damn closet. If she wanted to examine suits, we could do that at fucking Barney's.

She took the hint, stepping deeper inside and picking up several of the paddles. She lifted a wooden one off the wall, shifting it from one hand to the other, then swung it around, as if to hit someone invisible in front of her. When she was done, she put it back on the hook.

On the shelf below the paddles was an organizer for smaller objects. She peeked inside, shifted a few things around and took a step to move on.

"Yellow light," I warned. *Go back. Search deeper.*

She paused, stepping back and looking once more, opening the box that housed a new set of Ben Wa balls. I never bothered cleaning those ... they were gifts given to each new submissive. And when they were finished, I bought a new set to keep in my closet for my next submissive.

The box of new Ben Wa balls had a ribbon on it and a handwritten tag that said 'For Marly.' She flipped over the tag and looked up at me before returning her attention to the box. She looked curiously at the balls as she opened the lid—they weren't the silver kind most people knew of. They were silicone and ribbed both for better grip inside and also for a more enjoyable experience. She closed the box, leaving it on the counter and lifted a cock ring. The lines of her throat visibly tightened. Oh, Jesus. Maybe I didn't think this whole idea through. Because seeing the sweet, innocent Marlena holding my bondage toys—her fingers around a ring that had sheathed my dick ... *Nope, don't go there.* I clamped my eyes shut, shaking the thoughts off like a dog shaking water off after a cold bath. Because that's exactly what I fucking needed; to be doused with cold water. She put the cock ring back down and wiped her hand on her jeans.

I almost laughed at that. Here I was, turned on at her exploring, while she was so disgusted, she was wiping her hands of me. Literally. She didn't quite look as deeply in that box as I wanted, but that was okay. There was time. Time for her to learn about one of my favorite toys later. And she had found her gift—that was what was important.

The game continued like that, with lots of green lights and yellow lights. It wasn't until she came upon Layla's collar again that I felt the sweat gathering at my hairline. I knew this moment was coming and yet, it was still hard as fuck to watch. And sit there helplessly.

She touched the soft leather collar briefly, her hands resting momentarily at the diamond studs. But much quicker than last night, she moved on.

No. It was too fast. She'd been so curious before and now? She must have been stifling that curiosity to try to protect me. "Yellow light."

Her brows shot up to her hairline and her eyes bounced between me and the collar. "Yellow. Light," I said again.

She picked up the collar, holding it in her palms, bouncing it around. Then, she put it to her own neck and wrapped it around over her choker. Securing it in place, she stretched her neck from side to side, feeling it out. It was a beautiful collar, but on Marly? It wasn't right. The antique choker I bought was made for her. This collar was clunky and took away from her delicate curves. I'd been so scared of that collar. For two years, it represented my failed marriage and no one who wore it after Layla had been good enough for it. But now? *It* wasn't good enough for Marly.

She didn't take it off, but continued deeper into the closet. At the very back, corsets hung in a line beside me. Marly was almost done, almost reaching where I was sitting—almost finished exploring when a curious frown dipped her face. She leaned over my shoulder and goddamn if my cock didn't respond as her breasts brushed my bicep. I followed the line of her outstretched hand to the red lace up monoglove hanging at the end of the rack. She lifted it, turning it over in her hands. Her head tilted, brows pinched together and knelt in front of me. She was done.

"Well?" I asked. "Any questions?"

"Two questions," she said. "The box … the little balls …"

"They're a gift for you. Your own set of Ben Wa balls. To … play with."

Her brows jumped, comprehension tightening her face. She knew what Ben Wa balls were. Well, that was interesting.

"And this?" she asked, holding up the monoglove. "It's too small to be a corset, obviously … and its shape, it's like a cone—"

"That's a monoglove. Also known as an armbinder. It locks your elbows and hands behind your back."

"Can you show me?" she asked. Still on her knees, she held the armbinder up toward me like an offering.

I nodded and stood, helping her to her feet as well. Her stiletto heels sunk into the plush carpet with each step until we were back out in the studio.

Spinning, her tight ass was now facing me as she placed her arms behind her back—legs spread just wide enough to have me sweating through my damn shirt. *Shit, shit, shit. This was a really bad idea.* I had to keep it together. Stay professional. It was all research, dammit.

"Okay," I hesitated. Since when did I hesitate? No. I was in control of this situation. And she was an engaged woman—even if their engagement seemed weird to me, I wasn't about to cross that line. Besides, she had enough rumors circling the mill about her without me adding complications to the mix. I'd heard the murmurings of those rumors, never paying them much attention. And now that I'd spent time with Marly? I knew they were bullshit. I stepped closer, pulling her arms tighter together at the elbow and laced it up, tying it firmly in place.

She spun in the mirror, trying to get a better look. "Wait—" I said. A low purr of sexual energy pulsed between us and as I scooped my hand into Marly's hair and brushed it away from her neck, she gasped. Rational thought was holding on by a tiny thread, followed loosely by my fucking self-control.

I brushed my finger across Layla's collar. "Do you like the feel of a collar better than your choker?"

She shook her head. "No."

"No, what?" She'd had the day off and granted, I hadn't been enforcing the 'Sir' rule that morning. But now? Here? With her arms bound and her chest rising and falling in heavy, rapid breaths? It felt appropriate. And also, wildly inappropriate.

"No, Sir." And for the first time, she said it without even a hint of sarcasm. "It's heavy. Uncomfortable."

"I agree." I hissed a low breath, lust simmering in my gut as I unclasped Layla's collar and removed it from Marly's throat.

"There," I said, my voice scratchier than ever. "Normally, you cinch the monoglove even tighter for reduced circulation to the arms."

She spun around, facing me, eyes wide and mouth rounded into a perfectly fuckable 'o.' Jesus Christ, I rolled my eyes to the ceiling just to divert my attention away from her swollen, kissable pout. "Why? Is that ..." her voice cracked, "… pleasurable?"

After a deep breath, I brought my gaze back to hers. "For some, yes."

She stretched her neck behind her, looking down her back at the bound arms. "It's pretty hot. Being trapped … unable to move," her voice dropped. "Completely in the care of someone else."

I gulped. *Fuck.*

"So, then what would you do?" Her voice was innocent but the question was a loaded gun, pointed directly at my balls.

I grunted, stepping back from her and carrying the remaining dishes from breakfast to the sink. Anything to keep busy and get away from the vision that stood a few feet away. "What do you mean, what would you do? You'd fuck."

"Well …*yeah*," she turned in the mirror once more for another glance. "But … I mean … just standing here? Or … like, face down on the bed?"

I sucked in a sharp, shallow breath. This was what Marly was here for. To learn. So I didn't have to do this shit alongside of Layla. I turned slowly, still finding Marly entranced by her own reflection. Her breasts in the low-cut tank top pushed up and swelled out of the neckline. Her nipples pierced the thin cotton and my mouth watered for just one taste. One lick. With a sigh, I stormed back into the closet, taking a moment to compose myself. I could feel the glowering scowl on my face. *Relax. This isn't real. It's a character study. You're Leo … not Jude today.* My racing heart slowed with several deep breaths and as I calmed down, I grabbed the spreader bar off the wall. "Well, I'd probably use this next," I said, exiting the closet and crossing to Marly. "It locks your legs in an open position." My mouth was like a sand dune and I wet my lips as best I could, despite my dry mouth.

"Do it," Marly said, voice as bubbly and innocent as though she just requested an ice cream cone from Mister Frosty.

I chuckled a wry laugh and shook my head. "You're not ready for this." I shook the bar as if that would demonstrate just how not ready she was. In truth? *I* was the one not ready to see her in that state. Spread wide. Bound. Flushed.

Marly's cheek flopped over to one shoulder as she shot me an exacerbated eye roll. "You're kidding, right? If I get this part, I'll most likely be in more compromising positions than this. And fully nude, too."

Jesus, don't remind me. The breath hitched higher into my throat and though it was air, I damn near suffocated. But she was right. "Okay … remember—" I held a finger to her nose. "Planner. If you need to stop …"

"Sticker to slow down. I know." Her eyes flashed. Nervousness, maybe? I nudged her legs apart and as I bent to slide the leather cuffs on, she turned.

"Wait!" I knew it. It was too much for a newbie. "If this were real … I'd be naked. I want to feel how it would be against my skin." She kicked her heels off.

"Uh—"

"Just take my jeans off. I'm wearing little boy shorts underneath … it'll be fine."

"Marly, I don't think that's a good idea—"

"First of all, if I have to call you, Sir, you have to call me Poppy." That brought a smile to my face. She liked her nickname. "Second of all, I'm telling you it's okay. Take my jeans off. I wear less than this when I go to the beach.

Trust me … *Sir*."

Fuck me. Those were the three magic words. Despite my hesitancy, I couldn't argue with her. She was a consenting adult and this was good … it was good for the movie and good for the part. Just not good for my damn cerulean balls. She was as naïve as Red Riding Hood befriending the wolf. My fingers brushed the bare skin of her taut stomach. Popping the button of her jeans, I tugged the zipper down and crouched as I hooked my fingers into her waistband. The denim slid down her slender legs easily.

On my next breath, I could smell her. Could fucking smell her excitement. Was it me that aroused her? The monosleeve? The anticipation of the spreader bar? Or a combination of everything? I inhaled that sweet, heady scent and pushed off my knees, taking her in.

Those "boy shorts" she claimed to be wearing was basically a lacy thong in which her curvy ass peeked out from. "If you wear less than this to the beach, what the hell beaches are you going to?"

She laughed and shook her head. "You sound like my dad when I was in high school."

Fuck. *Fuck*. I imagined an eighteen-year old, carefree Marly going to the beach with a bunch of friends. I suppressed a groan and gripped her shoulders, spinning her away from me. Kneeling, I attached each of her ankles to the spreader bar and stepped back to admire the sight. What a fucking sight it was. She was gorgeous.

Her hair fell in cascading waves down her back and she peeked over her shoulder as a wicked smile curved her lips. "Like this?" she asked.

She damn well knew like that. She *had* to. "Yep," I answered in a clipped tone.

"But ..." she glanced up and down at the bed. "... to have sex, I need to be bent, right? So, I wouldn't just be standing here. I'd ... oomph!" She bent at the waist and without her arms and feet to center her balance, she fell into the bed, face first.

Rolling her neck to the side, she burst out in laughter, face red and hair a wild mess of tangles. A strand stuck to her lipgloss and she laughed harder as she tried to spit it out. "Oh, God," she gasped between giggles. "I-I can't get up!"

My own laugh bellowed through the room as I rushed to her, grasping her waist and pulling her back up to a standing position, facing me. "There," I said, brushing her wild hair from her eyes.

She shrugged and freckles adorned her flushed face. "I guess it takes some practice, huh?"

Her body was pressed against mine, breasts pushed against my chest. They were soft—natural, and beautiful. Unlike so many other actresses I had acted beside. My hand splayed at her lower back and my fingers were dangerously close to the exposed flesh of her ass cheeks. Her pussy pressed into my growing erection and her giggles quickly morphed into panting—only making those glorious breasts heave harder with each breath.

Her eyes searched my face as she took her bottom lip between her teeth. "Thanks," she whispered. Her breasts brushed my chest, her nipples like pearls pressing against my ribs. I could almost taste our chemistry. It would be so easy to surrender to desire right now. To take her lips, slide my tongue into her mouth. My grip on her hips was tight and unforgiving, my fingertips dug into her soft flesh. From the counter, my phone rang, causing us both to jump. That piercing ring cleansed the thick, pulsing arousal between us. *Fuck.*

She swallowed. "Are you going to answer that?"

Fuck, no. I shook my head. "I'll call them back later."

So, what if I was physically attracted to Marly? Any man with a pulse would have gotten hard at the sight of a her tied and bent over. It didn't mean jack shit. I didn't want her. I didn't need her. And I'd be damned if I let another woman fuck with my career—not to mention my life. Hell, no. Never again. Especially one that was already spoken for.

I pushed her to arms-length and despite the scowl on my face, Marly's was soft, contemplative. "You okay, Poppy?" I asked. Even the nickname felt different now; more loaded. More suggestive.

"Yeah. I'm good." Though she was still wearing the monoglove and spreader bar, her shoulders were low and relaxed. Confident. Maybe the most confident and calm I'd seen her since the moment we met, and my thoughts lingered on what exactly that meant—that the most calmly confident I'd seen her was when she was bound and tied. "Interesting, isn't it?" I asked.

She tilted her head, brows lowered in question.

"How a bound body frees the mind." With three long strides, I was behind her, loosening the monoglove.

She hissed a long, low breath. "Why is that?"

"It's different for everyone. I've heard some people explain that it's because you have no choice. With your body bound, you are only able to control your thoughts and that release opens you to new sensory explorations."

She was silent, and I didn't interrupt her thoughts. Instead, I bent down to help her step out of the spreader bar.

"Let's take a break," I said. "Study our lines. It would be nice if we could have them memorized or mostly memorized when we run the scenes tomorrow."

"What else are we doing today ... Sir?" She added it as an afterthought. Like she wasn't sure if she was supposed to still be in character or not. Or maybe unsure if she *was* the character.

A fiery heat billowed through my chest. Sir coming from her lips was easily the most erotic thing I'd heard in years. Maybe ever. "We're going to study lines separately ... then, I want you to interview another Dominant. Maybe talking with someone new will inspire new questions. And I still want to take you to that public flogging tomorrow."

Unreadable silence stabbed the space between us. She'd said she was okay watching others, as long as she herself wasn't doing anything publicly. Had she changed her mind? "That is, as long as that's still within your comfort level—"

"Yes," she answered fast. "Sir. Yes, Sir. It's fine." She worked her jaw, like she was resisting the urge to say something. Then, without another word, she bent, retrieving her jeans from the floor and fled to her room.

CHAPTER FIFTEEN
Marly

S IR. ONE STUPID word. And yet the effect it had on me was consuming. For hours, I stared at the pages of my script, the words blurring together, memorizing nothing.

I tossed the pages aside and bent to the floor, scooping myself up into a long stretch. Closing my eyes, I listened for Jude in the other room. Was he in bed reading lines? Was he thinking of me? Was he as affected by all this as I was?

My mind grew still as I studied the sunlight pouring through the window, dousing the room in a golden hue. Outside, the sky had shifted from bright azure to brassy tangerine streaks cutting through the blue. If I closed my eyes, I could still feel Jude's touch on my skin. Still feel the way he laced up the monoglove and brushed my hair from my face. *I want him. I want him so damn badly.* There was only one person who could talk some sense into me.

I grabbed my phone and scrolled through my contacts. After a few rings, Omar's low voice rumbled. "Hey, boo. How's the whips and chains? Please tell me Rihanna is there?"

"I don't have time for Rihanna right now—"

"Whoa. No time for Rihanna? This must be serious."

"I want to sleep with him," I blurted out, clutching the phone tight against my ear with both hands.

Omar was silent on the other end of the line and I squeezed my eyes shut, dropping to a seat on the bed. "Say something."

"He's going to find out you snore."

"Say something *helpful.*"

"Okay," he said. "Use ribbed for her pleasure."

"Omar!" I fell back on the bed and stared at the white ceiling.

"Marly, you know I love you, but if you're actually interested in a man? He must be pretty spectacular."

"Oh, come on." I snorted. "It hasn't been *that* long."

"Well, you and I have been 'engaged' for six months, so it's been at least that."

"You've been laying low, too," I said, pointing out that Omar hadn't been on a date in six months either. "And I don't see you risking your career and jumping the bones of the first hot guy you see."

"I'm laying low, yeah. But I'm not celibate."

"And look how well *that* worked out with Simon." I cringed the second the words left my mouth. Silence rolled between us like a storm cloud. *Shit.* "Omar, I'm so sorry. I didn't mean to say that—"

"I don't want to talk about Simon right now. You called for help, right?" His tone was clipped, but not altogether angry.

"I know. I'm sorry." I sighed. "Please talk me out of this. I *can't* sleep with Jude. That would be crazy." Only, it didn't feel crazy. It felt right. His touch felt right. The spanking felt right. The way he brushed my hair before bed … even the BDSM stuff that felt *wrong,* somehow still felt right. Like him ordering me to drink water. Eating the scone off his lap. My pussy squeezed and my skin prickled with the memories.

Omar sighed. "First of all, this is your choice. You know that. But from my outside perspective? You need to ask yourself some questions and be brutally honest. Do you only want to get laid because you're horny?"

"Omar!" A blush crawled over my skin.

But Omar ignored my outburst and kept right on talking. "Because if you just need a dick in your cooch, then no, you cannot sleep with Jude. You can't risk your career and this role over a one-night stand."

I closed my eyes and sighed. *Yes.* That's what I needed to hear. "You're right, I can't risk my career—"

"That's not what I said," Omar cut me off, his voice a low rumble. "Are you just horny? Do you not care about Jude other than the fact that he's a hot guy who's paying attention to you? 'Cause, *girl*, we can go out tonight and toss a bottle cap into a crowd and find you a sexy, warm body."

I swallowed. Was that all this was? Was I just horny? I thought about Jude. His sandy brown hair and barely-there smile. The way his voice rasped when he called me Poppy. But beyond that? He was the first man in years, other than Omar or my dad, to care for me. To make sure I ate a decent meal. To talk to me, *really* talk to me, and ask questions that dug deeper than the typical press junket interview. He was deep and thoughtful and caring and kind—*and he could spank my ass until it was raw.* "No." The ache in my chest resonated in my voice. "It's not just that. I really like him."

"I figured as much," Omar said, his voice softening.

"Everything I've worked for. All those rumors I've tried so hard to dispel. And I'm going to … what? Play right into them? Do exactly what the whole industry expects me to do and sleep with the lead in the movie? Everything you and I have been doing with this engagement will be for nothing—"

"Whoa," Omar said. "Hold up a second. First of all, does Jude even have a say in the casting?"

I fell quiet. He resigned from casting, but that didn't mean he didn't still have power. A power over me that was inevitable when one person had more clout in the industry. "No," I whispered. "He told me he resigned from casting when he decided to help me this week."

Omar chuckled. "I have to admit, I like this guy more and more."

"But it doesn't matter if Jude isn't helping cast the movie anymore. The truth doesn't always matter in our industry. You know that."

"I also know that plenty of actors fall in love onset."

"Love?" I jerked back as though I'd been struck. "That's transference … not love."

"Sometimes," Omar said. "And sometimes it's real. And since you're not really the transference type …"

"Are you freaking kidding me? You can't possibly be suggesting I'm in love with Jude. I've known the guy for three days!"

"I know. It sounds crazy. But the way you two were looking at each other at the club that night? The way he leaned in and kissed your cheek. There is mad chemistry there."

"Chemistry isn't love—"

"And whatever the hell BDSM mind games you two were playing with the chocolate caramels, that shit was hot."

My blush deepened. "You knew about that?"

"Marlena Taylor. I've known you for years. I've held your hand when you wore heels that were too high. I've held your hair when you puked. I've held your body when you've cried. Tell me one damn time I've bought you those caramels that you haven't ripped through that box like a T-Rex on a feeding frenzy?"

I laughed, but Omar didn't let me respond. "I *know* you. And you would not even be considering sleeping with this man if you didn't feel something substantial." He paused, then added, "And stop chewing your damn nails."

Aw, hell. I didn't even realize I'd been doing it and I dropped my hand into my lap. "How'd you—"

"Because I. Know. You. How many times do I have to say it?"

Oh, boy. I was about to get very real with Omar. He was my best friend. Of course we've talked about sex. But never in detail ...

"But what if these feelings I have aren't so much about Jude as much as they are about this, um, lifestyle he's introduced me to."

I could practically hear Omar's smile on the other end of the line and I grimaced. "You liking those whips and chains more than you thought, boo?"

"I don't know yet. Some of it I like. Some of it pisses me off ... which strangely, I also like." *And some of it I love*, I thought. Some of it makes me so wet, I'm afraid I'll leave a saturated spot where I'm sitting. "I read that a lot of submissives think they fall in love with their first Master ..."

Omar whistled. "Wow. Listen to you. You really think you're a submissive?"

"I might be. I mean, as a fun kink with someone I trust? Yeah …" *Someone I trust. Someone like Jude.*

"So, look," he said. "Here's what I think. You need to get out that pretty little planner of yours and make a pro-con list that you continue to add to during the week until you reach a conclusion. And while you're with Jude, you need to be really mindful. Is it him that's turning you on? Is it him you're attracted to? Or is it the acts he's introducing you to?"

Why didn't I think of that? Omar was one hundred percent right. I needed my planner. A pro-con list was just what I needed to help sort my thoughts. And I needed more time with Jude—which I had—to figure out if he has me hot and bothered or if it was his lifestyle. The week was far from over. Because I couldn't put myself through this for nothing … and I couldn't put Jude through it either.

I HAD MY pen between my teeth, chewing the cap as I reviewed my list. Writing down the pros and cons helped. If for no other reason, than to calm my nerves. Organize my thoughts.

Cons:

1) I may not really love him.
2) I may ruin my career.
3) I would prove all of Jack's stupid rumors correct.
4) Jude may just be using me.

But even as I wrote that last con down, I didn't believe it. Jude didn't seem like he was out to abuse his power. If anything, he was dubious about keeping me at arm's length and remaining professional, despite the odd position we were in. That was the weird thing about method acting—or truly any type of acting. Sometimes lines blurred.

Besides, it wasn't *just* my job in danger. Jude could get in some serious trouble with the studio's non-fraternization policy. Somehow, that fact made me feel a bit better. I wasn't the only one risking everything to potentially be with him.

Oh, God. Maybe he doesn't even want to be with me. The thought hadn't really crossed my mind until just now. It seemed so obvious that he was at least attracted to me. But much in the same way that I wasn't sure if I really liked Jude specifically, or if it was the introduction to the lifestyle … maybe *he* was infatuated with the acts I'm participating in and not me specifically? It's been seventeen months since he was with a submissive … maybe he's just rekindling his love of being a Dominant?

A cold numbness drained from my face down to my belly. It shouldn't have hurt—to think that he didn't want me. Especially when I wasn't even sure I wanted him. But it did. It was cold and sobering.

I shook the unwanted thoughts away. Okay … Pros. There were a lot of them—and they extended beyond just how freaking hot he was.

Both my mind and heart raced as Jude's boyish grin popped into my thoughts. My mouth kicked up in a smile at the thought of his. I liked spending time with him. I liked pleasing him. I liked how free I felt around him. This open, unbarred version of myself was limitless and I felt like infinite possibilities existed when I was with him.

I like him, a little voice whispered inside of me.

I shook my head. No. Stick to the facts. Stick to the

pro-con list. And don't let schmoopy poopy emotions cloud rational deductive reasoning.

There was a knock at my door and I jumped, the pen flinging out of my hand and rolling across the floor. Sighing, I stood and walked over to answer the door. The front door. Not Jude's side entrance. The only time Jude had used that door was if he was bringing food in from outside.

I opened it carefully, peeking out and standing there wasn't Jude ... but Ash. I squeaked a weird little sound and slammed the door shut.

I slammed. The door. Shut ... in the director of the movie's face. *What the hell is wrong with me?*

He knocked again, this time louder and through the door, he said, "Marly, let me in. Jude sent me with dinner so that you could interview another Dominant."

Jude sent Ash? He said I'd be interviewing another Dom while I was here ... but freaking Ash Livingston?

Carefully and with a deep breath, I opened the door again. He didn't wait for an invite, but barged through, swinging the plastic bag of takeout in his hand. "There we go," he said, breezing past me and set the food on a little bistro table in the corner of the room.

"Kale salad with quinoa and black beans for you ... Jude was insistent on all three, saying you need protein somehow or another. And a burger for me."

He climbed onto the stool and opened a plastic box containing his burger. Even the smell of that charred meat was enough to have me recoiling away from Ash. Combine that with the fact that he was the director of the film? And I literally wanted to be *anywhere* else but here.

"Sit," he said and lifted his burger in one giant hand. A

hand that probably spanked women. Or worse. I swallowed and sat across from him, opening my salad and feeling like a lamb sitting down for dinner in the slaughterhouse.

"So ... do I use my safe word with you if I'm uncomfortable?"

His gaze jerked up from over his bite of burger, eyes wide. "Safe word? Jesus, Marlena, what do you think we're going to be doing in here?"

I stabbed my salad with the fork. "I don't *know*, that's why I'm asking you."

"I promise you, we won't be doing anything that requires a goddamned safe word. Think of this like ... another meeting for the role of Holly. Except that nothing you ask me will weigh in on whether you get the part or not. Within these walls," he circled his finger in the air, "you're safe."

"That's what everyone keeps saying."

"Everyone?"

"Well ... Jude."

"He says it because it's true. The people up here? They would never shame you. They'd never make you feel bad for your kink or lifestyle and they trust you not to shame them." He licked some ketchup off his thumb and raised his brows.

"Trust. That's the other thing Jude keeps talking about."

"It's a big one." He grabbed a few fries and put all of them in his mouth at once.

"So, Jude said he doesn't really do one-night stands, but that some Doms do. How would that even work inside these walls? Where secrets and identities are so protected?"

"Ah," Ash said. "Now we're talking my language." He

leaned back and cracked his knuckles animatedly. "So, for the one-night stands, the subs who you bring up here—it's like they're on lockdown. They're only allowed inside the Dom's two private rooms—her room and your room. While entering and exiting the building, the sub is blindfolded."

"That sounds dangerous. For a woman to enter anywhere with a man she barely knows, blindfolded."

He shrugged. "One night stands usually are seasoned subs. There's communication beforehand, conversations about what to expect. In our community, blindfolds are the least scary. And they aren't surprised by secrecy."

I took a bite of my salad. "The girl you had with you the other night, she wasn't blindfolded and she was in the common room."

He nodded, swallowing another bite of burger. "The club has some submissives—both male and female—who are regulars. They've signed the contracts. They know the deal. Some of them are professional submissives hired by the club to be available to its patrons."

Whoa. I must not have been hiding my shocked expression well because Ash rolled his eyes and gave me an annoyed look. "What?" he pressed.

"That sounds a lot like prostitution." *Has Jude ever hired one of these professional subs?* God, even the thought had my stomach turning. Granted, the thought of Jude with *anyone* else made me uncomfortable.

"Every state is different, but the short explanation is that professional submissives and professional Dominants don't have sex—in the legal sense, there can be no exchange of bodily fluids." He smirked, then added. "At least not while they're on the clock."

"Has Jude ever—"

"I'm not answering any questions about Jude," Ash said. "You want to know about him? Ask him yourself."

Damn. Ash was testy. He seemed so nice at the audition, but now? He was short. Irritable. Maybe he didn't get laid last night with that professional submissive. I pressed my lips together, suppressing a smile and looked around the room. What the hell else should I ask? Maybe instead of that stupid pro-con list, I should have been scribbling out questions to ask tonight.

"What Jude's been teaching me about BDSM is so much more than leather and whips and stuff. I had no idea there were so many subsets of kink under this umbrella."

Ash nudged his fries across the table as an offering and I didn't hesitate to grab a couple—they smelled way too good to ignore. "Is there a question in there?"

Right. Questions. "Well, I'm mostly learning about Jude's, um, preferences. But that seems like it's only a small scope of what's out there. I'd like to know what other Doms enjoy."

Ash arched his brow as I nibbled on the tip of my fry. "You want to know what my specific kinks are?"

I shrugged in a way I hoped was casual. It felt so wrong to be asking my potential future director how he liked to fuck.

He sighed, leaning back in his seat. "I like administering pain. I like pushing my submissives to the edge of pain and then shoving them over the other side where it melts into pleasure. But not just a little spanking like Jude gave you the other night. Real pain. The sort of pain that makes most people cry and wince and they can't even watch as I clamp the jagged metal to her nipples."

The French fry turned to sand in my mouth. "You're a sadist," I said, surprised at how unshaken my voice was.

He nodded. "Spanking is fun, I guess. But paddling is even better. And the leather riding crop is my favorite because it can hit her clit just right and it leaves the most beautiful rectangular welt on her ass."

My stomach hollowed out. Ash Livingston just said *clit* in front of me. This week was getting weirder and weirder.

Omar's words echoed in my head. *You need to figure out if it's Jude you want or if it's just the lifestyle.* If I could experience what Ash was talking about … turning pain to pleasure in a magical way, like Jesus turning water into wine … maybe I could know. Maybe I could discover if it was this lifestyle or Jude that had me so mixed up inside. I stared at Ash closely. His dark hair and even darker stubble poking through his jawline. Clear blue eyes assessed me right back in a shrewd way. He was handsome … I'd be blind not to notice. But seeing him did nothing for me. Not like with Jude.

Ideas churned in my head. I wasn't turned on by Ash at all. So, if *him* hitting me could get me hot, then I'd know it wasn't Jude turning me on after all. That it was the kink.

I jumped to my feet and rushed for the small closet. The door slammed against the wall as I threw it open and lunged inside. I rummaged around, searching through the items I'd perused earlier that day. It wasn't as full as Jude's closet of toys was, but it had a handful of clamps, restraints, paddles and … aha! There it was. The riding crop.

I grabbed it and rushed over, handing it to Ash. He stared blankly at the crop in his outstretched palm and then back to me, blinking. "What the fuck is this?" he asked.

"Your favorite toy," I said.

"Yeah, no shit. Why am I holding it right now?"

I needed to know. I needed to understand, needed to experience what the hell he was talking about without the fog of Jude Fisher. It couldn't be my ass or anywhere intimate, so instead, I tugged my hoodie off, and threw it on the bed, standing there in front of Ash in only my tank top. I extended my arm, offering him the inside of my wrist. "Hit me. Hit me with the crop so I can feel the whole edge of pleasure into pain thing you were just talking about."

Ash looked at me like I was crazy. Maybe I was. This was my director. And here I was begging him to smack me in the arm with a freaking riding crop. "I'm here to research the damn role, aren't I? So *hit* me!"

Ash stood, his blue eyes turning gray and dismal like a storm cloud overtaking a bright, blue sky. His mouth thinned into a firm line and he dropped the riding crop at my feet. "You're asking me to do something that should be reserved for your Dom and only your Dom? This just tells me you're not ready for this part yet." His voice was so quiet and threatening, it made the hairs on the back of my neck stand up. Silently, he moved to the door.

"But he's not my Dom. Not *really*. And I'm here to learn." I followed him, still holding my arm out like an offering.

He spun around to face me, his hand gripping the door handle so tight, he could have dented the metal. "I *know* sharing is a hard limit for Jude. And for this week, you *are* his submissive. You might think you're the student here, but Jude Fisher hasn't stepped foot in this club in over a year. *You* got him here. So maybe you could stop and think for a second about more than just doing what it takes to get this fucking role."

With that, he slammed the door behind him, leaving me feeling embarrassed, foolish, and gutted, standing in an empty room.

CHAPTER SIXTEEN
Jude

IT WAS ANOTHER night of almost no sleep. But instead of dragging, I was energized the second I saw Marly over breakfast, wearing her antique choker. We ran lines and ate lunch, but something felt off. Like she was pulling away. Keeping me at arm's length. And even though I knew that was for the best, it still unnerved me.

After lunch, I stood over Marly where she was lying on her bed, her wrists and ankles restrained at each corner. And thank God for the blindfold covering her eyes, hiding my intense erection. Even fully clothed in that position, she was the sexiest, most sensuous woman I'd ever seen. She wore a fitted t-shirt that was tugged up just beneath her breasts, revealing her slim stomach. Her tight jeans sat low on her hips. And the Victorian cameo choker rested at the base of her elegant throat.

She was beautiful. Sexy in an unassuming way. Funny. Smart. Talented.

And engaged.

And I am a total piece of shit for staring at a blindfolded engaged woman like this.

I cleared my throat, and tore my eyes away from her body. On the table beside the bed, I had laid out various sensory toys so that she could feel them—experience them in a blindfolded setting where her mobility was restrained.

I'd gone through about half of them already, when I leaned down to grab the feather.

She had been so odd last night when I was brushing her hair and tucking her into bed. She seemed ... lost. Lost in her own thoughts. Like she was hiding something. Had Ash noticed it last night? Did Ash tell her something about the lifestyle? About me?

I dragged the feather across her taut stomach, watching as her abdominal muscles twitched with the skimming sensation. Her mouth twisted, then pressed into a firm line. The restraints snapped as her hands jerked against them and she snorted, her chest bouncing with suppressed laughter that left me smiling right along with her. "Ticklish?" I asked.

She grinned wider. "A little."

"Breathe through it," I instructed. "In through your nose ... out through your mouth." After a few deep breaths, she seemed to calm down, despite the strokes of the feather across her belly. "Better?"

She nodded. "Yeah. It actually feels nice now."

"Good." I set the feather down and grabbed the candle that was burning on the nightstand. A wicked smile curved on my lips. Was she ready for this mind phuque? "I'm going to drizzle some hot wax next."

If I thought her muscles had jerked with the feather, I hadn't seen anything. All four of her limbs tugged hard against the restraints, but she took another deep breath and asked, "Will it hurt?"

"Only for a second and then the wax cools and dries on your skin."

Silence. Maybe she wasn't ready for this, yet. I set down the candle quietly onto the nightstand. "I also have a glass of ice water here in case it burns more than you expect and you need it."

I waited patiently, enjoying the view as she thought it over. In a few days, she'd be back home with Omar. Even though our time together was only a slice of reality, a partial truth, being with Marly made me happier than I'd been in years. And in less than a week, I'd be back to my miserable self.

She was quiet for another long moment, chewing on the inside of her cheek before she finally nodded. "Okay. I-I think I'm ready."

She was definitely not ready. I could see it in the way her fingers clutched the edges of the headboard. The white knuckled grip. The way her chest heaved with shallow, nervous breaths. "Trust me?"

She nodded in one sharp, succinct movement. "Yes."

"Okay. I'm going to count down from five. I'll pour the wax on one. Five …"

She transitioned from chewing her cheek to nibbling her bottom lip. "Four …" She sniffled, her toes spreading against the bottom of the bed. "Three …" Her knuckles turned an even ghostlier shade of white. "Two …" Her face drained of color, leaving her normally pink, freckled cheeks a sallow gray.

I lifted the glass of water. "One." I tipped the cold water and drizzled it on her belly. She gasped, her lower back arching off the bed. It only took her a second to realize that it wasn't hot wax and in that moment, her rounded mouth shifted into a surprised laugh.

"Was that ice?" she asked through her laughter.

"Cold water," I said, leaning down and peeling the blindfold from her eyes. Then, leaning over her, I undid the restraints. "You didn't seem ready for the wax, yet," I added with a quick wink.

She sat up after being freed of the wrist restraints and I sat on the bed, undoing her ankles. Even though I kept them loose, she rubbed at her wrists and little red marks were angry against her alabaster skin. I grabbed some lotion from the bathroom and went to work massaging it into her wrists.

"You don't have to do that," she said. Sadness trickled into her voice ... sadness and was I imagining guilt?

"I do, actually. It's part of my job." I applied pressure across her palms, massaging each finger. I grazed the engagement band on her ring finger, the lump in my throat dropping to my stomach.

"Yeah, but you're not really my Dom—"

"For this week, Poppy, I am." I dropped her hands and moved my attention down to her feet where there wasn't an engagement ring catching the light like a big ol' *fuck you*. I ran my thumb against the outside of her ankle up her calf and she moaned. *That's more like it.*

"Why don't you check the top drawer of your nightstand?"

She gave me a skeptical look, narrowing her eyes, before reaching over and sliding the drawer open. She gasped, pulling the small plastic box of salted caramels out and cupping them in her palm.

I expected a smile. Or at least a thank you. But instead, she yanked her foot from my grasp and swung her legs around the edge of the bed. "No. Shit. I'm so ... I'm sorry," she said. "I need to tell you something."

My blood turned icy in my veins and my stomach concaved, like a wrecking ball connected to my gut. "Tell me what?"

"I screwed up. It was an accident, I didn't realize what I asked was so bad until after. But ..." her voice cracked and with it, my guts twisted. I'd never seen her like this. She was distraught. Her full, pink lips twisted, lines furrowing between her brows and tears filled her eyes.

She took a deep breath and said, "Last night ... with Ash ..." her voice faded. Not that I needed to hear a whole lot more. Oxygen punched from my lungs and I felt instantaneously light-headed. It was happening. Again.

No. Not Marly. Marly wasn't Layla. I took a deep breath and looked at Marly. *Really* looked at her. She clutched her trembling hands, trying to stop the violent tremors. She chewed the inside of her cheek and her eyes were wide and panicky. It was the look of guilt. No ... not guilt. *Remorse.* "Last night, with Ash ..." I repeated, urging her to continue and trying to keep the tight edge out of my voice. But right now, this confession was an unsheathed blade, pressed to my belly, ready to slice me open.

Her eyes drifted closed. "Last night, I asked Ash to hit me with the riding crop." She swiveled to face me and draped her palm over mine. "But it was only on the wrist so that I could feel the difference between how *you* hit and how he hits." Her confession came out so fast, the words ran together. She sniffed and blinked, tears dancing at the edges of her eyes.

She asked Ash to hit her.

I'd been sucker punched once in the seventh grade. By Tommy Martin the morning after my mom was elected to city council. She beat out Tommy's dad and as I closed my locker ... there was Tommy, towering over me and slamming his fist just below my ribcage. I fell to the floor, the wind literally knocked out of my lungs.

It had been my only sucker punch ... until Layla. But even that wasn't a total surprise. There were signs with Layla; small details I slowly started picking up on and piecing together the truth. The light, lingering scent of male cologne on her neck when she got home. The way she would come in late and run to the shower before even kissing me hello, as though she could rinse away her infidelity. This? Here with Marly? This was totally unexpected. And it hurt a hell of a lot more than Tommy's thirteen-year old fist. And in a weird way ... it even hurt more than with Layla. Differently. Not nearly so publicly.

"I'm sorry," she said. "When I asked him to do it, I didn't realize it was a betrayal. I just ... I just was researching. Curious what the different type of pain would feel like with a Dom who was a sadist. It wasn't until he explained how terrible of a betrayal it would be to you ..." she sighed, cutting herself off. "Well, not explained as much as shouted and stormed out of here."

My gaze jerked back to her eyes. "Ash yelled at you?" The thought of that made me furious—not at Ash necessarily. My friend was watching my back, like any good buddy. But the thought of anyone shouting at Marlena was the equivalent to watching a puppy get kicked. I sat there staring at her, at a total loss for words. This whole thing just seemed so unlike Marly. Her face was white, like a crumpled piece of tissue paper. I hated that expression. Hated the way her beautiful, plump mouth turned down at the corners. Hated the single tear that escaped and cascaded down her cheekbone to the corner of her frown.

I pressed my eyes closed. This couldn't be happening. Hell, Marly and I weren't even *together* and I somehow felt cheated on.

If you're not together and you feel cheated on ... maybe that's not Marly's fault, a little voice echoed in my head.

"I'm sorry," Marly said again. It sounded genuine. Then again, so did Layla the first time she apologized. "I get it now and it won't happen again without discussing it with you first."

Not 'it won't happen again' ... but 'it won't happen without a discussion first.' Somehow, that statement felt more honest than an empty promise of faithfulness. Anyone can make a promise to not do something again—many have made that promise. And many have broken it. But a promise to communicate? That was good. It showed growth and knowledge of the lifestyle and a trust that she can come to me with her desires.

But I still didn't fucking *like* it. "I thought you didn't share, either," I said. "I thought it was one of your hard limits, too."

She shrugged. A small gesture, bringing one frail shoulder to her ear. "If I was truly in this Dom/sub relationship, I wouldn't want to be with anyone else."

I swallowed hard. "But?"

"But ... we're not. And I'm here to learn for the sake of the movie. For the sake of doing Holly justice onscreen. And ..."

There was more to this. Something beyond the words she had just said and I narrowed my eyes, studying her. Staring at her.

Marly shifted her weight, twitching and chewing her nails. "And ... I gave you hard limits when this was all just a theoretical thing." She gestured around the room as if it was a symbol for BDSM. "But how can anyone really know what their hard limits are, when you're only just beginning to open your eyes to things you never thought you'd like."

Oh. Oh my God. Of course. *I* knew Marly was a natural submissive. But *she* didn't know that. I could tell she was enjoying our little games—everything from her flushed cheeks, to her tight nipples told me so. But for as much as I knew and could read her reactions … she was still figuring it all out. "You're surprised at the fact that you like this." She didn't even wait for me to finish speaking as she nodded, her eyes drifting to the ground.

Something between us was shifting. The way she was opening up to me. Relinquishing control. That planner she was so obsessed with had been beside her bed every morning, as if she was scribbling in it every night … but this morning? It was in her bag by the sink. Was she letting go of that obsessive need to dictate every minute of every day?

I scrubbed a hand down my face and paced to the window. Was it truly a betrayal if the person didn't realize she was betraying you? My mind said no … but it didn't change the sick, aching pang just behind my ribcage. Taking a deep breath, I said, "Okay."

Her gaze jerked up to meet mine. "Okay?"

"Okay," I repeated. "I can't say I like it. But I understand it." *I can't say I like it?* It was the fucking understatement of the century. "I had planned for us to go to the public flogging tonight. I think it would be good for you to see, if you're still up for that—"

She nodded. "I am."

"I'll arrange something for you tonight afterwards. For you to feel another Dom's … style. I'll have some clothes brought up for you to wear."

I turned, heading for my room, but Marly's voice stopped me. "Jude—" she said. I looked over my shoulder, catching her wobbled expression. "It's not that I want someone else, you get that, right? This is truly just curiosity."

It's not that she wants someone else. Of course she didn't. She belonged to Omar. And it tore my heart in half. How fucking stupid was that? I was falling for another man's fiancée. Maybe I was more of a masochist than I thought. Then again, where the hell was Omar in all this? What sort of man allows his fiancée to go to a BDSM club with another man and doesn't ask to see the place first? I didn't like judging other couples—God knew plenty of people made judgments about my lifestyle. But she and Omar? Something wasn't adding up there. "I get it," I said quietly. "Omar's a lucky man."

"Omar," she whispered and touched her ring. "Right."

I paused, my eyes traveling to the untouched salted caramels on her nightstand. "Marly," I said. She tilted her head in response. "Have one caramel now. Text me with how it is."

She still needed some nurturing in her aftercare. I couldn't let that slip because of this conversation. But I also couldn't stay there and watch. I couldn't take another second of hearing Marly talk about being with someone else—whether that was Omar or wanting to feel Ash hit her.

I left, shutting the door quietly behind me. I leaned over the sink and splashed some cold water on my face.

How can you truly move on from the past, when it keeps finding ways to creep into your present? I grabbed my phone and punched a text to Ash.

I need a favor.

If history was going to repeat itself, then I was going to be prepared. No more sucker punches.

CHAPTER SEVENTEEN
Marly

I EXAMINED MYSELF in the mirror. The dress Jude sent up still had tags on it—seven hundred dollars. For a dress in a private club that no one would ever see and I'd never be photographed in. What was the point of that? My dad would be rolling in his grave right now. He understood the occasional splurge and he loved buying me presents ... but he loved a good deal even more.

Instead of tearing the tags off, I tucked them into the dress. Just in case Jude decided he wanted to return it. At the most, I'd be wearing this for what? An hour? Two tops? How late can a public flogging go?

Holy shit, just listen to yourself! I scolded myself. A public flogging. Forget the stupid dress, Dad would be rolling in his grave about *this*. I could still hear his voice—his Dadisms. In the ninth grade, my boyfriend threatened to break up with me if I didn't let him cheat off my math homework. For weeks, I let him copy my work until one day after school, my dad came home early. He walked in on my boyfriend copying my homework. The anger and disappointment in Dad's eyes—I hated that look. I never wanted to be the source of that expression on anyone ever again. *"Marlena, if you were meant to be controlled, you would have come with a remote,"* he'd said. Then, he took our papers and the next morning, he turned us *both* into the principal for cheating all year. I had to do extra credit for weeks to climb out of those zeros I received. But Dad wasn't wrong. I was raised to be independent. In control of myself. So then, why in the hell did it feel so damn good to lose that control within these walls?

"Sorry, Daddy," I whispered, then tugged the tags off the dress.

There was a knock at the side door—from Jude's room. I rushed over, opening it to find Jude standing there in his usual starched white shirt with the sleeves rolled neatly to the elbow. Charcoal dress pants. Sleek silver and black leather belt. Matching black leather shoes.

He towered in the doorway, taking up most of the space—both literally and metaphorically. His shoulders rolled back, his chin high and his eyes fixed onto me. His jaw twitched.

"Well?" I said, doing a twirl for him in the new dress. "What do you think?"

His gaze swept briefly down my body, then jerked back to my eyes. "I think … you don't look like you."

"I'm not supposed to look like me. I'm supposed to be Holly."

"Right," he said. His voice was stern, but his eyes were pensive. "Can I come in?"

"Oh, yeah. Sorry," I said, stepping back to give him room to enter. Then, I looked around the room to escape those searing jade eyes of his. I wanted to know about him and yet that damn commanding nature of his managed to turn me into a blubbering idiot with a simple glance. "Before we go, I was wondering what your favorite toy is? I've been studying them and there's so many. How do you choose?"

Jude's head jerked with the question, eyes wide and momentarily stunned. "Are you asking Leo? Or me?"

"I'm not so sure there's much difference between the two anymore." I responded in a moment of bravery.

That stunned look of his quickly morphed into a grin. "We're pretty similar at times, huh? It's why when the script rolled across Ash's desk, I was the first person to pop into his mind to play the role."

"So?"

"Even with that," Jude walked to my bed, "Leo and I have very different answers."

He had one hand in a pocket and the other was brushing across his top lip. "Leo tends to be more about pain. Whereas, I'm more about the power in bondage and control. So, for Leo, I think his favorite toy is right here." Jude held up a hand, palm out.

"His hand?"

A smile twitched on across Jude's mouth and the smug grin sucked the wind right out of my lungs. God, he was breathtaking.

"Yep ... the crops and stuff are fun. But I think Leo would love to feel the pain he's administering on his palm with each strike. *And* since he's a control freak on top of a sadist, he would want to know just how hard he was hitting; so that he didn't go too far."

I nodded, my mind drifting back to the other night when Jude's hand came down on my ass in the common room. A shiver rolled over me like water sliding down my body in the shower. I never considered myself to be masochistic, but when it came to Jude? I trusted him. I trusted him to know just what buttons to push and how far to push them. Which was ... *holy shit*. I didn't trust anyone other than my dad and Omar. He stood over my bed and I swallowed, that warm feeling zinging into my veins and swirling around in my stomach like the first sip of hot coffee.

"So, then for *you?*"

He inhaled a short breath before leaning down to my nightstand and pulling something small out of the top drawer. "This," he said, holding a small toy out.

I took it in my palm—some sort of small ring with a silicone ball on it the size of a pea. It could *maybe* be a cock ring, for a man with a micro-penis. But even still—I hadn't ever seen a cock ring with a little ball on it like this one. And based on when I had felt Jude's erection pressing against my belly when he spanked me? He did *not* have a micro-penis. "I didn't even see that in there."

Jude shrugged. "It was in the back of the drawer. It's small, so it makes sense you would have missed it. But that's my favorite toy. That along with the bed restraints."

I turned the small ring over in my hands. Only, by the time I looked up again, Jude had moved in, towering above me, so that his hot breath cascaded down my neck.

"Why would Holly need to know about Jude?"

I swallowed. It was a damn good question. And the bottom line was that I didn't *need* to know. I *wanted* to know. I held up the small silicone ring, hoping to change the subject. "What is this?" I asked, ignoring his question.

He took the toy from me, holding it up. "It goes on your tongue. Or my tongue." Then hitting a small button on the side, the ring vibrated in his hands. "For oral pleasure." He turned it off, placing it again in my hand. "Now, I'm going to ask again—why would Holly or Marly need to know about *my* personal tastes in the bedroom?"

Because I desperately wanted to. If I was a stronger person, I would have just said that. Boldly. But instead, I cast my eyes down and shrugged one shoulder to my ear. "I figured it would be helpful to know everything."

He nodded, but his jaw clenched. "Research."

I followed his lead, nodding along with him. "Right."

"Just like the other night with Ash." This time, he didn't wait for my response. He simply crossed to the front door and held it open. "Let's go, then."

Ten minutes later, we were silently walking down the dark hallway. "You look beautiful."

"Thank you," I said. "And thanks for the dress. It was ... it was way too much."

Jude shrugged. "Technically, it's a tax write off." He slid me a smirk, but it was missing that extra bit of warmth. Missing that spark. That chemistry.

With each step, the heavy bass of music grew closer and closer until we were standing outside an unmarked door. It looked like the door to any other room in that hallway. "You ready?"

I nodded and with his hand still hovering at the small of my back, Jude opened the door, guiding me inside and down the rabbit hole.

Everyone who had been in the common room a few nights ago was inside that room, including Ash and a different sub than I had seen him with the other night. There were a few extra faces that I didn't recognize and some men and women who looked like they weren't there with anyone.

The woman who had been Ash's sub the first night in the common room stood across the room. This time, alone. Her shiny, white-blond hair was trimmed short, and tonight those bangs covered one of her eyes almost entirely. Her leather jumpsuit was cut off at the tops of her thighs and cut high, revealing the bottom curves of her ass.

"There's a bar in the back corner," Jude said. "Do you feel comfortable enough to order me a martini while I find us a good spot near the stage?"

Across the room, the pixie-cut submissive stood beside the bar. Under normal circumstances, I would have said no. Would have preferred to have Jude by my side the whole time. But I wanted to meet that girl. And based on how Jude reacted when we saw her the first night? I doubted he wanted to talk to her. "I'll be fine," I said. "May I order something?"

Jude smiled. "Is that a good idea?"

No. Yes. Maybe ... nerves rippled in my stomach like the ocean before a storm. Not that alcohol was necessarily the best thing to calm excitement. But it couldn't hurt at this point. A little liquid courage. Instead, I simply answered, "I like having something to do with my hands."

"How about you start with a glass of sparkling water. Then you can have a bourbon later."

"Thank you, Sir." The words rolled off my tongue effortlessly and I froze, startling myself.

Jude's brows jumped. "That almost sounded sincere," he said, chuckling.

"It was," I lifted my chin to meet his gaze. "It just ... slipped out without even thinking."

He blinked, his thoughtful, green eyes darkening. "Go on, then," he said, tipping his head to the bar.

I scurried across the room, weaving around the bodies dancing and mingling. Instead of sliding up to the bar at the gaping hole on the right side, I slipped into the corner on the left where Pixie-Cut Girl was standing, sipping a tumbler of something pink. I racked my brain, trying to remember the name Ash called her the other night ... Ava? No, that wasn't it.

"That looks good," I said, hating the quiver in my voice. Other than Jude, Ash, and phone calls to Omar, this was the only person I'd had a conversation with in days. That, combined with the dirty looks this girl had given me and Jude the other night? Well, those waves in my belly had turned into a damn tsunami. "What are you drinking?"

Pixie Girl's dark brow arched and disappeared beneath her side-swept bangs. Her eyes were icy blue and cold, just like her raspy, low voice. "You aren't supposed to talk without permission."

I paused. "Permission ... from you?"

Pixie snorted. "Hardly. From your Master." She took a long, slow sip from her tumbler, the pink liquid sliding over her blood red lips.

"Oh, well—"

"What can I get you, Angel?" The male bartender interrupted me. Angel? That was weird.

My face must have showed it, because Pixie leaned in and whispered, "They call all subs Angel."

"Right. I guess that makes sense." Yeah, in the way that fucking trigonometry makes sense. It was stupid and generic and I hated it. *Angel.* It was the sort of bullshit nickname sleazy men gave you the morning after when they can't remember your name. "I'll have a martini, up, very dry, extra olives. And a sparkling water, please."

The bartender nodded, then dashed off.

"Ah, yes. Martini, very dry. So dry, you should just swirl the vermouth in the glass and throw it out. Jude

Fisher basically just wants ice cold gin, am I right?"

"Uh … I'm not one hundred percent sure, but I'm going to guess that if I'm supposed to have permission to speak to anyone, then I probably need permission to discuss his drinking habits."

Pixie held up her hand, palm out and nodded. "Sure, sure. Makes sense. I can't say you seem like his type, though. I'm surprised he lets you out like … *this*." She punctuated the word with a flicked finger and her eyes shifted up and down my dress.

She was baiting me. It was so obvious. And also, *so* freaking effective. "Does Jude have a type? I hadn't really noticed."

Pixie snorted and spun around, resting her elbows on the bar. "Does Jude have a type," she repeated, laughing. "Sweetheart, for months that man has been seen with only brunettes. They had to wear leather. And they always wore the same stupid red shade of lipstick."

An ice-cold shiver tumbled down my spine. Brunette. Leather. Red lips. They were all like—

"All to remind him of his ex-wife," Pixie finished the thought for me.

I thought back to that first night in the hallway when we ran into Ash and this sub. I'd been wearing that dark-haired wig that Jude had been so disgusted by. It had been the first thing he wanted me to remove, along with the heavy makeup.

I glanced at Pixie through the corner of my eye, not needing to turn my head fully to see the triumph gleaming in her crystal blue eyes. I slid my hand down the silk fabric of my dress, gliding my clammy palm over my hip bone. Thank God he hadn't given me leather to wear tonight.

"Well," I cleared my throat and tossed Pixie my most confident smirk. "I guess it's safe to say he's moved on."

Pixie huffed a laugh. "Jude Fisher is a fraud. A sorry excuse for a Dom. I'd tell you to watch your back around him, but really it's your heart you've got to watch out for." She tossed her head back and guzzled the remainder of her drink in one swallow before slamming the glass on the bar and disappearing into the crowd.

A few minutes later, I was grateful to be back at Jude's side with my sparkling water in hand. But wherever I landed in the room, I could feel Pixie's eyes burning through me. Hell, I couldn't even remember the girl's name—and the nickname *Pixie* somehow wasn't cutting it. I tapped Jude's elbow. "Who is that?" I asked, tilting my chin toward Pixie.

Jude followed my gaze. Even through the layer of his button-down shirt, I could feel the undeniable knotting of muscle under my palm. "That's no one."

"Is she a professional submissive?"

"Yes," Jude said, his voice tight.

"I'd like to interview her."

His head whipped around to look at me, startling me. "Interview Eve? Why?"

Eve. That's right. Was that her real name? "Because who better to explain this lifestyle to me than someone who does it for a living?"

"How about someone who does it because they love it, not because it pays well," Jude said.

"You don't think she loves it?"

Eve was still staring directly at us and she tilted her head, a small smile splayed on her lips. She lifted her hand to her mouth, pressed a kiss to her fingers and blew it in our direction. Jude stepped into my line of sight, blocking me from Eve. "Would you stop staring, please?" he hissed.

I could've gotten mad. I could've seen his anger and bossiness as a way of trying to stifle me from learning. And a few days ago, I probably would have. But now? Now that I was getting to know Jude better, I saw right through his act. And instead of yelling back at him or storming off, I squeezed his arm harder and looked up into his green eyes. "We don't have to do this tonight," I said with a shrug. Truth was, I *did* want to see the public flogging. I was nervous and excited and while I didn't envision public BDSM parties becoming a weekly event I penciled into my planner, I did have an odd fascination to learn what it was about.

But not at Jude's expense. I liked him too much to hurt him. *Again.* I'd already hurt him once. His eyes lifted to mine, bright and beautiful and shock lifted in his expression. I smiled encouragingly at him and said, "We can go back to the room and order takeout. Or rehearse our lines. And do this another night. Or not."

His eyes burned into me and a dozen emotions twisted on his face. But with a blink, his tightened features smoothed out and the pinched expression in his jaw relaxed. "They only do this on the weekends, so this is our last night for you to see it." He paused. "You *do* want to see it, right?"

I swallowed, feeling the lump in my throat fall to my stomach and ricochet off my gut. "I do …" I said. "But not at the expense of *you*."

He smiled at that and for the first time since he left my room that afternoon, he seemed to relax. "I'm fine, Poppy. I promise you. This room isn't my favorite part of LnS, but if I couldn't handle it, I would tell you. Part of that whole trust thing we keep talking about." His smile widened and lifting a hand, he brushed my hair away from my eyes in that gentle way I was growing so fond of. "But thank you for looking out for me."

"It's what a good sub does, right?"

"It is." He nodded.

Our eyes stayed latched for a few more seconds before I glanced away. "So," I said, "when does the 'show' start?" With a look around the room, I noticed it was crowded enough that I didn't feel as singled out as I did the first night in the common room … but not so crowded that the room was cramped. It was the perfect amount of people. In front of them was a stage with three steps up. On the far wall was a window and a hand rail in front of the glass— like they were in the reptile exhibit at the zoo or something. And on the wall opposite the stage was a giant mirror.

"Right about now," Jude said, his hands falling to my hips and he spun me to face the stage. A woman crawled onto the stage on her hands and knees. Cuffs pinched her wrists and ankles so tightly, that I could see her pink flesh straining against the thick leather. A man was walking in the lead, tugging a leash that hooked to her collar. Black dress pants clung to his muscular hips and accentuated the lean muscles of his bare torso. I recognized the internet mogul from the other night in the common room and his submissive—the same woman who gave him a blowjob in front of the whole room.

I inhaled a sharp breath and Jude squeezed my hips. "If you want to leave at any time, you just say so, okay?" he said.

I nodded, not trusting my voice, but also watching in

fascination as the submissive stood to her feet, her chin firmly tilted down her sternum. The Dom clipped his sub's wrist cuffs to a rope hanging from the ceiling and each of her ankles to their own restraints, spreading her legs wide. She wore nothing but garters and high heels.

A loud noise clanked through the room and whatever small chitchat was left grew silent as the rope attached to her wrists tugged up, drawing her arms over her head. For a moment, I didn't think the rope would stop stretching her until her feet were off the ground. But just as one heel slipped out of her stilettos, the cranking rope stopped, leaving her there, stretched. On display. Her perky breasts and tight nipples round and lush. Her pussy swollen, pink, and exposed for everyone to see.

The center of the stage started spinning, like some sort of Lazy Susan, revealing all her angles to the crowd. Her Dom stroked her skin gently at first, running the paddle over her bare, ripe flesh as the stage spun slowly with both of them on it. Then, lowering the ropes, he gave her a command. One simple word. "Bend."

The ropes released and she didn't hesitate for a moment and hinged at the hips, exposing even more of herself to the crowd. He stroked her hair, murmuring something in her ear. Then, using his fingers, he spread her wide for everyone to see. Her pink, wet core tightened visibly. Then, pulling back, he hit her with the paddle. In the center of the ass. He hit her hard. Much harder than Jude had spanked me. An immediate red welt surfaced on her skin and he hit her again. And again. Sometimes right on the pussy. Other times on the ass cheeks.

Jude was standing beside me, his hands possessively positioned on my hips. It felt good having him there.

Reassuring, like a safety blanket. His hips brushed against my ass as he shifted his weight from one foot to the next. Was he nervous? Enjoying the show?

The first round of paddling only lasted about a minute before the Dom tugged the ropes and she was standing straight up, facing the audience once more. Her face was flushed, her lips parted and she was panting. With her legs spread, it was easy to see how turned on she was; how swollen and pink her clit looked. Chloe entered the stage, wearing almost the same outfit I had seen her in the first night—tight leather corset. Short black skirt. Fuck me heels. She held a small basket which the Dom took a clothespin out of. One by one, he placed the clothespins on his submissive's body, starting with her nipples. One on each breast. One on each earlobe. At the base of her neck. And two on her clit.

I shivered and felt Jude take a step back from me. *Please don't pull away from me*, I thought. *Not now.* I could barely understand what I was feeling and I needed him beside me. Needed to feel him with me through this whole experience. Reaching around, I grabbed Jude's lower back, pulling him back into me. His sharp breath was hot against my ear and as I tugged his body back against me, I understood why he pulled away. He was hard. So fucking hard and now it was pressed right against my ass. I squeezed my eyes shut as a flood of arousal rushed through my body like a hit of pure caffeine. The show was interesting—informative and sexy in its own way. But Jude? Hard as steel and pushed against me? *That* had my body singing.

"Sorry," Jude whispered and once more tried to pull away. But I held onto him, pulling him harder against me.

"No," I said, my hand sliding dangerously lower … I

wasn't grabbing his ass, but my hand was close. "Stay. Just like this."

"Marlena," Jude growled a warning.

"Please," I begged, my voice a hoarse whisper.

He didn't say another word, but he also didn't pull away and his fingers splayed wider over my hips, stretching against the tight skin of my lower abdomen.

With the clothespins pinching the submissive's most intimate erogenous zones, Chloe pulled a large vibrator out of the box, while the Dom resumed paddling her ass. Bending, Chloe undid the right leg restraint and put the submissive's leg over her shoulder as she placed the vibrator against the clothespins at her clit. The subs moans cried out through the silent audience and were soon echoed by others in the crowd. As I looked around, tearing my eyes away from the stage, I saw that almost everyone in the audience was touching each other. Every Dom had his fingers inside his sub. Or their subs were bent, getting fucked as they watched. Jude and I were the only two not being intimate.

And yet in other ways, we were potentially the most intimate of anyone else in that room.

I stole a glance over my shoulder at Jude and his eyes weren't on the stage. Or any of the others in the club fucking. They were on me. Watching my every move.

My breasts felt intensely sensitive and heavy. My pussy was so achy, begging to be touched. God, it had been so long. I wanted to be stretched, filled, taken to the brink of ecstasy and pulled back just before I fell over the edge.

Chloe now had the submissive's leg straight up in the air with the vibrator still against her clit. Her moans morphed into screams—pain or pleasure, who could tell? Chloe slid the cuff on her ankle up around her knee and attached it to the girl's collar as she held that position in a standing split.

The Dominant walked forward, unzipping his pants and I gasped. No. They wouldn't. Are they going to fuck here in front of everyone?

I was turned on. And ashamed. And hot. And embarrassed. And … oh, God. *I need to get out of here.* Spinning, I dropped my face into Jude's chest. "Can we go?"

He grabbed my hand, weaving me through the small crowd to the door we entered through and once again, we were in the dark hall. I released a breath, pacing a few steps each way.

"What's wrong?" Jude asked.

"What's wrong?" I repeated his question. "What's *wrong*? Jesus, Jude. There is a woman on a stage getting beaten and pinched and she's about to get fucked, while a crowd of people watch and also fuck each other."

"Yes," he said, blinking. "That's what people do here, Marly. They fuck. They get fucked. They take the lines of pain and pleasure and control and submission and meld them together like two pieces of clay and before you know it, you can't tell the two apart anymore." His words were heated, passionate and he took a step closer as he talked. "Don't tell me you didn't know what you were getting into by walking into that room." His voice was almost threatening in its quietness.

"I knew," I said. "I just didn't … *know.*"

"And? What did you think?"

I crossed my arms over my chest, the pressure a brief reprieve from the heavy ache. "I could tell you liked it," I said, my voice breathier than I meant it to be. It wasn't meant to be an accusation, but somehow, it came across that way.

"In case you didn't notice, I didn't spend much time watching the stage," he said, his chest lifting with a deep breath. His neck was tight, thick and veined with restraint. He was watching *me*. I knew it. He knew it. So why was I resisting when it was so clear I wanted him back? "But we're not here to talk about what I liked about being in there. We're here for you. For your *education*. So, tell me ... what did you think?"

"It was sexy to watch ... at times. But also hard to imagine that feeling good for her. The clothespins ..." I shuddered, imagining how much that would hurt.

Jude took a deep breath in through his nose. "Not everything in this world is for everyone. You have to try things. See what works for you, what doesn't. Sometimes you know before you even try it that it's just not a turn-on. Other times, you surprise yourself with what's arousing."

"Like watching public sex," I said.

"And being watched," Jude added. "Are you having second thoughts about that hard limit, too?"

Absolutely not. "No," I said. "I'm an actress. I crave the spotlight, but ... someone watching as I—" My voice cracked and I couldn't even say it. Instead, I shook my head. "I could never."

Jude exhaled. Relieved. He was relieved that I hadn't changed my mind.

"Besides," I said, "even if I was considering it ... there is no dipping your toes in with that. It's all or nothing. Head first into the deep end and if you regret it ..." I shrugged. If you regret it, you're just screwed. Left with that regret for the rest of your life.

Jude flashed a quick smile. "Not exactly," he said and

walked past me to a door beside the public party room. A light overhead was green and Jude turned the knob, opening the door. The room was smaller than the other room. More narrow. Along the wall was a floor to ceiling window, facing into the public flogging area.

I was silent as we entered. On the other side of the mirror, people applauded. The Dom and sub and Chloe were gone from the stage. Some people in the crowd were dancing. Others were in the corner. Some of the submissives were on their knees, sucking their Masters off.

"In here?" Jude said. "It's a good place to see if something public would be appealing to you. On the other side of this window, it's a mirror. You can see them. They can't see you."

Excitement tightened in my core. The thought of Jude and me in here, where no one else could see us, but we could see everyone else. It satisfied some chaotic need that was clawing at my core. "Does that excite you?" he asked. "Appeal to some tiny, quiet voyeuristic part of you?" I nodded as my nipples pushed against the silky fabric of the flimsy dress and my blood heated in my veins. I stepped closer to Jude, feeling that same heat fill my cheeks. *I want him.*

"I figured …" Jude said, his voice tight. Restrained. In some ways, I loved that restraint. It was tight and sexy and then in other ways, I wanted to see him go nuts with wild abandon. The restraint is sexiest because you know the monster lurking beneath the calm. "And I thought …"

"You thought …" I said, stepping in closer and looking up into Jude's eyes.

"That this was a good place for you to experience Ash."

Ash. Well, if that wasn't a bucket of ice water thrown

onto my fiery sex drive, I didn't know what was. "Ash?"

Jude nodded. "You want to feel the difference, right? Between two Dominants? How a sadist paddles versus a Dom more into control, like me?"

Shit. I did ask for that. Under the guise of researching the role. "Right," I said, quietly. "Will you ... um, be here with us?"

"Absolutely not. I'll be out there," Jude said, inclining his chin to the room beyond the mirrored window. "I filled Ash in on everything, including your safe words. He also has a spare key to your room, in case you need something." Jude stepped forward, cupping my jaw and kissed my forehead. "I'll be right out there if you need me. I trust Ash with my life. He's the only person outside of Chloe that I would allow anywhere near someone I care about within these walls."

I swallowed and tears burned the backs of my eyes. Jude didn't share. He'd made that clear from day one. Granted, we weren't boyfriend-girlfriend. We weren't a real Dom/sub partnership. But sometime in the last few days, we'd grown close in an odd limbo state that was neither friends nor boyfriend-girlfriend. And he was sharing me. Because I had asked him to. "You care about me," I said, looking up at him.

"Of course I do." He gave me a tight smile.

Was this it? Was this my moment? Panic swept through my body and the jitters were so severe, I could actually feel my knees shaking as I lifted my eyes to his. And there, in the depths of his jade stare, I absorbed his calm stoicism. I fed off of it. He was my Dom; he was there to protect me, care for me, and service me. I was safe with Jude—my body, my emotions ... maybe even my heart.

I took a deep breath and stepped forward into his body. For the first time since I got the callback, I felt like I was finding my place in Jude's wild, chaotic world. And the fact that he was willing to put my needs before his, touched something deep inside me that had been neglected for years. Since even before Jack. I didn't have to step far before I was pressed against him. My silky dress and his crisp shirt were hardly any barrier for my piercing nipples. "You care about me like ... more than a friend?" I blinked, looking up at him through my lashes.

"Marly," he whispered and dropped his forehead to mine. "I am doing everything in my power to keep this situation professional ... or at least as professional as two method actors studying for BDSM roles can be." Reaching up, he cupped my face, dragging his thumbs over my cheekbones. "This world of dominance and submission and bondage is amazing and eye-opening and bizarre and challenging. Especially when you first enter it. You start to feel all these crazy new intense feelings. And it's hard to decipher."

"What if ..." I swallowed, gathering courage. "What if it was feeling less and less like acting between us for me?"

He swallowed and I watched carefully, holding my breath. Watched every little line of his face. Every little twitch of his jaw. Every tightened muscle within his neck.

"You're engaged," he said, his voice hardening and his hands fell to his sides.

Oh, God. This was it. I had to tell him the truth. The lies were swallowing me—drowning me. And if what I was feeling for Jude was real? He needed to know sooner rather than later. Heat pulsed through my veins, my blood turning to molten lava and my face grew flushed. The nerves were getting to me. My palms were moist and I wiped them on the dress. "What if I wasn't?" I whispered. "Engaged, I mean."

He narrowed his eyes. "But you are." He took another step back. Like I was posing a threat to him. Like I was an encroaching hurricane ready to tear his world apart. Hell, maybe I was. Maybe he should be backing away from me. What kind of hot mess lies publicly about an engagement to her gay best friend? "... Right?"

This was it. He was flat out asking. I opened my mouth to answer, but before I could, Jude turned on his heels, facing the other way. "It wouldn't matter," he said. "We'll be acting in the same film together if you get this role and Silhouette Studios has strict non-fraternization policies."

"Actors and actresses date all the time. Look at Brad and Angie ..."

"Yeah," he said, interrupting. "Look at how that ended."

"Will and J—"

"Marlena," Jude said, rubbing his hand over his brow. "None of this matters. Because you *are* engaged, right? And *that* is my hardest limit."

Before I could say another word, there was a quiet knock on the door. Jude pushed a sigh through his tight lips and rushed to the door to open it. Ash stepped silently into the room, his gaze fastened onto mine. Intense blue eyes that scrutinized me in the most unnerving way.

Jude flashed me a weak smile, standing in the doorway, almost as though it could offer him some sort of protection. Some sort of shield. That doorway was his sanctuary, his escape away from me. "If you need me, I'll be in that room. You can look out there and see me at any moment. You can text me. Or just tell Ash and he'll come and get me."

I shivered, hugging my arms into my chest. Why Ash? Of all the Dominants out there in that public flogging room, why did Jude want me to do this with the one other man in this club I would have to see on a daily basis if I got this part?

"Ash is my best friend," Jude said, answering my thoughts. Was I that readable? Was I so transparent, that my questions were written all over my face, unspoken? "I trust him with my life."

I nodded, but said nothing more as Jude left.

The space between us was thick and wrought with tension as Ash sauntered toward me with practiced casualness. But I knew better. He was *anything* but casual. Each smooth step was calculated and controlled like a tiger in the wild moving in on its prey.

"I'm surprised you told him," Ash said.

Panic climbed up my throat and with my mouth open, I gave a little gasp. How did Ash know about Omar and me? I jerked my chin up to look at Ash and his eyebrows cinched together in the middle of his face. "About our discussion last night," he clarified. "How you wanted to feel another Dominant's force." I released a quiet breath.

Right. Of course he knew nothing about me and Omar. That was my own stupid, self-sabotaging paranoia. "And I'm surprised you didn't," I returned. "Tell Jude about our dinner and what happened." I'd been certain all night last night that Jude was going to storm in at any moment and yell at me. Kick me out of the club.

He shrugged. "I would have eventually. I just wanted to give you the chance to tell him first."

I narrowed my eyes. "Why?"

Ash snorted and twirled a riding crop that was in his hands. "Because I had to be the one to tell him last time and I never want to be the reason my best friend's face crumples like that ever again."

"You're the one who told him? About Layla?"

Ash's eyebrows lifted at the mention of her name, disappearing beneath a dark patch of hair that had fallen over his forehead. "He told you about Layla?" Ash sounded skeptical.

"A little," I admitted. But I wanted to know so much more about the woman who crushed Jude's heart. Wanted to know why Jude had tensed up when those tourists came through Silhouette on the backlot tour and why Eve hated him so much.

Movement on the other side of the mirror caught my eye and I watched as Jude moved through the crowd, from the bar to a leather armchair in the corner. Lowering into it, his eyes remained on the mirror. Burning into me as though he, too, was watching me.

"God, I could use a drink," I murmured.

"Would Jude be okay with that?"

I thought back to the public flogging. "He told me I could have one tonight after I finished my sparkling water."

"And did you finish your water?"

"Yes."

"Well, that's easy enough," Ash said and moved to a small cabinet in the far corner of the room. "Normally, I wouldn't give another Dominant's submissive any alcohol—that's a pretty big no-no ... but if he said you could have one, I don't see the harm." Ash tugged open the carved wooden door and pulled down two tumblers. "What's your poison?"

"Woodford on the rocks. Or any bourbon they have is fine."

Prior to that, his face had revealed nothing. A stoic trap, ready to catch anything that dare cross his path. But now? Surprise etched across his features. "Bourbon, huh?" He pulled a bottle off the shelf and dropped a few ice cubes into my glass. "I'm surprised. I would have pegged you for a Cosmopolitan girl."

I snorted. "The only things I like pink are my lips, my shoes … and after this week? Maybe my ass."

He tipped his head back, laughing and delivered me the bourbon, touching the edge of his glass briefly to mine. "I'll drink to that."

I lifted the edge of the glass to my lips, drinking down the cool, spiced bourbon. After a few sips, I crossed to the window, looking out at the party happening around Jude. He wasn't participating. His eyes were steadfast, latched onto the mirror. He sat straight in the leather chair, one leg crossed over the other with a martini in hand. One finger drifted mindlessly across his bottom lip, like he was deep in thought. "How often does he go out into that room?" I asked.

I heard Ash walk up beside me. "Before Layla, never. But part of Layla's kink was voyeurism. She always wanted to go to the public areas and he bent one of his soft limits for her."

I swallowed hard, taking another drink from my bourbon. "Like he is tonight—with me."

"Sort of. But sharing you with another Dom? That's a hard limit for Jude. And you made it pretty clear last night—this isn't real. He's not your Dominant. You're not his submissive. This is research." Ash paused so long, I turned to look at him, making sure he was still beside me. He arched his brow. "Right?"

"Right," I repeated, but my voice was hollow. My answer was simply a reflex. Because it *wasn't* right. Nothing about being in this room with Ash felt right.

"So," Ash cleared his throat and set his nearly empty scotch on the table, lifting the riding crop once more. "Ready?" He tapped the edge against his palm, like a Catholic school teacher.

I stared into my half empty bourbon. "Is this the only drink I get for the night?" I asked Ash.

His eyes fell to my glass and a smile twitched at his lips. Then, grabbing the bottle of Woodford's he tipped it over the edge, topping off my drink. "Yes, but I'll give you a tad extra. Seems like you could use it."

"Thank you."

I took another long sip, the alcohol buzzing through me. In theory, it should have eased my nerves, but it had the opposite effect, leaving me more jittery than before.

"So ... where do you want to feel this?" he asked, waving the riding crop. "You mentioned your wrist, but that could be more painful than, um, well, a fleshier area of your body."

"Fleshier?"

His grin widened and he shrugged. "There's a reason the doctor gives you shots in your ass, not your wrist."

Oh, God. I felt my face drain of color and my stomach tightened, twisting like wringing laundry. "Can you ... I don't know ... hit something else first? Like, that chair or something?"

"You want me to strike a chair?"

I nodded, swallowing more of my drink. It should have

warmed me—but I still felt cold. So damn cold.

Ash shrugged. "It's your learning experience." He walked over to the leather arm chair, spinning it so I could see. "Usually, I start by dragging my hand over the area I will hit," he explained and slowly, he slid his fingers over the leather, grinning. "I have to admit … it feels ridiculous doing this to a chair."

I gave him a wobbled smile. "I know … but I think it'll help me."

He shrugged and continued. "So, next … if it was my submissive's ass I was striking—I would have her bend at the waist. I might put clamps on choice areas of her body, too. To really enhance the sting. Then … I wait." He stepped away from the armchair, circling to its other side. "I don't touch her. I don't move. I hardly breathe. I stand there and admire her beauty. I watch as her tight, little body trembles in anticipation. I make her wait. Wonder when it's going to happen. Most of my submissives love this moment. They writhe in excitement for it. Their little thighs wiggle together and I yell at them when they squirm."

My breath deepened, my chest heaving with the inhalation. My pulse was thunderous in my ears. He wasn't even hitting me yet and I was petrified. He was so different than Jude. So much more … threatening. Was that the difference between a sadist Dom and Jude? "How long will you wait before you … strike?"

"As long or as short as I want," Ash answered. "Sometimes I make them wait a couple minutes. Sometimes I'll give it longer."

"What was the longest you've made a sub wait?"

"Twenty-seven minutes."

My mouth fell open. Holy shit.

"And that was only because I was so turned on, I couldn't wait anymore."

He took another sip of his scotch, then pulled the riding crop back and whipped it toward the chair. The slap of leather on leather was so loud, it made me jump. My heart plummeted to my stomach. That hit was *hard*. That wasn't a playful spank. That was legitimately forceful. The sort of hit that a passerby would call the cops about if they didn't know any better. He did it again. This time, the sound didn't startle me, but it was just as loud. He hit the chair four more times and when he spun to face me, his face was flushed red. Little specs of perspiration pushed out of his pores along his forehead and his breath heaved, pushing oxygen in and out of his lungs violently.

"You don't hold back, do you?"

"No." One simple word. One simple answer. But God, it held so much intensity. "Well?" he asked, walking toward me. "You sure you want that sort of force on your wrist?"

I shook my head no. I wasn't sure I wanted that sort of force *anywhere* on my body. That kind of hit? It would leave welts on my skin for days. Maybe even weeks.

"We could do the backs of your thighs. Not quite so intimate."

I nodded, looking out the window at Jude. His eyes were on me. Almost like he could see me, even though I knew that was impossible. It was a mirror on that side … he had no way of knowing I was standing against it looking right back at him. I heard Ash's approach. Heard his deep, heavy breaths. Saw his shadowed silhouette behind me in the reflection of the window.

That sick feeling twisting in my stomach deepened.

No, I couldn't do this. Not to Jude. And not to myself. It just felt ... wrong. "Planner," I whispered.

Ash froze behind me. Then, he backed away. I could feel the space he put between us. Feel it in my gut ... in my bones. I stared at Jude in the other room. His tightened brow. His down-turned mouth. His white knuckled grip on the martini. This wasn't right. I didn't want Ash. I didn't want to feel his force. I didn't want to be sharing a drink with him. That chilled nervousness that plagued me for the last few minutes lifted and warmth filled my cheeks. "This isn't right," I said. "The very first time Jude and I talked, my gut told me that this would be one of my hard limits and I didn't listen to it ... I-I would never do this. And Holly would never do this. Neither of us would share ourselves with someone other than the man we love." I placed a hand on the cool window, dragging my finger down Jude's cheek on the other side.

"The man you love," Ash said, his voice softer, farther away.

That warm feeling ignited into an inferno inside of me and I whipped around to face Ash. Love. *Oh, God*. Did I really just say that? "I—I mean, the man Holly loves ..." but my voice faded away and I shook my head, dropping my gaze. The alcohol buzzed in my mind, clouding my thoughts.

"That's not what you said," Ash said.

"I know, okay? I just—I'm feeling confused. And ... dizzy."

Reaching out, Ash took the almost empty bourbon glass from my hands and set it aside. "Let me take you back to your room," he said—more like a demand than an offer. "Jude will come in for aftercare soon ... I'll buy you a little time, but can I make a suggestion?"

I nodded tightly. "I suggest that you figure out what the hell you're feeling. And soon."

When I dared to look up at Ash again, his stern expression had been replaced with something new. Compassion, maybe? Despite his hard words, his mouth and eyes were soft. Without actually touching me, he guided me out the door and down the hall back to my room. "You made the right choice," he said, finally breaking the silence. "You're right—Holly would never want another man to lay a hand on her. It's a trust that she and Leo have worked hard to build and she'd never compromise that."

He pulled a keycard out of his back pocket and as he slid it in the lock, my door lit green and clicked open. I walked inside and turned to face Ash. "I guess I've still got a lot to learn," I said quietly.

Ash shrugged. "So does Holly," he answered. "That being said, Jude is my best friend. And I haven't seen him look at anyone like he looks at you in two years. So before you slip up and use the four letter 'L' word again ... make sure you mean it."

I nodded, tight, staccato movements. "But what about the non-fraternization policy at Silhouette?"

"There's a consent contract. A non-disclosure that consensual couples can sign," Ash said. "Richard Blair would prefer *no one* date within the studio of course, but ..." Ash shrugged and rolled his eyes. "Let's be honest, in our industry? Actors, producers, directors ... date all the time. We practically live in the studio, so if we don't date each other, we'd never have any human contact." His mouth lifted in a grin. "As long as it's consensual and you're both willing to sign a contract stating such, you should both be protected."

I stood there in the doorway as the air conditioner

clicked on. Cool air brushed over my skin and billowed across the silky dress sheathing my body.

"The only question left is … do you love him?"

Do I love him? I closed my eyes and pictured his sharp, high cheekbones. His clean-shaven jaw, that occasionally, by the end of the day, had the slightest rasp of stubble poking through. His trimmed, styled hair. And those brilliant green eyes. I pictured him standing right here in front of me and the mere thought of his presence had my pulse racing. My heart slammed against my ribcage and my breath grew short.

I opened my eyes and put my hand to the ache beneath my breastbone. "I think I do," I whispered.

"You *think* you do?"

"I feel … like every time he's not around, I want him to be. And—when I think of him hurt or upset, sitting out there in that common room with his martini, I get this twisty-sick feeling in my stomach. I feel hot, but clammy all at once." I pressed my palms to my stomach and closed my eyes. I'd never been in love before—is this what it felt like? Like I was tied up in a million knots?

"I'm no expert, but that sounds like love to me. Just … don't fuck with his heart. You're engaged. And he's only just beginning to superglue the pieces back together after Layla. Whatever you do … end it with Omar first."

Omar. I needed to talk to Omar. Needed to tell him what I was feeling … he would know what to do.

Ash tapped the side of the doorframe, backing away. "I'll tell Jude we didn't go through with the riding crop and that you need a little time before he comes to tuck you in." With that, Ash grabbed the handle and pulled the door shut between us.

CHAPTER EIGHTEEN
Marly

I COLLAPSED ONTO the bed, the ringing phone pressed against my ear. "Come on … pick up. Pick up, pick up, pick up, pick up …" I dropped one foot to the floor in an effort to stop the room from spinning. Stupid bourbon.

"Marly," Omar said, his voice sleep-laden and graveled.

I sniffled, closing my eyes against the hot tears threatening to spill over my cheeks.

"What's wrong?" Omar asked, concern replacing the grogginess.

"It's Jude," I whispered. "Well … Jude and bourbon."

On the other line, I heard another man's voice, muffled … murmuring, "Who is it?"

I stiffened, pressing the back of my head harder into the pillow. "Oh, God. You have someone there with you," I whispered, as if Omar's date could hear me. Hell, maybe he could. Was that smart? For him to have taken someone home? Then again, was it freaking smart for me to be here at a BDSM club with Jude Fisher? "I'm sorry, Omar. I'll just—I'll call you tomorrow."

"Marly, wait," Omar said and I heard the rustling of covers and a door shut on the other line. "Talk to me. What happened?"

"Nothing," I sobbed. "And *everything*." I launched into the story of the last two nights. Everything from chatting

225

with Ash, to wanting to explore another Dominant's force, to changing my mind when standing there with Ash and looking out at Jude. "I want to be with him," I said, finally. "And not just to hook up for a night. I want to cook dinner with him. Go shopping together. Decorate a Christmas tree. Meet his mom, who by the way, sounds badass. Oh, God, Omar ..." I clenched my hand against the silk dress, the delicate fabric rippling beneath my tight grip. My other hand flew to the antique choker and I ran the tips of my fingers over the cameo. "I love him." My sobs deepened, heaving in my chest, and the tears spilled down the sides of my face.

"Then why are you crying?" Omar asked, his voice soft.

"Because I don't *want* to love him. I told myself I wouldn't do this again. That I wouldn't wind up with another Jack—"

"Whoa. Okay. I don't know Jude all that well, but Jack's an ass. And from the little encounters I've had with Jude, he is nothing like your ex. Besides, you weren't *in love* with Jack."

That was true. I cared about Jack. But we barely had a chance to fall in love before he was using his power as director over me. I inhaled a shaky breath, my tears quieting and swiped my palms over my damp cheeks. "What do I do? I tried to tell him earlier tonight about our fake engagement, but ... I don't think he's going to listen to me."

"Baby ... you're in *love*." Omar chuckled. "However you tell him ... it's got to be bold. Just because you're a submissive now, doesn't mean you're not *fierce*. Besides, you got that liquid courage thing going for you at the moment."

My eyes traveled to the nightstand and I opened the top drawer. A smile replaced my tear stained frown. *Be fierce.* Hell, this idea was fierce … it was sexy as hell. But was it smart? I would never do this sort of thing soberly. But with a glass of booze coursing through my veins? "I can be fierce," I whispered, running my fingers along the edge of the nightstand.

"Oh, I know you can. Go get him, Boo."

I disconnected the call and jumped to my feet, washing my flushed, tear-ridden face and splashed some cool water on my swollen eyes. "I love him," I said to myself. *The strongest people feel the pain, understand it … and accept it.* I closed my eyes. That's what this feeling of love was. The ultimate pain. Tearing my once wounded heart from my chest and placing it in another person's hands to tend to. Isn't that what BDSM was all about? Giving yourself, mind, body, soul—pleasure, pain, everything. And trusting your Dom to do right by you? Was there much of a difference between BDSM and love?

I launched myself off the sink and rushed for the nightstand, not bothering to change out of my dress. I tugged open the drawer, pushed aside the box of Ben Wa balls Jude had given me the other day—*later*. I'd use those later. Instead, I grabbed a collar with bells on it and the vibrating tongue ring.

Rule #6 – If Poppy chooses to masturbate, she must call Jude and wear her collar of bells so that he may listen to her as she orgasms.

Nerves collided in my belly, bouncing around and off each other until I thought I might be sick. I cinched the belled collar around my neck, over the Victorian choker. Then, laying back against the bed, I slipped the tongue ring on my thumb, pressing the small button to turn it on. Vibrations slammed against my knuckle, sending shivers up my arm.

Turning my head on the pillow, I dialed Jude's number and set the phone beside my ear. I then slid my hand beneath the tight elastic of my panties, gliding my finger over my clit. The sharp vibrations brushed over me and my sex clenched hard with wanton desire.

His phone rang twice before he answered.

"Marlena?" he said.

I sighed a quiet moan and the bells gave a light jingle with the movement. The low rumble of his voice sent nervous electricity shooting through me. What if he never spoke to me again after this? What if he hated me? Wanted nothing to do with me? Despite these doubts, the fears, my body responded to the vibrations against my clit, arousal budding. My hips pulsed as I used my thumb to circle the slick rubber toy over my tight, wet nub. My back arched, sending the bells on my neck into a chorus of jingles.

"Marly?" he gasped. "What are you doing?"

"Oh, God," I whispered and slid my free hand up my body to cup my breast. Tugging at the neckline of my dress, I freed one nipple, rolling it between my thumb and forefinger as I plunged my other finger deep inside my wet core. I tensed around my fingers, my muscles squeezing and aching for release. I pictured Jude's face. His stunning green eyes inches from mine, searing into me as he propped his body over top of me.

I slid a second finger inside, pumping them faster while my vibrating thumb worked my clit. His voice ... Jude's voice was so sexy, especially when saying my name. So deep and masculine with perfect diction—and I wanted to hear that proper voice lose it. Cry out my name. Convulse in pleasure. Gasp in my ear as his teeth came down scraping across the fleshy part of my earlobes.

I moaned again, my lower back arching off the bed. The jingling of the collar was getting faster, louder as I pulsed my hips in rhythm with my hand.

"Marlena, stop," Jude demanded and I could hear his pounding footsteps. Instead of stopping, I slowed my hand down to match the thud of each one of his steps, picturing his face. His eyes. His chest. His body pressed against me, writhing with my movements.

"No," I whimpered. No more stopping. No more slowing down. I wanted Jude—so badly I could taste it. He was so incredibly sexy—exuding masculinity and sexiness and control in a way that had me trembling with need. Omar was right—he had never been more right in his life. I had to be bold. If I sat down over breakfast and told Jude the truth? Would he even stay seated long enough to hear me out? Now? Now I had his attention.

"This isn't right, Marlena. You should be calling your fucking fiancé with this."

I let out a ragged breath. As pleasure bloomed between my legs, unease crept from my mind down my throat and they collided in my belly, like a tumultuous elixir. I was vulnerable in every way imaginable, baring both my body and soon, my soul to Jude. This was it. This was the moment where nothing between us would be the same ever again. *Be bold, be fierce.*

"I don't ... h-have a fiancé," I panted, my voice breaking against a brittle breath. Like a tension cable snapping, the emotional burden of that lie spiraled away from me. For the first time in months, breathing came easier. The air felt crisper, cleaner inside my lungs and without the soot of the lie darkening my path, I was able to bask in the glow of intense pleasure between my legs.

At this point, it almost didn't matter what Jude's response was. It just felt so damn good to have the truth out there.

"What are you talking about? What about Omar?" A bellowed snarl accentuated each question. I could hear the anger in his voice. But edging alongside of that anger was something more—something deep and wrought with tension. It coiled around my spine, tightening my skin and the tips of my breasts. Heat sizzled through my veins and stars danced behind my closed eyelids as I lost myself beneath the pressure of my fingers; against the buzzing tension of my clit.

"Marlena," he said. "Answer me. What do you mean you don't have a fiancé?"

But I couldn't answer—I was so close. I heard the jagged inhale of Jude's breath and his voice sounded further away as I writhed on the bed, bucking against my hand. Sensation pulsed in my belly as my core tightened. I drove my pelvis down, fucking my fingers harder with wild abandon, imagining Jude. His sharp, green eyes. His tight jaw. The way his neck tightened when he was deep in thought.

Reasonable, sensible Marlena was gone. All that was left was Poppy. Poppy who wanted to be tied to this bed. Poppy who wanted to be made to crawl on her hands and knees to Jude and beg for release. Poppy who wanted to eat a scone off his knee and be spanked when she was bad and praised when she was good.

It wasn't rational. But right now? It transcended want

and desire. I *needed* Jude. The sound of footsteps on the phone stopped.

Then, my front door clicked and he was there, standing in the rectangular open doorway, his chest heaving, phone still pressed to his ear. He stepped inside, slamming the door shut behind him. His hair was more disheveled than I'd ever seen. Rumpled and tossed like he'd been running his hands through it. His crisp white shirt was wrinkled and where the sleeves were folded up to the elbows, the left arm had slid slightly lower than the right elbow. As he lowered the phone from his ear and tucked it into his front pocket, his eyes scanned the length of me, throat bobbing. I lay there, legs spread, frozen with my finger inside of me and the elastic of my thong stretched to the side. It bit painfully into the sides of my hand. My silky dress rumpled around my hips and my breast pushed out from the neckline. *Say something*, I thought, unable to take my eyes off of him.

Hope peaked in my heart. He wouldn't have entered this room if he didn't want me.

"Do you want me to leave?" he growled.

I most definitely did not. Simply *thinking* about him had me drenched and throbbing—but now? With Jude standing here in front of me, I was so turned on, I wasn't sure I could last much longer. I resumed pulsing my fingers in and out of myself, then shook my head no, the bells rattling along with me, answering audibly where my words couldn't. His eyes steeled into me and his chest inflated with a suspended breath.

I stared into his jade green eyes, shivering against the cold, hard set of his jaw. "May I come ... Sir?"

His expression lit on fire, intensified by my question, and silence crawled between us like an unwanted guest. Did he want me to beg? Plead? I panted, awaiting his answer as his gaze stayed latched to my face. For the first time since this crazy idea entered my head, dread twisted in my gut. *He was going to say no.* To everything.

I dropped my gaze between his legs where I could see the rock hard outline of his cock pressing against the flat front of his dress pants, and my fears slipped away. My lower back lifted off the bed as I arched into my touch, moaning.

"Yes," he said, his voice dark and discordant, missing its familiar poise I had grown so used to. "Come, Poppy." His breath turned shallow and I was snared in the intensity of his glare. Hypnotized by the flex of his jaw and the way his hands fisted at his sides. He didn't bother to adjust himself—to hide his erection. Why should he? With me bared to him like I was, legs spread, breast in hand, and hips circling my fingers mercilessly, modesty was pointless.

My eyelids grew heavy, but I forced them to remain on Jude as I pressed the vibrating toy harder against my clit. Knowing the vibrator had been on Jude's tongue in the past made it so much hotter, second best to his actual tongue dragging across my body.

Heavy pulses budded between my legs, beginning deep in my core and ricocheting outward to light every single one of my nerve endings on fire. It didn't matter that he hadn't laid a hand on me. That his lips weren't pressed to mine. This moment of vulnerability and pure rapture was more intimate than any sex I'd ever had.

His eyes burned against my body as my limbs jerked with the convulsing euphoria. A gust of air tore from his lungs as he choked down a swallow, his eyes scanning across my flesh and landing on my pussy as it pulsed—tightening and releasing like an overworked heart.

Waves of pleasure rolled through me, lessening with each dissolving pulse until I was laying there, my body feeling like putty. Like it could be molded into any form or shape Jude wanted me to be.

He took two long strides closer to the bed, until he was only standing a few feet away.

I clicked the vibrator off, sitting up on my elbows and snapped my knees together. That liquid courage from earlier was wearing off.

"Now … what's this about you not having a fiancé?"

CHAPTER NINETEEN
Jude

W*HAT IN THE serious fuck was happening?* My head spun and even though I'd only had two martinis all night, I felt intoxicated. Marly was intoxicating. Her smile, her scent, the way her pink skin flushed as she came.

When I answered Marly's call and heard the bells ... I was instantly hard, dropping my martini into Ash's hand and rushing toward her room. Now, she was laying in front of me, her swollen clit begging for my tongue.

"Omar's not my fiancé," she whispered as tears filled her eyes.

"You're not engaged?"

"No, Sir."

I closed my eyes. I knew something was up with them. Whatever it was they had, it didn't feel right. And though this was kind of a shock ... it also wasn't.

"Have you *ever* been engaged to Omar?"

"No, Sir."

On one hand, I should be furious. She'd been lying to me. But on the other hand, my relief overpowered any sense of anger or betrayal. Reaching out, I curled my finger under her chin, lifting it until her gaze reached mine. Her skin was silkier than the dress that sheathed her tight little body. Her tongue peeked through the seam of her lips, wetting them.

Those dark blue eyes flashed a brilliant shade of cerulean, wide and wet and the intensity of her stare sent a tremble tumbling down my spine. "Why would you lie about that?"

She pulled her chin out of my hold and swung her leg around the side of the bed. The absence of her stare burned more than a branding iron on my flesh.

"Look at me," I demanded.

With her hands clamped in her lap, she looked up, searching my face. Looking for something I was careful not to reveal.

"Omar's my best friend," she said. And damn, I hated how her voice cracked. "He's gay and needed a beard. I was so sick of producers and directors treating my auditions like speed dating and as soon as we announced our engagement, all those propositions at auditions stopped." Her jaw tightened and she looked away, brushing away the tear that slipped over her razor-sharp cheekbone. "They were more concerned with not disrespecting Omar by hitting on his fiancée, than they were with respecting *me*." What a shitty, shitty industry we were in. "I'm sorry," she whispered. "I didn't think I'd—"

"You'd what?" My question was tighter than my clenched fists. She pushed to her feet, tugging the dress lower over her thighs and covering herself as if she hadn't just been finger fucking herself in front of me. As I took a step nearer, Marly backed away.

"I didn't think I'd … feel something for you."

My head was buzzing like thousands of bees were inside of me, swarming. It was no surprise that she had feelings for me. I'd felt it too, from the moment we'd met. My cock pushed painfully against my zipper, straining to be set free.

Straining toward Marlena. Fuck, I wanted her. More than I'd wanted anyone in longer than I could remember. I didn't even recall wanting Layla this badly.

She looked frightened as I took another step forward and her back hit the bedpost. I froze. Fuck, I didn't mean to scare her. I was just ... shocked. I placed my hands out in front of me. "Marlena," I said gently. "You're safe here. You know that, right?" She nodded, but the fear in her eyes betrayed the nod of her head. I spun away from her, needing a break from those soulful eyes and wet, pouty lips to think.

"Are you mad?" she asked from behind me.

"No," I answered without thinking. And I meant it. This wasn't the same as Layla lying to me. I don't know why it was different, but it was.

"Then ... what are you?" she asked.

I spun to face her. "I'm ... conflicted. I don't want to be yet another person in this industry who takes advantage of you." My voice was tight and my clammy hands flexed at my sides.

"I don't want that, either. But ..."

"But?" I prodded.

"I'm falling in love with you, Jude."

She's falling in love with me. My blood rushed, replaced with liquid gold and my lips parted in a gush of air. In the moment, it took for each of us to release a breath, I closed the space between us, my lips crashing down onto hers. Her body heat penetrated me and every breath was filled with her potent scent. My tongue moved along the seam of her mouth and with a low moan, I took her lips, claiming her pleasure as my own. With each stroke of my tongue, she fell heavier in my arms, responding with her own lips, sliding back and forth against mine. I swallowed her pleasure. Savored every moan. Every sigh. Every whimper.

"Why didn't you tell me sooner?" I gasped, tearing myself from her lips.

"I didn't trust you at first. And it wasn't just my secret to tell. I had Omar to consider. Besides, would you have listened if I told you sooner?"

"Yes!" I dragged a hand down my face, shaking my head. "I mean, maybe. I don't know ..."

Marly stepped into me and I held a hand out, stopping her. "No. Marlena, I meant it when I said I can't be with my co-stars anymore. Nothing good comes from it."

Looking down at the tongue ring in her palm, she slowly raised her gaze. "Marlena" She asked innocently. "Who's Marly? What have I told you about saying other women's names in our bedroom, Leo?"

Alarm registered on my face and despite the moment of surprise, the tiniest smile twitched on my lips. "Marly, be serious—"

She struck me hard across the face with the palm of her hand. Nerves and heat slammed together in my chest and surged down to my stomach. My cheek stung, but fuck was that hot.

"What did I say?" She raised a brow, pinching my chin and forcing my gaze back to hers. Those blue eyes were sharper than the edge of a knife and could cut me just as deeply. Pierce into me and ruin me in one swift movement. She had that power. Layla had had that power too. And she had wielded it with reckless abandon. "I don't want to hear another woman's name in this room, you understand me?"

That small grin curved wider toward my eyes. "Of course."

"Say my name," she whispered.

"*Marlena,*" I said, running a hand across my stinging cheek. Then, anticipating her movement, I caught her wrist as she lifted her palm to strike me again. I didn't squeeze her hard, but used that wrist to tug her flush against my body. Her breasts heaved, pushing against my crisp white shirt and if I closed my eyes, I could almost feel her tight, pebbled nipples through the thin layer of clothing. "I'm falling in love with *you*. Not Holly."

Her mouth formed a perfect o-shape and I sucked in a sharp breath. Most women would have gushed or cried. But not Marly. Not my Poppy. She snapped her mouth closed and lifted her chin. "Fine," she said, then tilted her head and looked me directly in the eyes. "But, I need to say one thing first. And you're not going to like it."

"Try me," I hissed.

"I'm not Layla," she whispered.

Layla. Her name—it was a bitter, acidic reality check coming from sweet Marlena's lips. Like shoving a dirty finger into a healing wound. I jerked back, retreating from her.

"I'm sorry I lied to you about Omar and me ... but I'm also not sorry. He and I did what we both had to do to get ahead in an industry that marginalized us. And I won't apologize for the act itself ... we made a decision that protected us. But I'm sorry for deceiving you and not telling you sooner."

I narrowed my eyes. "And what does any of that have to do with my ex-wife?" I couldn't even say her name aloud. Not here. Not in this room.

"Because I know she hurt you. I know she lied to you too. And even though I don't have all the facts about her ...

this situation is different. I didn't lie to hurt you."

She was right. It wasn't the same. Not every lie was created equal. I circled my thumb over her skin. "I'm not mad at you. And I know you're not Layla … to start with, she would have never apologized."

"Okay," Marly said, and curled her fingers over my jaw. My stubble scraped against her soft skin and I could smell the perfume clinging to the insides of her wrists. "So, you're not mad. And we've established I'm not Layla. I'm falling in love with you and you're falling for me …"

It was exactly what I'd been craving all week, but also exactly what I'd been dreading. "Come on, Jude," she said. "We didn't come this far to only come this far." Then, pushing onto her toes, she kissed me.

Marly

I KISSED HIM softly at first, Jude's mouth warm and inviting as he dove his hands into my hair, wrapping my red curls around his fist, tugging my head back.

"Fuck, Marlena." He dropped his forehead to mine and I put one hand to his cheek, stroking him with my thumb. His skin was unusually rough, his stubble poked into my hand.

"Jude, please," I begged, my sex throbbing for him. "I haven't been with a man in a year. Not since Jack—" he cut me off with his lips, swallowing my words.

"Marlena," he said, his mouth peppering kisses across my jaw. "I don't want to hear another man's name in this room again."

I grinned. He was thawing. I was chipping away at the

ice. "Except Omar's," I said. "He will always be in my life."

"Fine. But I still prefer not to hear his name if we're kissing. And definitely not if I'm inside of you."

"I can live with that."

"And Marlena ... if you hit me again, you'll get three more from me for each strike. Got that?" He flashed me a playful smile as I nodded, grinning. The thought excited me. His palm on my ass. Bare flesh on bare flesh and I considered slapping him once more just to feel his punishment. But my need to please him won out over my desire for punishment.

"Yes, Sir."

He slid an arm around the back of my waist, encasing our bodies together. His hard length pushed into my hip. "Besides," he whispered, bringing his lips to my ear, "Holly would have *never* hit Leo."

A grin spread on my face. "You're right," I whispered back. "That was all Marly."

His mouth came down hard onto mine, his tongue pushing past my lips and slicing into my mouth. This kiss was different than before. It was wild and frenzied with a low hum of agonizing tension. Like a wild animal having been released from its cage after years of captivity, that kiss resonated down my tingling body. My breasts grew heavy, my nipples tight against the soft, billowed silk and heat pooled between my legs. The flavor of him was raw, unbridled passion and the intensity of that single kiss left me panting and breathless as he pulled back.

I fumbled with his belt, struggling to undo the sleek black leather and silver buckle. It didn't take long until I had him stripped down to his boxer briefs as he slowly unbuttoned his shirt. A tanned chest peeked out from the shirt and contrasted beautifully against stark, white fabric.

I sank to my knees, my mouth burning a path of kisses down his chest and abs, his skin salty beneath my tongue. Delicious. When I was face to face with his bulge, my nose brushed the small line of springy hair leading down the middle of his belly and disappeared into the waistband of his boxer briefs. Curling my fingers into the elastic band, I tugged them down and his erection pushed free from the cotton. Hard and thick with veins straining against the velvety flesh. My mouth watered and I slid the vibrator ring onto my tongue, pressing the button on the side.

Brushing the vibrator gently along his shaft, I started at the base and licked up to the tip, circling his head slowly. He groaned, thick fingers diving into my hair and though the movement was commanding, he was gentle as he pulled my long hair off my shoulders and out of my face. "Marly," he groaned, as I increased suction, taking him entirely into my mouth. My sex throbbed, the emptiness consuming all my thoughts. I needed to be filled with Jude; I needed relief from the agonizing emptiness.

The tip of his dick grazed the back of my throat, a little dab of cum rolling around my tongue. As I pulled him out of my mouth, I scraped my teeth along his length a bit harder than normal. He hissed as a smirk played on my lips. "For a man who likes to give pain, you're kind of a pussy," I teased.

I nibbled along the edge of his head, flicking my tongue at the soft, velvety underside before pumping him slowly with my fisted hand.

"Aaah," Jude's knees buckled with the sudden thrust and his grip on my hair tightened briefly before he released the hold once more. I ran the tip of my tongue along my lips and slid him into my mouth once more. I started slowly again, using my hand and mouth simultaneously, alternating between fast and hard to swirling, leisurely licks as though I were finishing an ice cream cone that was melting in the sun. Each time the vibrator came in contact with his head, Jude's hips bucked and his hands squeezed whatever part of my body he happened to be grasping in the moment.

It was a weird sensation, the feeling of vibrating rubber against my tongue and teeth. But not altogether unpleasant. Jude's groan was like an aphrodisiac and I scraped my nails down the sides of his thighs. After his hiss of approval, I slowly dragged them up the insides, cupping his balls and gently rolling them in my palm.

Why did this feel so damn good? In my past experiences, blow jobs were something you did when you wanted to get it in return or if you were too tired for actual sex. But here? With Jude? I was so turned on, I found myself wiggling back and forth on my knees to get a little friction between my legs while sucking him off. My moan vibrated right along with the tongue ring and with that, something in Jude snapped. His hands on my shoulders tightened with one final squeeze and he pulled me off of his erection.

His cock still pierced forward, veiny and thick. Did I do something wrong? And slowly, I lifted my eyes to his. He growled—actually growled—as he raked his gaze across my body, pausing briefly at my cleavage, still spilling out of the silk dress before landing back on my eyes. Then, pulling me to my feet, he grabbed the hem of my dress and yanked it off my body as I shimmied out of my panties.

"I need to taste you. Have you. Before I come," he whispered, diving his nose into my hair and inhaling deeply as his hands skimmed my breasts, his fingers, rolling over my nipples. I parted my mouth, aching for his kiss, but he didn't indulge me. Instead, he hovered over my parted lips, waiting, breathing, until I was clawing at the back of his neck, moaning incoherent pleas for him to kiss me.

When he finally slid his tongue along mine, the movement was soft and controlled—as if I expected anything less from him. The slick sensation of his tongue touching mine combined with the buzzing tongue ring jolted down my body and his mouth followed the delightful wave of ecstasy, kissing down my neck and sternum until his tongue rolled over each nipple.

I was in such a foggy state, writhing and lost in his mouth, that I didn't even realize Jude was strapping me into the bed restraints. It wasn't until I went to cup his face and my hand snapped against the leather, inches from the bed post.

Jude chuckled, pulling back and inspecting me with a contented sigh. Then, turning, he fastened my ankles into the bottom posts, spread eagle. Goose bumps raced down my flesh and across my stomach. I was open, exposed. And so turned on, my body felt like it was on fire.

There was enough slack in the restraints that I could move my arms and feet a few inches in either direction and I tugged on the ties to test it. Before I had barely moved, Jude had his lips on my ear. "For now, you have some leverage. If you test that and wriggle beneath me, I'll pull these so taut that your knees won't even be able to quiver." His voice was nearly a whisper; deep, rough and filled with all kinds of sensual promises that made me feel like I was walking against the ocean current. With Jude, I never quite knew what I was getting. He kept me guessing constantly.

And damn, was that exciting.

"Do I make myself clear?" he continued, awaiting my reply with an arched brow and curved grin.

"Yes, Sir," I replied, and the words came out strained, like my throat was packed with cotton.

"Good girl, Poppy," he whispered as he lowered his lips to mine again. His tongue ravaged the inside of my mouth, exploring every little area and I moaned, aching to touch him. Aching to run my hands through his hair. With what little mobility I had, I gripped the headboard. His teeth grasped the base of my tongue and he slowly sucked the tongue ring from my mouth into his with a proud smile.

The buzzing was quiet. Barely audible and yet, everything in my body clenched with the soft hum.

I arched my back into his kisses as they lined a path down my neck and over my heavy breasts. His hand gripped the curve of my waist and he squeezed me before inching down between my legs. A soft breeze tickled my skin and I sighed as the coolness of it hit my heated, throbbing flesh.

A breath caught above me and Jude's grasp on my thighs tightened. "Holy fuck," he growled. "You are so gorgeous." He groaned and the muscles in his jaw twitched.

I rolled my hips toward him, but his hands at the junction of thighs and pelvis held me firmly to the bed. As if I could go anywhere, even if I wanted to.

"I want you completely silent during this," he said, his voice laced with need. "Not a peep." He met my eyes from between my legs.

His tongue drew slowly up my length, settling on my clit in a slow, lingering lick. The rapid vibrations of the tongue ring contrasted his slow, skilled tongue and sent stars popping at the back of my eyes.

The feeling was far more intense than I could ever have imagined. And without the ability to move—to stop him— to give him the ol' tap on the shoulder, 'you can stop now' motion, I felt powerless beneath his mouth. That must be the point. To give yourself over to the feeling entirely. To let your pleasure, your desire be completely in the hands of someone else—holy shit, was that liberating. My legs stiffened as Jude's pace quickened; he moved from thrusting his tongue in and out of me to sucking on my clit.

I ground my hips into his face as my sex tightened around his final tongue thrust. Spasms went off inside of me, clenching and relaxing in an orgasm so intense, I didn't even recognize my own voice calling out for Jude.

As he lifted to his elbows, a haughty grin stretched the length of his face. "Not exactly the silent type, are you?"

I moaned. My sex was swollen and hot. Limb by limb, Jude tightened the restraints until each arm and each leg was completely stretched out. I whimpered as he gave a final tug to the restraint.

"I told you to be silent," he said, after sliding the tongue ring off and setting it to the side. "What do we do about those vocal chords of yours?" Thrumming his fingers along my thighs, he mocked deep thought for a second before grabbing a ball gag from beside the bed. He dangled it in front of me, his face turning serious for a moment. "Do you think you can handle this?"

I swallowed, trailing my gaze along the leather straps and red rubber ball. Anxiety danced in my stomach like freaking Fred Astaire. But the answer was yes. I wanted it. I wanted more of this—whatever this was. I swallowed, nodding. "I can handle it."

The concern lifted from Jude's face, and was replaced with a sinful smirk. "I'll fasten it loosely so you'll still be able to speak a little. You can't use safe words, but do you remember what to do instead?"

"I snap my fingers," I answered, remembering our first night at the diner when we discussed the various uses of safe words and movements.

"Good girl, Poppy," he praised, as he put the gag in my mouth and strapped it behind my head.

The ball was small enough to fit comfortably in my mouth. It pressed my tongue down, but if I really wanted to, I could push the ball to the roof of my mouth and use my tongue to speak—whether or not he could understand me would be another thing.

Kneeling between my open legs, Jude stared at me. "So fucking beautiful," he murmured, before lowering his lips to my nipple.

I moaned from beneath the gag and it came out muffled. That wicked little smirk of his climbed higher as he met my gaze. And even as I tried to arch my breast deeper into his mouth, the restraints made it damn near impossible. They were tight enough to cause only the tiniest biting ache. Sort of like an uncomfortable yoga pose I held just a few seconds too long.

As Jude moved to my other breast, he dipped a finger inside of me, circling his thumb over my slick nub. My body jolted with the touch and a flash of heat encompassed my whole body.

With a quiet rip of a plastic wrapper, I glanced down to find Jude rolling a condom onto himself. He positioned his head at my opening, easing inside me.

A whimper escaped beyond the ball gag as he rolled his hips between my legs, brushing his hip bone against my most sensitive area. He pulled out slowly, painfully slowly, until he was barely even still inside me. Then with little pulses, he teased me, pumping in and out just barely enough that I could feel it.

With what little motion I had, I fisted the headboard and grunted, doing everything humanly possible to pull my hips down harder onto his erection. Bindings and ball gags do not call for slow, meaningful thrusts. I wanted to be fucked. Pounded. Hard and senseless, until my head slammed into the headboard behind me.

Jude chuckled from above me, his thick arms trembling under the restraint of holding back. Bending at the elbows, he dropped a feathered kiss to my jaw. "Delayed gratification, remember?" he said with another small pulse of his hips. "I want to fuck you senseless, but right now—I just want to watch you squirm another moment longer."

One thing about ball gags—it makes it really hard to catch your breath. I was panting, only, it was through my nose. Another groan gurgled at the back of my throat and I managed to say something that sounded like "Please."

With that plea, Jude entered me completely. A sigh of pleasure trembled in my belly and my head dropped against the pillow with the deliciously full feeling. *Delayed gratification*, I thought with an inward sigh. Damn, he nailed it. He stayed there inside of me for a moment. Moving in circles, hitting that knot deep inside before he dragged himself out slowly again.

I tightened my thighs around his waist, squeezing him as hard as I could. Not that it did much to restrict his movement.

"Are you ready, Marlena?"

I nodded, grunting once more. And with that, Jude pushed onto his arms, thrusting hard and fast into me. He groaned, the entirety of his sculpted muscles clenching.

And still, there was nothing I could do but watch. And feel. And enjoy. I had to trust Jude to know what I wanted and what I needed without being able to move or offer him any signals.

Each plunge went deeper, harder—and it was just what I needed. The ache pulsed with each thrust and just as I thought it couldn't get any better, a slight buzzing sound caught my attention. Jude had slipped the small vibrator onto his thumb and slowly, gently, he placed pressure onto my clit. The vibrations sent a voltage of electricity directly into my veins. It was almost too much to bear—if I thought that spanking was what the BDSM community was all about, I had it completely wrong. Being with Jude was like being on a road trip blindfolded. I didn't know where he was taking me; I didn't know what roads would be taken to get there—some would be bumpy, others fast, some slow and smooth ... but I trusted the destination would be fabulous. I trusted him to make it fabulous.

He was getting harder inside of me with each thrust and each one made me greedy for more. His rough voice was intense above me. "Marly—I'm so close. So fucking close. You feel amazing."

With his admission, my orgasm slammed into me, completely unexpected, rippling down my entire body. I curled my toes and fingers around the restraints, squeezing as my pussy clenched and relaxed around Jude's cock. With a groan, his eyes fluttered closed and he threw his head back, tight muscles around his neck working with his

ed himself, frozen inside of me as my body clamped down onto his erection. With a final blissful sigh, he smiled, unhooking the gag from my mouth and dropping his lips to mine.

I moved my mouth over his and my sweaty flush quickly cooled as he loosened all the bindings. Once my arms were free, I threw them around Jude's neck, holding him close and trailing my nails down his back. Not being able to touch him—to hold him during intimacy was the absolute hardest part of being restrained. I wanted my hands all over his body.

He sighed into my touch and brushed his lips down my neck. His whispers and praises rolled through me like warm, salty water. They were healing; healing the marks on my ankles and wrists from the restraints. Healing my raw nipples, sensitive from his teeth and mouth. Healing my bruised ego and years of doubt and abuse from Jack and the whole movie industry.

He stood, going over to the bathroom sink and returning with my hairbrush. I swallowed, sitting up, anxiety tightening in my belly. "You're not leaving tonight, are you?"

His mouth tipped into a smile. "No. Not unless you prefer to sleep alone—"

"No. Stay with me. Please."

"Then, turn," he demanded with a light tap of the hairbrush onto my arm. I did as I was instructed, turning my back to him as he started pulling the brush through my hair in long strokes from root to tip. When he finished our ritual—brushing my hair, cleaning my face, applying my moisturizer—he pulled the covers of the bed back and we both slipped in beneath them, his arm draped across my

249

bare torso.

His expression shifted, uncertainty tightening the lines around his eyes. "Are you okay?" he asked and even there in the dark, I could see the brilliant green of his eyes.

"I'm wonderful," I answered. "Are you?"

"I feel the best I have in years," he said. "But I also know … I can be a bit much, especially for someone new to this. And if you need everything to stop … if you need to go home to Omar tomorrow, I understand."

I shook my head. "I don't want to leave. I like it here. I want to be here, with you. And it has nothing to do with your position in our industry and everything to do with your soul. Your heart." I placed my palm flat over his chest, feeling the rhythmic pounding of his heart against his ribs.

Is this real? My body felt so full, so pleasantly achy, like after you stuff yourself on an incredibly decadent meal. That's how Jude made me feel. Nourished and satisfied. He pulled me tighter against him and I watched as his face lifted in a serene smile.

"Good. So you'll be ready to resume training tomorrow." This time, it wasn't so much a question as it was a statement.

"I'll be there," I said, "with bells on."

CHAPTER TWENTY
Jude

THE NEXT DAY, I was shocked by Marly's transformation. She took to this lifestyle—my lifestyle—faster and better than I'd ever thought she would.

I watched as she paced the room while we rehearsed scenes as Leo and Holly, picking at her cuticles every time she forgot one of her lines and I chuckled inwardly. Nail biting. *An actress.* Actors and actresses were supposed to be perfect, flawless from our whitened teeth, to our manicured nails. But Marlena was perfectly imperfect. She was real. Which won out over the myth of 'perfection' any day.

Before I knew it, the day flew by in a whirlwind of rehearsals and role-playing scenarios.

She recited Holly's lines, her eyes bright blue as she looked at me through a web of thick, black lashes. "I'm not whips and chains. I'm sunshine and roses," she whispered.

I swallowed as I stared down at her. The lines were similar to a conversation we'd had a couple of days ago. There was a tightness in her jaw; a thickness to her voice. Was she even acting? The more time I spent with her, the more convinced I was that she was meant for this role. She was not only an incredible actor ... but she *was* Holly.

"If you are the sunshine ... then I am the shady tree," I said.

Her brows creased and she moved to where the script

sat on the table, flipping through the pages. "Those aren't the lines," she said.

"No. But maybe they should be." I cleared my throat, taking a sip of water and shaking the scene off. "Let's take a break."

Her chin lifted and she smiled at me, lowering to a seat on the edge of the bed. I could still smell the scent of her arousal clinging to the pillows and sheets from last night. Fuck. I took a deep breath. *Control yourself. Right now is work time ... play time is later.* She tugged her heels off and rubbed her arches, kneading them with her knuckles.

"You should wear your slippers," I said, laughing. "Why give yourself calf cramps for rehearsals?"

Marly sighed. "The right pair of shoes helps me get into character. It's stupid, I know." Then, she added with a gulp, "Jack used to make fun of me in rehearsals for it, too."

My eyebrow climbed at that. "Marly, I'm not making fun of you—"

She nodded, slipping the other shoe off and repeating the massage. "No, I know." She shrugged. "Jack found me ... amusing at best. I was less a girlfriend and more like a project to him." A breath seemed to shatter within her chest. That didn't sound like fun Dom/sub play ... that sounded borderline abusive. And I hated the way her voice cracked with the memory. "Like I said, I know it's stupid to rehearse in heels. And maybe it's superstition, but it works for me—"

"Marlena," I interrupted. "You know yourself. Better than anyone. And if a pair of shoes puts you in the role, then own that."

Marly snorted, rolling her eyes and continued massaging her foot.

I had no idea if I was getting through to her. "You know—my mom used to always read me a quote: When a bird sits in a tree, it never fears the branch breaking. Her trust is not on the branch but on her own wings. Believe in your wings, Marly. Believe in your process. And don't fucking believe an asshole like Jack. People like him … just want to clip your wings and keep you grounded." I knelt on the floor in front of her and put my hands on her legs. "But you're not meant for the ground."

"Jude—" When she lifted her eyes again, they were wide and wetter than an ocean's wave. "I need to tell you—with Jack and me, I know you've heard the rumors …" she cleared her throat. "That I only *dated* Jack to get the part in his movie. It's not true. Jack made all that up because he was pissed I dumped him after the premiere. Honestly, I only waited that long because my publicist told me it would be terrible PR to do it before the movie came out." Marly clicked her tongue, shaking her head and tore her eyes from me.

I *ha*d heard the rumors. Honestly, I hadn't given them much thought. For starters, it was Los Angeles. Not that I approved of it, but people switched husbands and lovers like they were test driving cars. But Marly was different; there was an innocence to her. It was practically like pulling teeth to convince her to come to LnS with me in the first place. Maybe I was wrong about her, she didn't seem the type to use her sexuality to get ahead.

I broke the heavy silence. "I never believed a damn thing that man said."

"You know Jack?"

I shook my head. "Not really. But knowing you," I

paused, swallowing. "Well, let's just say that you don't come across as a woman who does this sort of thing often."

Heat flooded her cheeks and freckles the color of caramel splattered across her skin. I wasn't even sure what I meant by that cryptic message. Taking lessons from an incredibly strange man in a room that had more security than the Pentagon? Having incredible sex with someone she knew less than a week?

"Thank you," she whispered, wringing her hands in her lap.

"Look, last night was incredible. I think *you're* incredible. But if this doesn't work out, I can be professional on set. And if you prefer to end this now to avoid having to work with someone you're involved with—"

"That's not what I want."

My heart slammed into my ribs. "It's not what I want, either. But I'd understand. I'd hate to think you felt coerced into something—"

"No," she said, her voice stronger than I'd heard it all morning. "I don't feel that way at all. I wanted you last night. I still want you now." We froze, our breath severe and sharp and our faces only inches apart. I held her eyes, hypnotized by them and I couldn't resist a taste. Even though playtime was supposed to come later, I was helplessly drawn to her. Helpless, like a blade of grass in the middle of a hurricane. And she was tearing through my soul, destroying me.

I slanted my mouth over hers and she tasted—Jesus, she tasted incredible. I glided my tongue into her mouth and she opened to me. Her arms wrapped around my neck, clawing, pulling me tighter against her and her ankles hooked around my hips. Her bare heels prodded into the small of my back, urging me for more. And I was desperate to give her more.

But not right now, I thought, ending the kiss. We still had work to do. Work which could be playtime too.

She brushed her fingers across her lips, blinking, smiling at me. "Can I ask you something?" she questioned.

"Of course."

"I get why you went through all this trouble this week to avoid acting with Layla again," she said. "I don't know exactly what happened, but …"

"But you saw that TMZ report two years ago, didn't you?" I pushed off my knees and sat next to her on the bed.

"Yeah," she said. Her forehead puckered, and her mouth turned down at the corners. "But as you said … celebrity gossip is hardly ever accurate."

I shrugged. "Well, that one *was* pretty accurate, actually."

"You didn't know me at all that day at the first audition. So why would you trust me with your Rolex, Jude. That's … that's not normal."

"Normal." I hated that word. "No … I guess it wasn't normal behavior. But is it so weird that my gut told me I could trust you?"

She arched her eyebrow and gave me a look. No, not just a look, but *that* look. The one that said *yeah, it* is *so weird.* "The problem is," I said, trying again, "I've always trusted my gut … but I haven't always listened to it. When I was eighteen, I asked the most popular girl in school to prom. Jenny Weaver. She was head cheerleader, homecoming queen, basically every guy wanted her. I asked her, thinking no way in hell she'd say yes … but she did. And even though my gut told me I should have been going to prom with my best friend—the girl I'd grown up next to since I was five—I didn't listen to it. I went with Jenny. And she ended up leaving prom with her ex-boyfriend, not me."

Marly nodded, her expression lifting. "So, you learned to listen to your gut," she said.

I snorted. "You would have thought I'd have learned, wouldn't you? That watch I gave you was my father's. My family wasn't all that wealthy when I was a kid. My dad worked hard, but he was just an elementary school teacher. And my mom was a college professor, which contrary to popular belief, doesn't earn that much. Even so, we were comfortable. But any money we had as a family got shuffled into my mom's campaigns. Running for office takes a lot of money. And it takes even more time. They were always out—at events for charity and fundraisers."

"That must have been hard."

I shrugged. "Maybe. But I also grew up watching a strong woman work hard to achieve her dreams. My dad always talked about wanting a Rolex. He had this mason jar where he saved every extra bit of money he had. He started it before he was even married and I remember seeing him dump spare change into it every night from his pockets when he got home from school. Then when I was eight, my mom started her first city council campaign. He came downstairs with his jar of money and gave her his Rolex savings so she could afford to print lawn signs." I smiled at the memory, sighing and falling back against the wall, the comforter wrinkling around my legs. "That year for Christmas, my mom sold her wedding gown to buy my dad that watch. And I remember watching them on Christmas morning as my father opened his gift—he cried. I'd never seen my dad cry before. He held my mother as tears fell down her cheeks, too. And later that night, he told me to find a woman who would sell her wedding gown to make me happy. But in turn, I better be just as willing to give up a piece of myself for her." My fingers trailed over the bare skin at my wrist. The skin there was paler than the rest of my arm.

"Okay ..."

"The point is—I chose incorrectly. My dad gave me clear cut advice. Marry someone genuine and kind. Someone who understands the give and take of a relationship. And I married Layla. My gut told me I shouldn't. My gut was screaming at me on our wedding day that something felt off. But I thought it was nervous jitters. I should have listened to it. When she left me, I swore I would always trust my gut."

"Can I ask ..." Marlena started speaking, but quickly dropped her head.

I reached out, blanketing her hands with my palm. "You can ask whatever you need to," I said quietly.

She blinked, looking up, her eyes a shimmering, bright blue. "What did she do? You've mentioned a few times that she cheated?"

I gulped. "Her one goal was to use me to break into Hollywood. And I was dumb enough to think it was love. She required public everything in her submissive contract. She wanted to share, but that's where I drew the line. She didn't care about my lines though ... my limits. She was fucking every studio head and producer she could."

Marly gasped and when I slid a glance to her, she was covering her mouth. "I'm so sorry. I mean, I saw the footage a while back of ..."

"Yeah, I know. Everyone saw. Eventually, she started cheating on me with the President of Gary Brothers Studios ... she leveled up. And instead of ending our three-year marriage in a respectful way, she sold the footage of her and him to TMZ. Ash knows one of the production editors over there and managed to tell me before it aired, so I wasn't quite so blindsided. I was panicked, freaking out ... I rushed down to their offices, screaming at every production assistant working to give me that footage ... There was a studio tour happening. Everyone got pictures and videos. I made a fool of myself. It ended up as part of the story."

"That's why you panicked when the studio tour came through Silhouette?"

I nodded, hating that I still couldn't handle those stupid tours. "Yes. And that's why I'm helping you. This film could be amazing. I think you're the best actress for the part. And if I have to act beside Layla and pretend that we're in love—" My voice broke and I went to the sink, turning it on simply to give myself something to do. I washed my hands, flicking a glance to Marly in the mirror. "I can't do it. And there would go any hope of the film winning any sort of best actor nods for me. I'm good, but I'm not that good."

Marly's wet eyes glistened from the other end of the room, and my stomach clenched. "You remind me a lot of my mom. You're the kind of woman that a man could give his life savings to help achieve your dreams. I want to see your dreams come true."

I trusted my gut this time. Marlena would never climb those social ladders. It was how I knew Jack was a lying piece of shit. I knew from personal experience the kind of women who would fuck to get ahead. And Marlena Taylor? That girl simply wasn't the type.

Spinning away from the mirror, I turned to face her and helped her to feet. She stared at me, her cheeks flushed, mouth wet and parted, her eyes shrewd. "You seem like the kind of man I would sell my wedding gown for."

I closed my eyes, my chest squeezing at her admission. Did she mean it? It was too early in our relationship. Way too early to be feeling this intense. But I could see us in the future. Could see Marlena in a simple white dress, a small wedding at my parent's Montana ranch. No fanfare. Just us. A couple of rings. And a lot of love. I could see her belly swollen with my child. I could see her coming home from filming, just in time to help me tuck the kids into bed. I wanted to give her everything.

I opened my eyes and found her still staring at me. But giving her everything she wanted? It began with this role. Right now, that was what she wanted. And I was going to make sure she got it. Even if I had to destroy myself to do so.

Leaning down, I lightly brushed my mouth over hers. "You ready to continue the lesson?"

She nodded, tilting her head.

"Good." I stepped back, releasing her hands. "Undress."

CHAPTER TWENTY-ONE

Marly

I STOOD THERE, completely nude in front of Jude who was still fully dressed in his flat front slacks and crisp button-down shirt. It hung open, revealing the 'V' where his throat melted into his muscular chest. The sight of him, even fully clothed, left me panting. Wanting. Desiring.

He circled me, not touching, but I could feel his gaze just as surely as if it were his fingers skimming along my heated flesh. His eyes flashed as they slid down over my breasts and landed between my legs. I resisted the urge to cover myself. To squirm. But a hot blush over my cheeks and neck gave me away.

"Fuck, you're gorgeous," he said. I could hear the adoration—the lust—in his voice, deep and graveled. His jaw flexed as he walked in a circle behind me. I closed my eyes, shivering despite his hot breath on the back of my neck. "You know what you do to me, right?" he asked.

He stepped so close to me, that his cotton-clad erection brushed against the bare, sensitive flesh of my ass. I whimpered and nodded, then cried out as something whipped against the backs of my thighs.

I yelped, my body jerking in response.

What the hell was that?

"That's not how you answer your Dom, Poppy."

I swallowed as he continued pacing, circling me until

he was back in my field of vision, in front of me. "Yes, Sir," I whispered.

"Better," he said. His voice was different somehow. Jude in Dominant mode was deeper, raspier. More raw, like potent, undiluted testosterone. He oozed sex and power in a way that had my knees trembling and weak.

In his hand, he clutched the leather riding crop, similar to the one Ash had used last night. I gulped, my throat going drier than a bale of hay left out in a Los Angeles drought.

"Eyes stay straight ahead," he said. "What are your safe words?"

"Planner for stop. Sticker for slow down ... Sir."

"Good girl, Poppy." His voice was hoarse as he praised me.

He smacked the insides of my thighs with the leather crop. "Spread," he said, and I immediately complied, wet heat pooling between my legs. My clit was swollen and achy and my sex throbbed, begging for any contact he was willing to give. But I knew better than to ask. He would give me what I needed. Jude wouldn't tease me only to not deliver. If there was anything I had learned this week, it was that. As my Dominant, he had my best interest in mind; he had my pleasure in mind. Even if pleasure meant a little pain beforehand.

He continued circling, and with my eyes straight ahead, after a couple of steps, he was once more out of sight. "Normally, I use the riding crop as punishment for my submissives," he explained. "Normally, it's a means of discipline. But you, my gorgeous, scarlet Poppy ... I've learned you seem to enjoy the punishments. Which means for you as my submissive, it doesn't quite work the same way. Am I right? Do you enjoy a little bit of pain?"

I had never considered myself a masochist. It seemed so … depraved. But I couldn't deny that when Jude spanked me that first night, my panties flooded. "Yes, Sir … at least, I think so." Then I added, "With you."

He gave an approving hiss. "Have you ever been spanked before me?"

I shook my head. Another smack, this time on my other thigh. I yelped, a satisfied cry. It hurt—and yet it felt so fucking good. "No, Sir," I corrected.

Jude chuckled. "I'm so used to administering pain for punishment, but for all I know, you're intentionally answering incorrectly because you like getting hit. Is that why you keep forgetting to answer with 'Sir?'"

"No, Sir," I said quickly. "I'm just not used to it yet."

Thwack! This time on my left ass. I moaned as the sting lessened, melting into a buzzing bliss on my backside. "But you enjoy it? The so-called punishments?" He circled to the front once more, staring directly into my eyes as he awaited my answer.

"Yes, Sir. But I enjoy pleasing you more."

He shuddered. Visibly shuddered as a smile curved at the corners of his full, lush lips. "That makes me so fucking happy."

Thwack! He smacked the crop against one nipple, then the other. It was the hardest hit yet and the feeling whipped down my core to my pussy. My nipples stung, the aftershocks tightening my belly and the pain melting into a simmering euphoria. My breath caught. An intense need to move, to squirm overtook me and I locked my knees to stop myself from shaking. A single drop of arousal slid down the inside of my thigh. Like a two-headed dragon fighting with itself, I was turned on and ashamed all at once. My calves knotted into tight little balls as I curled my toes against the carpet.

The corner of the riding crop dragged slowly against my inner thigh, catching the drop of arousal. Jude brought the rectangular riding crop to his mouth and licked where he had caught my cream.

His mouth turned in a quick smile that vanished almost instantly. "Delicious," he whispered, his eyes blazing. Then without warning, the crop sliced through the air, landing hard against my clit. I cried out, my hips bucking with the sharp, tight sensation that sent pleasure jolting down my legs. My knees gave out and I landed on all fours on the floor, panting ... quivering.

"Up," Jude demanded in a sharp tone. I dug the pads of my fingers into the carpet and even though my legs were wobbly, I pushed to my feet, taking a deep breath and spreading my legs once more.

Even though I was staring straight ahead, my vision was blurred; I was so aroused, I literally couldn't see straight. My pussy clenched, craving that again. The sudden, hard contact was enough to have me throbbing for more.

"Did you like that?" he asked, and there was genuine interest in his voice.

"Yes, Sir," I panted.

"Good." He stroked his hand through my hair, gently brushing his fingers beneath my eyes where mascara-laden tears streaked down my cheeks. I wasn't crying—at least, it didn't feel like the sort of tears I was used to. They weren't tears of sadness or even joy—it was simply too much emotion. Too much too soon and I wasn't able to process everything I was feeling. "When I do something that makes you feel good, what do you say?"

Without thinking, I glanced sideways at Jude. *Thwack, thwack!* He smacked each nipple. "Let's try that again," he said. "If someone gives you a gift, you say …"

"Thank you," I said. The quivers of excitement had morphed into full-on shivers now and my body was convulsing with need. Never in my life had I felt this turned on. *This alive.*

"And when it's *me* who is giving you that gift … what do you add to that?"

"Thank you, Sir."

I wanted to sneak a glance at his cock. I wanted to see how hard he was. To get a glimpse of whether or not his cock was straining against that proper suit of his.

When the crop came down, it smacked against my belly. Each hit went lower and lower down my abdomen, over my pelvis, until he smacked the crop against my clit once more. This time when it reached my bundle of nerves, I braced for it. Was ready for the jolt of pleasure and pain. It was like a current of electricity surging through my whole body. I moaned with it and immediately thanked Jude for the gift.

"Turn," he said. "Bend over, grasp the edge of the bed and spread your legs."

I did exactly what he said, completely exposing myself to him; bare and vulnerable in a way that was utterly intoxicating. Though I couldn't see Jude, I felt his greedy gaze on me, burning me from behind. Blood rushed in my head, my pulse pounding in my ears. Waiting. Anticipating.

"You only have to thank me at the end," Jude said.

"The end?" I turned to look at him and in one swift

motion, he had his hand wrapped in my hair. The sharp bite of his fingers at my roots made me gasp as he tugged my face forward. My nipples grew even tighter, my breasts heavy and achy.

"Eyes ahead," he said roughly.

Then with no warning, the crop came down hard against my spread pussy. Each hit managed to connect with a slightly different area of my sex. Behind me, I heard Jude's satisfied grunts with each hit, and a ripple of heat snapped through my body. Everything was so sensitive—heightened. My sharp breath punctuated the sound of leather slapping flesh. My skin erupted in a fiery burn that was somehow diffusing and melting into velvety bliss. My traitorous body should be in pain, and yet all I could feel was the sensation of pleasure. My pussy was drenched, my clit full and hard. Out of reflex, I bucked my hips against the hit, leaning more into it and my wails echoed within the room. I heard his zipper behind me, then the soft rustle of his pants falling to the floor and the sound of a wrapper tearing. I was desperate to see him, to feel him. The feeling of release was right there in front of me, like a beast, ready to claw up my core. I was wet and aching and my pussy was ignited in more ways than one. Climax was just out of reach—ready to explode within me; ready to buck my hips and curl my toes.

"Are you going to come?" Jude asked, as he resumed hitting my sex with the riding crop.

"Yes, Sir. Please, may I?" I managed to cry out.

"When? Tell me when you're going to."

"Any second now. I can't hold on," I said. "Please—"

"*Come,* Poppy."

The moment the words left his lips, I felt that undeniable clench of my core. "I'm coming," I panted as my orgasm crashed over me like a rogue wave. He plunged his cock inside of me just as I released around him. My pussy convulsed against his unbearably thick length, rippling as he sunk deeper, harder inside of me. Then he withdrew, hard and fast, pumping in and out of me as I held onto the bedpost with clenched hands. My knees quivered, my thighs tightening as each one of his sensational strokes extended the orgasm. I screamed, as the blissful shocks receded into mere flutters. Even in the wake of my climax, I still throbbed for him, yearning for more.

His fingers bit into my ass, clenching my tender flesh with his grasp, and his hips wedged between my spread legs. He plunged in and out of me furiously in hard, punishing thrusts that slammed his cock against the wall of my cervix. Those same hands that were gripping my hips and ass so hard, swept over my body in long caressing strokes.

Together we were all sweat and skin and pure, undiluted lust. Both of our grunts filled the otherwise silent room.

His fingers glided over the side of my hip and clamped down on my clit once more. The stroke of his skilled finger was such a contrast to the riding crop—it was just too much. "I-I can't. Not again," I whispered and shook my head, gripping the bedpost tighter.

"That phrase doesn't exist within these walls," Jude said. "You remember what you say if you need me to stop or slow down, right?"

I nodded and my body shuddered, my pussy clenching beneath his fingers. I was achy and tight, and the feeling was right on the edge of being so good that it physically hurt.

"So, do you have something you need to say to me right now?"

My body had never been so responsive, so sensitive to sensations. It was an intensity I wasn't prepared for … but it also wasn't bad. Actually, it was good. *Really* fucking good. Jude would take care of me. He wouldn't leave me needing and wanting without the payoff. With a deep breath, I shook my head no.

Hot air hit the back of my neck in a deliciously agonizing way as he whispered, "Then just let go, Poppy." His fingers moved against my clit once more, clamping it, and stars flooded my vision. I gripped the bedpost tighter, my thigh muscles shaking with suppressed need. My spin curved, arching into the bewildering pleasure.

It shouldn't feel this good. Being hit with a riding crop—being ordered around, commanded, owned. Slamming into me from behind, Jude was in a frenzy, thrusting wildly.

"Oh, fuck, Marlena," he moaned. That was all it took. My pulse raced as another orgasm peaked, shattering through me.

His cock plunged inside once more in a final deep thrust. He jerked, his body shuddering as he groaned my name, grinding into his own climax. I could feel his release deep inside my body, despite the condom. Feel his pulsing euphoria in rhythm with my own.

His forehead fell to my back, and he pressed a lingering kiss to my spine before reaching up and taking my hands in his, pulling me away from the bent position I'd been in. Lifting me in his arms, he laid us onto the bed, stroking my hair and kissing me, murmuring "Good girl, Poppy," over and over again.

I melted against his lips, against his strong arms beneath my body, letting my weight fall into the tender strokes of his hand through my hair. My body shook violently; the tremors rocking through me, uncontrollably.

I lifted my gaze to find Jude composed in that way he always was. His eyes were closed, his lashes black against the tanned skin of his sharp cheekbone. My shivering muscles slowly subsided and I allowed Jude's calm demeanor to seep into me. The hypnotizing rhythm of his fingers brushing through my hair calmed me with each stroke.

I felt so ... alive. Like for the first time in years, the pieces of my heart that Jack shattered were being glued back together again.

On the outside, I was welted, red and bruised in areas that I'd never thought to explore. But on the inside? I was invigorated and nourished. He had given me something precious. The ability to let go of control. He had gifted me with a way of releasing the tension of constant worry and concern and the militant organization my father had pushed on me all those years. I loved my dad—with all my heart. But he was wrong. Giving the man I loved control of my body wasn't shameful. It was sexy and I *enjoyed* it. It didn't make me any less of a feminist or any less empowered. And really, I held the cards here—Jude couldn't take something I wasn't willing to give. If I used my safe word, all playtime ended. *I* had the ultimate control.

"So, Poppy ... what do you say to me after that?"

I inhaled deeply and closed my eyes. "Thank you, Sir."

CHAPTER TWENTY-TWO
Marly

THE NEXT DAY, I knelt on the floor with a pillow Jude gave me tucked beneath my bad knees. And I was fully naked in the center of the room. My new set of Ben Wa balls were deep inside my pussy, pressing against my knotted bundle of nerves. With every wiggle, every little movement, they rolled over my g-spot, causing me to gasp. My hands were behind my back, my forehead was against the plush carpet and a blindfold shielded my eyes.

Jude had left a while ago—I had no way of knowing how long. Maybe fifteen minutes? The only thing I had to go on was how my knees ached from being in that position, and the tiny bite at my shoulder joints from keeping my hands tucked at the small of my back.

Finally, the side door from Jude's room creaked open and heavy footsteps thudded behind me. "Poppy," Jude said. "You can stand up." I released my hands, my fingers chilled from the lack of circulation, then pushed to my feet.

Jude's hands curled on my elbows, guiding me, ensuring my balance.

"Where are we going?" I asked.

"We just have one more exercise for the day," Jude said.

"I don't know if I can handle any more lessons for today," I said.

I couldn't see a thing beyond the black eye mask pressing against my closed eyes. But behind me, Jude stopped walking. Stopped prodding me forward. His grip on my elbow tightened ever so briefly. After a moment's silence, his gruff voice whispered in my ear, "I think this exercise will be good for you. But if you'd rather wait, and do it another day, then use your safe word." His lips brushed against the curve of where my neck met my shoulder. "I've told you before ... use your safe word. Marly. That's what it's there for."

"But sometimes I need to talk through what I'm feeling. I'm not sure if I even *want* to use my safe word yet."

He let out a jagged breath, and his thumb circled the sensitive skin at my elbow. "On one hand, you are a natural at this. There is some innate part of you that so fundamentally connects to Holly and to being a submissive, that it's almost reflexive ... right?"

My stomach tensed. Goosebumps raced down my arms and I could practically feel them raising against Jude's flattened palms. I thought of my dad, how ashamed he would be of me, but I couldn't ignore this side of myself any longer. For years I tried to compensate for it. Buried myself in structure; in organization. My yearly planners were like siblings I never had. One came every year in my Christmas stocking. They played such a pivotal role in my life and in my relationships. They made me feel like I had control, even if it was completely in my head. And in less than a week, Jude had managed to crumble it. "Yes, Sir."

Tension melted from my shoulders with the admission. "I saw it in you," Jude said. "That very first day we met, outside of the audition room. I saw it in the way your gaze wouldn't meet mine. I saw it in the way you dropped your chin, clenched your hands into fists, and the way your cheeks turned an adorable shade of pink. But the real clincher? Was when you saved me from that tour coming through. You saw my discomfort, and you reacted quickly, absorbing the attention for me. That quality, that ability to read me, doesn't just make you a phenomenal submissive … it makes you a phenomenal partner."

His words crashed through my body and a sweet jolting sensation shimmied over my flesh. It wasn't until that moment that I realized how hard I was chewing on the inside of my cheek. His hands gently slid up my arms, then down again, as if his movements could rub away my goosebumps. "But why? Why am I like this?" I asked. It was like there were two versions of myself, and they were so different, yet so similar, that they were like twins.

"Does there need to be a reason? If it feels good, and the relationship is established with trust and consent, then who cares about silly definitions of right and wrong?"

There was such certainty in his words, in his stance, that his confidence punched through to my core. "Right. That little matter of trust you keep talking about," I said.

"Which brings us back full circle to your safe word," Jude said. "Because you can be Marlena—who is in control—a Type-A planner-using woman by day, and Poppy—who is submissive—and enjoys unbidden ground-shattering BDSM fun by night. But if you don't learn to use your safe words, we'll never get there." His voice grew louder as he circled in front of me, lacing his fingers into mine. "Surrender yourself to me," Jude said. "Surrender yourself to the lifestyle. Stop overthinking and relax into who you really are." He leaned in closer, his minty breath hot as he whispered. "The truth is, even when we're playing … even though I'm the Dominant … *you* still have all the control here. You dictate when we stop. When we go. How far we go. How intense playtime is. And part of the game is I do my best to read your signals so that I can get just to that line without crossing it. *That's* what's so fun."

"You make it sound so sexy."

He lifted my fingers and pressed a kiss to my knuckles with his warm mouth. "It's the truth. *You* are in total control ... it just looks like I am. And right now, I don't see a submissive who can't handle one more exercise. I see a submissive whose cheeks are flushed, whose lips are wet, whose nipples are hard, and who is using exhaustion as an excuse to back away from the lesson. But if I'm wrong, and you really do need a break, then use your safe word. I think I'm good at reading you, but only you truly know yourself. Using your safe word will never make me disappointed in you. If you use it right this second, I won't think any less of you. Do you understand?"

"Yes, Sir." My fears slipped away. There were so many of them, I could hardly keep track anymore. Fear of not seeming strong enough. Fear of intimacy. Fear of trust. But deep inside of me, Jude managed to unravel something. His reassurances stripped me bare. These feelings were no longer my deep, dark secret. Jude had lifted the rock and shined a light on all those dark, ugly things I thought I needed to keep hidden. Not only that, but he saw the beauty in them and helped me see their beauty, too. He put them out there and not only still loved me for them, but was willing to go on the ride with me. "I'm ready to continue the lesson. And I'll use my safe word if I need to."

"Okay then. For this exercise ... you have to trust me. Trust that I will take care of you."

I released a long, slow breath and nodded. "Yes, Sir."

Then we were moving once more. I was aware of every little brush of his hands against my naked flesh. Every little breeze that tickled my goose-pebbled skin. It was so weird to be so exposed on such a regular basis. To be naked, literally and figuratively when Jude stood there, nudging me forward, very much still clothed.

"Reach out your hand," he said.

I tilted my head, not able to help my smirk. I reached out, expecting to come in contact with a choice body part of Jude's. Only instead, my hand connected with the front door.

I pressed my fingertips to the smooth, painted wood and shrugged. "Okay," I said, drawing out the syllables.

"Find the doorknob … and open it."

His words swam in my murky mind and it felt like I was submerged underwater. I must have heard him wrong. He'd been so clear—sharing was his hard limit. And mine, too. I opened my mouth to object, then in light of our recent conversation, snapped it shut.

This was an exercise in trust. I needed to trust him. Or if it was too much, I needed to use my safe word. So was this too much? Maybe he had arranged something with the club. Had asked that no one exit their rooms for this window of time. Whatever it was, Jude would not betray a hard limit. Ever. I trusted him enough to know this. But he would push the boundaries.

Sliding my hand along the door, my breathing was sharp and short, echoing the erratic beats of my heart. I found the doorknob and turned, pulling the door open.

His lips brushed against my neck, sending waves of pleasure undulating down to my belly and my wet cunt squeezed the Ben Wa balls within my body. "Good girl, Poppy," he praised and that approval was an even bigger hit of pleasure than his lips were.

He guided me through the open door, two steps into the hallway. My bare feet were cold against the tile floors—such a stark difference to the warm, soft carpet inside my room.

I swallowed, the tension of my throat taking hold of other areas of my body. *Trust him, trust him, trust him,* a little voice chanted inside of me. He would never allow someone else to see my naked body. *Jude doesn't share.*

But just as the thought crossed through my mind, I heard footsteps. Fast and assured, they walked right by us in high heels. Chloe maybe?

I whimpered and out of instinct took a step back, connecting with Jude's firm body. He caught me, his fingers digging into the flesh at my waist. "Breathe, Poppy," he said. "And trust me."

"Hey, Jude," a voice said. Chloe. Yes, it was definitely Chloe.

My face twisted, and even though I wore the blindfold, I opened my eyes—still unable to see anything.

"Hi, Chloe," Jude said back. Maybe when he said he didn't share, he meant with other men? But he did share with women.

Oh, God. I was going to have to clarify that—no threesomes, not with men, not with women, not with Chloe, and *definitely* not with Pixie—Eve ... whatever her name was.

His hand skimmed across my belly, trailing lower over my body until his fingers brushed between my legs.

I whimpered, my traitorous sex twitching at the first

signs of attention. "Sticker," I whispered.

Jude moved his hand away from my sex, resting it on the outer edge of my hip bone. "Are you okay?" he asked, and Chloe's high-heeled steps became softer as she walked away from us.

I blurted out, "When I said sharing was my hard limit, I meant with everyone. Women, men, everyone."

Jude chuckled. "Me, too."

"Then what the hell—"

"Do you want the game to stop?"

"I don't want anyone to see me naked."

"I know your fears, Poppy. And I would never push you beyond your limits. But I might just push you right to the line." He kissed my jaw, his lips lingering there. "If you get the part of Holly, a lot of people are going to see you naked."

I swallowed hard, my breath becoming solid and heavy. Fuck. He was right. Everyone would see my body. There would be screenshots all over the internet. Memes. Who knows what else.

"Do you want to stop?" he asked. His arms slid around me, embracing me from behind. "I'm proud of you with either decision."

A trembling exhale tore from my lungs and I shook my head. "No. Let's continue."

Jude hugged me a few moments longer before releasing me from his hold. "Take one more step forward," he demanded. "Then spread your legs."

I did as he said, my sex pulsing with excitement, despite how nervous I felt. I froze as I heard more footsteps. This time, more than one set. Jude's fingers moved between my legs once more. This time, I surrendered to the intense jolt of pleasure. It felt so wrong. So sexy. He gathered my juices and used my own arousal to circle over my clit. Inside me, with his fingers and the Ben Wa balls, I felt full, and as the blood rushed lower in my body, I tightened my muscles.

"Hey, Jude," a man's voice said. This one, I didn't recognize.

"David," Jude said.

"Baby girl, say hello to Jude," the man said.

"Hello, Sir." This time, a woman's voice. And she had some sort of baby-ish voice that made me cringe.

Their footsteps faded down the hall and I relaxed into the game. I wasn't sure how he was doing it, but there was no way these strangers could see me. Jude would never allow that to happen. I smiled to myself as Jude's fingers flicked at my clit faster, circling over me and my nerve endings sprang to life.

"Are you going to cum like a good girl for me?" Jude whispered. His hot breath rushed against my ear and neck and I shivered as his other hand found my nipple.

"Yes, Sir."

More footsteps. Only now, I was more turned on than before. My breathing increased, in short sharp pants. *A recording.* That must be how he's doing this. I smiled wider and my eyes cinched from beneath the blindfold. *Yes!* He must have recorded the footsteps and this dialogue earlier and all these voices were just some prearranged prank to teach me about trust.

That's why I wasn't being addressed directly. Why no one was talking to me.

"Jude," it was Ash's voice this time and he sounded startled.

"Hi, Ash," Jude said, plunging his fingers inside of me.

He hit the Ben Wa balls and the pressure mounted, pushing against the inner walls of my pussy. A moan escaped my lips at the welcomed intrusion and Jude rolled my nipple harder between his fingers, pinching, then whispering in my ear, "Do not make a noise of pleasure. Or pain. You only speak if spoken to."

"Um … Hi, Marly," Ash said, hesitancy in his voice. No doubt part of the recording.

"Hi, Ash," I said, almost giggling at the absurdity of it all.

Smack! Jude's palm connected hard with my ass. "That's not how you address another Dominant at LnS, Poppy."

"Hello … Sir," I tried again.

"Eve, say hello," Ash demanded. I froze, my knees locking. Eve? Pixie was here?

"Well, hello again," Eve said, her voice smooth and calculating.

"Eve," Jude said, his voice was tight and his hands paused over my body.

No way. There was no way Jude would have asked Eve to be a part of that recording. Not with how he reacted to seeing her the other night. His fingers had slowed against my clit, but he quickly resumed. Only now, my arousal was once again being replaced with the fear. The mistrust.

"I like your choker," Eve said, "I mean, I'm surprised Jude went with an antique cameo, rather than leather—"

"Ash," Jude growled a warning.

"Come on, Eve," Ash snarled. "You're going to pay for that one."

My hand flew to my throat and my fingers brushed over the choker. *It wasn't a recording.* There was no way that was prearranged. Which meant ... oh, God. Did Eve and Ash just see me naked? Here with Jude's fingers inside of me. My throat closed and my mind raced as tears rose from deep in my chest. "Planner," I said. "Planner ... I-I need to know that this isn't real—"

"Okay," Jude said quietly. "Breathe, Poppy. Good girl." And with the soft, crooning praise, he tugged the blindfold off. My body was shaking violently and I blinked as light flooded my vision.

In front of me was a divider ... an old dressing room divider with blacked out sections, blocking us from the hallway. My chest collapsed with the heavy exhale and a single relieved tear sprung from my eye. "I knew it was something," I said, exhaling a long, low breath. "I knew you wouldn't have let me be just ... out here. Like this." I gestured down at my body and Jude slipped a robe over my shoulders. Sliding my arms inside, I hugged it tightly around myself as Jude slid the divider open, allowing us to walk around the other side.

"I was setting this all up while you were inside the room, kneeling on the floor," Jude said, taking my hand and guiding me. We stopped on the other side of the divider and Jude curled his arms around me, cradling my body with his. On the other side, facing the hallway were large signs, instructing passersby on what they could say to us, including complimenting me on the antique Victorian Cameo choker. *That's* how Eve knew. "It's what we call a mind phuque," Jude explained. "A way of playing a game that's like a trust fall—only more intense."

"And I failed." I clenched my fists until my short nails dug into the palms of my hands.

"You didn't fail," Jude said, taking my shoulders and

looking in my eyes. "This isn't a clear win-lose scenario. It's all to continue building our relationship. You did *great,* Poppy. You were calm and collected and … tell me the truth … it was a little fun, right?"

My smile twitched. "A little. Until Eve came."

Jude's expression soured and he sighed. "Yeah. Ash will handle her for that. But technically, she didn't do anything wrong. She read what I put on the cue cards." He laced his hand into mine and gently tugged me back into our room, then folded up the dividers and dragged them inside as well.

I watched him carefully. What the hell was up with Eve? Was she his rebound after Layla?

"Why is Eve so interested in you?" *And me.*

Jude's gaze jerked up from the dividers. "She isn't."

Yeah, right. "Okay …" I said, trying again. "You can't possibly think that I don't see the weirdness between you two?"

He shut the door behind him and sighed. "Look … I was a really bad Dom to her."

I swallowed the lump forming at the apex of my throat and it went down hard to my stomach. "What do you mean?" Jude was so responsible. So calmly in control at all times. It was hard to imagine him as anything but responsible. He didn't answer—he simply leaned forward, placing his palm against the wall. "Did you hurt her?" I pressed.

"Not physically, no," he said, still facing the wall.

"Did you not stop with her safe word?"

"Of course not," he snarled. "I always respect the safe word."

"Then what? What did you do to make her hate you so

much?"

"I tried to force her to be someone she's not."

I was silent, waiting for more of an explanation. But it never came. "Someone like ... Layla?" I pushed. I knew I shouldn't. I could see his discomfort, even though he was good at hiding it. And part of a submissive's job was to look out for the well-being of her Dominant—but wasn't part of his job to be open and communicative with me, too? I gulped. We were both failing—already.

"Yes."

"You don't want to talk about it?" I prodded more.

"No."

More silence. I never thought that silence could be deafening—but this was. The silence was actually *loud*, roaring between us. "Okay," I said, taking a careful step toward him. Jude eyed me warily, his gaze never once leaving mine. "I can drop this for now ... *if* you promise me that you will eventually tell me the whole truth there."

His jaw ticked and I could practically *feel* him thinking.

"I deserve to know your whole story," I said. "It's part of this trust thing going both ways."

With that, his stony expression softened. His down-turned mouth lifted briefly into something that could *almost* be called a smile. With a sigh, he said, "I promise I'll tell you everything. Just not right now. As you can imagine, it's not fun reliving some of your darkest moments."

I nodded, but didn't press the issue anymore. He knew where I stood; he promised to tell me. That was all I needed for now. "So what's next on our agenda?"

That almost smile curved into an actual smile and he stepped into me, pressing his lips gently to mine. "I'm going to tuck you in for a much needed—very earned nap.

And when you wake up, you're going to get dressed up for me. Chloe brought some clothes for you to wear. I took the liberty of hanging them in your closet and there's a small bag of makeup on the counter. Put that on, along with that wig you brought."

"My wig?" I drew back and his arms at the small of my back held me firmly in place. "I thought you said I had no use for that within these walls."

"And I meant that," he said. "But we're not staying inside these walls. Tonight, we're taking this downstairs to the LnS Club."

CHAPTER TWENTY-THREE
Marly

A FEW HOURS later, I was rested and dressed, spinning in front of the full-length mirror on the inside closet door. I gasped for breath, looking at my reflection. *Literally* gasped for breath. The black leather corset was so tight, I couldn't take a deep breath if I wanted to.

Leather. Eve's voice from last night echoed in my mind. *Sweetheart, for months that man had been seen with only brunettes. They had to wear leather. And they always wore the same stupid red shade of lipstick.* With the wig and the leather—I was two-thirds of the way there.

Was he dressing me to look like Layla? No. No, that was crazy. And I was the one who brought the wig to LnS, not Jude.

I gave another turn in the mirror, looking at my ass in the short leather skirt. *Holy shit*, I barely recognized myself. But that was sort of the point. If we were going in public, no one could recognize me or else we were both in deep shit.

The leather was smooth beneath my palm as I ran my hand down my corseted waist. My waist was cinched, creating that all-too-alluring hour glass shape. The short skirt was complimented by thigh-high black stockings and a seam that went up the back. I wore a scrap of fabric that I supposed some women would call underwear ... though, honestly, I might as well have gone commando. My gaze flicked down my legs, and I closed my eyes, picturing Jude's face. All sexy stern mouth, thick brown hair, and chiseled jaw. Between my legs, my panties grew slick—at this rate they'd be soaked before I ever left the room. When I opened my eyes, I truly didn't recognize the girl standing in front of me—but my reflection grinned wickedly back at me. Then I shimmied out of the thong, giving a quick check in the mirror to make sure I wasn't exposed in the short skirt and thigh-highs.

I moved to the sink to finish my makeup. Grabbing a tube of lipstick, I swallowed, turning it over in my hands. *Sunlit Poppy.* In other words... *red. Dark wig. Leather clothes. Red lips.* I dropped the lipstick and it clattered as it hit the porcelain sink. There was no way I was putting that lipstick on. No fucking way. A thought hit me hard like a bucket of ice water in the face. *What if he only came up with the nickname Poppy because it was Layla's lip color?* I swallowed hard, forcing myself to look at my reflection. No ... he couldn't. He *wouldn't* do that ... would he?

There was a knock on the door. On *Jude's* door. "Come in," I said, but my voice sounded hoarse.

Jude entered, a grin spreading large across his face as his gaze locked onto me. "Wow ... you look ... *different.*"

I swallowed. "Good different?"

"You always look gorgeous. But I prefer your natural hair color." Even though he was being nice, the compliment rubbed like sandpaper over my skin. "You almost ready?" he asked.

I took a deep breath. I had agreed to table the conversation about Eve ... but that was before. Before the leather outfit. Before the red lipstick. I turned, holding up the small black tube in Jude's face. "What is this?"

His throat worked, Adam's apple bobbing as he inspected the tube in my hands. "Um, lipstick?" he said, clueless. There was genuine confusion in his face. His brow tilted down, forming a 'V' between his eyes. Maybe he wasn't doing this on purpose. Maybe this wasn't some crazy, intricate plan to get me dressed up like Layla.

"The other night when I was getting your drink at the bar, Eve was there. And she told me that you had a type. Essentially, Layla's type. Dark hair." I tugged at the strands of the wig. "Leather." I slapped my palm over the leather stretched across my hip. "And red lipstick." I punctuated the last sentence by holding up the lipstick again.

The confusion on his face shifted, turning into a scowl. "Eve talked to you at the public flogging?" His tone was dangerously dark and his eyes simmered a deep shade of green.

"*That* isn't what matters right now. I was willing to talk about Eve another time. But now? In light of all *this*," I gestured at my outfit. "I need to know the truth about what happened with her. Why does she hate you so much? Why did she call you a fraud?" When Jude didn't answer, the knot in my stomach rose to my throat.

"Because I *am* a fraud," he whispered.

I waited, needing more of an answer than that. But it never came. Jude stood there silently, staring at the floor. The imminent threat of tears burned in my sinuses. "I *need* to know you're not dressing me up like some fucking doll to look like your ex-wife—"

"No," Jude growled the word as he stepped closer. But I countered by stepping back. "Fuck, *no*, Marly. That's not what this is. *You* brought the wig, remember?"

I nodded. "Yes. I remember. But what about the leather?"

"Chloe picked out the clothes," he said. "I gave her my credit card and your sizes and she went shopping for me yesterday. Leather corsets and black skirts are basically her uniform here, so I can't say I'm surprised at her choice." I looked down at the outfit. It did look like something literally out of Chloe's closet—at least from the little bit I knew about Chloe. Relief was imminent. Scratching at the surface. But the lipstick still remained. The lipstick and my nickname.

"And this?" I gestured to the lipstick. "Sunlit *Poppy*?"

Jude swallowed hard, his jaw ticking. "It looks bad, I know—"

That was all the answer I needed. It was Layla's lipstick. Tears sprang to my eyes, hot and salty. The tube slipped from my fingers and hit the floor. "Is that why you called me Poppy?" I looked up into his eyes, refusing to shrink back from his gaze, despite the distortion from my tears, like seeing him through blown glass.

"Marly," he said gently, and this time when he moved toward me, I didn't back away. He cupped my jaw, his hands large and warm, and his thumb stroked across my damp cheeks. "No," he said—his voice was soft, but firm. "I kept that makeup bag stocked here for the last couple of years. Yes, some of the items in there were Layla's brands and colors. I always try to have makeup replenished for any submissives."

"And this is Layla's shade, isn't it?" My voice cracked. Why did that hurt so damn much? It was a stupid tube of lipstick for God's sake. It wasn't like he was out fucking Layla. But I couldn't help the burning ache at the hollow of my stomach.

"It was," he answered, honestly. "But I don't want you to wear it because of that. I was going through the new makeup Chloe keeps stocked for me and when I saw that the shade was called Sunlit Poppy, I smiled. Because it was such a beautiful coincidence. That's why I tucked it into your bag of makeup."

I wiped my fingers beneath my eyes, wiping away my tears. With all the stupid eye-makeup I'd just put on, it was probably running down my face now.

Jude bent and kissed my forehead, my nose, and both my cheeks. "Please don't cry. I'm so sorry—I clearly wasn't thinking. Do you want a new nickname? We'll find you one. That outfit? Throw it in the garbage if you want. That wig? I'll go buy you a blonde one right now."

I believed him. I believed every word he said. This wasn't intentional. Whatever had happened with Eve, this wasn't him repeating old behaviors. Even still—I had to know. "Tell me what happened with Eve."

"Okay," he said, tugging me to the bed, urging me to sit. I lowered to the edge, my muscles tight and alert. "Just please know … what I did was fucked up. And horrible. And I know that. I apologized to Eve many times for it. Layla had just left me, had just cheated on me—"

"*Jude*," I interrupted. "I understand. Now, tell me."

His hands clenched at his sides and for the briefest moment, his eyes shut. "After Layla left, I hired Eve as my submissive. My life was unraveling. I was losing control of everything—and, as you know, that's a Dominant's worst nightmare."

"That's *your* worst nightmare," I said. My stomach was tight and I clenched my clammy hands in my lap to stop myself from biting my nails. Whatever he was about to admit to went so far beyond him just dressing Eve up to look like Layla. He wouldn't be acting so nervously if that's all this was.

Jude started pacing the room, back and forth across the carpet. It was the most fidgety I had ever seen him. "As I mentioned, I don't do one night stands. I don't do casual encounters. And so that left me with one choice—a professional submissive. I chose Eve specifically because at the time, she had dark hair, like Layla. They were about the same height, build, everything. I asked her to wear Layla's clothes. I gave her Layla's makeup to put on."

"Sunlit Poppy?" My throat closed with the question and I barely managed to get it out.

"No. It was another darker shade of red. Like a deep burgundy."

I exhaled the breath I'd been holding. "Good."

"I've never been a sadist," Jude continued, but with that admission he stopped pacing in the center of the carpet and looked straight at me. His body crumpled as he fell to his knees. Crawling over to me, he dropped his head in my lap, and my palm instinctually fell to the top of his head, my fingers diving into his thick strands. "But with Eve— night after night, I would dress her up as Layla and I would paddle her until she used her safe word. I used clamps. I used the whip, the crop, my hand—anything that I could use to close my eyes and imagine I was beating Layla back into submission. Beating Layla back into loving me."

A gasp popped through my loose lips. "You pretended she was Layla and *beat* her?"

"Yes," he admitted. His head hung in shame. His voice, tight and ragged. "Eve is a masochist. She likes pain. She told me she could handle it, but I took it too far. I always took it too far. It's my job as her Dom to get close to the line without crossing it. The goal is for her not to use her safe word. And I don't think there was a single night we spent together where she didn't use it." His voice cracked, and with that, he tilted his eyes to mine. "It was fucked up and irresponsible. And every time I see her, I'm reminded of what a terrible human I turned into after Layla left."

I ached for Jude … and for Eve. I knew heartache, but never like that. I'd never had a boyfriend cheat on me so shamelessly, so mercilessly without some sort of contrition. But even still, something wasn't adding up. I narrowed my eyes, examining Jude. There was more. "How long did this go on?"

"Every weekend for six months."

Months? My fingers stilled at the back of his neck. I hadn't even realized I was still stroking his hair; unknowingly comforting him. "So if this was going on for months … what else happened? Something must have been the breaking point for you to leave the club and not come back until … until now." *With me.*

"The last weekend I saw Eve," he paused, clearing his throat and his eyes were wet with a sheen of unshed tears. "She told me she was falling in love with me." He shook his head, his eyebrows low over his wet, green eyes. "Why the fuck she was falling in love with a Dominant like me was beyond my understanding. But in that moment—she was wearing Layla's clothes. And her lipstick. And through my gin-fueled haze, if I squinted my eyes, she almost looked like Layla. I was drunk and sad—and I lost control."

I gasped and felt a throbbing pain on behalf of Eve. "What did you do? Did you hurt her?"

He shook his head. "Not how you're thinking. I-I kissed her. I made love to her," his voice broke and once again, he dropped his eyes from mine—unable to look at me. "Professional submissives aren't supposed to be intimate with their Doms. I told her I loved her, too ... because in my mind, she was my Layla. And I had accomplished what I wanted. I had beaten her back into loving me."

Oh, my God. Poor Eve. No wonder she's so bitter. But I understood. I didn't condone what he did—but I understood it. Understood why, in that moment of desperation, he would succumb to the feeling of love and affection from the person that for weeks he was pretending was Layla.

Jude clutched me tighter, and continued talking. "As she slept that night, I felt so utterly and completely sick with myself. I left. I left her here in this room, alone and confused with no aftercare."

"Did you ever explain?"

He rubbed at his bloodshot eyes and nodded. "I tried to apologize. To explain a couple weeks after. But as you can imagine, she didn't want to hear it. She had cut off all her hair and bleached it blonde."

"You didn't love her at all?"

"No. I mean, there's always a bond with a submissive. Even if it's only for a weekend, but—I didn't love her. Not like she loved me. I used her. When she gave herself to me and I took it, it was reckless. What she was giving wasn't mine to take. But I was selfish. For the first time since I began as a Dom, I acted with only my interests at heart. I betrayed everything a Dominant is supposed to be. She's one hundred percent right ... I'm a fraud. I have no business teaching you this lifestyle, when I've barely been a part of it myself for the last seventeen months."

"That's not true," I said, my voice a raspy whisper. "You're allowed to make mistakes. As long as you own them and apologize. Which you did."

He pulled his palm down his face and the stress had aged him. He looked tired. Distraught. Vulnerable in a way that I had never seen him before. Hearing about Jude's monumental fuck up was comforting. From the moment we'd met, he'd been so composed. Even when anxiety was taking hold of him with the studio tour, he was rigid and together in a way that I never was. But this? This made him human. It made him more like me. And in a way, I loved him more for his mistakes and his ability to own them.

I shifted my weight on the bed, restless and wriggling beneath Jude's clutched arms at the sides of my thighs. Jude's fingers bit into my hips, holding me tighter. "Please, Marlena. I beg you, don't leave me. I know I messed up, but don't leave because of this."

"I'm not going anywhere," I said. How could I? Jude had taken me by the hand and opened my eyes to a whole new part of myself. A part I never knew existed. And a lifestyle that was healing a part of me I never realized was broken. All those acerbic concerns that were piercingly loud, howling in my mind faded to whispers. Jude had revealed a vulnerable side to himself—and did so in a way that he wasn't justifying his actions. He was claiming them.

"I take it Eve didn't accept your apology?"

He shook his head. "No. I tried several times and eventually gave up. I assumed it was just part of my penance. Honestly, if I was her, I wouldn't have accepted my apology either."

I slid off the edge of the bed until I was kneeling with Jude on the floor. "Sometimes that's part of fucking up," I said. "The fact that sometimes people can't or won't forgive us. But that doesn't mean you can't forgive yourself."

We were nose to nose, my hands curved tightly around the back of his neck, his palms planted on my hips. The carpet which seemed so plush beneath my feet, now bit into my knees, already raw from our games earlier. He scooped his hands up the sides of my body until he was cradling the backs of my shoulders. "I don't want to let you go—but Marly, you need to get away from me. Lately, I destroy everything I touch and I can't do that to you. I love you too much to see that happen."

"Why don't you let me worry about what's bad or good for me?" I said, taking his lips—cutting him off from those bitter words; those dark thoughts. I swallowed them, drinking them down and forcing them to disappear. He was scaring me with the warning—because that's what people did when they faced a new mountain. A new scary, beautiful mountain to climb—and I wasn't going to let him back away from the thrill. Not this time. If he needed me to be strong enough for the both of us, then I would be.

I deepened the kiss, sliding my tongue along his and those ugly words of his morphed into moans of pleasure. My breasts, already flattened by the corset pressed into his body and I became all too aware of the fact that I wasn't wearing panties anymore.

Jude groaned a satisfied sound and his touch, feather soft, skimmed the insides of my thighs as he found a path up to my bare sex. His gasp resonated down to my toes and he broke the kiss as he growled, "No panties?" He dove his greedy, lustful fingers inside of me, not bothering to wait for an answer.

It took every ounce of fortitude I had to pull away. To take his hand and remove it from the sweet bundled knot inside of me. "Delayed gratification, remember?" I said, smirking. I stood, smoothing my leather skirt and moved to where I had dropped the lipstick.

I bent slowly, methodically over to pick it up. With a peek over my shoulder, I made sure Jude had a good view of *everything*. He was exactly where I had left him seconds earlier, biting his lip, hair rumpled and strewn, crisp shirt wrinkled and untucked. Fuck, was he sexy.

"Marlena, no," he said, his voice still gruff. "You don't have to wear the red."

"I know I don't. But now that I know the whole story, I want to."

He pushed to his feet in a graceful movement that if I'd blinked, I would have missed. "You're just saying that."

"Jude," I snapped. "I don't *just say* anything. You told me the whole truth. You showed me I have nothing to fear in a silly lip color. You told me that the name Sunlit Poppy reminded you of me. And it feels like we're taking something that *was* Layla's ... and making it *ours*." I leaned into the mirror, lining my mouth just slightly over my natural lip line and Jude's eyes followed the movement. When I was finished, I turned to face him, blowing Jude an air kiss. "Well? What do you think? Does Sunlit Poppy suit me?"

He crossed to me, his steps strong and purposeful as he closed what little space was left between us. His panther-swift movement both thrilled and scared me, my heart fluttering at all his masculine beauty. He quite literally robbed me of my breath as his massive arm curved around the small of my back and pulled me into him. With his other hand, he tore the wig off my head and tossed it to the ground. "You're gorgeous. Red lips, glossy lips, no lipstick—you're stunning. Wear whatever the fuck you want." I feathered my fingers over his breastbone, brushing across the hard wall of his chest.

He tugged me even harder against him until my body was flush with his in a searing closeness, enveloping me; owning me. He rocked his hard length against me, his rhythm pulsing with slow, intentional thrusts until each grinding movement was synced with our heaving breaths.

It was hypnotic and intense and I descended into his mesmerizing movements. His rigid cock pressed against my pelvis, occasionally brushing my clit, hard and ready. And those eyes. His green eyes were so shrewd—so scorchingly beautiful, that they could have branded me. They were intoxicating and I sunk deeper into the trance, submerged in his gaze.

Sex with Jude was always an adventure. Each time had been exciting and new. But this? This intense, intimate rocking was different and it left me aching for more of him—his lips, his cock, his eyes. If I had any self-control, I would have ended it there and walked away, ensuring that he was the one wanting for once. But I couldn't. My blood roared, searing hot through my veins, my heart hammering against the stupid, tight corset.

My head fell back as his hands dipped below my skirt once more. "Don't you dare look away," Jude growled. I snapped my gaze back to his, my eyelids heavy and hooded as his fingers circled my clit in soft, measured strokes. Barely touching. Barely bearable.

Just as I was about to pull away, to end this oddly intoxicating dance we had going, Jude launched forward, brutally taking my mouth in a bruising kiss. I gasped, opening for him, driving my tongue against his. It ended just as abruptly as it started and his teeth bit down on my bottom lip, catching it as he pulled away. Pain pinched at my swollen lip, and I stood there panting, gasping for breath. His hands tugged free from beneath my skirt. An aching space opened between us, and I whimpered with the lost connection, losing my balance with shaking knees.

"*I* say when gratification is delayed," Jude said, the tiniest smile splayed across his lips and he brought his fingers to his mouth, sucking my juices off of them.

There he was. My Jude was back. "Yes, Sir," I whispered. Catching my reflection in the mirror, I sucked in a biting breath. Was that really me? My cheeks were flushed, my eyes bright and dilated, my hair was a tangled mess, and my lips—they were swollen and smeared with red. I oozed lust and arousal, like an animal in heat. I would quite literally drop to all fours and howl at the moon if Jude asked me to.

CHAPTER TWENTY-FOUR
Marly

ONCE I CLEANED myself up, I followed Jude out of the room and shut the door, locking up behind me. "Is this safe? Going out in public tonight?" I tugged at my wig, making sure it was secure and pulled some of the dark bangs further down on my eyes. Nerves smacked around in my belly. What if someone recognized me?

His smirk climbed as he lifted my hand and dropped a kiss to my knuckle. "Don't worry, Poppy. I checked with our bouncer, Pete, not too long ago and he assured me it was a quiet night. And if it gets busy, we'll come back upstairs."

Jude's hand trailed across the small of my back as he guided me down the stairs. His touch sizzled against the slim strip of bare skin that peeked between my corset and the skirt. I was still hot from before; itchy and unsatisfied and so freaking wet, that I could feel my arousal dripping between my legs. As we approached a door at the end of the hall, the thumping music grew louder and louder, until I could feel it vibrating against my toes. I breathed in deep as the door swung open and I was finally met with a room other than the one I had been quarantined to. I understood why, of course … I couldn't just go walking around Los Angeles with Jude without speculations and tabloids popping their pictures. But it was a bit imprisoning.

Jude nodded to the bouncer—Pete, I guess. He was a massive man, whose arm was the size of my waist. Taking my hand, Jude laced his fingers with mine.

From over his shoulder, he sent me a smirk, eyes roving down my body. As we descended the hall, Jude's hold curved tighter around my waist, pulling me close into his side. Our steps fell in sync with one another's as his thumb circled my hip bone.

The hum of chatter and blaring music grew louder with each passing step and the hallway filtered into the dark club. A horror movie played on huge flat screens above the bar. A dance floor writhed with a small group of bodies clad in leather and lace. My feet cemented to the floor as I scanned the room, wide-eyed. "Holy shit," I said, on an exhale. In a weird way, *this* was more shocking than the public flogging.

Jude waited patiently, his hand still claiming my left hip. "Wild, right?"

"Yeah, but not more than the other night. So why does this seem so much more intimidating?"

"That happened to me the first time I explored the private areas, then came back out to the public club. I'm not sure why, but I think we just get so used to the privacy upstairs—and how small the crowd is, that coming back down here is jarring. Even on a quiet night."

"This is a quiet night?" I had to practically shout to be heard over the music. Then again, I could see what Jude meant—it was dark with strobe lights flashing on the dance floor. It was hard to see Jude right here in front of me, let alone for someone else to recognize us from farther away.

"Are all these people ..." I stepped closer into his side, finding comfort in Jude. "Are they all BDSM folks, too?"

He shook his head. "No, probably not. They're most likely people who dabble and enjoy edgy without actually moving into a lifestyle. Which is fine … there's room in the community for all types."

On the side of the dance floor was a cage with a Dita Von Teese style pin-up dancer inside. She shed her jeweled corset, then placing a full glass of champagne on her head, continued with the dance, not spilling a drop. "What do we do now?" Our bodies were pressed flush together. Though I wasn't sure if that was a result of the crowded club or our own doing. He didn't seem to mind. He angled his face down, his breath warm against my lips.

"We get a drink."

I grinned. "We? Does that mean I can have a bourbon?"

He matched my smile. "If you ask really nicely," he said.

"May I please get a bourbon?" I nibbled my sore bottom lip, directly on the spot that Jude bit, not thirty minutes earlier, loving the dull snap of pain. His mark. Branding me as his. I knew I should have added a Sir to that, but God, I wanted his hand on my ass. I wanted to feel his punishment, maybe even slightly more than I wanted to please him tonight. The thought was so thrilling and terrifying all at once, that I was willing to act out in the hopes of some attention—like a toddler. That's what this stupid delayed gratification shit was doing to me. Turning me into freaking Benjamina Button.

Despite the fact that I withheld the 'Sir,' I felt his approving hiss all the way down to my toes. Hooking a finger under my chin, he lifted my eyes to his, locking into my stare. His arousal pressed against me and I wanted to close my eyes; to disappear beneath that chilling gaze of his. "Add a 'Sir' onto that question and you've got a deal," he murmured, appearing lost in his own thoughts.

I took a breath. "May I please get a bourbon, *Sir*?" Why was a three-letter word so powerful? Even as I said it, the chill crept through my veins, halting my blood flow like a frost sweeping over a field. Through the leather corset, my breasts tingled and I was certain my nipples were hardened peaks beneath the restrictive fabric.

Jude wasn't smiling, but his eyes flashed as I said the word. His breath turned shallow and his full lips parted in approval. "You may. I have a tab here—just put it under my name."

"And what would you like?" As if I needed to ask.

"Martini, straight—"

"—up, dry with extra olives?" I finished the thought for him with a smirk.

He nodded slowly, that one dimple appearing below his creased eye. "That's right."

And with that, he leaned in, gently brushing his lips across mine in a kiss so gentle, the tenderness of it skated across my skin leaving goosebumps in its wake.

THREE BOURBONS AND ten songs later, I was on the dance floor with Jude pressed against me. Sweat dripped down the back of my neck, the fake dark hair sticking to my skin. The DJ took residency in the corner of a stage, four feet up from the floor. A spotlight popped on center stage as a curtain pulled back, revealing the Dita Von Teese look-alike dancer wearing retro panties and pasties. She had a massively large feather fan and managed to keep herself covered in a vintage burlesque dance.

Jude hugged me closer, moving in rhythm to the slow, crooning beat. His hand roamed down my hip to the edge of my skirt, his fingertips brushing my skin. A breath croaked in my throat as I tightened against him.

"Come here," he said, pulling me to a quieter lounge area, elevated in the back where there was a circle of leather club chairs, protected by another bouncer. He nodded at Jude as we took the steps up to one of the chairs. Even though there were clearly two chairs available, Jude pulled me onto his lap, fingers drawing little circles over my stockinged legs.

"It's getting a little too crowded out there. We should head upstairs soon."

With a quick glance around the room, my eyes landed back on Jude, who stared directly through me as though he could read every thought I'd ever had. "Is this the VIP area?"

He nodded. "It's a little more private, but I'd rather not take the risk for much longer."

As his fingers on my legs moved north, the strip of skin between my thigh highs and skirt tingled and I wiggled in his lap. Damn, that felt good. Too good. I scratched at the base of the wig, making sure it was still in place.

His jaw twitched and he shook his head, muttering a curse. Falling onto his elbow, a hand raked through his sandy brown hair. "Fuck," that same hand fell to his eyes, pinching the bridge of his nose.

I tilted my head. "What?" I asked, threading my fingers into his hair. When my nails skimmed across the back of his neck, he gave a violent shiver.

"I just can't believe I'm here with you. After everything

that happened with Layla, I promised myself I would never again get involved with an actress. Especially not one I was acting alongside." His grip tightened on my hip as he dragged his other hand down his face, a smile curving from behind his fingers. He shook his head and a rueful chuckle parted his gritted teeth. "But with you—Jesus, I dunno. You're different. I want everything about you. I want to do things to you." His hands roamed my body, hungrily. Possessively. And it made me shiver as that touch scraped up my body to my ribs.

"I want you to do things to me," I said. "BDSM things."

"Don't you worry, Poppy. I'll show you the ropes."

I snorted, laughing at his cheesy joke, but my laughter immediately stopped when he nipped my ear. "I need to get you upstairs to our room immediately," he growled, the heat of his breath sending goosebumps rippling down my neck.

Using the armrests as leverage, he pushed to his feet, backing me into the wall. It was cool against my bare upper back and Jude's muscular thigh pressed between my legs, where I throbbed for his touch. He nudged me with his knee to open my legs wider. "Let's get out of here," he whispered, and his hot breath breezed across my lips. I couldn't wait until we made it back to the room. I needed him now. Even if it was just a taste.

Without thinking, I kissed him. Our lips crashed together, and my nails scraped up the back of his neck, tugging his hair while pulling him deeper into the kiss. It didn't take much coaxing before he was parting my lips, delving his tongue into my mouth, stroking me to widen for him. I whimpered into his lips, collapsing all my weight between his body and the wall.

"I warned you," he whispered, ending the kiss. His mouth curved into a sexy, devious smile. "I need to get you in private. I don't share—not in *any* way." I panted, catching my breath, and blinking as the room came back into focus. The music played in my mind louder than before and laughter and conversation flooded my ears. The club was busier now than it had been when we first arrived.

"You're right," I said, my voice husky and low. "It's more crowded now. Too risky—"

Jude's voice cracked with a laugh. "Look at yourself," he said, shaking his head. "One week ago, would you have ever believed you'd be here with me? Wearing a leather skirt with no panties. Craving a paddle to the ass. Your mouth watering to call me 'Sir' …

"No," I answered quietly, and my eyes were wet with emotion I couldn't quite explain. "But then again, I never had anyone I was this passionate about. I never had anyone I loved so much."

He kissed me hard once more and the loud click of a camera shutter came from beside us. I blinked my eyes open to find Jack standing beside us. My ex-boyfriend. Ex-director. And the man who made my career in Los Angeles a living hell for the past year.

And he had his cell phone in hand, taking our picture.

CHAPTER TWENTY-FIVE
Marly

T HE SARDONIC CURVE of Jack's mouth angled into a sharp grin and fear froze me in place. *Maybe he doesn't recognize me.* Maybe he didn't even see me. I spun, facing the other way and pulled the wig in front of my face.

Jude was right—we should have waited until we were back in the room. What the hell was I thinking? Publicly making out with a man I wasn't even a co-star with yet? Spreading my legs for him in public with no panties on? How many actresses had I seen flash the paparazzi accidentally? And each time, I judged them—couldn't believe how stupid they were for taking that risk. *Now look who's stupid.* The whole night screamed of poor decision. I knew the moment Jude saw my ex by the way his brows pulled together and his touch on my spine went stiff.

"Marlena Taylor." Jack's smoother than-butter voice was quiet, but it managed to cut through the ambient noise of the club easily. "I thought that was you. The hair almost got me—threw me off for a hot second. But I'd know those freckles anywhere."

Jude reached out a hand, an uncharacteristic smile crossing his face. "Jack," he said. "I'm surprised to see you here."

I was frozen. Physically frozen and unable to move like someone had shoved me into a meat locker. "Jude Fisher."

Jack's smug smile kicked up higher at the corners. He placed a palm to his chest, introducing himself. "Good to see you again."

"I wish I could say the same," Jude snarled.

Jack looked to me, his eyes blazing and his mouth twisted into a calculating grin. "Marlena. Aren't you going to say hi?"

My lips pressed into a firm line and the exhale that crept from my nose flared my nostrils.

"What do you want, Jack?" I whispered, even though I doubted anyone could hear us over the music.

He lifted a chin toward Jude, waving his phone in the air. "Oh, I'm sure your fiancé would love to see what you're up to tonight." Jack sneered, scrolling through his phone, he paused and held up an image he had snapped of us moments before. His grin was as slick as his hair.

There was a low growl that came from Jude and I put a hand to his chest, rolling my shoulders back and squaring off in front of Jack. "Omar *knows* where I am. This is just research for a potential part."

"Yeah. I know all about your 'research' for roles, don't I, babe?" Moving past us, he clapped Jude on the back. "Enjoy her while you've got her, man," he winked. "She *really* gets into her roles."

He barely got the words out before Jude swung his fist at Jack's face. The cracking of knuckle on jaw was unlike any sound I'd ever heard. Jack hit the floor, without even an attempt to get up or fight back.

Jude bent over his body, fisting his maroon Prada shirt. "Shut the fuck up with these lies about Marly. We all know they're total bullshit. Be a fucking man and stop pissing and moaning because you got dumped. If I hear from even one more person that you're still perpetuating this bullshit, you'll *never* direct for Silhouette Studios or anywhere else I am connected again."

He didn't wait for Jack to respond, simply tossed him back down like he was a piece of lint from his sleeve. Taking my hand, he tugged me beyond the bar toward the back exit. "Come on," he whispered, kissing my forehead as we shoved through the murmuring crowd.

Looking over my shoulder, I saw a crowd congregating around Jack and camera phones snapped picture after picture. "What the *fuck*, Jude?" I tried to wrench my hand out of his hold, but Jude held on tightly, pulling me to the back door.

"Stop it! *Stop!*" Pete was already waiting by the back door, his foot propping it open.

Jude spun to face me, cupping my jaw. "Marly, listen to me ... we need to get out of here before someone gets a picture of us here."

"Maybe you should have thought about that before *punching* him," I hissed. "No one would have noticed if we had just slipped out!" Oh, God. This wasn't happening. Cameras were going to be everywhere. They could check security footage or other patrons would be looking for my face in the crowd now. I squeezed my eyes shut, mirroring the squeezing shame in my chest.

Jude pulled his hands from my face and sighed. "I know, okay! I know ... can we talk about this on the way?" he gestured to the door, grabbing keys from his pocket. The commotion grew louder, coming toward us. I nodded stiffly, rushing out the back door.

We were in Jude's car, racing through the streets within seconds. Anxiety fluttered in my chest. No, fluttered was too delicate. It stampeded my chest, making it hard to breathe.

Jude sped down the streets of LA, fast enough to get away, but not so quickly that we would get pulled over. About fifteen minutes later, he pulled up to a locked gate, punched a code into the keypad and sped into his driveway. The house was massive. Almost three times the size of mine and with another push of a button, a garage door lifted. He slid in between an SUV I didn't recognize and my own car on the right. It looked like the nerdy girl stuck at the cool kid table beside these amazing vehicles.

I got out of the car and Jude opened the side door to his home. Jude Fisher's house. I had to give myself a mental slap to snap out of it. We entered an enormous white stone and marble kitchen; the sort of kitchen that was so pristine, I wondered if it had ever been cooked in, even once. "Jude." My voice was hoarse and he ignored me, pulling his cell phone out.

"Yes, we're here," he clipped, holding a finger up to silence me. "We're fine. How is Jack?" There was silence as I strained to hear the mumbled voice on the other end of the line. "What are the chances he'll press charges?"

Dress shoes clacked against the marble as Jude paced back and forth around the kitchen island. "Grab Marlena's things from our room upstairs. Rosie will meet you in the garage to bring them inside."

He hung up and tossed his phone onto the island, dragging a hand down his face, then landed both hands on his hips. "Dammit, I never should have taken you out in public to the club. It was stupid and risky and I'm so sorry, Marlena."

I swallowed. "I never thought Jack would be in a place

like LnS. He was always so … vanilla."

"This is my fault. I should have been more careful. It was my job to be more careful."

"This isn't your fault. I wanted to go downstairs to the club. And *I* kissed *you*. Everything was going fine until I did that." I gulped and fear clung to the inside of my throat, refusing to be swallowed down. "I don't think Jack's going to call the cops. He wouldn't want the press to find out that he got his ass handed to him. And leaking that photo would mean people would come forward with seeing him hit the floor." God, I hoped I was right. Hoped Jack's ego and self-preservation weighed stronger than his sense of revenge.

Jude grunted a curse and resumed pacing. "I hope not. Chloe said she doesn't think he's going to press charges, even though his nose was spurting blood like a geyser."

"Good," I added quietly, and Jude froze, lifting his eyes to mine.

He raised an eyebrow, humor twitching at the corners of his mouth. "Good?"

I nodded. "Yeah, fuck him. He deserves it."

He held my gaze before sighing, smoothing a finger across his brow. "We need to get you home. Before the studio finds out about our week together. Before the media finds you here—I mean, you and Omar might not be legit, but the world doesn't know that yet."

"Jude—"

"It'll look terrible. Be bad PR for you, and could severely ruin your reputation if people caught you here with me. It could ruin your chances of getting the part—"

"Jude, stop!"

But he didn't. He kept rambling, gathering various

items into a duffle bag. "I'll call for my driver to come get you from the back driveway. We can find a way to get your car back to your place in the morning …"

"I'm not going anywhere," I shouted over Jude's rambling. He froze, bent over his cell, before turning to face me.

Alarm furrowed his brow, and his jaw dropped momentarily before a smooth grin lit his face. "You're not?"

"No," I whispered. "We have a contract stating that I'm here until Thursday." Despite the false sense of dominance I had at the moment, my belly was quivering. It wasn't easy standing up to a man like Jude. "No one followed us here," I continued, "we are completely alone and safe in this house. You have gates surrounding the whole property for Christ's sake. As long as Jack doesn't call the cops or the press, we're fine." I lifted an eyebrow. "Besides, I still have a lot to learn, don't I?"

He moved in slowly, approaching me like a jungle cat circling cornered prey, his eyes glowing nearly as bright. "You certainly do." Rotating his wrist, he circled my hair around his fist until my neck was pulled tightly back in his grasp. Despite the fire in his gaze, a tender smile curved his lips. "Marly," his gruff murmur rumbled through me.

His lips slid down my cheek to my jaw and he flicked a tongue out, caressing the tender skin at my neck.

My head fell back as I fisted my hands into his silky hair, the hard muscles of his neck clenched at my touch.

"Did I say you could touch me, Marlena? Drop those hands and touch yourself instead."

Air sucked sharply into my lungs, but I did as I was told, lowering my hands to the tops of my thighs. Slowly, I pulled my skirt up and brushed my fingers over my wet opening. "Yes, Sir," I answered quietly and through a thick web of lashes, I looked up, meeting Jude's eyes.

Any sort of finesse or control Jude had exhibited before was far gone; in its place was a new primal urge, a hunger that claimed me as he brought his mouth down hard onto mine, groaning.

My fingers twitched, aching to stroke his thick soft hair, but I braced my arms, keeping them on my pussy instead. I gasped a breath of thick air, pulling oxygen in through my parted lips in a pant. Hunger ached in my chest for him. His pale green eyes dilated, then impossibly darkened as his mouth tightened into a hard line. He pulled back, examining me, dragging a single finger down my bare shoulder, drawing a teasing, provocative line. Blood roared in my ears and my belly quivered with a shaky breath until his mouth found mine once more, tongue thrusting rhythmically into my mouth.

His hand flanked mine and he guided my fingers from where they fluttered at my clit, inside my damp opening, until I was fingering myself with quick thrusts. A high-pitched whimper managed to escape, even though I was biting my lip. At which point, Jude pulled my hand from between my legs and dipped it into his mouth with a satisfied hum. His tongue worked my fingers in and out, rolling his tongue over the soft flesh of my fingertips, as his hard cock strained into my hip from behind the zipper of his pants.

Then, releasing my fingers from his mouth, he leaned down, kissing me deep with long, silky strokes of his tongue. Through the fog of our frenetic kisses, I grasped Jude's dick through his pants, stroking against the fabric up and down his impressive length. A look of pure, undiluted pleasure slid over his features as he threw his head back and let out a groan. That noise, that groan, was like an aphrodisiac and my nerve endings sparked to life at the sound.

His hands found my breasts, squeezing them through the tight corset. "Fuck," he growled, cupping my ass. Then he hissed, pulling back as his hand trailed over the bare flesh, brushing my seam. "What did I say about keeping your hands to yourself, Marlena?"

Whatever thread of composure I had left combusted and anticipation buzzed through my body. I hadn't meant to disobey him; it was reflexive, touching him. But now that I had, the thrill and threat of punishment fired off little sparks in my core.

A fog of greedy lust engulfed me, so hazy I was nearly blinded by the need for his touch. For his lips. His tongue. Impossibly, in the last few days, I had found myself not only drawn to Jude in a way I never thought possible … but trusting him. With my secrets. With my body. With my desires. In such a short period of time, he'd had such impacted and change on my life.

Jude sucked in a hard breath, his eyes traveling to where I clutched my hands behind my back. His mouth came down hard onto mine once more and my lungs struggled for air as our kisses slowed. His fingers dipped between my legs, exploring into my slick, hot center, gathering moisture before trailing along my backside. It took every ounce of energy not to tear my clasped hands free and grip his shoulders for leverage. "God, that's hot," Jude hissed. "We should institute a no panties rule forever."

"If you want, Sir." *Forever.* The word left me breathless. I clenched my laced fingers tighter behind my back, forcing myself to remain still.

"Good girl, Poppy," Jude crooned. My reward was his lips on mine, in a soft kiss that was no less intense than the others. "Move those hands around my neck." I did what he said. Squeezing my ass, he lifted me and my legs wrapped around his lean waist. Rocking against his rigid length, I rubbed my cleft against the outline of his erection and his low chuckle rumbled through my mouth, vibrating down to my core.

"Patience," he whispered, as his hands snaked around my midsection, locking me into his body. And then, we were walking—well, *he* was walking. I heard the distinct creak of a door opening and then the silky feel of a bed beneath my bare flesh.

I started to kick off my heels, but Jude's hand caught them around the arch, pushing them back up. "Leave them," he whispered, lowering his body down slowly over mine and bracing his weight on his elbows. Hooking his fingers into my skirt, he tugged it down slowly, the smooth leather scraping my nylon thigh highs. "But this needs to go." Then, he tugged the wig from my head, throwing it aside. "And this." Grabbing a tissue from his nightstand, he swiped it across my lips. "And the makeup. I want the real you."

Curving a hand under my neck, he slowly removed most of the makeup from my face before sitting back, examining me with a sigh. "There," he said. "That's much better. That's Marlena. My Poppy."

I stretched my arms overhead, curling into the silky bed and allowing it to absorb my weight. My skin was too tight and absolutely everything on me tingled under Jude's approving gaze. "And this?" I trailed my touch down the middle zipper of my corset, my fingernail gliding over the swell of cleavage.

Jude nodded, eyes blazing. "That has to go, too."

Slowly, I undid the zipper, dragging it halfway down to my belly, but keeping my breasts covered. "You sure?" I whispered, a hint of a smile in my teasing question.

"I have never been more fucking sure of anything in my life," he said, chest heaving with each breath. In seconds he was on his feet, tugging his shirt over his head and unzipping his dress pants. He pushed them down to the floor. His cock pierced forward, long and hard. I tightened at the sight of his taut body before me.

He nodded. "Now you."

Pushing off my elbows, I stood, spinning my back to Jude. Stealing a look from over my shoulder, I tossed the corset to the floor. When I twirled back to face him, he had closed in on me, only a foot away, eyes fierce and glittering in the sliver of moonlight slicing through the window.

Sweat glistened on his chest and the muscles of his shoulders and biceps strained with whatever restraint he was holding onto.

"Lay down," he commanded, his voice even darker than his shadowed eyes.

I swallowed. "Are you going to punish me?"

An eyebrow lifted at that. "Do you deserve to be punished?"

The breath stilled in my chest. "Maybe. Maybe I want to be."

His eyes clamped shut and he grunted a curse. "Don't say things like that to me, Marly."

"Why?"

When he looked at me once more, his jaw eased into a

tight smile. "Because I'll never let you leave this bedroom."

With a shiver, my blood rushed hotter, faster through my body. My pulse raced and my nipples pebbled toward him.

Amusement sparked in his eyes. He flicked a glance to the bed. "On your hands and knees, Marlena."

I did as I was told, crawling slowly onto the bed and arching my back, looking over my shoulder at Jude. He moved to the other end of the room, opening a closet and pulling out some sort of curved paddle. It was smooth as he trailed it up my thigh and I shivered as he caressed the edge along my too-tight sex.

"Eyes forward," he growled. "In the interest of continuing our lesson, this is one of the toys many Doms use to punish their subs." He held the paddle under my gaze so that I could get a good look and anxiety clenched low in my belly.

"Does that make me Holly again?" I managed to ask, keeping my eyes forward despite the urge to look back at him.

Jude hooked a finger under my chin and gently dragged my gaze to his. "Absolutely not, Marlena. It's just you and me here." He brushed his lips across mine in a final gentle kiss before moving behind me once more.

"This can sting," he said. "Don't be afraid to use your safe words." And then, as quickly as the words left his mouth, the paddle came down across my ass. The pain sliced through me, then quickly receded into a hot, sweet ache. He paused, skimming the paddle's edge up the backs of my thighs. He was testing me—giving me the opportunity to catch my breath ... use my safe words if I needed to.

But I didn't. I craved more. Faster, harder. I wanted the pain as much as I wanted the pleasure … maybe even more.

He hit me again. And again. Between each strike, he trailed his fingertips gently over my ass, sliding them against my wet clit. The alternating between pleasure and pain was too much and I found myself wriggling, shifting my weight back and forth on my knees. With one final strike, I cried out just as Jude's lips landed between my legs, his tongue laving at my clit and thrusting inside me. The yelp quickly morphed into a moan and I rolled my hips into his face.

"Oh, God," I whimpered. The tension coiled deep and low; pulsing, building like a house of cards ready to tumble at any moment. In alternating motions, he licked the length of me, taking his time to suck my clit into his mouth, working his tongue in circles, while his teeth held me gently in place. My toes pushed into the comforter, fingers digging in and clenching the bedding in my fisted hand. Jude's hand brushed up and down my spine, finally landing on my ass. And with a final low moan, I shivered with pleasure, my sex clenching and desperately rippling around his tongue.

When the spasms finally slowed, Jude guided my hips around, turning me onto my back. He ripped the foil with his teeth and hissed as he sheathed his cock in latex. His biceps roped, clenched with the entirety of his body weight above me and just as I was about to roam my hands over the landscape of his body, I stopped myself, my hands pausing in mid-air. "May I touch you, Sir?" I asked, arching my neck to meet his gaze.

A satisfied grin curved toward his eyes and he nodded. "Yes, you may, Poppy." Slowly, I brought my hand to his shoulders, and as I rolled my fingers over the tight muscles, he trembled. With his first thrust inside of me, I reflexively curved my lower back off the bed. His hiss of pleasure tingled a path from my ears down my chest and my calves tightened, toes curling as he withdrew his thick cock from inside me.

"Fuck, Marlena."

Everything strained for control from his face to his toes. I wanted to immerse myself in every second of the evening. Remember every tiny detail. He was impossibly gorgeous and I found myself staring, transfixed at his chiseled face as he pulsed his hips deep inside me once more.

He gasped, gripping at my waist when I started rolling my hips around him. "No," he grunted. "I-I'm too close."

After a deep breath, he pulled back, sliding slowly out of me and then thrust once again.

I quivered, the pulse hitting deep in my belly. Slowly, he tugged each of my hands overhead, lowering his lips to mine, his eyes searing into me. "Trust me." It wasn't a question, but I nodded all the same.

With each thrust, he rocked his hips back and forth, stroking my deep knot of nerves from inside. I lifted my hips, tipping my pelvis so that he was able to drive deeper and I squeezed his waist with my knees. "Fuck, yes," he coaxed, driving harder into me.

Though he was measured and controlled in his movements, each thrust grew more wild. Faster. Like an inferno that began as a single, controlled flame, it was quickly growing into an uncontrollable wildfire.

My body clenched with another orgasm. I gripped onto him, convulsing against his body, shivering in ecstasy. I moaned, crying out Jude's name with the final moment of pleasure.

His lips touched my ear and he whispered, "God, I love seeing that."

With each pump, his pace quickened, taking me again and again in deliciously wicked thrusts. His hands tightened around mine and with a final roll of his hips, he threw his head back as an orgasm swept his tensed muscles. Blue veins stood out against his tanned skin and he shouted my name, dragging my mouth to his. Even through the kiss, I watched in awe as the final tremble shook his body. Scraping my lips down his jaw, I sank my teeth into his shoulder.

Sweat slicked along his face and shoulders and he wrapped his arms around my waist, holding me tight against him. "I don't know that I'll ever let go of you."

CHAPTER TWENTY-SIX
Jude

MORNING CAME FAR too quickly. Warmth pressed into my chest and as I blinked my eyes awake, Marlena's body was nestled against me, spooning. I sighed, pulling her tighter and snaking my arm around her bare waist.

She was so fucking soft. So gorgeous. And when she moaned, she wiggled against my hard cock.

Rolling to face me, I was met with her sweet smile. In the morning light, the spray of freckles across her nose and cheeks seemed to be even more highlighted. "Good morning," she said quietly, a morning rasp invading her normally clear voice.

"Morning," I returned, my lips curving, and pulled her in for a gentle kiss.

My erection pierced forward, nestled between her thighs and pushing into her saturated folds. I wanted her. I wanted her over and over again. But she might still be sore from last night. "Coffee?" I asked. "I had Rosie stock my fridge with half and half."

"In a minute," she rolled over, straddling me and lifting onto her knees. Leaning over my nightstand, she grabbed a condom from my stash and slipped it over my cock. With a sigh, she lowered herself onto me. Fucking heaven. I lifted my hips, pushing deeper into her wet heat.

"My God, you're fucking beautiful," I said, diving my hands into her red hair and pulling her down to my lips. The tips of her breasts brushed against my chest and I took a nipple into my mouth, circling my tongue around her peaked nub.

From above me, she panted, quickening her pace. I moved to her other breast, wrapping my lips around the rosy tip and giving it the same attention. How did I get so lucky? I didn't deserve her. But that didn't mean I wasn't going to keep her.

She lifted up, straightening her spine and rolling her hips, her body rippling over top of mine. Wetting the pads of my thumb, I put pressure to her clit, circling the slick area. Her soft belly tightened visibly. With my other hand, I brushed the mole on her thigh before gripping her hip and guiding her body rhythmically over mine.

Like a rubber band, I was stretched too far, knowing that with this woman my fate was entirely up to her. I would either snap or shoot forward and only hope she'd be along for the ride. She was different than the rest. Marlena Taylor was genuine, kind-hearted. More than just a Hollywood starlet out to climb the ranks to stardom.

A flash of light came from behind her and her shriek rocked me from our blissful state. She turned toward the window, shielding her breasts as another pop of light came from a small opening where the curtain hadn't pulled entirely over to the window frame. "Oh, my God," she said, covering her face.

I leapt up, pulling Marly down, using my body to shield her from the photographer, and tucking her into the blankets. "Stay down," I growled, grabbing the other sheet and wrapping it around my waist. I ran to the window pulling the curtains flush to the sides. How the fuck did they get beyond the gate? Did they climb over top? I ran to my cell and dialed the police when a whimpering from under the covers caught my attention.

"Poppy." I pulled her out and took her into my arms. "It's okay. Here." I grabbed my robe from a hook on the door and put it around her shoulders. "Look at me." I tilted her chin, angling her gaze to mine. Anxiety clenched my stomach as my eyes connected with her sparkling baby blues. They were wet and shimmered like sunlight along the top of a lake. "It's okay, Marly. It'll be okay."

She shoved my chest and pushed to her feet. "It will *not* be okay. Are you kidding me? I have a reputation in this town for sleeping my way into roles. And now? They have photographic evidence of just that. Even though it's not true. Even though it was *never* true." She sobbed and pulled the robe tighter around her body, moving toward the door. Her shoulders trembled violently with her tears. "What was I thinking? This isn't the girl I want to be."

I hated seeing her so upset. Those tears broke my heart. I jumped in front of her, holding my hands out. "Wait," I boomed, stopping her before she ran out of my bedroom. "Let me make sure the windows are all covered." I reached into a drawer, pulling out a pair of pajama bottoms and slid them on.

Slipping into the kitchen, I nodded at Rosie, my housekeeper and the only woman I allowed a key to my home. "Mr. Fisher!" she exclaimed. "There must be dozens of reporters out front. What happened?"

I rubbed my forehead, checking each window and pulling the blinds. "I had an overnight guest," I said quietly, and Rosie nodded, comprehension flashing quickly along her face. "Can you call Joe? Have him bring around the sedan with the tinted windows. Make sure he pulls into the garage—the spot all the way on the left so they don't see her car within it when the doors open."

"Yes, sir," Rosie said, concern tilted in her brown eyes.

I ran to the closet next to my bedroom, grabbing some of Layla's clothes she had left here. Yoga pants, a button-down shirt … they were maybe the only things Layla had ever worn that were down to earth. They were also probably the reason she left them here.

Marly was pacing when I got back to the room, still clenching my robe. "Oh, thank God," she rushed to me, grabbing the clothes. "I thought I was going to have to drive home in this." She pinched the corset as though it were a cockroach; gross and impossible to kill.

"You don't have to drive anywhere," I said. "My driver will take you home—it's a tinted car. He'll drive you around for as long as it takes to lose whoever is following you."

Her harsh, humorless laugh cracked like a whip between us; the smile on her face was sour. "Like that matters. They got a photo of us in bed together."

I clutched her shoulders, tugging her into my chest. "We don't know that. They *took* a photo, that doesn't mean they could see anything in it. The curtain only had a tiny opening."

A breath dragged through her open lips and she shook her head. "Even still, someone must have leaked the image Jack took of us at the club. Otherwise, why would they be here?"

Anger squeezed in my chest. Someone. Yeah, right. It had to have been fucking Jack. That was his payback. Even without me punching him in his smug fucking face, he probably would have leaked that photo.

Her eyes were wet as she looked up at me, and it was worse than a punch to the spleen seeing her in that state. Everything inside of me simply wanted to hold her until every tear had shed.

"This isn't me," she said quietly. "I've just been caught up in this role. And in *you*. I'm not whips and gags and paddles. I'm lace and silk and … and … teddy bears."

If her tears were a punch to the spleen, then her words were a knife to the gut. "I warned you," I said, in a hoarse voice. Even after I cleared my throat, it didn't help much. "But for a girl who claims that this isn't you, you seemed to really enjoy yourself. Besides, I can do fun things with lace and silk too." I leaned back to look into her bright eyes and gave her my best smile. "Teddy bears might be a little creepy though."

Marly laughed, dropping her head with a small shake. With a final sigh, she broke free from my hold, sniffling. "Thank you for this week." My stomach dropped, empty and hollow as she lifted her hand to my jaw. "It was amazing."

I swallowed the lump in my throat. Maybe if I pretended it wasn't there, it would disappear. "Why does that sound like a goodbye?"

She blinked, not answering. And that was answer enough. *Because it is goodbye.* "I-I've got to get to Omar," she said. "He'll know what to do. We have to arrange something with our publicists—"

"Marly, slow down." She couldn't leave me. This couldn't be over. "Maybe it's best if you wait it out here. They'll lose interest and go away after a few hours.

Something new and shiny will inevitably pop up. It's tinsel town, remember?" I didn't say it ... but I needed her. A group of paparazzi outside my home was my fucking nightmare. I needed Marly to get me through it.

"I just need to get home. I need some space. Some time."

"Well, that might be hard since we're auditioning together in a couple days."

She pulled her hair into a ponytail and smoothed it back with her palm. "Maybe we shouldn't be," she whispered. "Maybe this was all a huge mistake."

She moved past my shoulder and I grabbed her elbow, gently stopping her. She spun to face me, eyes flashing as she looked between my grasp on her arm and my eyes. "What about us?" I asked. "Can I see you before the callback on Thursday?"

A bitter laugh bubbled and exploded as Marly rolled her eyes. "You don't get it, do you? Even if I get this part now, it won't be because they consider me to be the most talented. Or the best for the part. Even if that's *why* they cast me. All people will see is a girl who's had two leading roles and two fuck buddies in each respective part. No one will take me seriously after this." Her voice cracked and tears welled in her eyes as she lifted her gaze to the ceiling. "It's my fault, Jude. Really. I should have known better than to sleep with you." And with that, she spun, yanked open the door, and walked out.

CHAPTER TWENTY-SEVEN
Marly

I SPENT TWO days in the comfort and security of my bedroom. I didn't leave. Not even once. Thank God for en suite bathrooms and roommates who bring you food.

A groan wailed through the room, and I wasn't sure if it was my stomach, my voice, or the bed. Then I heard footsteps padding across the floor and the mattress sagged on the edge.

"Time to get up, sunshine," Omar whispered.

This time it was *definitely* my groan. "No," I mumbled, stuffing my face into the pillow.

"Yep," Omar stood, throwing the covers off me and I squealed, reaching for the corner to cover myself. It wasn't like I was indecent or anything, but still. "C'mon, baby. It's your big day."

I sniffled, pulling myself up to a seated position. My eyes were swollen and my vision blurred from two full days spent crying. "I'm not going. What's the point? Even if I get the stupid part, everyone will think it's because of Jude, anyway."

Omar shuffled around the room, pulling out two different outfits and hanging them on the back of the door. "The point is to pick yourself up and show the world that their stupid accusations don't mean anything. You know the truth. You know if you get this part, it'll be because you researched and worked hard to understand Holly. Isn't that what matters?"

Stupid Omar and his logical reasoning. I snorted, falling back onto the pillow.

"Speaking of Jude … he's been calling," Omar said quietly. "He even stopped by yesterday." My throat grew tight as I glanced at his watch, still sitting on my nightstand. I knew he'd been here. I heard his voice from the hallway. "He's really worried about you." Omar tossed something on the bed by my feet. "And he brought you a weird fucking gift."

I lifted a teddy bear, the fur soft as silk against my hands. Only the teddy bear was hog tied; bound up like some sort of submissive sexpot. A laugh exploded from deep inside me and it was the first moment of happiness I felt in almost two days. With a final swipe of my eyes, I set the teddy bear to the side, shaking my head. "He shouldn't have come here. Not with the reporters watching this place so closely."

"He came in a tinted limo. No one could see him. Besides, while you were in here wallowing—"

"I am *not* wallowing." Omar shot me a look and I snapped my mouth shut immediately. "Okay, fine. I was wallowing."

"Exactly. While you were wallowing, Kyle and I released a statement."

"Without asking me?"

"Please, boo. It's not always about *you*." He shot me a playful grin, still rifling through my drawers. "Besides, how could we ask you anything? You wouldn't listen. You wouldn't talk to me." He pulled out a bra and panty set that were basically just scraps of lace and string, gave them a quick once over and nodded, tossing them onto the bed at my feet. "So Kyle and I came up with a plan. And you need to know before you go out there." He stopped and with a deep breath, turned to face me. "I came out. To the public." He shrugged nonchalantly, but there was a tight twitch to his jaw.

"Omar!" I was up and out of the bed in seconds, my arms flung around his neck. "What—how? I thought you wanted to wait a couple of years? I mean, I think it's great, but please tell me you didn't do that for me." As I pulled back, his muscles bunched under my hands.

He shook his head, kissing the top of my hairline. "I did it for me, not you. And really, I should have done it a long time ago. For the sake of my community. Hell, for the sake of my *sanity*. It does nothing for me to remain quiet, hiding who I am."

"And Simon?" The nerves bounced from my belly to chest, then back again.

Omar's grin widened, his teeth a bright, pearly white. "Simon's got nothing over me anymore. I just wish I'd been brave enough to do this when he first blackmailed me. *But* I've saved every email and every text from Simon since we met." He held up his finger and produced a stack of stapled papers that were rolled up in his back pocket. "And extortion is a felony in the State of California. The statute of limitations isn't for five years."

Yes! Oh, thank God. Simon deserved every bit of bitchy Karma coming his way. "You're the bravest person I know, Omar. I'm so proud of you." I brushed my fingers over his shaven head. "So, you're out?" I grinned and warmth spread through my limbs.

He curled one shoulder to his ear and flashed one of his

breathtaking smiles. Omar's phone buzzed and he pulled it out of his pocket, pressing it to his ear. "Hello? Yes, this is Omar ..." He covered the speaker and mouthed, *be right back*, as he stepped out of my bedroom.

I wandered to the dresses Omar had pulled from my closet and ran my hands over the silky green fabric. Facing Jude again after all we'd been through? It tied my stomach in about a million different knots. I overreacted to the paparazzi. It wasn't Jude's fault they had found me—it was Jack's. All Jack. And if I stayed in bed, avoiding this callback, then Jack would get just what he wanted. If I left Jude, gave up on that sweet, sticky love I felt heavily behind my ribcage, Jack would win. *Again.*

I examined the dresses, picturing Holly. Would Holly wear these to an audition? I shook my head. No ... they were too formal. I threw open my closet, rifling through my clothes—I needed sexy, but understated. Classy with a little bit of edge. *That* was Holly. I paused in the middle of my closet and grinned. *There it is*, I thought, snatching leather leggings from a hanger along with a pearl beaded sleeveless shirt. Sexy without being too revealing. Classy—what girl doesn't love pearls? But also edgy with the leather pants. And of course, a killer pair of heels.

I changed quickly, finished my makeup and smoothed my hair with the straightening iron before stepping back and examining myself in the mirror. I looked like Holly. And Marlena. Somewhere in the last week, the two of us were a bit indistinguishable. I took a deep breath and smiled at my reflection, hearing my dad's voice. *Push yourself. Because no one else will do it for you.* I smiled. "You're wrong about that one, Daddy." That's what friends and loved ones do. Omar was always there to nudge me forward when I stalled. And Jude—I swallowed, feeling the twisting emotion rising up from my chest. A Dominant's job is to anticipate a sub's needs. And a sub's job is to please and support her Dom. You're supposed to push the ones you love—as long as it's not away from you.

Which was exactly what I did to Jude. I pushed him away. Left him when he must have been reeling as much as I had been.

I walked to my nightstand to where Jude's Rolex rested beside my turquoise planner. I can be both women—I can be the organized, controlled woman by day, and the submissive crawling on my knees toward Jude by night. Being one doesn't mean I can't be the other. Being Jude's submissive doesn't mean I have to abandon everything I've known about who I am or what my dad taught me. And that was a relief. I grabbed the planner and the Rolex, tucking them both gently in my purse when Omar barreled back into the room, his phone still clutched in his hand. Holy crap, if I thought he'd been smiling before—now it looked like he had a cantaloupe wedging his mouth open. I laughed, unable to help myself from giggling and smiling along with him. "What? Omar, what's going on?"

"I got the part," he said, his voice so calm, it betrayed the news he was giving.

"You got it? The six-movie franchise?" I squealed and launched myself into his arms. He squeezed me tightly, spinning us in circles around the bedroom. "Congratulations. You deserve it."

He slowly lowered my feet back to the ground, his chest heaving, panting, both of us catching our breath. "Now, it's your turn. Go get 'em, Marlena Taylor."

TWO HOURS LATER, I was going down the same line of producers and casting directors, shaking hands again.

I paused as I reached Eve, sitting behind the table, spine rigid, and extended my hand to the professional submissive. I'd been shocked when I found Eve in the audition room. But I had only stalled briefly. Only stuttered for a moment before I picked myself up and continued.

Eve took my hand slowly, her frosty pink lips curving into a small smile. "That was incredible, Marly," she said.

"Thank you, Eve."

I *nailed* the audition. I knew it. Eve knew it. Everyone behind that table had to have felt it. Every line, every movement, every feeling I had in that reading was spot-on. Perfectly imperfect Holly. There was only one problem.

Jude wasn't here. His absence in the audition was like a storm cloud over my head. Maybe he was too busy managing the PR shitstorm himself? My stomach squeezed in spite of this rational and totally plausible possibility. But something just felt wrong. After how hard he worked to help me land this role? And how adamantly and vehemently he didn't want Layla to have it? Why would he miss the callbacks?

Maybe he was giving me space—hell, I had a*sked* for it. And he said he removed himself from casting. Maybe that removal meant he couldn't be in the audition room at all? But of course, this was my own fault. He had tried to call. He had stopped by. And I had ignored him. I inhaled a deep, calming breath, feeling his absence like a gaping hole in my chest. I assumed that I'd be reading for the role of Holly with Jude.

Richard Blair, the CEO of Silhouette Studios took my

hand firmly in his, snapping me out of Jude-infused thoughts. Mr. Blair's smile was firm as it lifted to his eyes. "That was a damn fine audition, Marlena. I hope you didn't mind us throwing a few new faces into the mix today," Richard said, gesturing to Eve and a couple other new people I didn't recognize. "We thought it would be a good idea to have some people in the lifestyle in the callback room today."

"It didn't bother me at all. That's a great idea," I said. It would have been better if it was a submissive who didn't have it out for Jude and his happiness ... but my only solace was that however much Eve didn't like me ... she must hate Layla more.

Warmth flowed through my veins like I had taken a shot of tequila. "Thank you so much again," I said to Mr. Blair, trying not to sound giddy. On one hand, I wished I could have read those lines with Jude. Looked into his eyes as I recited and repeated lines that I now felt in the depths of my soul. On the other hand? Reading the sides with the random production assistant reassured me that I was meant for this role. It reminded me that I was a good actress. It wasn't just my real feelings for Jude shining through when I read the lines—I had found my inner Holly, even without Jude being front and center.

Richard Blair gave another smile before releasing my hand, and I moved to the last person in the line-up. Ash Livingston.

"Great job, Marlena," Ash said, taking my hand firmly. He leaned in, whispering, "And don't worry. Jack's been officially blacklisted from ever working for Silhouette."

A blush crawled up my chest, heat flooding my face. Omar had forced me to look at the photos the paparazzi took of Jude and me in bed before I came to the audition. The image from Jude's bedroom was dark—blurry at best. Jude's face was clear, but all they could see was my back. All you could see was that Jude was in bed with *someone*. And yet, the magazine still ran the story.

And the photo Jack took in the club was blurry. Just two people making out—one of which looked like Jude and the other looked like a nondescript brunette. Jack's petty, vindictive bullshit backfired, and not only was he banned from LnS, but apparently Jude had kept his promise and blacklisted Jack from Silhouette.

"Thank you, Mr. Livingston."

Even though he released my hand, his gaze still bore into mine. "I look forward to seeing you soon."

I swallowed, ducking from Ash's gaze. As I dipped my hand into my purse to grab my keys, my fingers brushed the cool metal of Jude's watch.

The leather pants scuffed against the insides of my thighs with each step, and I could feel Ash's hot gaze on me as I headed toward the door. My blazer was slung on the chair near the exit. I blinked, swallowed, and turned back, making eye contact with Ash once more before flicking a glance at my jacket and walking out the door, intentionally leaving it behind.

On a slow breath, I counted to ten and as I made my way down the hall, a recognizably husky voice called for me from a few feet away. "Marlena Taylor," the voice said, low and sultry.

"Layla Hutson," I whispered, my throat dry as I turned to face the brunette bombshell. And like a bomb, she was just as volatile, ready to explode at any moment and take out everyone in her path.

Even though Layla's smile was spectacularly beautiful, it was hollow. She flipped her long raven hair behind her shoulder and quirked her red-stained lips in a condescending smirk. "Well, well, well … hello. You must be the woman fucking my husband." Layla held out a hand and I took it, jaw dropped and speechless.

"Excuse me?"

Layla rolled her eyes. "Oh, sweetie. Come off it. LnS? That dark wig? It's pretty obvious what you two were up to this past week."

I swallowed, tipping my chin higher. "We weren't *up to* anything," I said. "And last time I checked, he was your *ex*-husband."

Layla checked her reflection with a compact mirror, not even bothering to look up. After smoothing the blood colored stain on her lips, she snapped the compact closed with one hand. "Right, yes. Ex-husband. Whatever." She snorted a half-laugh kind of thing, her lip curling with it and strode to the door. Pausing, hand to the doorknob, she spun back to face me. "Tell me again—what color was that wig he put on you? And let me guess—red lipstick? Probably—" she tossed me the tube of lipstick she just put on and I caught it, turning it over.

"Sunlit Poppy…" I read aloud the same time Layla said it.

Pushing her bottom lip out, she shot an exaggerated pout toward me. "Don't be too sad, cupcake. I'm hard to forget. Jude was madly in love with me … and he always will be."

With a click of her tongue, she moved to pull the door open, but I was there first, slamming it shut before she could go inside. "You know what's really interesting?" I asked in a whisper. "I actually brought the wig myself. You know, for anonymity's sake. And when I put on that dark hair and Sunlit Poppy lipstick … he pulled away from me. The first thing he had me do was take off the wig and wash my face before he made love to me. That's right—made love. He loved you at one point in his life, but believe me … he's over that." I smirked and pushed off the door, backing up. "So, yeah … maybe you are hard to forget. But if I had to guess, I'd say it's for all the wrong reasons." I tossed the lipstick back to Layla whose mouth hung open like a caught fish.

She recovered quickly, snapping back into that menacing smirk. "Well, unfortunately for you, Jude quit the project yesterday. Whatever extracurriculars you two did will have absolutely zero sway on these guys."

Ice cold chills slammed into my chest. Jude quit? Why the hell would he do that?

Layla tutted and shook her head. "Oh, I guess he failed to mention that during your week of playtime? Yeah. He's gone." Her voice hardened and transformed from raspy pin-up girl into bitchy broad. "He's gone. You lose."

I shook my head. *He quit.* Now if I got the part, no one would question if it was because of our relationship. A hoarse, melancholy chuckle pushed past my lips. "No," I said, shaking my head. "I didn't lose." I blinked and met Layla's confused glare. "You don't get it," I said. "That's how much Jude believes in me. He *knows* I'm going to get the part, even without him being connected to the film." I took a step closer to Layla, my confidence building. I didn't care what this woman thought of me. I didn't care what anyone else in the industry thought anymore. *I* knew the truth. I was a good actress. The best who auditioned for

Holly. And I was sick and tired of letting the Jacks and Laylas of Hollywood push me into the corner. "And let's be honest, Layla," I whispered. "Only one of us has slept her way to the top. And it sure as fuck isn't *me*."

Layla opened her mouth to respond, but I cut her off. "Oh, Jude told me everything. And I mean … *everything*." Layla's mouth hung open and the red line of lipstick contrasted the pale pink inside where the color didn't reach. "You're not only a terrible submissive and an awful person … but I've *seen* you act. And as bad as your personality is … your acting is even worse." I smiled wider, diving my hand into my purse and pulling out Jude's Rolex, slipping it over my wrist, holding it for comfort. For strength. "Let the best submissive win," I finished.

Layla's gaze dipped to the watch and the color drained from her already paling face. "Is that Jude's watch?"

I winked at Layla and before I could answer, Ash popped his head out, nearly slamming into Layla with the door. "Layla," he hissed, then quickly gained his composure with a deep breath. He nodded politely, but tension coiled between them.

"Hi, Ash. Have you missed me?"

"Missed you like a cold sore," he grumbled. Ash stepped aside, holding the door open for her. My blazer was draped over his other arm. "Come on in, we're ready for you."

Layla glanced into the room and her shoulders visibly bunched around her ears. She pointed inside at the table. "Is that … Eve? From LnS?"

Ash's grin widened. "Sure is. Richard and I thought we needed a female submissive on the casting committee. Someone who could help us determine the actress who really understood the submissive role within the community."

Layla swallowed, her gaze drifting briefly to me, before landing back on Ash. Her lips tightened, puckered into a pout. She looked ... nervous. Layla Hutson was fucking nervous. *Good job, Ash.*

"Good luck," I said quietly, and Layla's head snapped around to look at me from over her shoulder, glaring. "You're going to need it."

Instead of following Layla into the room, Ash exited into the hallway, handing me my blazer. "We'd like for you to stick around, if possible." A smile creased his eyes and he held up two hands. "Officially, I can't say anything yet." Then, lowering his voice to a whisper, he grinned wider. "But unofficially, you got the part. There's no way Layla can beat that performance in there."

Holy hell. I knew I'd done well; knew I deserved that part, but for them to have made the decision so quickly? To finally be respected and seen for my talent? My eyes drifted closed as tingles traveled down my limbs. When I opened my eyes, Ash was smiling. "You were good. *Really* fucking good. Even Richard, who was your biggest critic last week, thought you were mesmerizing."

"Thank you," I said, my sinuses burning from beneath my flaming cheeks.

"You're welcome." He turned back for the room.

"Ash, wait!" I finally shook myself from the daze and yanked his sleeve back into the hallway. Amusement lit in his eyes and he patiently waited. "Jude ... where's ..." my voice cracked and I tried again. "Layla said that he quit. He *can't* quit!"

Ash's smile dropped and that spark of excitement simmering behind his eyes quickly extinguished. "He did quit. Said something about not wanting his influence to be a part of the decision making." Ash swallowed. "He wanted you to have the spotlight."

"Oh, God." I rubbed circles over my temples. "What have I done?"

Ash sighed. "When Jude falls, he falls hard. He's willing to give up anything to make the woman he loves happy."

The Rolex was heavy and thick on my bony wrist and I clutched it in my other hand. This part was his Rolex. And he gave it up for me. I gulped down a tear, forcing myself not to cry. Not here. Not in an audition. And certainly not when being offered the role of a lifetime. "I have to go find him." I spun to take off out of the building, but Ash dashed in front of me, stopping me.

"Wait, wait," he said, laughing. "First, you have to wait for us to call you back in there and officially offer you Holly. *Then* you're going to go find Jude and get him to take back the role he deserves."

"You're right," I nodded. "I have to … I have to do something."

"Something drastic," Ash said, his blue eyes bright as he regarded me warmly.

"I have to sell my wedding dress," I whispered, thinking of Jude's mom.

Ash frowned. "You have a wedding dress?"

"Never mind. Just … tell me where he is."

"I will," Ash said. "After you wait here and accept the part."

CHAPTER TWENTY-EIGHT

Marly

I SPED DOWN the road, past Daisy's diner until I swung into the almost empty lot at LnS where Ash promised me Jude was hiding out until all those paparazzi outside his gate disappeared.

I slipped in through the club's front door and even though it was morning, there were still staff working ... did this place never close? I recognized the bartender from the first night, Andrea, and gave her a little wave. Then I rushed beyond the bathrooms until I bumped into Chloe at the bottom of the stairs.

"Good morning, Marlena." She was kind, but not overly warm. "What can I do for you?"

"I just need to slip upstairs to Jude's room ..."

"I'm afraid I can't allow that." Though her words showed regret, her tone certainly didn't. Prickles of awareness covered my flesh.

"But I was *just* here—"

"Right. Last week. But you're not an official member."

Oh, hell no. I did not come this far just to get turned away at the door. One way or another, I *was* finding Jude today. "Actually, if we're going to get technical about things, my contract was through Thursday. Considering we didn't specify a time, I am legally allowed to be upstairs until tonight at 11:59 pm." There was a pause as Chloe chewed the inside of her cheek, rolling that thought around in her mind. "Am I wrong? Go ahead and check the paperwork … I'll wait here."

Chloe's eyes narrowed and she stepped aside. "No need. Go on up."

I slid by her shoulder and made my way up the stairs slowly so not to appear too hasty. But as soon as I turned the corner, I took off on a run down the dark hall. I slowed as I approached his door and pressed my ear to it. There was silence on the other side, not that that surprised me. These rooms were made to be sound proof. He could be in there screaming at the top of his lungs and I wouldn't know the difference.

I placed a palm to the door and a shiver tumbled down my spine.

"What are you doing here?" Jude's low voice growled from behind me. I spun, my back pushing against the door.

God, he was beautiful. Tall, sculpted, with features that looked to be carved by some Greek god. But now a dark cloud hovered over him, and those features I loved to get lost in were fogged with grief. "Jude," I whispered, and threw my arms around his neck.

To his credit, he didn't push me away, but he also didn't hug me back. I gulped, releasing him. "Okay, I deserve that," I added quietly.

Pulling out his keycard, he unlocked the door and sipped the cup of coffee he had in hand. "What are you doing here, Marlena?" he repeated.

"I needed to see you," I said, without thinking.

Two eyebrows climbed higher over his jade eyes. Though his expression was tight, there was a sadness that lingered there. "Well … here I am."

Damn. He wasn't making this easy. "I-I wanted to bring you back your watch. Since you weren't at the audition. I know what it means to you."

His face softened, if only for a moment. "Thank you. You could have sent a courier." Then after another moment, he asked, "How'd it go?" His thoughtfulness touched something deep inside me. He was mad at me— rightfully so. I took off, abandoned him when he'd given me so much; had opened up so much to me. And despite that, he still wanted the best for me. He still wanted me to have the role.

"It went great." Though I was smiling, an ache settled in my chest. I couldn't feel elated. Not yet. Not without Jude. "I was offered the part of Holly almost on the spot— right after Layla left her audition."

His mouth twitched, and though he offered me a small smile, it didn't reach his eyes. "That's wonderful, congratulations."

"But I didn't take it," I blurted out, before I lost my nerve. "I said I would only accept the role if you played Leo."

Jude cursed, turning his back on me and storming into his room. "Why would you do that?" he grunted. "You *had* it. You had it without me. Isn't that what you wanted?"

"I thought it was." I rushed toward him, pulling his shoulders close to me. His broad back pressed against my breasts and I heard his hiss. "But without you, I don't have it. Without you, I don't have … anything." The last word came out in a whisper and I clenched my eyes shut at how stupid I sounded.

"That's what you wanted. You wanted to get the role all on your own. You chose your priorities," he said, not turning around, barely acknowledging my touch on his body. Then, softer, he added, "And those priorities weren't me."

So that's what this was really about. For the second time in Jude's life, a woman chose her stardom ... her career over him. My hands traveled down from his shoulders to his ribs and over his abs. The muscles there rippled under my fingers. "I freaked out," I said. "After what happened with Jack and all the tabloids printing that stupid picture, I couldn't handle another public scandal."

"I know," he said softly. "I'm just trying to give you what you want. And what you want is to not have to deal with another reputation in this fucking town."

"But I realized something at that audition." I dropped my cheek to his shoulder blade, clutching at his back. "I don't care. I don't care about any of that anymore. I know the truth. I haven't slept with anyone to get a role. I never have. I never will. And this week ... with you ... it's given me a new sense of confidence I've never had before. I was good in that audition room. These stupid rumors don't matter as long as I have *you*." After a moment of silence, I swallowed another trembling sob. "Please, tell me I still have you."

"It was one week, Marly," he snorted, and it was an odd combination of a chuckle and a grunt.

I shook my head, backing up. "Don't do that. Don't trivialize what this week was." His words stabbed me in the chest, the pain resonating through my body like a poisoned dart and just as paralyzing. "I don't think you mean that."

"Marly," he whispered, finally spinning to face me. "You'd be so much better off if you just took this role and didn't look back."

He lifted a hand, brushing the backs of his knuckle across my cheekbone. Electricity surged from his touch on my skin down to my heart. It was a small victory, but I'd take it. At least he was looking me in the eyes again. "Not a chance, Jude. The studio wants you in the film. And I want you in the film. Either I do this movie with you, or I don't do it at all. If you're not in it, then the part is going to Layla and someone else."

Jude groaned, and I knew I hit him in a soft spot.

"Is it me? Do you not want to act beside me now?" My stomach wobbled with the thought, but unfortunately, it was a very real possibility that I had to face. "Because if that's the case, I'll decline the part—you can have Leo back. I'll sell my wedding dress for you," I whispered. "I'd rather not have the part, if it means having you."

Jude rushed toward me and crashed his lips to mine. His tongue plunged into my mouth, devouring me in a kiss that made my toes curl within my Chanel pumps. His lips worked around mine before pulling away gently. "That," he said, his breath nearly a pant, "is not the case. I can't do this role with anyone *but* you."

A smile twitched on my lips. "So … you'll be my Leo?"

"Yes," he said quietly. "As long as I can also be your Jude. And you—my Marlena."

I pushed up on my toes, brushing my lips gently to his. "So, how do we get my LnS membership bumped into full time?"

EPILOGUE
Jude

I WOKE UP even earlier than I had planned to on Christmas morning.

Today's the day. The day I'd been planning for months. It was a lot of firsts all rolled together. My first Christmas with Marly. Her first Christmas without her father. Her first time meeting my parents. Her first trip to Montana.

I slid out of bed as quietly as possible, so as not to wake her and crept across my childhood bedroom to the bag which housed seven small, wrapped presents—all for Marly. It was only six a.m. My sister was spending the morning with her in-laws and she and the rugrats wouldn't be here until lunch.

Despite my light footstep, Marly stirred, rolling onto her left side, blinking her eyes open and yawning. "Jude? What time is it?"

I dropped the bag near the door and knelt beside the bed, pressing my lips gently to her smooth, makeup-free forehead. "Early. Too early. Go back to sleep."

"I'll get up if you're getting up."

My cock stirred, seeing the way she lifted her slender arms over head, her small perky breasts stretching with the movement, her perfect rosebud nipples hard and pushing against the thin cotton of her shirt. "Stay," I said, smoothing my palm over her hair. Then I grabbed two quarters from the nightstand and placed them on her closed eyes. "Stay. Go back to sleep. And I expect those quarters to still be there when I come back up."

Her mouth tilted into a smirk. "Or else what?"

I flicked her nipple—hard enough to cause her to gasp. To cause the small of her back to arch off the mattress. "Try me and find out." I whispered the threat, my voice playful and my body wanting to forget all about my plan for today and instead sink my cock deep inside of her.

"I'm excited about our gift to your mom," she said, out of the blue.

"Me too. She's never going to see it coming." I leaned down, kissing Marly deeply. "Now, go back to sleep."

"Yes, Sir," she murmured, her voice thick with grogginess.

I waited there another few moments before gathering the gifts and tip-toeing my way downstairs. Even though I was thirty years old, there was something about being back in my parent's house that made me feel like I was eight again. As though I wasn't supposed to be awake at this hour, sneaking around the house like a cat-burglar.

"Morning," my mom said, nearly giving me a heart attack.

"Holy shit." I clutched my chest, feeling each heavy thudding heartbeat slam into my palm from behind my breastbone. "Mom, what are you doing awake so early?"

My grip on the bag of gifts tightened.

Mom shrugged, taking a sip of her coffee. "I'm usually up at six every morning. Especially with guests visiting. I like to have the coffee brewed and breakfast made in case someone wakes up."

I shook my head, laughing. "You really are supermom,

you know that?"

"If we're comparing me to superheroes, I'd rather be Wonder Woman. Without that stupid leotard, though."

"You can be whatever the hell superhero you prefer, mom."

My mom stood up from the kitchen table and shuffled over to the French Press, pouring me a mug of rich, black coffee and sliding it across the kitchen island. "This girl's the real thing, isn't she?" she asked.

"Yeah, mom. She is."

She held my gaze for a long moment—her eyes a slightly darker shade of green than mine. "Good. I like this one."

I smiled. Most people assumed I inherited most of my attributes from my dad—they couldn't be more wrong. My mom and I were so similar that it was sometimes painful. She needed the control, the power. She ran this family as well as the State of Montana.

"I love her," I admitted. "I love her more than I ever thought I was capable of."

"Oh, sweet boy." Mom brushed her palm to my jaw. "Just you wait until you have kids. You don't even know what love is yet."

I smiled, imagining Marly pregnant with our child.

"She's good for you," Mom said. "I can tell." Then she added after a pause, "We just need to get her to stop with all that yes ma'am and yes, sir crap. What is this, the military?"

My grin widened. Oh, hell no. I'd worked hard to get Marly to a place where she answered me 'yes, Sir' reflexively. No way I was reversing that.

"I have to put her gifts in her stocking. Want to help me?"

Mom raised an eyebrow, taking a long sip of coffee. "Why do you need help stuffing gifts in a stocking?"

"You'll see."

A FEW HOURS later, almost all the gifts had been opened. All except our stockings—and our gift to my mother. Beside me, sitting cross-legged on the floor, Marly wiggled and flashed me an excited grin. "Now?" she whispered.

I nodded and she leapt to her feet, lunging for the large wrapped box still beneath the tree, and handed it to my mom.

Mom slid a narrowed gaze to me. "This huge thing is for me?"

"Yes, ma'am," Marly said, clasping her hand into mine as she sat back down.

The gift had been entirely Marly's idea, sparked when I was showing her my parent's old wedding album.

Mom tore open the wrapping paper, the slim wardrobe box nearly as tall as she was. Then, lifting the lid, she gasped. Her eyes grew wet and Marly squeezed my hand.

"What is it, sweetheart?" Dad leaned over her shoulder to have a better look. "Oh my—"

"How did you find this?" Mom asked.

I smiled, feeling the tears and emotion climbing up my throat, burning my sinuses. Marly's cheeks were already wet, stained with tears. Mom didn't wait for an answer, she stood and pulled her wedding gown out of the large wardrobe box, holding it up to herself and laughing. "I don't remember ever being this thin, though!"

"It was all Marly's idea," I said. "I told her the story—how you sold your wedding gown to buy dad's Rolex—"

"Your Rolex now," Dad said.

"And we had the designer on the movie recreate your gown for you, mom."

My mom hugged the dress tighter into her body. She wasn't ever a woman who wore her emotions on her sleeve, but for the first time in years, she looked downright giddy. She rushed toward us, crushing me in a hug and kissing my cheek. Then, leaning down, she cupped Marly's face and pulled her in, holding her tight, the dress crushed between them. "You did good. This is the best gift I've ever gotten," she said.

Marly's smile stretched wide over her beautiful face. "We had her sew it to my measurements. Jude said you were my size when you got married."

Mom snorted, her gaze drifting down to Marly's waist and I coughed to catch her attention before she blew the rest of the plan. It didn't take more than a quick look to set her back on course, and Mom nodded, saying, "Yes, of course. I think I was about your size. Give or take a couple pounds."

"I'm so glad you like it," Marly said, still beaming. "When Jude told me your version of the 'Gift of the Magi,' I just knew—we had to find a way to get you that dress back."

"Do you still have your mother's wedding gown?" Mom asked.

Marly shook her head. "I always wanted to wear my mom's wedding dress, but she was actually pregnant with me when they got married—so her dress wouldn't exactly work in a conventional way. I actually saved the fabric— I'm hoping to sew some of her dress into mine so I can walk down the aisle with a little piece of her history. And I had the thought that I could sew the rest of the fabric into a Christening gown for my children."

"That's a wonderful idea," Mom said. Then, wiping her eyes, she added in a very thinly veiled change of subject, "Hey, don't you still have your stockings to do?"

My heart raced. This was it. Months of planning and it was finally here. Mom handed us our stockings and I set mine aside, wiping my sweaty palms across my pants. "You go first, Marly." I nodded toward her stocking and she didn't hesitate, digging in immediately. "Yep, that one first," I said pointing at the small envelope in her hand. She tore into it like she was five years old, pulling out the gift card.

She gave me an odd look, tilting her head. "A Chipotle gift card?"

"You know," I said. "For your *Burritos.*"

"Um … okay." She laughed, but clearly wasn't catching on yet.

I had placed all the items in order in the stocking, so as long as it didn't get shuffled around too much, it should be perfect. She pulled out the next wrapped gift and opened it. "Doritos …" This time, a smile began tilting the corners of her lips.

"That's right. Another favorite." Mom and Dad exchanged quizzical glances and shrugged. "Burritos, Doritos …"

She laughed, opening the next gift—a Snickers bar. "Burritos, Doritos, Snickers …" She got it now and as she tore into the next gift, she was shaking her head. "And M&Ms."

BDSM. Mom and Dad still seemed clueless across the room. But I wasn't finished. "Keep digging. There's more."

"More than all this?" Marly asked, waving around the junk food. "You spoil me, Jude Fisher." She dug in and pulled out the final wrapped gift and sighed as she opened it. "A planner," she whispered, hugging it to her chest. "Thank you."

I leaned over, kissing her. "I couldn't let the tradition fade away. I hope you're okay with someone other than your dad carrying it out."

"I couldn't be happier."

"There's more …"

"*More?*"

My pulse kicked up. God, I love this girl. The fact that she was happy with a few bags of junk food and a planner as her Christmas gifts was reason enough to spend a lifetime with her. She didn't expect thousands of dollars of gifts. She didn't expect any gifts. Time together was gift enough for her—and it only made me love her that much more. "Open it up to today's date," I instructed.

She gave me a smirky side-eye. My racing pulse could now officially win the Kentucky Derby. I slid my hand into my pocket, wrapping my fingers around the velvet brocade box. My stomach was tight with nerves and I ground my teeth together as she did what she was told. Stickers fell out of the marked page. Wedding planning stickers. And there on December 25th, I had scribbled the words:

Marlena Taylor, will you marry me?

Dropping to one knee in front of her, I pulled out the box, flipping the lid open to reveal her mom's antique engagement ring that Omar had helped me sneak out of her jewelry box in her bedroom.

My hands trembled as I knelt there, holding the open ring box. Her expression was surprisingly calm, blue eyes glistening. "Marlena Taylor, when we met, my heart wasn't supposed to race like it did. I wasn't supposed to kiss you. I wasn't supposed to love you. But I did. You brought sunlight back into my dark, shaded world. My whole life, I'd been chasing the wrong dreams until I met you. From the moment I saw you, my gut told me you were the one. That I could love you. And so, for the first time in my life, I'm listening to it. Will you marry me?"

Her bottom lip trembled, her throat tight, and a blue vein became visible from beneath her alabaster skin. "Do you have a pen?" she asked my Mom.

Startled, my mom scrambled to the side table, handing her a simple ballpoint pen.

Marly set the planner in her lap, scrolling through dates and then scribbled something into the calendar before holding it up for me to see. There on May 29th, she had written *Mr. and Mrs. J. Fisher* and scribbled a heart around it.

"Does this date work for you?" she asked, sniffling.

I recognized the date as her parent's anniversary. She could have asked for a wedding this afternoon and I would have said yes. "Any day that ends in 'y' works for me, Poppy."

"Then yes. My answer is yes," she squeaked, tears sliding down her cheeks.

I slipped the ring on her finger. The same ring she'd been wearing when we first met. The same ring that had symbolized a fake relationship and a world of lies, now represented our burgeoning marriage. And it couldn't be more perfect.

We both stood and Marly slung her arms around my neck, kissing me.

My mom draped the wedding dress across the chair. "Something tells me you might want to try this on today."

Marly gasped. "You would let me wear it?"

"Let you?" Mom asked. "Sweetie, you're *family* now."

Marly's eyes drifted shut and more tears spilled across her wet, spiked eyelashes, falling down her cheeks. "I love you so much," she whispered. "I'll always be your sunlight, as long as you're my shady tree."

"Always, Poppy. Always."

Can't Wait for more from
the Silhouette Studios Series?
Here's a Sneak Peek of Role Play (Book 2)

CHAPTER 1
Ash

I WAS BORN a daredevil. Always the risk-taker, I exited the womb so fast, the doctor only just barely caught me as I shot out of my mom's vagina like some sort of infant Evel Knievel.

Needless to say, not much rattles me in life. Not when I challenged the largest kid in fifth grade to an arm wrestling match. Not when I was caught cheating on my PSATs. Hell, I wasn't even rattled when my sister walked in on me beating my meat in the bathroom while flipping through her Teen Beat magazine.

So then why the hell am I sweating like a pig in a bacon factory the first week of directing my first major motion picture?

I rushed down the halls of Silhouette Studios, sweat pushing out of my pores and dripping down the sides of my face. The headset encasing my ears bounced off my jaw with each heavy-footed step and the clipboard tucked under my arm was quickly becoming saturated with sweat.

We were only a week into filming this movie and already, I was in over my head.

I briefly squeezed my eyes shut, taking a breath. *No,* I told myself. *I've got this.* The second I started doubting... started believing the whispers of insecurity and doubt, Hollywood would swallow me whole.

My cell phone was practically affixed to the my palm, checking updates and communicating with my executives.

Around me, the lights were on full blast and hotter than the goddamn Los Angeles sun at the beach. This movie was my baby. I had directed at least a dozen movies already in my career—but none like this. My reel consisted of college aged comedians getting high and doing stupid shit. But this script was different. I knew it from the moment it landed on my desk; from the moment I flipped open the first page. This BDSM introspection was my career making film.

"If you can keep your dick in your pants," my boss and the president of Silhouette Studios, Richard Blair had joked. That booming voice resonated in my head like a snare drum. Okay, yeah. I had a reputation... but it wasn't that bad, was it? This was fucking Hollywood after all. And I was certainly fucking my way through Hollywood. Including, but not limited to our costume designer— Callie. Or was it Katie? Shit... better remember her name and fast. But in my defense, I met her *before* the movie was in pre-production and I had no clue we'd be working together this soon after.

I paused, gripping the small wedding band that barely fit around my pinky. Hammered white gold. Classy. Understated. Just like Brie was. Emotion clogged my throat and I had to swallow twice before it dislodged. Five years. Had it already been that long? It felt like a lifetime, and yet, also like it was only yesterday that we were laying on the couch together as she threaded her fingers through my hair.

I released my hold on her wedding band, pulling my attention back to the here and now. *Here.* On the lot of Silhouette Studios directing my biggest film yet. *Now.* Now Brie was gone. *Here.* Surrounded by my crew and employees. *Now.* Now I wore her wedding band as a constant reminder of the woman I lost.

Now... I was miserable. Five years and I was still as miserable as the day she died.

Some men became hermits after a loved one died. I on the other hand, dove head first into sex as my escape. I felt guilty the first few times, but ultimately, Brie had been the one to teach me that sex and intimacy weren't exclusive. She had been the one to show me how emotionally freeing sex and the power play relationship dynamics could be. I told myself daily that I needed it to move on from her, but the truth was? Being an active Dominant in the community was what kept me *close* to her.

"Ash." My name boomed over the headset. "I need to see you in my office," Richard said.

I looked at my phone for the time, thankful to my CEO for the disruption as I was about to wander down memory lane. For some people, it was paved in candied, sweet memories. For me? It was dirty, bumpy and I was bound to get lost there in the twisting, winding darkness.

My eyes adjusted on blue backlit numbers on his phone. Shit, was it already ten am? I needed to get the lead out of my ass. We were prepping for tomorrow's shoot— the sexiest scene of the movie. When I was done with it, Jude and Marlena would go down in sex scene history with Sharon Stone and Michael Douglas.

It was a closed set tomorrow and everything needed to be perfect to make sure Jude and Marlena were comfortable. It needed to go perfectly. Hell, if I was being honest, I needed *every* set day to go smoothly, but if I only had to choose one day out of the three month schedule to go well? It would be tomorrow. If this film earned Silhouette Studios an Oscar nod, Richard would have to consider me for other more serious movies. Even with Jude on my side, I had only ever managed to assistant direct the serious films, being looked over time and time again.

Until now.

I hit the rubbery button on my headset. "Sure thing, Rich. I'll be there in a minute."

"Make it thirty seconds."

I all but ran down the corridor to Richard's corner office with the view of Hollywood hills. When the CEO of your production studio asks you to be quick... you haul ass. With a light knock, I opened the door and slipped inside. "Rich," I said, finding my boss sitting at the large mahogany desk watching yesterday's scene on his monitor. He looked tired. More tired than usual for him. Though he was older than me, the lines on his face seemed deeper today and he wasn't smiling and offering to pour me a scotch like he usually did.

"Come on in," he paused the video. "And shut the door behind you."

Uh oh. This wasn't good. I did as I was told and slid into the seat opposite Richard. "What's going on?" I didn't often feel nervous, but right now? With Richard's glare not faltering from the monitor... I squirmed in my seat like a schoolboy being sent to the damn principal's office.

"I've been reviewing last week's shots. And... they're

lacking a bit of nuance in my opinion."

The air punched out of my gut. In his *opinion*? What fucking opinion was that? My hands balled into fists, my chest tightening painfully. Everyone on the crew had been working tirelessly—nonstop—for three months in pre-production. Those shots were gorgeous. The script was perfect. *Deep breaths, baby,* Brie would have whispered if she'd been here. She would have squeezed my knee, forced my stupid, irrational temper to calm down.

I listened to that voice deep in the back of my mind and dragged a shaky breath through my tight lips. Every day it felt like her voice was growing further and further away. Like each morning, I was forgetting something so minor, so small—the way her voice would be rough in the morning before coffee, or how she would crack trying to sing karaoke—and with each fading memory, she was slipping further and further away from me.

Which only pissed me off more.

I had to calm down. I forced my balled fists to un-curl—even if I didn't agree with my boss, I had to remain professional. "How do you mean, Rich?"

Rich chuckled and lifted a cup of coffee, sipping it before continuing. "BDSM is a weird thing, isn't it?"

My shoulders knotted around my ears. I wasn't exactly protective of my lifestyle, but I didn't like it being called weird either. It was kink. A damn fun one if you asked me... and I wasn't broken or emotionally damaged because I enjoyed it. I was broken because of other shit, but not because of this. When I started in the lifestyle, I was fine. Healthy. Emotionally, in tact. *Happy. So fucking happy.* So, hearing my boss... someone I admired and respected call me weird wasn't exactly what I was ready for this morning before I'd even had a chance to have my fucking coffee.

Richard examined me, his eyes drifting to my arms briefly. "Relax," Rich said. "I know you're a Dominant. I'm not calling *you* weird... I'm saying that the different perceptions of it can be strange."

I inhaled a sharp breath. "You know I'm a Dom?"

Rich shrugged. "Of course. I recognized it in you the second we first met eight years ago. Which club are you a member of? Dynasty?"

"LnS," I said quietly. Jude and I had been exclusive members there for years. As far as I knew, there were only ten clubs similar to LnS in all of California. Lns had private quarters in the upstairs section of the fetish club. Downstairs was a normal kink bar—kind of goth, but in a playful, voyeuristic way. Upstairs? That was the real thing. A place for high profile Los Angeles personalities to get their kink on without being outed. It was highly secretive. And the club made sure that you didn't mention a word about its members to anyone. They had files of dirt on every member and revealing anything could result in them leaking your darkest secret to the tabloids.

Out of reflex, I touched my fingers to Brie's ring again, cursing myself for the nervous tick.

I stood, moving to the French press Richard kept in the corner of his office and poured myself a cup.

From across the room, still seated behind his desk, Richard nodded. "LnS. Of course. Nice place... I was there for a few years, too. Moved onto the Los Angeles Tennis Club."

I took a sip of coffee. I had heard rumors the tennis club was a front, but this was my confirmation. "So, then you're a...?" I let the question dangle between us like a swinging pendulum.

"A Dominant," Richard answered. If he was fazed by the question, it didn't show. It wasn't exactly a shock—that Richard was also a Dom. Everything about his personality screamed it. From the strict regimens he had in the mornings to the way he commanded a room from the moment he walked in. But just because someone was powerful in a boardroom didn't necessarily mean they were like that in the bedroom. Hell, I knew high powered attorneys and senators who spent so much of their professional life in charge that when it came to the bedroom, they wanted a someone to dominate them.

Even still... I kicked myself for not picking up on Richard's cues. And for being so easily readable by my boss.

"Back to the issue at hand," Richard said, "There's something lacking in last week's shoot."

"Lacking?" Defensive anger inflated in my gut once more like a helium balloon. "We've been working our asses off—"

"I know, I know. But I see what I see, Ash. Don't take this the wrong way. The studio has a lot of money in this and we want it to do well." He cleared his throat, setting his coffee mug down and resting his elbows on the desk. "Ash, I'm going to ask you something personal. Have you ever broken a sub?"

A breath pushed past my lips as I fell back in the chair. Involuntarily, my knee bounced and I squeezed my hand over my thigh to stop the movement. "I've been with newbies."

"That wasn't the question. Have you ever taken a woman with submissive tendencies and truly taught her what the lifestyle is? Shown her the pleasures within pain and submission? Have you ever watched it in her eyes as she shifted, stopped fighting, and gave in?"

The line of my throat was dryer than if I had swallowed sand in place of my coffee. I'd never had any desire to break a submissive. Brie had already been in the community as a sub when we met. If anything, she had trained me. Introduced me to the lifestyle. Training a new sub? Breaking someone in? That was a little too close to home. None of the sex I'd had in the last five years ever felt like I was betraying Brie. But training a new submissive? Introducing a new partner to the life Brie and I had started together? I swallowed, ignoring the buzzing sensation in my sinuses. It would cross the emotional line I had drawn in the sand.

I shook my head, focusing not on the burning emotion in my chest, but on the cool metal of her ring on my pinky finger. My rock. Both in life and in death. "No. I've never broken a sub. And I don't plan to." *I fuck*, I wanted to say. *A lot. But I don't commit.* Being a Dominant; feeling the power over a woman… over her pleasure, her pain… was my Xanax. It gave me control in a chaotic world where I had zero of it. It gave me a piece of Brie. It gave me a fake reality where maybe, just maybe, I could have saved her.

Rich nodded, his expression impassive, revealing nothing. But for a brief moment, his gaze dropped to Brie's ring. Rich had known me five years ago. Not well, but I had been one of his associate producers. Did he suspect? Did he know that Brie was in the community back then? No. Her dad made sure that never leaked out. "That's what I thought," Richard said. "Look, moving on isn't easy. I know—"

I snorted, shaking his head. "What do you know—"

"Ash," Richard's voice boomed, rich with authority. "*I know.*"

Oh. Understanding washed over me like a warm, healing wave, lapping at my toes. Rich knew. Knew like I knew. I could see it in the way Rich's mouth tightened. The way his brown eyes filled momentarily with moisture. I wanted more details. Wanted to know every painful memory and ask about who Rich had lost. Whoever said misery loves company knew what they were talking about. Five years later and I was still drowning in pain—and more than anything, I wanted to grab the ankles of other people around me and pull them under water, too. But instead, I just sat there, listening. Sinking.

"The first time breaking a sub is never easy. They cry, they fight you, you have to explain everything to them. In some ways, it's downright annoying. But that moment that you give them their most intense orgasm ever? When they look you in the eyes and call you *Sir*?" Rich paused, his eyes drifting closed and I swallowed, feeling the tight movement travel the line of my throat. "Experiencing the moment that another person enters this crazy world of ours is empowering and that feeling is indescribable. This movie is all about that process. It's not about the lifestyle… it's about the entry *into* the lifestyle. From a submissive woman's perspective. Not a Dominant man's."

I sat silently, taking another sip of coffee. The hot liquid burned a path to my stomach. "Well, that's what we're doing with these," I said, gesturing at the monitor with my coffee cup. But I didn't buy it myself. What Rich had just described? It was nowhere near what I had directed last week in those shots. I cleared my throat, not ready to admit that aloud. "Maybe when you see some of the scenes cut together—"

"You're not succeeding," Richard interrupted. "You think it's what you're doing… but it's not reading that way."

"But I've been using the script—"

"Nope," Richard interrupted again. "Whatever you're doing isn't working."

I threw my hands up. As they fell to the armrest of my chair, I leveraged my weight and pushed to my feet, pacing across the room. I fucking hated being wrong. It pissed me off to no end. "Well, what the hell do you expect me to do, Rich? We're a week into filming. Should we reshoot last week's scenes? Or maybe spend the night at LnS… go find some newbie submissive and break her just to see what the hell it is you're talking abou—"

"That's exactly what I want you to do," Rich said.

I snorted, shifting my gaze out the window. But I couldn't even focus on the beautiful view of Hollywood hills. My eyes clamped shut. "You've got to be kidding."

Richard shrugged. "Look, I know legally I can't tell you to do this. I can't enforce it in anyway. But if you're up for it… I would highly recommend that tonight and for the next few weeks after filming, you go to LnS. Find a new girl… someone to break. Take the time and turn a woman with submissive tendencies into a true, honest to God sub. It will help the film."

"Then what? What do you expect me to get out of that?"

Richard lifted his eyebrow. "Perspective."

Excerpt from

Capturing You

(A Maple Grove Romance, Book 1)

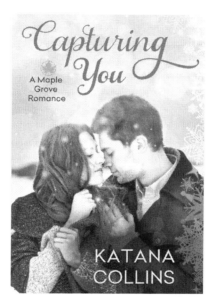

PROLOGUE

THE EDGE OF the heavy card stock bit into Lydia Ryder's palm as she gripped the pamphlets. Numbness crept up her body, beginning with her toes until it nearly swallowed her.

"There are alternatives when and if you're ready to be a mother. Premature ovarian failure doesn't necessarily mean you can't have children. There are plenty of options. In vitro, adoption…" Dr. Seaver's voice faded into the recesses of Lydia's mind. Even though the doctor only stood only a few feet away, it may as well have been miles.

Lydia stared, hypnotized by the pamphlet in her hand. *Coping with Infertility…*

She wasn't even thirty years old, too focused on her photojournalism career to consider a serious relationship, much less a family. Hell, she didn't even know if she *wanted* children, and yet here she was—with nature making the choice for her.

"Depression can be very common in the wake of a discovery like this. I'm referring you to a therapist— someone you can talk to. And in the meantime, we'll start you on estrogen therapy. You'll feel a lot better once your hormones are balanced. Lydia… are you listening?"

She jumped at the weight of Dr. Seaver's palm on her shoulder. With rapid fire blinks, she raised her gaze to the gynecologist. "Yes. Yes, I'm listening. Thank you, Dr. Seaver."

She pushed off of the exam table, hiking her leather camera bag and laptop case onto her shoulder and draping her blazer over an arm. Taking the prescriptions the doctor held out, Lydia tucked it into her purse along with the folded pamphlet.

There was another few minutes of chatting, but she could barely focus enough to listen. It was as though she was submerged in water, straining to hear those above her.

When she left the building, the roar of New York City traffic was like white noise, as comforting as the sound of waves crashing or crickets chirping.

The prescriptions and pamphlet—merely three pieces of paper—weighed heavily in her purse. It was a boulder on her shoulder. Moisture welled in her eyes, the tears burning like acid, but she blinked them back. She would not mourn. She would not cry over something she never had and didn't know she even wanted.

With a glance at her watch, she felt the relief that she wasn't yet late for Noah Blue Tripp's press conference. She passed by a Newsstand off of Hudson; that horrible article that her name was now attached to sat front and center, nestled between *People* and *Us Weekly*. *Noah Blue: Hot Actor, Cold Heart.* She cringed at the cover; at the differences between the portrait she took, a smiling Noah against a simple white backdrop, paralleled against the dingy, dark photo that the ghost writer had found of him drunk at a club.

It was her first ever mainstream magazine article. She understood why the *Daily View* wanted one of their veterans ghosting her. But did they have to so utterly botch her article?

Not to mention the fact that they used *off the record*

information. By the time Lydia had read the new copy, the article had already gone to print and it was too late. The ghost writer claimed that it would be their word against Noah's.

She pushed on, ignoring that queasy feeling in the pit of her stomach. To make matters worse, a rival magazine, *City Star*, saw the Noah Blue article and liked it so much that they offered her a full time job.

She hadn't said no, but she also hadn't said yes. Gotcha journalism and TMZ reporting was the last thing she had expected her life to become when she graduated with her BFA in photography and writing. Her throat tightened, sweat forming beneath her button down shirt as June's hot sun beat down on her. But now? These medical bills were going to add up if she didn't get on a better insurance plan. And how often did photographers get the opportunity for salaried jobs with paid vacation and sick days? It was a good opportunity; even if she only did it for a short time to pay off some bills. Lydia pushed her eyes to the ground, watching carefully as she huffed down the city sidewalk toward the press conference. The building was just ahead— a tall, corporate looking building that was plopped right in the middle of the West Village's old city charm.

She froze, waiting at the stop light from across the street as city traffic whizzed by. She blinked as dark hair, olive skin and dimples came into view. Noah Blue. Standing just outside the building, talking to another man. Oh, God, she felt sick about what had happened. The *Daily View* using that story about his sister-in-law's funeral was just appalling. And even though the magazine's lawyers had warned her to stay far away from him, she just couldn't. She owed him an explanation; an apology.

The light turned green and she rushed forward as Noah walked into the coffee shop that was in the lobby of the building. Her laptop and camera bag bumped her hip with each bouncing step. What the hell was she even going to say? What *could* she say?

She shook the doubtful feelings away. It didn't matter. She needed to apologize; even if it opened herself up to a lawsuit. She needed to look this man in the eyes and tell him that she had nothing to do with that story—but even still, that she was sorry.

She pushed through the glass doors as the familiar smell of heady arabica wafted around her. Scanning the bustling cafe, she looked for those signature blue eyes and dimples that made Noah Blue Tripp famous. How did he manage to disappear so quickly? There was a huge line of people waiting to place their orders. Then again, he was a star... maybe they let him through to the front of the line? She weaved her way through the crowd, just in time to see a glimpse of Noah getting on the elevators in the lobby.

Damn. But maybe it was better this way. She didn't even want to go to this press conference—she knew exactly what happened with that article. What else was there to learn?

That nauseous feeling flooded her core once more and she leaned against the wall beside the restroom door. Was it the hormones Dr. Seaver had injected her with today? Or was that her stupid conscience rearing its head? Either way, it felt horrible. *She* felt horrible.

Pushing off the wall, Lydia turned and reached for the bathroom door just as it swung open. A broad-shouldered man in a plain white T-shirt and perfectly fitted jeans barreled toward her. He didn't look up as he shook his hands of water. Defined muscles pushed against the shirt in the most delicious way, and she stood frozen to the floor as he collided with her. Her ankles wobbled over the pencil thin heels she wore, and she yelped, stumbling backwards as a strong hand darted out, steadying her just in time.

She began an apology as he said at the same time, "I'm so sorry." His voice boomed over hers, and her mouth went dry at his tone—one hundred percent masculine and utterly delicious. She could dip that voice in chocolate and eat it for dessert.

He smiled. A genuine smile from a stranger in New York was not a common thing. Two dimples formed on either side of his mouth. Heat raced across her body, and Lydia's skin tightened under his gaze as it swept her face.

His chest was heavy with each breath and she watched as his expression shifted into something more melancholy, reminding her of where she'd just come from. She placed a palm on her purse, remembering the pamphlet.

"My fault," he said as he dropped his hand from her elbow. She'd barely noticed he had still been touching her—it felt that comfortable, like his hands were simply meant to be on her body.

A heaviness sat in her belly as a thought hit her hard like a bucket of ice water. Dating—meeting men... it would never be that easy, flirty thing again. Sooner or later, if things got serious, she'd need to have the infertility conversation. She was suddenly very thankful that his hand was nowhere on her anymore.

Shrugging, she gave him a small smile. But even as she lifted the corners of her lips, she could feel the quivering sob forming in her chest. Like a striking match, it started small, but given the circumstance could quickly form into a roaring fire.

His jaw tightened as he swallowed and creases settled across his sun-weathered face. "You can do this," he said, almost as though he knew; as though he understood.

Her fake smile sagged, and for the first time all day, Lydia allowed herself to feel the full weight—the full sadness of her loss. She didn't bother brushing off the runaway tear.

The man stepped to the side. Slowly, she reached for the doorknob, pausing just before she opened it. "Thank you," she answered, looking up into his bright blue eyes once more. She smiled, warmed by the kindness of this stranger, before closing the door behind her.

After splashing some cold water on her cheeks and taking a moment to collect herself, she exited the bathroom and moved to the end of the long line. Somehow, the crowd was comforting. And even though there wasn't a single friend in the coffee shop, Lydia felt far less alone in the presence of strangers.

Two people ahead of her, she saw the man from the bathroom. Just as she looked up and caught his eye, he turned his head back toward the menu board. Lydia exhaled a silent breath. Of course he wasn't interested in her, not in that way. No man wanted to date a crying woman.

"Mommy! *Mommy*! I want a blueberry muffin!"

The child's voice came from directly behind her and cut right through to her heart. With a stiff spine, she turned to find a little girl with light brown hair, ruddy cheeks, and light eyes. Heat flushed across Lydia's face, and her chest expanded with a held breath that felt like a bubble lodged just to the right of her heart.

"Is that how you ask for things?" the mother asked, her voice razor sharp.

The little girl groaned, and the next thing Lydia knew, the kid was stomping and thrashing her limbs around. Her screams pierced through the low, chattering hum of the café.

The mother gave a weary sigh and somehow managed to talk over the screams. "You have until *three*. One—two—"

Lydia shifted, looking to the board uncomfortably. What do you do in this situation? Pretend like it wasn't happening? Ignore the tantrum? Hardly any of Lydia's friends had kids yet—she could count on one hand the number of times she'd held a baby. The noise abruptly stopped.

"Now apologize to Mommy."

Mommy. Mom. Mother. Mama. Lydia clamped her eyes shut, squeezing as hard as she could as though this subtle movement could completely eradicate any thoughts of children or motherhood from her mind.

"Kids," the man in front of her murmured with a snort. "Who needs 'em, right?"

Lydia's eyes snapped open, excitement pulsing in her brain. Was bathroom guy talking to her again? But instead, she was met with the gaze of a different man directly in front of her. He was handsome in a much different way than the guy from earlier. *Kids, who needs 'em.* Was he kidding? She scanned his body—he was in great shape, even if a little pretentious in the way his shirt was rolled just perfectly to the elbow.

Lydia gave a polite smile. "Right. Who needs them," she answered. She could barely read her own inflection.

Was that sarcasm? Hesitancy? Hell if she knew her own thoughts anymore. And she suddenly felt exhausted.

"No, I'm serious." He spun to face her. His gaze flicked down to the child before meeting Lydia's once more. "The planet is far too populated as it is."

Lydia swallowed hard, her throat burning. She considered that statement for a moment. She supposed he wasn't wrong about that.

His eyebrows lifted. "Don't get me wrong. Kids are cute and fun for like, an hour. But I love my life. I'm fulfilled by my job, my friends, romance... I don't need a kid to satisfy some weird biological clock."

Up until an hour ago at the doctor's office, Lydia had been pretty pleased with her life, too. She didn't love her new gig freelancing for trashy magazines specifically, but she loved photographing and reporting. She loved her friends and the freedom to date as she pleased. Maybe this would be okay. Lydia's breath became heavy, and she examined the men in front of her. Both offered her exactly what she needed to hear in a moment that she needed clarity more than anything. Two very different sets of advice... advice they hadn't even realized they were giving. "Thank you," she whispered before she could stop herself. There were plenty of men who didn't want children. She didn't have to be destitute of love and relationships just because she couldn't have kids.

He gave her an odd look, confusion marring his handsome features.

"Sorry, Mommy," the little voice whimpered. "May I *please* have a blueberry muffin?"

There was a rustle as the woman peeked beyond Lydia at the glass case. At least seven people were ahead of Lydia, and there was only one muffin left. Lydia hoped she was gone before the next tantrum started.

"I swear," the guy said, "there should be an area where kids are strictly not allowed."

Lydia felt a small smile flick at the corners of her mouth. "There is. It's called a bar."

Ahead of them, she heard the quiet snort of a laugh from the bathroom guy.

The man in front of her grinned, his gaze traveling the length of her body. "I'd drink to that." He slipped a hand into his front pocket as the line lurched forward. "I'm Jason."

"Lydia." Brushing her hand to her clavicle, and rolling her neck to each side, she tried to ignore the noise as the little girl's whining behind her grew louder once more. To be fair, the line *was* taking forever.

The line moved again, and they were nearly to the front. From his back pocket, he pulled out a business card and handed it to Lydia. His smile softened, crinkling around striking eyes. "Lydia, I hope I'm not being too forward… but I'd love to take you out to dinner. Call me sometime."

He didn't wait for her answer before turning to one of the open baristas. The man from the bathroom finished paying and crossed toward Lydia. His bright blue gaze met hers and for a moment, everything stood still. She swallowed, taking the final opportunity to memorize the way his dark hair curled around his ears; it looked like he had been running his hands through it all day. Angled features and stubble dusted along his chiseled jaw. A grin lifted his face, and those damn dimples flanked another breathtaking smile.

And he was headed directly for her.

He paused at Lydia's shoulder, so close that she could smell the traces of cedar and smokiness on him—like a campfire. Something heavy buzzed between them as he held her gaze. Warmth seethed through her body and despite this heat, she shivered.

Blinking, he brushed by her, crouching in front of the little girl, holding out the last blueberry muffin. He grinned wider, looking up at her mother. "Here ya go." He dropped it into her hand with a wink. "Blueberry muffins are my little girl's favorite, too."

Lydia's stomach knotted as smile lines creased his face. Though he looked tired, he also had a peace to him that she didn't find very often in Manhattan residents. "Be a good girl for your mommy, okay?" He pushed off his knees, standing once more as the mother thanked him.

With a final look at Lydia, he left the coffee shop. Without saying another word to her. Heat and embarrassment rose like high tide from her belly. But for what exactly? She hadn't done anything wrong. She gulped. Or had she?

Stepping up to the counter, Lydia ordered her tall, sugar-free, soy vanilla latte as memories of her mom and her shitty childhood consumed her thoughts. Looking on the bright side, at least now she wouldn't end up pregnant with a baby she didn't want like her own mother had. She couldn't do that to any child. And maybe she *didn't* want one. Maybe that parental gene was absent in her family. And this was nature's way of taking care of the decision for her.

Lydia sipped her latte, savoring the warm flavor. Its comforting steam billowed around her mouth, and she sighed. This was okay—*she* was okay. She didn't know the first thing about kids or babies. And if she changed her mind... well, just like Dr. Seaver said, she had options. In the meantime, she needed to find a way to pay for these medical bills.

Through the window, she watched as the man walked confidently down the street, sipping out of his to-go cup.

She lifted a chin and reached into her purse for the pamphlet, dropping it into the trash along with the referral for a therapist. This was a good thing, Lydia thought as she rested a hand to the door.

"I love you, Mommy."

Lydia's belly tightened, and her grip froze on the handle. *You can do this*, she repeated to herself, grabbing her cell phone and dialing.

"Yes, hi, Mara? This is Lydia Ryder. I would like to formally accept your offer with the *City Star*. I can start next Monday."

Excerpt from

Healing You

(A Maple Grove Romance, Book 2)

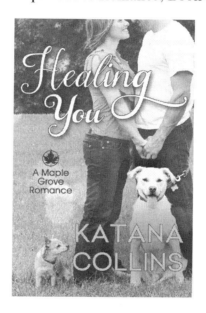

CHAPTER ONE

IT WAS ONE of those stunning New Hampshire summer mornings. You know the kind—the air was fresh and cool, but the sun was warm. Sky so blue you could damn near dive into the center of it and go for a swim. And Maple Grove was swarming with tourists and lovebirds walking hand in hand around the cozy little town.

Steve Tripp groaned as he passed by the third couple kissing over bagels and eggs that morning. And it wasn't even nine AM yet. Sitting outside at a local cafe, a couple twined their hands together and the woman batted her eyes as the man fed her a bite of his eggs. Grunting, he shoved his hands deeper into his pockets as he strolled past them.

An outsider wouldn't think their small New England town had much in the way of tourism, would they? But they'd be wrong. From the months of May through September, tourism in and around their lakes region boomed. And since Maple Grove was notoriously dog friendly, and Steve Tripp owned the only veterinary clinic in town, his business likewise was almost too busy to keep up with.

Steve rolled the kinks out of his neck as he crossed the street to Latte Da, Lex's new cafe and bakery. He'd been up before the sun this morning taking care of a horse's broken shoe over at the Wilson farm. When the call woke him from his deep sleep, he'd barely been able to throw on yesterday's clothes, on the floor by his feet, before running out the door. And now that it was time to open up shop? Well, he needed some serious caffeine to do so effectively.

A cheerful bell chimed at the top of the door as Steve skulked in. Lex looked up from behind the counter and over the sea of heads standing in line, sent him a grin. He held a finger and jerked his head, signaling for Steve to come around.

"Good morning, doctor," Lex grinned and his British accent rang through the cafe as he ran a hand through his rusty brown hair.

Steve grunted something that resembled 'good morning' in response. "I see business is doing well, huh?"

Lex shrugged and delivered a lopsided grin to the crowd. "Well, considering I only opened up shop earlier this year, yes. But ask me again when Old Man Winter comes for a visit."

Steve gave a hoarse chuckle. "You'll be fine, man. Once the first snow of the year hits, we'll get all those ski bunnies in town."

Lex nodded and grabbing the filter from the espresso maker, banged out the muddy coffee grounds from within. "Your usual?"

Steve eyed the line he was so blatantly cutting in front of, but Lex swatted away his concern immediately. "The man who saved my cat from the pound of chocolate she swallowed will always cut to the front. So... your usual iced latte and bagel?"

Steve sighed and felt a smile curve on his lips. "You got it. Aw, hell. Add some cream cheese to that bagel, too. And an iced coffee for Amanda. I'm feeling generous today." His assistant worked damn hard for him at the clinic, and he liked to give her as many incentives to stay working for him as possible.

"You know," Lex leaned forward, resting an elbow atop of the glass bakery case. "I just finished a new chocolate pistachio spread—it's like Nutella, but better. Why don't I give you half your bagel with the cream cheese and the other with the chocolate?"

Steve groaned dramatically and dropped a hand to his belly. Though it was still flat beneath his button down shirt, he may have to pop open his pants button if he continued on this eating spree. "Twist my arm. But if Ronnie kicks my ass at the gym tonight, I'm blaming you."

Lex lifted both hands in surrender, backing away. "Don't you dare sic your sister on me." His eyes flashed at the mention of Steve's sister, and though it was subtle, he saw how Lex wet his lips. Nodding, the baker rushed off to complete the order while his two employees—a couple of students from the high school—tended to the tourists in line.

Steve leaned against the wall facing the counter, and with his peripherals scanned the tourist crowd this season. It was their busiest year yet, that was for sure. With the economy bouncing back, more and more people were swarming to the small town for their summer getaway. In line ordering were two women—girls? Steve inspected closer, narrowing his eyes. Women. Definitely out of college. Or at least, he hoped they were out of college. No way he'd be caught dead checking out someone young enough to be in school with his baby sister.

The brunette had curly hair that was piled on top of her head in a messy bun. A mole was to the right of her eye in a very Marilyn sort of way, and when she smiled one dimple creased the upper part of her cheek.

Steve chuckled to himself. Oh, yeah, baby? Two can play at that game. He grinned back and flashed her the Tripp signature dimples, one on either side of his mouth. She dropped her eyes, catching her bottom lip between her teeth.

Steve sighed. Damn, how long had it been since he'd been with a woman? He did some quick math in his head… St. Patrick's Day. And since it was now July, that was… shit. Five months. Otherwise known as *too damn long*.

He caught his reflection in the window beside him; the scar slicing down his face stared back at him. Angry. Creased. Red. *Hideous…*

He ducked from his own stupid reflection as his phone buzzed from within his back pocket. Tension melted from his shoulders as Steve relaxed, happy to have the distraction. A text from Amanda: *You have a walk-in appointment who just arrived. How long should I tell her?*

Yep. The job that never ends. Nor did he want it to. In a way, Steve always felt more connected to the animal kind than humans… not that he'd ever admit that out loud to anyone. He'd sound like a lunatic. But it was the damn truth. He typed a quick response to his receptionist and vet tech in training. *5 minutes away. Just getting coffee.*

He tucked the phone back into his pocket, looking up just in time to see Lex handing a couple of to-go cups and a paper bag over the top of the bakery case. His friend's grin widened and he flicked a glance over to the brunette in line. "It seems you have an admirer. She took care of your bill."

Well, that was an interesting role reversal. Steve arched a brow in her direction, catching another one of her high voltage smiles. "Thank you," he mouthed from across the room.

When he lifted the bag, he saw a phone number and the name *Sophy* scribbled onto it with black sharpie.

"Maybe today won't be as bad as I thought, after all." Steve tossed one more wink toward the brunette and shouldered the bakery door open with a nod goodbye to Lex. Crossing the street, he shuffled over to his veterinary practice.

Pushing through his own front door, he smiled at Amanda and set her iced coffee down on the front desk. He eyed the handful of mail she had left in his tray for him and debated leaving it until after lunch. "Good morning, how are you today?"

He looked up to catch her wobbly expression. Eyes turned down, she swallowed hard and gestured to the back corner of their waiting area.

Steve pivoted slowly. The first thing to catch his eyes was an older yellow lab laying on the tiled floor. As he rose his gaze, he met the wet eyes of Yvonne. His high school sweetheart; his first love; and the girl he'd nearly killed almost a decade earlier.

Want a Free Maple Grove Cookbook?

Sign up here for my newsletter and get your copy today!

madmimi.com/signups/9988d924b2a24d3f8c1864f00dcb603d/join

Also, be sure to check out the Maple Grove Prequel

Meeting You

It's available for free on Smashwords, Barnes & Noble, Kobo, iBooks, and Amazon.

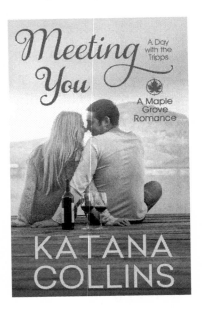

Other Books by Katana Collins

Silhouette Studios
Callback
Role Play (Coming Soon…)
Outtake (Coming Soon…)

Soul Stripper
Soul Stripper
Soul Survivor
Soul Surrender

Wicked Exposure
Wicked Shots
Wicked Exposure
Wicked Release

Harrison Street Crew
Ex-Con
Outlaw
Enforcer

Standalone
Blind Spot

Acknowledgments

You might be surprised to learn that the hardest part about writing a book for me is not, in fact, writing the book. It's everything else that orbits around the writing. Writing comes easily. It's fun. But editing? Marketing? Social media? Graphics? Oh, man. The list goes on and on and on. And for that reason, I need a whole team of people to make these books happen. I wish it was as easy as writing a book and poof! Being done! But it's not. It's so not.

To start with, I have to thank my marketing assistant, Heather White. You have been so valuable to this process. Thank you from the bottom of my heart. And to Danielle Eaton—your brain works in wild and mysterious ways and I love how you can come up with ideas over a single roll of sushi. (Sidebar: When can we get sushi again? Now I'm hungry).

Melissa Rheinlander—you're the boss and you know it, girl. Thank you for all you do. There's no one I'd rather be bossed around by! Becca Mysoor, editor extraordinaire and above all, friend. You are my rock and not only do I need you to stick around to edit my books, but I need you to hug me and slap donuts out of my hand when I got to eat a whole box. Derek Bishop, thank you for stepping in on short notice and editing this long ass book in less than a week! Your knowledge of the English language is stunning. Krista Amigo, thank you for reading and giving me insight into how Hollywood and filmmaking and Los Angeles are!

To my amazing beta readers—Caitlin, Sarah, Sasha, Kris, Sonal, and Sharon—thank you! You helped shape this book into something coherent! Anyone who knows me knows what a hard job you had, haha.

To my family—Mom, Dad, Bo, Bridget, Adam, Harrison, and Adelynn... you guys are the best. Love you so much!

And to Sean: Thank you for bearing with me through this wild process. For being my sounding board and my own personal hero (I also know you just made a gagging noise when reading that! Stop rolling your eyes and keep reading!). I love you. Also, why, oh why did we get another puppy??

I'm certain that I am leaving people out and for that, I apologize! Thank you to everyone! And most importantly, thank you to you, my amazing readers who love romance and read voraciously! I've said it before, but without you, I'm merely a writer. You all make me an author.

Thank you.

About the Author

When Katana Collins was younger and stole her mother's Harlequins to read beneath the covers with a flashlight, she wanted to read about the tough as nails heroine. The perfectly imperfect girl with quirks and attitude and sass. And the anti-heroes who were anything but "Prince Charming." Forget the knight on a white horse … she wanted the bad boy on a motorcycle.

So, now, she writes those romance novels she craved to see on the shelves all those years ago—the sassy heroines. The badass heroes. She penned her first romance novel back in 2012 and now, a few years later, she is an international author with 15 published books, in a wide range of contemporary romance genres (Paranormal, New Adult, Small town, Erotic Suspense … you name it!).

She lives in Portland, Maine, with an ever-growing brood of rescue animals: a kind of mean cat, a doofy lab, a very mellow chihuahua, and a very *not* mellow cairn terrier puppy … oh yeah, there's a husband somewhere in that mix, too. She can usually be found hunched over her laptop in a cafe, guzzling gallons of coffee, and wearing fabulous (albeit sometimes impractical) shoes.

She loves connecting with booklovers like herself, and fellow sassy storytellers, so feel free to drop her an email, visit her on her website (katanacollins.com). She also loves connecting on Instagram (@katanacollins), Twitter (@katanacollins) or Facebook (@katanacollins) or in her reader group, Kat's Kittens!